THE
WOLF
KING

BY ALICE BORCHARDT

Devoted

Beguiled

The Silver Wolf

Night of the Wolf

The Wolf King

THE
WOLF
KING

ALICE
BORCHARDT

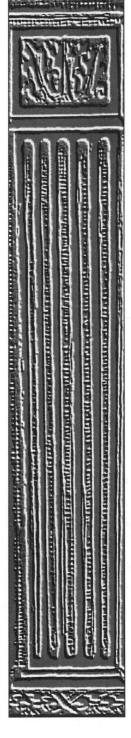

THE BALLANTINE PUBLISHING GROUP

NEW YORK

A Del Rey® Book
Published by The Ballantine Publishing Group

Copyright © 2001 by Alice Borchardt

All rights reserved under International and Pan-American Copyright Conventions.
Published in the United States by The Ballantine Publishing Group, a division of
Random House, Inc., New York, and simultaneously in Canada by Random
House of Canada Limited, Toronto.

Del Rey is a registered trademark and the Del Rey colophon is a trademark of
Random House, Inc.

www.randomhouse.com/delrey/

LIBRARY OF CONGRESS CATALOGING-IN-PUBLICATION DATA
Borchardt, Alice.
The wolf king / Alice Borchardt.—1st ed.
p.   cm.
"A Del Rey book"—T.p. verso.
1. Rome (Italy)—History—476-1420—Fiction.
2. Young women—Fiction.   3. Werewolves—Fiction.   I. Title.
PS3552.O687 W65 2001
813'.54—dc21   00-051860

Manufactured in the United States of America

First Edition: March 2001

10   9   8   7   6   5   4   3   2   1

I

WHEN HE FOUND HER IN THE SNOWBANK, HE was sure she must be dead.

These Franks were fools about bad weather. True, they had come from beyond the Rhine and conquered Roman territory; but too much soft living since then had ruined them.

He was surprised and angry. Not with the gentle creature he was sure she must have been, but with her menfolk and guardians. Because she must have been surrounded by those dedicated to her interests. This girl was obviously a noblewoman. To be abandoned here to the fury of winter's last blizzard seemed an impossible fate for such a woman.

In the name of God! No, that name was bitter on his tongue. The woman-skirted priests told him the powers his people honored were demons, that they were somehow evil. They claimed that their Jesus was the only god. But his own gods—whatever their moral stripe— were better suited to the sort of life his people lived than this fool Christ.

He quickly brushed the snow away from the woman's face, wondering if she was dead. He pulled off his glove. He was warming to a fine fury; he would have no problem with the cold. What manner of men had charge of this slender beauty, that she was left here to die? He touched her cheek, then her forehead. Cold. Cold and hard as marble.

She was wearing a silk gown trimmed with sable, and a white

brocaded mantle. The wind was howling around him and the world was sinking into a cold, gray blueness as the sun set somewhere beyond the clouds. He lifted her hand. Icy but still flexible, not stiff yet. His outer mantle was a thick bearskin, somewhat worn and stained. No, very worn and stained, but warm.

He leaned over her, lifted her head, and tried to see if her breath fanned his cheek. The hard, wind-driven pellets of sleet, mixed now with the blowing snow, stung his uncovered nose and lips.

He couldn't tell anything. He paused for a second, then vented his frustration with one sharp curse word. He could put his hand down her dress, but to touch a young woman in certain places, even with her permission, was considered a particularly vile offense. He was hesitant, not wishing to dishonor her family even if she was a corpse.

Then he spat out another curse, this one directed at himself. If she wasn't already dead, she might easily die while he stood over her dithering about the proprieties. He pushed his hand down her dress, feeling for the heart where the throbbing can most easily be felt, on the left chest below the breast. He was rewarded by warmth and a slow but steady throbbing. After that he wasted no time. He pulled off his outer bearskin mantle, threw it on the snow drifted at the roadside, then lifted her and wrapped her tightly in the heavy fur. He reflected that both he and the mantle were probably harboring a few fleas, kept alive by the warmth of his big body. This girl didn't have nearly the healthy temperature he did; maybe the little bastards would die. At any rate, the extermination of his vermin companions was the only benefit he was likely to derive from this particular adventure.

He had planned to avoid the monastery at the foot of the pass, to find some secluded place to sleep through the blizzard, then continue on his way unobserved by the Franks. No possibility of that now. If he didn't get this girl to someplace sheltered and warm, she would soon die. Well enough for him to curl up inside his mantle and let his own body heat seal out the cold. He could survive almost subzero temperatures wrapped in the skin. That was, after all, why he'd killed the animal in the first place.

He'd met the bear in the mountains when he was no more than fourteen. It had been an old animal, humpbacked and silver about the muzzle, but well fed, with a thick winter pelt.

"It seems," he had said to the bear, "I am your destiny."

The bear reared on his hind legs and roared a challenge.

"You may go if you wish," he told the bear. "I will not hinder you."

But the bear dropped down on all fours and trotted forward to wrap him in a lethal embrace. He knew he would get only one chance, then the creature would kill him. He stood his ground and drove his spear into the bear's side as it reared again to tear him apart. The spade-shaped blade sank in to the cross hilt but the bear didn't die.

He thought, *I did not reach the heart,* just as the bear stripped the skin from his ribs with one claw and made a serious attempt to disembowel him with the other. *So,* he thought, and remembered himself as calm. *This is death.*

But it wasn't, because then the bear died and left him with the biggest and best skin he'd ever seen. At least it was the best after he'd tanned it and sewn up the hole made by the spearhead. He was glad he'd clung to it along the many roads his life had taken since then.

He struggled downhill with the woman over his shoulder. The icy, vicious wind in his face attempted with almost conscious malignity to blind and freeze him, but he was too proud and annoyed to give in to his discomfort. His own anger warmed him. *I could have searched the drifts where she lay,* he thought at whatever guardians and companions had been with her. *But I didn't.* "Fools, you deserve to die," he whispered in the teeth of the wind. He spoke to their souls, their ghosts, if they happened to be following him.

Frank means free, so they say. Frank means fool, idiot, if you ask me.

Hear that, woman? He shook the limp body draped over his shoulder. *I think your people are stupid. I think your people are dirty. I think your people are lazy. I think your people are—*But then night and the storm didn't hear the next insult because he ran face first into the monastery wall.

He staggered back and sat down in a snowdrift. He eased the limp body from his shoulder and cradled her in his arms.

She was breathing. The bearskin had done its work. Her skin was warmer than his now. He was clad only in his shirt, woolen mantle, trousers, and cross-gartered leggings. And more tired than he realized or was willing to admit.

He lifted her, got to his feet, and went in search of a gate.

HE FOUND IT AT LENGTH AFTER A SEARCH ALONG the walls, a search in which his principal terror was of straying away into the icy darkness and freezing to death before he could find the building again. Yes, he could lie in the cold and wrap the mantle around them both, but he didn't think even the bearskin would serve to warm two people on a night like this.

Women were, in his experience, fragile creatures, and he had no desire to lie in the darkness and feel her life drain away as her body grew colder and colder. When the Frankish slaveholders had driven him across the Alps to sell him to the Lombards, he'd had just such an experience with the man chained next to him, who had been old. Beyond a certain age the body loses the power to keep itself warm. Used to frigid winters and violent blizzards, he'd warned the slave dealers that the older men in the party might not survive the climb over the pass. But all he got for his pains was a blow to his face with one end of the driver's whip—a blow that nearly broke his jaw and made eating the biscuit and dried meat they were thrown every few days both difficult and uncomfortable. Then he was roundly cursed when three of the slaves died at the top of the pass. He had woken one morning and gazed into two ice-glazed blue eyes empty of life. He remembered he'd been lying there when the older man began to whimper and moan in the night. He spoke not one word of the man's language; he had not even been sure what it was. All he could do was share part of the bearskin with him. He didn't like to remember he'd cursed and threatened the old one, trying to make him shut up, fearing he'd bring the driver's punishment down on all of them.

At length his neighbor was silenced. He had thought the old one slept. But when gray light from beyond the boiling clouds began to fill the high rocky track—not like the sunrise, more the way water fills a cup—he had realized he was chained to a dead man. Then it was his turn to shout and scream and he'd been duly punished. And worse yet, laughed at by the slave drivers for being frightened of a corpse.

He remembered the way the old one's stiffened body bounced from ledge to ledge until it finally vanished into the thick, pale ice cloud filling the valleys below. He tightened his arms around the woman and prayed to meet the slave dealers again. Prayed to his own stubbornly held gods that he might be able to meet them sometime when circumstances favored him. He didn't ask for any special advantage, only weapons and no chains to confine him. He would solemnly thank his gods and handle the rest. He also prayed to find the door in this wall. By now it was night and black as a pig's asshole.

He circled the structure, rapping with his right hand. At length his knuckles struck wood—oak planks by the feel of them and bound with iron. He slammed his fist against it, and the door swung open. He found himself in a shallow courtyard almost as dark as the night he left behind.

There was a little light, enough to show that the pillared walkways sheltered from the wind held a half-dozen men. One of them reared up and shouted at him, "Kick the perdition-bound door shut, you fatherless bonehead. It's cold enough here without a fool like you letting the storm in."

He was in no position to argue. He kicked the door shut.

A lantern with a very low flame hung on a rack projecting from the wall. By its light he could see the huddled figures lying against the walls.

"Is this how guests are accommodated here?" he asked contemptuously.

"This is how the smart ones are," the reply came from above—the one who'd shouted at him. "This is not the best of stopping places. Nor is the lord abbot the friendliest of men. At least we will survive here and can press on to more comfortable places in the morning. What have you there?" He pointed to the bundle in the bearskin.

"A . . ." He paused. This wasn't the most respectable bunch he'd ever seen.

"A . . . what?" Someone from behind him lifted the lamp from the wall, held it up, and looked down into the face of the figure.

"A woman!"

The man who had shouted at him stood up. "A what? A woman! You motherless one. How do you bring a woman into this of all places and on a night like this?"

"I found her."

Someone in the shadows gave a nasty laugh. "My cousin found eight pieces of gold, or at least so he said. But the king's judge cut off his right hand anyway."

"Is she pretty?" the man who had called him motherless asked. "If she is, you might be able to sell her for a few coppers, a night's lodging, and some food. If she's amiable enough, they might even let you keep her when you leave."

Just then something struck him a hard blow in the upper back. He felt the point enter his skin. He dropped the woman and spun around. As he did so, he felt the knife rip out of his back as it was torn free of the hand of his attacker. The skills that had kept him alive in the Lombard slave pens served him well. He slammed the heel of his hand into his assailant's chin, snapping his head back, while he brought his knee up between the fellow's legs.

His knee thudded painfully into a spiked leather cup. *A professional,* he thought. Therefore he had no compunction about slamming the knife man's head against one of the stone pillars holding up the porch roof. It broke like an egg hitting a cobbled floor. Brains were flung everywhere.

Screaming. He was hearing screaming. His opponent shouldn't be screaming. He should be extraordinarily dead. No, the screaming was behind him. He spun around. The woman was up. She had a foot-long knife and was driving it up into the throat of the man who'd shouted at him to shut the door. She didn't look steady on her legs, but the hand holding the knife was accurate enough. The steel had gone in below the Adam's apple and the point had broken through next to the spine.

She wasn't screaming. No, the one doing the screaming was another of the "guests," the one holding the lantern. Blood poured from his face. The blood from four long gashes on one of his cheeks dripped onto his shirt. She must have gotten him with her nails. He snatched up the bearskin, threw it around her, grabbed her, and ran across the courtyard to the inner door.

It opened in front of them. A man stood behind it holding a wax light. One of the monks, he surmised. When they were safely inside, the monk slammed shut the door and shot the bolts. The monk, if that's what he was, let them both catch their breath.

"We come," he gasped, his arm wrapped around the woman; she sagged against his shoulder.

He could smell a faint perfume in the darkness. She was growing warmer, and the scent was being released from her clothes and skin. It was a shock to him, a delicate scent like the incense of the Christian churches he'd been forced to attend by his Lombard masters, but not so musky, leaning more toward flowers.

"We come," he gasped out again, "in search of food and shelter—"

"Be quiet," the old monk whispered. "What were you two playing at out there? Were you trying to rouse the abbot and his whole house?"

Someone or something giggled in the darkness. The monk, if that's what he was, muttered something unintelligible under his breath. "Too bad for you both now," he muttered.

The woman took a deep breath and pulled the bearskin around herself. "My husband and I—" She indicated him. "—got lost . . . We were coming over the pass . . . and . . ."

"Husband? Tee-he-he. Oh, my, what a deception."

The figure materialized next to them. It carried a torch. He could see enough and smell enough to tell it was dirty, crippled, and old; how old, he couldn't tell. It limped and had a head of thick, white hair. Crippled: the back was hunched and twisted, the shoulders were higher than the head. Dirty: the stench of unwashed flesh was a vile reek in the stone-walled corridor. He'd never encountered any human quite so aromatic, even in the slave barracks where men went for months without washing.

It giggled again and reached a filthy paw toward the woman.

He was just getting over the shock of hearing he had a wife, but he instinctively interposed his body between this thing and the woman. It turned toward the monk with the wax light and chuckled horribly.

"He says he's her husband?"

"Yes, my lord abbot," the gatekeeper answered obsequiously. "We should honor the sanctity of the marriage bond as Christ . . ." The porter spoke gently, slowly, as if to a child.

"Abbot?" the woman whispered. He found he was holding her hand; it tightened on his own.

The creature turned away from the gatekeeper and began to try to pull the bearskin away from the woman's body. A thread of drool ran down from the corner of its mouth to the chin. The mucus glistened in the light—the light coming from behind them.

Something smashed into the side of his face. He felt her hand pulled free of his as he lost control of his body and went down. The back of his head struck the stone floor of the corridor; his vision dissolved into flashes of light. *No,* he thought. *No.* Twisting, he tried to fight off the stunning effects of the blow and regain control of his arms and legs.

Someone screamed. A woman.

He had a moment's sorrow that he couldn't have offered her better protection. He was still struggling, but couldn't feel his arms and legs; and when he could, it seemed only a few seconds later—he found he was tied hand and foot and being dragged along the corridor feet first, his head bouncing uncomfortably along the cobbled walkway.

"My lord, I beg you . . ."

Everything was black as the bottom of a well. He wondered if he'd been blinded by the crack on the head . . . but no. It was just dark because he could see a little.

"My lord!" The old man who'd opened the gate continued to remonstrate with his captors.

"Drive that fool away!" The command came from the one he'd heard addressed as abbot. "Drive him back to his cell. I don't want this one to get away." The creature sounded like a peevish child.

"You know, you know how I love to hear them scream. You can hear them for a long time afterward. After we drop the slab some of them go on all night, screaming and screaming and screaming."

S HE WAS NOT AS FRIGHTENED AS SHE OUGHT TO have been. This was her first clear thought. She'd awakened when he pushed his hand down her dress. She'd believed for a moment, for a joyous moment, that he was her husband taking familiar liberties while waking her from a nap. But that happy, carefree moment quickly faded.

The other memories were a jumble. He was carrying her. It was cold, oh so cold. He was saying insulting things. They were dragging him away, down the hall. Now three women appeared, coming out of the darkness. One carried a candle, but she could see them all clearly. She must see well in the dark, she thought.

They were questioning her, tugging at her clothing, trying to get her to accompany them.

"Is he really your husband?"

She felt an odd sense of dislocation. The questioner was an older woman. She seemed respectable enough in her brown mantle and linen veil. She smelled of soap, perspiration, and wine. The other two stank only of drink. They went unveiled and their gowns were shapeless and none too clean. They walked in such a heavy aroma of alcoholic deterioration that she wondered how they managed to stay upright. She was sure they had both been drunk almost constantly for months.

One was dark with lank, greasy hair; the other might have been a blonde but she was so filthy it was impossible to tell anything about her original appearance.

"Is he your husband? Really your husband?" the older woman asked again.

No. The idea, for a number of reasons, was ludicrous. But she wasn't about to tell them that. She'd spoken in hope of protecting them both from any opportunistic lechery among what she was sure, by now, must be a nest of brigands.

"What is it?" the woman shrilled. "Are you dumb like poor Morgana here?" She indicated the more wretched of her two companions, a child.

"No, I'm not dumb," she heard herself answering. "Yes, he is my husband. What are they doing to him? Where are they taking him? All we ask is shelter for the night, then we will leave in the morning and never trouble you again."

The blond one, the one called Morgana, began to whimper. She sounded like a dog, a dog whipped too often.

The lank-haired one leaned toward her. "Look, look, Lavinia. She . . . has . . . jewels."

The woman reached forward haltingly, to fumble at her neck. The idea of being touched by any of these women was repulsive. She eased backward.

"Don't like us, do you?" the older woman taunted. "Don't worry. When you've been here as long as we have, you won't look much better. Fact is, you'll probably look worse.

"Sully here probably isn't much older than you are. But right now *he* won't be able to keep his hands off you. Forget about your man and be nice to the abbot. He rules here.

"Sully, Morgana, bring her along now. Girl, you come with us. Don't give us any trouble now and you won't get hurt. Be a shame to spoil your pretty face."

Then the two slatterns closed in on either side and began to hurry her along the corridor.

Again the weird feeling of dislocation. Her memory was a jumble of images, images she couldn't sort out. Every time she moved, she felt dizzy and her head hurt. Every step sent a dagger of pain into one side of her face. The horse reared. She saw its head against a sky streaked with red, orange, and black, a sunset sky. The snow was blue in the failing light. She was a good horsewoman. Somehow she knew that she should have been able to control him, but this animal was insane with terror and it was falling. Falling. And there was pain. Pain then as now, like an ice dagger driven into her ear and cheekbone.

Then he was fumbling with her dress. At first she was overjoyed, thinking it meant the end of the rearing horse, the pain, the cold. Not passive cold but a stinging burning chill in her hands and feet. A cold that crept, preceded by a buzz of agony, through her fingers and toes, then feet and hands. She had known she was freezing to death. Not a peaceful death, but an awesomely agonizing one as ice crystals formed in her flesh, bringing paralysis and pain on top of pain . . . driving deeper toward the bone.

Then she was sure all this was part of a nightmare and she would wake safe and warm in her bed . . . with . . . and then she lost the trail in confusion. But he would be there and she had simply been dreaming. It took only seconds for her to realize warmth and safety had been the dream and the nightmare . . . reality. But he did have her over his shoulder, and he was insulting the Franks, her people, in Saxon. He'd wrapped her in this bearskin and seemed to mean her no harm.

Then they were in a room and God, God, the stench. But the older woman, Lavinia, was lighting a many-branched oil lamp with her taper. The lamp flared temporarily, throwing a blinding light into what had been darkness only seconds before. When her vision cleared, she saw the older woman had something like horror in her eyes. Morgana crouched down near a fireplace in one corner of the room, shivering. Sully was pointing again at her neck.

"Jewels, Lavinia . . . jewels. Can I have some?"

Lavinia shook her head, was shaking her head over and over. She ignored Sully. "I knew it would happen one day," she said. "They'd bite off something too big to chew or sink their fangs into, something strong enough to eat them. And now, by the look of you, woman, they have. What is your name, girl, and of what family are you?"

She looked down at herself, trying to see what inspired such horror in the woman's eyes. She was wearing a dalmatic of green silk brocade trimmed with sable over a divided riding skirt of soft suede leather embroidered with gold. Her mantle was white brocade, heavy material lined with ermine. She reached up to her throat. Sully was right. Jewels, at least a half-dozen necklaces; her hair was done up in a snood of soft metal chains; and if the necklaces and snood were a match for the rings on her fingers, the count was seven. They were all made of silver or gold and embellished with precious stones.

"That's a lot of jewels," Sully said. "You think he will give me some?"

"No," Lavinia snapped. "What are you, half-witted like her?" She pointed to Morgana. "You could well be looking at all of our deaths. Do you think women dressed as she is wander about the mountains at night, free for the taking? No, her family will be looking for her and they won't stop until they find her.

"Girl, are you fool enough to let yourself be carried off by some pretty-faced scoundrel like the slave dragged off to the chapel?"

"No, I wouldn't run off with anyone."

"Husband. Husband indeed. That slave is no one's husband. No, you belong to some great lord, husband or father, and he will be wild until he finds you. And when he catches up with you, he will probably kill every single one of us." She slapped her forehead. "What to do? What to do? What is your name?"

"Regeane." The word passed lips that seemed to belong to someone else. "Regeane," she repeated hesitantly. "Regeane is my name."

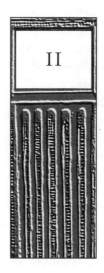

II

WHEN MAENIEL RETURNED TO HIS STRONG-
hold, a few of his people greeted him. Gordo, a huge,
bearded man, gave him the news.

"What do you mean, she left? Two days ago? Did no one accompany her? What are you thinking? What were you thinking?" he almost screamed.

Gordo managed to look pained and taken aback at the same time; it was rare for his leader to show strong emotion about anything. Maeniel's present conduct amounted almost to hysteria. Disapproval crept into Gordo's expression of concern. This simply was not done. "You forget the dignity of your position," he admonished his lord.

Maeniel ran his fingers through his hair. He raised one hand, then let it fall to his side. "Where is my wife?"

He sounded dangerous. Gordo was unperturbed. "I'm trying to tell you. Please listen."

Maeniel took a deep breath and let it out slowly.

"She worried about the weather," Gordo continued. "She worried about you. She was afraid you might not return in time to join the king. She worried about the great Charles's army, saying that one good blizzard could wipe out the Frankish warriors. We told her we thought that no great loss, these kingly quarrels being nothing but a nuisance to humbler folk. If they all died, so much the better for us, Matrona said—that, I didn't."

Maeniel nodded. "I'm familiar with Matrona's sentiments. Continue."

"The weather grew worse. We could all feel the storm but Matrona said they would beat it to the foot of the pass if they hurried. So she went."

"Not alone!"

"No, not alone," Gordo explained patiently. "She took Matrona. Gavin whined and moaned a lot about it being cold, but he, Antonius, and several others went with them. The storm came that night, and it's been blowing ever since. With Matrona not here, there is no one to cook." Gordo sounded disconsolate. "With your permission, I'm going hunting," he said as he ambled phlegmatically out of the room.

Maeniel hurried to his bedchamber. His wife could write. Possibly, just possibly, she'd left a note for him.

His room was empty but not cold. The fireplace, a shallow opening in the wall, was overhung by a huge marble hood. Even in the coldest weather, the stone—once warmed—trapped enough heat to keep it comfortable. Assuming, that is, someone kept the fire burning. Someone had.

The Romans who built the fortress hadn't envisioned this room as a bedchamber. It may have been the *tablinium* office belonging to the general who commanded the fortress.

The room was lit by three large, round windows set high in the wall on one side. Each window was plugged with thick glass to keep out the wind and cold. One couldn't see much through them, but they let in a lot of light. A door and two more windows were below. All were now closed by heavy oak shutters against the bad weather.

When he'd first come here, the room attracted him. Not only because of the light, but the windows and door opened onto a private balcony with a view of a beautiful valley and the mountains beyond. Over the years he'd made the room into a place of luxury. Silk rugs from somewhere in the east covered the floor and hung on the walls, insulating the cold stone. The bed was a giant carved four-poster made of cedar and comfortably equipped with three layers of hangings. Silk gauze for warm summer nights; silk brocade for nippy spring and autumn ones; and heavy, woolen and silk tapestry for the worst winter weather.

Fine, thick feather ticks filled the bed box. They were covered by silk sheets and a heavy fur comforter.

She'd left no note, but her nightgown was thrown across one of the chairs by the hearth. He lifted it, brought it to his face, and inhaled deeply. It was permeated with her. She followed an ancient Roman custom, lavishing particular attention on it because she knew it especially delighted him. She rubbed oils of different fragrances into separate parts of her body. Her arms roses; hands citron; neck myrrh, as were her breasts; lavender, from the Frankish kingdoms, on stomach and thighs; sage and bay on legs and feet. A ravishing mixture of odors: food, fruit, and herbs at the same time.

There were four chairs near the hearth and four board games scattered on a table. Her attendants each had an accustomed chair. Matrona, the one facing the fire; Barbara, across from her; and Antonius, her chamberlain, with his back to the fire. Gavin also left traces near the hearth. Maeniel considered him with a touch of jealousy. He was a bull in rut and would take anything offered, but Matrona kept him on a short leash.

He could almost see them of an evening, laughing, drinking together, sharing a game of chess or backgammon. Gavin liked to gamble and sometimes played for high stakes, but Antonius, who usually took his money, kept him from plunging too deeply around the women. There had been an unpleasant moment when Antonius first came to the stronghold from Rome, with Regeane. Gavin accused him of cheating at cards and threatened Antonius with a sword. Maeniel wasted no time. He picked up Gavin and heaved him through the nearest window.

Antonius had been horrified. But Maeniel conducted him to the window—the same window he'd thrown Gavin through—and pointed out the red wolf struggling in a snowbank. "He doesn't like it," Maeniel said. "His fur is short. And it takes him hours to work his way back to the gates. He won't draw on you again." Then he ambled away, but before he left he asked Antonius, "Did you cheat?"

"Of course," Antonius replied.

"Don't," Maeniel said.

And as far as he knew, Antonius hadn't cheated again. But he won anyway, since he was—on his slowest day—at least twice as intelligent as Gavin—or any of the rest of them, for that matter.

Maeniel moved back toward the bed. Regeane and Matrona had perfumed the sheets and coverlet. In their world few people slept alone. When Regeane retired for the night, she normally took one of her women with her when he was not there.

Outside, the wind pounded the shutters. He could hear its whispering scream through walls five feet thick. "No," he whispered. "No." He didn't care who had gone with her. He would leave tonight and . . . He turned and saw Barbara sitting in her chair by the fire.

His body jerked in a startled reply; he averted the change with an effort of will, a conscious effort.

"Barbara! You didn't go?"

"No." She shook her head. "You forget. I'm not up to dealing with the weather.

"Antonius is a lot younger than I am," she said. "I tried my best to keep her here, but no one would listen, least of all Regeane." She rolled her eyes heavenward. "And as for the rest, when I suggested they restrain her ardor for travel in howling blizzards, all I got were some very peculiar looks."

"They can't imagine interfering with another's freedom of action," he explained as he walked over and settled in Regeane's chair across from Barbara.

"That Gordo," she went on, "that fool nearly didn't bother to tell me you'd arrived. He just happened to mention it as he passed through the kitchen on his way to God knows where."

"He's going hunting," Maeniel said.

"In this?" Barbara gestured toward the shuttered windows.

"It's probably not blowing as badly down in the valleys. Even if it is, he can always pile up somewhere and sleep."

"At least she rode Audovald," Barbara commented.

"That makes me feel better," Maeniel said. "Audovald is a very responsible creature. That mare I gave her is a flighty female, too young and nervous—"

"If she weren't a horse, I'd call her a bitch," Barbara said. "She's only interested in one thing—"

"I told her," Maeniel said, "not until spring."

"Er, yes," Barbara said slowly. "You told Regeane—"

"No! I told the mare she might as well forget about it . . . and not to go stretching her neck out of the stall to lift the latch or try to jump over the half door."

"Yes," Barbara mused. "You told the mare . . . Amazing. I'd like to know how you did that."

"I'll show you sometime," he answered absently. "But Audovald is sensible. He can find his way down the mountain in the dark. I'm glad he's with her. What is this business about the meat? Why is Gordo going hunting? And don't you find it disconcerting to live with us?"

"I don't know why he's going hunting, and no, I don't normally find you or your friends disconcerting. Compared to the average husband, you're a breath of fresh air. Any other man would probably be taking out his temper on the rest of us."

"No," Maeniel said. "I'll just go after her. Right now."

"In this? With night coming on?" Barbara objected.

"Doesn't matter," he replied.

The shutters rattled and slammed as wind battered the building.

"I hope none of them has started on the livestock," he muttered as he was rising. "You tell them the sheep are here for wool and milk, the same goes for the bull, cows, and goats. No snacking, on pain of my grave displeasure. Got that?"

Barbara nodded. "I believe they're all present and accounted for. The livestock, I mean. As far as your followers are concerned, I can't say."

"Need any money?"

"No," Barbara said. "I promised I'd stay here while she was gone."

"Fine. I'll bring her home when I find her."

Barbara followed him downstairs, across the great hall, down another flight of winding stairs, and watched him as he melted into the night.

I T WAS BAD, HE THOUGHT AS HE MADE HIS WAY down the trail, but the wind was at his back and he could see fairly well. As wolf, he could travel even in a howling blizzard—as Barbara put it. But this wasn't that severe a storm. "Of course," he grumbled to himself deep in his throat, "there should be no storm at all. It is spring. The sky should be clear, not a pall of rolling billows shadowed by mist. The sun should be out during the day, warming the air and melting the frozen rivers and streams and turning the valley fuzzy green with new growth. But no, here is this last gasp of winter . . ." Abruptly he hushed himself. He stood stock-still. He waited for the

wind to drop. It was blowing the thick ruff of fur at his neck up
around his ears and battering his sensitive tympanic membranes inside
with its harsh fluttering sound.

The sound came again. A scream, a horse scream, a cry of pain,
terror, and distress.

Above the wolf the mountain towered, its top lost in cloud.
Beside him on one side, an only half-seen gorge fell almost straight
down to a river still locked in ice. A wolf can see in almost pitch
darkness, but now there was little light for Maeniel's eyes to use. He
maintained his position on the trail by touch: the feel of his paws
on the snow, his sense of wind direction, and the slope of the trail
under his feet. He couldn't travel any faster without putting himself
in danger.

He pushed his pace. He knew he was heading roughly in the
direction of the sound he'd heard. That was all he could do at the
moment.

This was his domain.

His domain in the human, legal sense. As the man Maeniel,
he held it, courtesy of Charles, king of the Franks. Those coming up
and over the pass followed his road and his rules. He'd not heard of
any travelers coming this way, so the horse must be his and with his
wife's, Regeane's, party.

Audovald? He didn't want to think so. No, Audovald was not
simply a horse, he was an old and trusted friend, and Regeane—God,
oh, God, Regeane had been on his back. He paused, a particularly
vicious blast of wind flattened his fur, and the cold ripped at his skin.
He shook himself violently to clear the snow from his pelt, thinking
he had spent too long in the Roman city. *The mild climate there softened
me. If it is Audovald, he will know my voice.* Maeniel lifted his head and
howled. He gave the cry all he had, beginning in the deep baritone
hunting call up and up, ululating through loneliness, then moving
into the highest registers of grief and inconsolable longing, up, up
almost beyond the range of human ears.

He was answered. The sound was a whistling neigh of deep
distress.

Despite the wind and cold and darkness, he began to run.
First bound was fine, but the second carried him out over and into
nothingness.

REGEANE," SHE WHISPERED, AND TURNED TOWARD the bed.

"I wouldn't look there, noble lady," Lavinia said. "She was one of the abbot's favorites and took poison. He likes them better dead than alive. So she's still here, but smells bad and has bits and pieces falling off her now."

"What?" Regeane whispered, knowing as she did so that Lavinia was telling the truth. A set of preternaturally sharp senses warned her there was a corpse in the room, and it was in the bed.

She lifted one hand to her face; she felt a sense of drunken disorientation, but she hadn't been drinking. She'd been riding along a trail at the pass. The horse reared. Her last horrifying memory was the realization that the horse Audovald was toppling over. The earth that formed the narrow road must . . . must have . . .

Regeane touched her cheek. Her hand was cold, icy. The bite of her own cold fingers on her skin startled her and brought her back to full alertness. She moved as far away from the bed as she could.

"Is there no place cleaner and better favored than this . . . this death chamber, hereabouts?"

"No," Lavinia whispered. "We women come here because it's safe. Even if she—" Lavinia indicated the bed.—"isn't the most pleasant company in the world, at least she won't beat and rape us. Something I can't be sure won't be done by the abbot's livelier companions."

Yes, Regeane thought. This was a nest of brigands, if not something worse. *Worse,* the idea troubled her clouded mind. What could be worse, this side of death? But just possibly she was not this side of death. Perhaps she had died when the horse . . . fell? She wasn't sure it had fallen, but then—no. Yes, she was, she was sure: the horse fell. How far down was it into that valley? Someone, she couldn't remember who, said almost a mile down. No, nothing could survive a fall like that. So she was dead. But how so? Since she could still feel, think, move, and yes—she took in a deep breath of the freezing air— yes, she could also breathe.

But she might as well be dead, she was so cold. She eased toward the low fireplace where the child Morgana crouched. The woman

Lavinia picked up a log from a metal rack near the hearth and threw it on the almost-dead coals. It hissed, sputtered. The bark must have been wet. Then it caught and flamed up, sending a burst of heat into the room.

Regeane stretched out her hands gratefully toward the radiant heat rising from the newborn fire. She closed her eyes, seeing the hot redness behind her lids. The chimney smoke in her nostrils and clinging around her clothing had a far cleaner odor than anything in the putrid room around her.

"Ahhh, that feels good," Lavinia whispered.

Regeane felt her mind was beginning to clear. "My . . . husband?"

"Don't be a fool," Lavinia snapped. "I'll bet you don't even know his name."

"I don't, but he tried to help me. He may even have saved my life. So where did they take him? And what are they going to do to him?"

"Hush. Be glad they have him to occupy them until morning. Let them finish killing him and tomorrow I'll . . ." She turned back to where Regeane had been standing and gave a harsh gasp of surprise. The girl was gone!

T HE SAXON WAS NOT AN OPTIMISTIC MAN AND, indeed, his worst fears had been confirmed. He'd heard—even among the Lombards—dark tales about this place, the so-called monastery at the foot of the pass. Those tales had bothered him not at all, for he had planned to avoid at all costs the functionaries of the Frankish king. He didn't know if they would return him to his Lombard owners, but he didn't plan to test their charity. Nowhere in this harsh world could a friendless, kinless man hope for shelter or even compassion. This was his firm belief, and nothing in his life had even begun to persuade him otherwise. Certainly not this experience.

He'd managed to get sufficient control of his reflexes to prevent his head being battered to a pulp on the floor, but he remained tied. On the way to wherever they were taking him, he simply concentrated on keeping his tender skull away from the cobbles; otherwise, he ceased to struggle and tried to let himself go limp. Tied or not, he was still entangled with the bearskin, and the thick pelt kept him from being bruised or brained by his captors' careless handling. The thing was lucky, or maybe it wasn't. He'd been captured wearing it, but then, it probably saved his life when he was sold to the Lombards. But in the slave pens, he'd had to fight three men over the damned thing—or was it four? The whack on the head had been hard . . . But then his speculations were ended, because he found himself in the monastery chapel. He was stretched out on the floor.

The *thing*—that was how he thought about it—the thing that giggled was examining him. A finger prodded him in several places. "You sure you didn't hit him too hard?" it questioned the servitors who'd been dragging him along. "He looks dead."

"Dead, my ass," a voice he recognized as belonging to one of the men by the gate snarled. "Open your eyes, pig."

Somebody, probably the speaker, drove a boot into his ribs.

The Saxon whispered the vilest epithet he knew and opened his eyes. They were gathered in a circle around him. He'd never seen a worse band of cutthroats. They were all scarred, missing eyes, hands, noses, even lips. But what sent a frisson of sheer terror through his body was the fact that the speaker, one of the men he remembered from near the gate, was the man his companion had stabbed in the throat. And not only was he alive, but he seemed in reasonably good health.

The thing, the giggler, laughed a nasty titter. "Odd, he cannot believe you are alive."

Odd hawked and spat a disgusting mixture of phlegm and blood at the Saxon. "No thanks to him and his pretty pussy."

The Saxon twisted his head aside just in time to keep the mess from splattering in his face.

"She's a fair hand with the knife, that woman of his," Odd said. "Maybe she'll stay awhile, keep us company."

Yes, the Saxon thought, *there's the hole in his throat, almost like another mouth, where her knife went in.* Someone had stitched it shut. It was a red line from his Adam's apple to just below his ear. No, he should be dead. How was he not?

"Too bad," Odd said. His voice sounded thick, harsh—as if cutting his throat had interfered only with his ability to speak. "Too bad we couldn't get Gui back. The pig spilled too much of him against the post."

"Was that the one I brained?" the Saxon asked.

Odd laughed, an odd bubbling sound. Then he hawked and spat again. "I'm not all fixed. I'm still bleeding," he whined.

"Cut me loose," the Saxon said. "I'll fix you like I did Gui. You won't bleed anymore, you bastard."

Someone else kicked him. A good kick, vicious, it knocked some of the wind out of him.

"Beg for your life, pig," the giggler said. "They did." He gestured toward the choir stalls along the wall of the chapel.

Yes, the Saxon recognized it as a church, one of the Christian kind. He and the other slaves had been herded into one every week on the estate where he had been imprisoned. These places reminded him of nothing so much as cowsheds, but with higher roofs. They were long and fairly narrow. All along the walls there were seats with high backs carved of wood. These were for the priests, who were the only ones allowed to sit down. The slaves, and those few peasants who had braved the service intended for the villa's lowest field hands, knelt on the bare stone floor while the skirted Christian priests engaged in some complicated rite at an altar on one end of the room.

The cold, the pressure on his bare knees, and the stink of his fellow slaves' unwashed bodies, not to mention the presence of the taskmasters paid to keep the slaves from creating a disturbance, had rendered the whole ceremonial experience miserable. At certain times during the service—he was never sure which parts—the overseers struck with their whips at any slave unfortunate enough to make the slightest sound. Once, after seeing one of his more half-wit fellows who cursed the Christian god in the middle of the rites deprived of his eyes and tongue, he concluded this god was worse tempered than his people's spirits of wind, cold, storm, fire, desire, and fruitfulness. They, at least, were indifferent to human suffering. The Christian god was downright malicious. In fact this maggot-brained abbot, surrounded by what he was now sure were dead men, was a fitting servant for that god.

"Beg for your life." The abbot kicked him this time.

"Piss on you," the Saxon said.

"Beg," the abbot squealed. Snot ran from his nose, drool from his lips. He seemed disappointed. "By now," he whimpered, "they were all begging."

"Shit on you," the Saxon said. "I wouldn't give you piss, it's too good for you."

"I know, I know," one of the men near Odd shouted. "Let's show him our guests." He pointed to the choir stalls.

"Yes," the abbot said.

The abbot jumped up and down with glee, but on the second hop the Saxon saw where this was leading and managed to roll. The abbot landed on his ribs. The Saxon bucked like an angry horse—tied or not, he could move—but then they all took turns seeing if they could stay on top of him. He gritted his teeth, twisted and turned, trying to stay alive while the whole crew tried stomping him to death. Fortunately, only a few of them had boots heavy enough to do damage, but he heard one rib snap and then another; then he lurched up face first against the wooden rood screen in front of the altar, retching and gasping for breath.

The rest backed away, sounding winded, but the abbot got in a few more kicks in the region of his kidneys. "My, he is an entertaining one," the abbot burbled happily. "We haven't had one with this much energy in a long time. Yes, let's show him our guests."

Two of them got him by the arms and towed him back to the middle of the long room.

"The torch," the abbot shouted.

A torch flared somewhere near the altar and arced through the air in the abbot's direction. With surprising skill, the abbot plucked it out of the air, then shoved the flames in the Saxon's face. The abbot's companions looked even worse in the light. They all must have died at one time or another. One's head lolled strangely on his shoulders. Hanged? Another's skin was blackened, had an oily sheen, and part of a charred bone was visible at the elbow. Burned?

Death didn't seem to have altered their drinking habits. They were passing around a flagon. When it got to Odd, he took a hefty pull, then danced up and down, gagging and screaming, when some of the wine ran out of his cut throat and down his chest. The rest found this hilariously funny.

"It stings," he screeched. "It stings."

The Saxon imagined it did. Parts of the gash in his throat must still be raw. They were all, dead or alive, much taller than the abbot, but even so, he dominated them, for all his idiot gaze and constant drooling.

"Look," the abbot said, moving toward the choir stalls lining the sides of the church. He thrust the torch at what sat there.

The Saxon got only a glimpse, but the brief sight was almost enough to unnerve even him. He was almost sure he himself was going to join the things seated in the stalls before morning, if indeed the sun ever shone on this cursed place. And if morning ever came, it probably wouldn't for him. He turned his face resolutely away and closed his eyes.

The abbot gave a screech of fury and charged back toward him. "You'll look. You'll look or the first thing I'll do is put out your eyes." He slammed the torch into the side of the Saxon's face.

He heard himself scream as he felt and smelled his hair and skin burning. He could hear the abbot laughing.

"I knew I could make him scream. I make them all scream sooner or later."

"I can believe that," the Saxon said when he recovered enough to say anything.

"Do, oh, do believe it."

The torch was between himself and the abbot. All he could see were flames.

"Pull him up," the abbot ordered. "Get him on his feet. Bring him over so he can look at the other guests."

He was jerked to his knees. It took at least five or six of them. The Saxon was a big man. As they did, a thought occurred to him. The critic in his brain told him it was a rotten plan, but the more optimistic part of his mind suggested since he was fresh out of bright ideas, he might as well try this one.

He screamed loudly.

They let go of him and he fell, fell hard, and he screamed again. Not difficult. He had two broken ribs and they were excruciatingly painful.

Normally he wouldn't have screamed, being something of an iron man. *But screams seem to entertain these monsters. So give them a few,* he thought.

"What's wrong?" Odd asked drunkenly. "We didn't hurt you that much . . . at least not yet." Then he began laughing and spewing droplets of wine and blood from his cut throat.

"I'm hurt," the Saxon moaned. "Hurt inside. When you jumped on me, you must have broken something."

Odd kicked him and the resulting scream satisfied the rest that he was really hurt and not faking, because Odd put his boot toe into one of the broken ribs. The reflex of sheer agony arched the Saxon's back, and he almost fainted.

This aroused the abbot's anxiety. "Come on, get him on his feet. I want him over there before he dies on me.

"He," the abbot said, indicating the darkened altar, "will only let me play with them till they die. He won't let it go on any longer. He won't bring them back. If this one dies," he sniveled, "I won't get him back again. And I want to keep him for a while.

"So get him up," he screeched.

The corpse gang, because that's how the Saxon thought about them now, jerked him to his knees again. The Saxon made his body go limp. He fell, fell hard.

"Get up," the abbot screamed, and battered him with the torch.

The Saxon screamed and moaned but made himself lie still, then let out an absolute roar of sheer agony when the abbot pressed the torch against his side.

I MUST BE DEAD, REGEANE THOUGHT. YES, THAT would explain everything. *I must be dead; otherwise how could I see so well in the dark?* She was following the curve of the wall away from the room where the women had conducted her, but she was able to see the long hall around her. In fact there even seemed to be a light ahead, and she heard the distant sound of shouts and screams. Yes, there was a light. Regeane made herself hurry but found when she reached the silver glow it was only the moon shining through broken rafters above. Outside, the storm must have blown itself by. Now the moon shone fitfully through the swiftly moving cloud rack above.

The wind slashed through the broken roof, raising gooseflesh over every exposed inch of her skin. The cold was bitter, but the breeze was clean and it deadened the smells around her. Snow had blown in through the hole in the roof and drifted on the floor. It was frozen, slippery, and she tried to ease her way around it. Her riding boots were clumsy on the frozen surface.

"What? Woman? Are you mad? I tried to get you away from him." The whisper came from the shadows near the patch of moonlight.

Regeane recognized the voice, that of the old monk who'd let them in at first. "I must find my husband," she replied.

"Don't repeat that lie to me," he answered with some asperity. "I sent you away with the women to try to save you from our so-called abbot and his demonic crew, and here I find you rushing back. Are you in such a hurry to meet your doom? The man is a runaway slave. I felt his collar when he ran into me at the door. He's no husband to a woman like you."

"Doesn't matter," Regeane said. "I must help him. He tried to save me."

The man, only a shadow in the gloom, clutched at her arm, but she pulled away with surprising ease. Just then a terrible scream ran out.

"No-no-no," the old man moaned. He snatched at Regeane again, but she was already running toward the chapel. She saw big double oak doors just ahead. One was closed, the other open just a crack. Faint light spilled out into the empty hall.

She stretched out one hand and pulled it open.

To MAENIEL, THE SENSATION WAS MORE LIKE FLY-ing than falling. A fall is the primal terror, yet he was still not as afraid as he might have been, because the snow-filled darkness was so thick. It seemed to him that the trail just vanished, then he was flying, then he landed. The wind went out of him in a rush. He might have lost consciousness, but he wasn't sure. He only knew he'd been slammed hard into a pile of rocks, the wind completely knocked out of him. He did what a human would do in like circumstances: he lay very still and tried desperately to get his breath.

While he was doing so, his vision began to clear. Not much help, he thought, since all he could see were long draperies of blow-ing snow whipped like gigantic lengths of fabric by the storm winds. But when he looked up, he was able to see, even in the misty gloom, that the trail was gone, wiped out by a monster avalanche that had plunged down from the glacier-bound mountain slope above.

Regeane, he thought, and began to struggle. But it seemed an eternity before he could manage to get to his feet. By then the light was getting better, and he was able to see what saved his life. He was on the spread of snow from the avalanche itself. The whole topography of the landscape was altered. Not only had the trail down the mountainside been swept away, but part of the peak was gone, spread fanwise across what had been a steep drop to the valley with its mountain torrent in the gorge below. Now the slope was no longer so steep, and the river was trying to carve a new path over the debris of the glacier fallen from the mountain.

The wolf crouched and howled again.

And again he was answered.

The light was growing, though the snow was still falling. It was less a curtain than a haze, and not far away he saw a dark spot against the snow. It was Audovald. The horse was half buried. Only his neck and one forehoof were clear.

The horse blew through his nostrils when the wolf approached. *Is it you?*

Yes. They touched noses.

Audovald was reassured. *Are you angry?*

The wolf touched noses with him again. *No. I'm frightened.* This was a body movement by the wolf and otherwise untranslatable.

I lost her. This was a cry of pain from the horse.

The wolf touched noses with him again reassuringly. *We are all mortal. I trust you did what you could.*

The whole mountain fell. The horse was in distress. *The trail vanished from beneath my feet. The rest fled. Antonius tried to lead them to safety.* Audovald moaned, a single terrible sound from a horse. *I cannot know if he succeeded, but she'd pushed the others ahead and we were too far back. I tried to ride it down. I failed.* He stretched his neck out, rested his chin on the snow pack, and closed his eyes.

The wolf began to dig.

All my legs are probably broken.

Horses are pessimists, the wolf thought. He paused in his labors and asked, *Are you in pain?*

No.

Then we will try. The wolf continued digging.

She heard it coming. So did I, the horse continued. *The problem was the ice fall was so big we didn't believe our own senses, but she turned, pushed them past us, and cried out a warning. Antonius acted quickly. But by the time it was upon us, she and I were last in the column and were swept away. I do not know what happened to the rest.*

The wolf freed the horse's other forehoof. Audovald tried to lunge forward, but then cried out in pain and fell back.

Don't struggle till I ask you to, the wolf said.

Yes, my lord, the horse replied. The wolf noted, however, he seemed heartened.

THE SAXON SAW HER OPEN THE DOOR. BY SOME miracle the rest of the midnight court didn't. The abbot had just jerked the torch away from his side, and he and the corpse gang were avidly watching their victim's responses. The Saxon sagged back and lay on his side, eyes half closed, gasping for breath. She was a spot of pure beauty in a dark universe. Briefly he cursed her guardians again. How had they let such as she—certainly a noblewoman—fall into such utter peril? He hoped that seeing what they were doing to him, she would run. She should be terrified by this ghastly crew, but she didn't seem frightened. Instead she reached around and drew her knife.

A table knife, he guessed despairingly, but no, this thing counted as a short sword, a single-edged sax, and deadly.

"Leave him alone," she commanded.

Blessedly, they did.

The Saxon went through guilt that they'd concentrate their attentions on her, wild joy that she'd distracted them for a few moments, then hope that she was good enough with that pigsticker to hold them off until he could free himself. He'd tested the ropes during the earlier melee, and he was sure he could free himself, if only he could get a few moments alone.

True, he was injured and, if he'd spared thought about it, in pain, but he was boiling with fury and an absolutely blind thirst for revenge.

The whole crew surged toward her in a wave.

He rolled on his back, drew his knees up toward his chest, and thrust his bound hands up over his feet. When they were in front of him, he snatched at the ropes at his ankles. They gave with a hard pull. *Half rotten, like everything else in this filthy place,* he thought, and then he was on his feet.

Odd had a sword of sorts. It didn't look like a very good one; it was crusted with thick rust. Coming up behind the man, the Saxon ripped it out of his hand.

Odd spun around, surprised.

The Saxon swung the sword one-handed. *Gods of my people, it's good to have a sword in my hand. It's been so long,* he thought as his downstroke tore through Odd's shoulder, sliced through his ribs, and finished slicing his torso in half just above the hip.

Not such a bad sword, after all, the Saxon thought. It must once have belonged to a true warrior. *Wherever you are,* he spoke to the warrior's spirit, *I will avenge you.* So saying, he sliced the abbot into four pieces.

To his horror, they lay on the floor, wiggling, trying to draw together, rather the way a sundered snake thrashes and coils long after it is dead. Blood bubbled in the dead man's throat, pouring out on the stone floor. Blood, more blood than could have been in a man's body, came spurting from the hacked corpse, spraying in every direction.

Regeane saw the terror in the Saxon's face. She had her scramasax out. Heedless of the thing's value, she wrapped the white brocade mantle around her left arm. The man whose head hung at a strange angle struck at her with a spear. She parried with her mantle-wrapped arm, facing the spearhead up while she jabbed with the knife at his abdomen. She succeeded better than she'd hoped. A second later, he was tripping over his guts.

The Saxon seemed paralyzed with horror.

"The torch," she screamed. "Use fire. They are afraid of fire."

She was remembering Rome, black wasps on a woman's face, and a tomb that was there and then not there. She'd fought this thing before.

The Saxon lunged forward, snatched up the torch, and flung it at the wooden rood screen in front of the altar. The wood was old, brittle, and must have been tinder dry, and matters were helped by the fact that there were linen curtains on the bottom of the screen. They roared into flames, and, in a few seconds, the chapel was lit like day. What Regeane and the Saxon both saw was horrific.

The Saxon decided these must be the abbot's trophies. The choir stalls were lined with corpses. Some recognizable, dead possibly only a few months; others were only garments and dried skin, teeth, hollow eye sockets, and brown bone. What was very clear was that they had all died horribly. One recent corpse seemed unmarked, but from the expression of insane fear on his face and the position into which his hands had stiffened, it was clear he had been buried alive.

Regeane looked. Next to him was a woman. She was naked. She was nailed to the wooden chair by a dozen spears, none through a vital spot. She might, Regeane thought, have lived for days.

The remaining members of the corpse gang fled toward the altar.

Not a wise thing to do.

It reared up ahead of the corpse gang from the defiled altar, visible only because the flame racing over the rood screen outlined and defined it. A bear, but the biggest bear Regeane or the Saxon had ever seen. A bear with a pelt of flame. It roared and the walls seemed to shake. The corpse gang fell to the floor and groveled at its feet.

"Killed," it roared. "You have killed my votary, my worshiper, my priest. I have kept him and his creatures living for a hundred winters while I dwelt here."

"Yes," Regeane shouted. "He was a stench in the nostrils of all that is good."

"What care I how my creatures entertain themselves?"

The pleas from the corpse gang only seemed to annoy the bear creature. "Die," he said, and they did, collapsing to the floor in a heap. "I found you on the gallows. Go back."

They vanished.

"Pity I cannot make you do the same," it shouted, "but perhaps my minions can."

Both Regeane and the Saxon watched in terror as all around them the corpses in the choir stalls began to move.

I T TOOK THE GRAY WOLF ALMOST AN HOUR TO free the horse's hindquarters. They both suffered, fearful one leg would turn out to be broken. Then neither one of them would have known what to do.

The gray wolf didn't know how he could bring himself to kill a friend—even to save him terrible suffering. And the horse knew a shattered leg would be the end of him. Even a human with such an injury stood little chance of recovery. Blood loss and infection took a terrible toll even among those lightly injured. But as luck would have it, when the wolf had freed all four legs, Audovald found himself able to stand comfortably.

I cannot think, he told the wolf as he tested each leg by stamping and bending, *how I did not take mortal injury. But it appears I didn't. Now let's see if we can make it down into the valley. I must search for the rest.*

They were both balanced on the steep fanlike surface of the slide. By now the snow had stopped and the sky was clearing. The moon shone brightly. Both horse and wolf had no more trouble seeing than they would have at midday.

They may be miles from here or buried deep, Audovald said.

Horses are pessimists, the gray wolf thought again. He was about to begin circling when he heard a sharp yip from above.

Here and there some small bits of the trail remained. A black wolf was on one of them. Her tail waved back and forth in a graceful gesture, not an enthusiastic one.

I am alive, come.

He did. They were in a shallow cave, a natural grotto. Antonius was lying down, his head pillowed on a saddle. Gavin was tending a small fire. The black wolf—Matrona—and Maeniel both turned human. Maeniel borrowed some of Gavin's clothes, a heavy wool tunic and trousers. Gavin looked guilty and miserable at the same time.

"We lost her," he said, and began to weep.

Antonius opened his eyes once, shook his head, then closed them again. Matrona dressed in a white silk dalmatic and brown suede divided riding skirt.

"We will mourn later," Maeniel said firmly. "When we are sure. She is one of us, and we are difficult to kill."

Antonius's eyes opened. "You mean you think she might still be alive? But did you see what a drop—"

"As I said," Maeniel repeated. "When we are sure one way or the other, there will be time enough for grief and recriminations. In the meantime, we search. Antonius, can you ride?"

"Yes." Antonius was on his feet in a moment.

"Good," Maeniel said. "Audovald is making his way here."

"The horse survived?"

"Yes, I freed him. We—" He indicated Gavin and Matrona. "—will go as wolves." They dropped their clothing.

Moon dazzle filled Antonius's eyes, then they were gone into the night.

A NIGHTMARE. THIS WAS A NIGHTMARE, REGEANE thought as she brushed her hand over her eyes. "Might we be dead?" she asked the Saxon.

He nodded. "I have thought so myself. Dead in the wilderness without offerings and unmourned by kin. Without the proper sacrifices and lauds to tell the gods we were both noble and well-conducted, we have been consigned to the wilderness as outcasts."

"I have always been an outcast," Regeane said. "I am not afraid."

"As it happens, so have I," the Saxon answered. "Being reduced to the lowest slavery possible, sold only for my bodily strength, working chained in the Lombard wheat fields, I once took the part of a horse and drew a plow."

The conversation was very calm.

Blank-faced, jerking like a marionette, the first of the corpses, the one whose face was a mask of terror, began coming toward them. Meanwhile, the flames that had, at first, seemed to be confined to the altar screen and the cupola above it began slowly creeping over the beamed ceiling above.

"We should be having trouble breathing," Regeane said. "Instead, the smoke is being drawn out of the room."

They were both backing away from the oncoming dead man.

"I imagine there are holes in the roof," the Saxon said. Then he cried out in terror and disgust when he was seized from behind by something composed only of blackened bone with a few tattered remnants of flesh and cloth.

The head was half covered by a hooded cape. With a courage she didn't know she had in her, Regeane slammed her fist into its skull. The thing struck the floor and the Saxon stamped it to bits with his boots. Then he sliced the oncoming corpse into three pieces with his sword.

A second later, Regeane screamed.

The abbot's head, shoulder, and one arm were still together. Glaring malevolently, he seized Regeane's instep with his teeth and bit down hard.

The thing among the flames consuming the altar laughed loudly. "There is still some life in my creature and much malice."

"Stand still," the Saxon commanded Regeane. Then he sliced the top half of the abbot's skull off. "Not any longer," the Saxon said as the remains rolled across the floor.

"We must," Regeane whispered through stiff, pale lips, "find some strategy for dealing with these things."

"Yes," the Saxon answered.

And so they did.

Above, the fire was slowly consuming the beamed ceiling. Flaming brands and embers were filling the air around them. The choir stalls caught with a flash and a roar, incinerating the dead too decomposed to be of any use to the evil thing at the altar.

Regeane and the Saxon were forced backward into the hall. By now it was clear all that remained of the monastery was burning down.

"I'll cut," the Saxon said. "You burn."

"Yes," Regeane said, and kicked two torches out of the crumbling door frame as they moved away from the inferno through the ancient, doomed structure.

Everything in the ruin not exposed to the elements was tinder dry. He mowed down the horrors surrounding them. She set afire sheets of mummified flesh, rags of cloth, and dry bone.

The Saxon was an iron man, and his "Courage, woman, courage" kept Regeane going through the long night of pain, terror, disgust, and exhaustion.

The worst moments were when the thing from the bed in the first room to which Regeane had been taken rose and attacked them. The putrefying corpse was too wet to take fire from Regeane's torches, so she tore down the bed hangings, threw them over the foul thing, and set them ablaze, then added the ticks and linens. By then the whole building was engulfed, the roof of the chapel fallen in.

Regeane and the Saxon fled past the gate and out into the snow-covered countryside. To their surprise, there was light in the east and it was morning. They paused across from the gate, taking deep breaths of the clean, cold air. The Saxon sagged against a stone pillar set before the abbey, but then started up when he saw three wolves coming toward them at a dead run.

He wasn't terribly afraid. He'd fought wolves before and knew these three who looked full fed and in good condition would probably run from two adults, one of them an armed man.

"No," Regeane said. "Don't attack them. That's my husband and two of his friends.

"I told you," she said, clutching his wrist. "I told you I have always been an outcast."

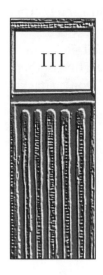

III

I SUPPOSE . . ." THE SAXON SAID LATER AS ANTONIUS was freeing his neck from the iron collar. "I suppose I am not dead?"

Antonius's eyebrows rose. "Indeed, did you believe this?"

"Yes," the Saxon answered hesitantly. "I did for a time last night. Are you a priest?"

Antonius's eyebrows rose rather higher. "No," he said. "Though my stepfather was a pope."

The Saxon said, "Unla?"

Antonius took pity on what he saw as a rather bewildered barbarian. "I am my lady's chamberlain. Her lord rules a duchy here in the mountains. He would not call it a duchy, but in size, prestige, wealth, and power it is."

Then the Saxon asked the question that had been burning in his mind ever since Regeane greeted a huge mountain wolf with a sloppy kiss and a hug. "Am I captured again?"

Antonius knew well enough what the collar meant, and the same for the question. "No," he answered at about the moment that the collar slipped free.

For a few heartbeats it looked as if the Saxon might cry. Antonius turned away quickly, not wanting to see such a massively powerful creature break down.

"But the collar?" the Saxon asked.

"What collar?" Antonius said.

"Come," Matrona said. She was clad in a long black silk gown with a gold and garnet necklace, an elaborate construction decorated with winged sphinxes. Like much of Matrona's wealth, it looked impossibly old.

The Saxon indicated it with one forefinger. "What . . . ?"

"One hot night in Babylon," she said, "I loved a king."

Then she reached toward his cheek, where the abbot had burned him. He flinched, but when she touched him the pain went out of his wounds—all of them. While she was tending him, he fell asleep, but he dreamed he was back in the slave pens on the great Lombard estate. He woke with a wild start and swung at Matrona, but she caught his wrist with a grip he knew could easily have broken it, had she chosen to do so.

"Who is god?" the Saxon asked.

"The mother," Matrona answered.

"The mother is all powerful," he said.

"I'm glad you know that. We will get along."

Regeane walked toward him. She had some clothing and the bearskin over her arm. "I have fresh clothes. Hold up his mantle, will you, Matrona, while he dresses?"

"Perhaps I will," Matrona said. "But then, perhaps I won't. I'd like to see what else he has."

Regeane blushed, but the Saxon blushed even more violently. His clothes were in rags. He colored all over his skin.

"Matrona, you're terrible." Regeane laughed.

All around them the sun was shining brightly, so brightly it had begun warming the air and melting the snow. The road was clear, and many of Maeniel's people were investigating the burned-out monastery.

"What are they finding?" he asked.

Regeane shuddered and clasped her body with her arms as if cold.

"Nothing, or at least nothing new. Bones, scraps of rotted flesh. They must once have thought about booty, for there is some gold and silver there, but we will not take it. We will bury it with the human remains in the cemetery within the enclosure."

"The old monk, the women?" the Saxon asked.

Regeane shivered again. "I think they were not real but shadows of the bear spirit. His servants. They all tried to keep me from helping you."

The Saxon nodded.

"Now get dressed," she directed. "We are going to Geneva to tell the Frankish king that his best road over the Alps is in ruins. You must look like a warrior of our party, a gentleman, so that your presence will not be questioned. We will protect you. And you may resume your journey when it is possible, if you wish."

He took the bearskin and the clothing from her. She turned and walked away.

"Dress," Matrona said, holding up the bearskin. "Your delicacy does you credit. Some chastity—not too much, mind you, but some—is attractive in a young man."

"Now I understand." He was pulling off his shirt and pants. "Now I understand," he repeated.

"Understand what?" Matrona asked from behind the bearskin.

"Everything," the Saxon said. "Everything. I wondered why the gods put such a heavy burden on my shoulders. The loss of all I was and had. Now I know. Someone had to be there to pluck her from the snowbank. To be sure she would live. I was chosen and must never count the cost."

On the other side of the bearskin, Matrona frowned.

A FEW DAYS LATER THEY LOOKED DOWN ON GEneva. The town wasn't much, but the lake was pretty. It mirrored the mountains and the dying light. When he found Regeane and the Saxon, Maeniel had sent for his people. Some had been out on a hunt with Gordo, but they joined the rest at his summons. So he had thirty warriors in his train. Most were part of his pack. A few like Antonius and Barbara weren't.

Matrona rode with the Saxon. She had remained beside him over the last two days. True, he had no more pain, but the burn inflicted by the abbot was a bad one and needed watching. So did he, Matrona thought. He rode like someone in a dream, one lifted out of himself by great sorrow or joy. At first she couldn't tell, but by the second day she was sure it was joy.

On the first night in camp, the gray wolf and the silver had vanished into the fir trees along the trail. "She is the silver, he the gray, you the black, and the captain of the guard is red," the Saxon said to Matrona.

"Yes."

He nodded.

"Do you know Irmunsul?"

"A tree of note," Matrona said.

"The tree of life."

"No," Matrona said. "You don't believe that?"

He didn't answer. Instead he asked, "Her father?"

"One Wolfstan," Matrona said.

He asked no more questions but when she looked again, she saw tears in the Saxon's eyes. "Very emotional, these wild men from beyond the Rhine," she told Maeniel a few days later.

"Her father was a Saxon," Maeniel answered. "He was murdered by Gundabald."

"Her late uncle?" Matrona asked.

"Her very, very late uncle," Maeniel answered.

They were alone, walking in the snow together. The rest were gathered around the fires, getting ready to bed down for the night. Regeane and Maeniel had an elaborate pavilion to themselves. Maeniel glanced toward it and saw a shape moving within. "She will be undressing," he said. "I wouldn't want to keep her waiting."

Matrona smiled. "No, that wouldn't do at all."

"What is his interest in her?"

"What is yours?" Matrona asked.

"Don't play games." The moon was full. It painted the snow with blue light; the shadows were gray shapes etched on silver. His face was flushed and his nostrils were distended like those of a stallion. "If that's the case, encourage him to leave. He has my permission. Give him anything he asks for. Money, weapons, horses—except Audovald—otherwise, I don't care."

"I don't think that will help," Matrona said. "Her father was sacred to his people."

"She is a Frank," the gray wolf said.

"Half Saxon by her father's blood. I think maybe the important half."

"No," Maeniel said. "I killed more than one man for her, and I'd kill a thousand rather than see her parted from me for even an hour without my consent. I waited for her for a thousand years."

"Don't kill this one," Matrona said. "She wouldn't forgive you."

"No," he said, the "no" a snarl in his throat.

"No, I warn you."

"That bad?" His eyes filled with a cold, pale light and glowed like a predator's in the dim flare of the campfires.

Matrona laid a finger on her lips. "Not a word; she doesn't know. Now go to bed."

"Yes."

There was no further movement in the tent. The lamp dimmed.

When he turned back to Matrona, he saw her clothing hanging from the stub of a tree limb, but the black wolf was gone. He knew she would watch the Saxon, but then, she watched everything.

He hurried into the tent. The lamp was out, but even through the canvas the tent was filled with a moonlit haze. She was wearing a silk nightgown, but only for a little while.

WHEN THEY LOOKED DOWN INTO CHARLES'S CAMP at Geneva, everyone turned to Antonius. As chamberlain, he alone had met the powerful Frankish king whose name was resounding now throughout Europe.

Antonius scratched his head.

Gavin, the red wolf captain of the guard, began to laugh. "He doesn't know how to approach him, either."

"Shut up, Gavin," Maeniel said.

"You say that a lot when Gavin's around," Regeane said.

"Yes," Matrona interjected. "And it never does any good. He just keeps talking."

"Not this time," Maeniel said firmly. His eyes were on an approaching party of armed horsemen. They were led by an older man, but the troops were young and the quality of their arms and clothing proclaimed them as the kin of some of the great families of the Frankish realm.

"All of you except for Antonius stay here. Antonius must accompany me." Maeniel was riding Audovald. "Go on," he said to the horse, and Audovald did. Antonius followed.

When they reached the horsemen, both parties drew rein.

"The *scarae*," Regeane said as they watched from above. "I've heard of them, the king's personal guard."

They surrounded her husband and Antonius. Regeane watched anxiously. "Matrona?" she asked. "Barbara?"

"Something wrong?" Barbara replied.

"I can't tell," Gavin said. "The wind is blowing the wrong way. I can't smell them."

"It's possible he's being treated with honor by the king," Barbara hazarded.

Just then Maeniel turned. He caught his wife's eye first, then switched to Matrona. He and the rest galloped away into the encampment of the Franks.

"Something is wrong," Matrona stated flatly.

"Should we flee?" Gavin asked.

"In a way," Regeane said. "Find a campsite and set up the tents." She looked up. The moon was visible, an almost transparent orb against a blue sky so clear it seemed formed of fine enamel work. The last sun was blazing gold in the west, and darkness blazoned with a million stars held the east.

"And?" Matrona asked.

"Change," Regeane said, but when she turned her horse she saw more members of the *scarae* were behind them.

Gavin pulled on his reins and the horse half reared. He reached for his sword.

Regeane guided her mount in front of him and rode toward the one she was sure must be the captain of the *scarae*, a burly man with a face that was a mass of both scars and wrinkles. She bestowed a dazzling smile on him and was gratified to see the hardened warrior turn the color of a ripe plum.

Barbara made a small sound of approval deep in her throat.

Matrona whispered between her teeth to Gavin, "Fool, not here. You will get us slaughtered."

"My lord," Regeane said. "You startled my husband's captain."

"I was sent to conduct you to a campsite," the warrior said. His smooth, cultivated accent belied his battered looks. "I am Arnulf of the Breton Marches."

Regeane smiled again and offered him her hand. The old warrior bowed over it in a courtly manner. "I will try," he said, "to take you to a place of comfort."

It wasn't a place of comfort where they were lodged. He led the party to the center of the camp. On one side were the tents of the *scarae* nobles, but on the other, the ox-drawn wagons holding the armies' "comfort women" and purveyors of food and drink, especially drink. Once it had probably been an open meadow shaded by scattered groves of trees near the lake's marshy shore, but now the winter-seared grass was trampled into mud and the trees cut for firewood, and the site was unbearably noisy, stinking of a combination of odors: human waste, spoiled food, liquor, and clouds of smoke from the fires nearby.

Maeniel's men gathered tightly around Regeane, Matrona, and Barbara. Gordo sneezed. Joseph, a formidable warrior who wore a heavy beard and long mustaches, looked as if he might be ready to challenge Arnulf to single combat.

"I cannot think," Regeane said haughtily to Arnulf, "that the Frankish king would consign a kinswoman of his to such an unpleasant spot."

"My lady, in the absence of your lord, I and my men will see to your safety," Arnulf said smoothly. "And I find it difficult to believe that a man of such high position as your lord would expose his wife to the rough and tumble of an army camp, rather than leave her safely bestowed at home with her weaving women."

Then he directed a gaze at Regeane that made her blush and turn away. He tried the same thing with Matrona. He was used to using an insolent stare to cow women.

She gave him a look of cold-blooded appraisal, then spoke softly and all but inaudibly to him. "I wonder which is smaller, your prick or your brain, that you would insult a kinswoman of this king? I cannot think he is so weak a man that he will suffer it tamely."

"She but boasts of her connection." He also spoke softly between his teeth. "Their relationship is both distant and dishonorable."

"That is not for you to judge," Matrona said. "Now go away. It is not proper for my lady to suffer the insolence of underlings." Matrona turned her back on him and addressed Regeane and the rest.

"We are here, my lady, and had best settle in for the night." She pointed to a few small trees remaining at the water's edge. "You men cut some firewood and pitch the tents. We women will need to start supper."

Arnulf was still sitting on his horse, staring at them.

"Go," Matrona said. "We neither need nor want anything further from you." When Matrona was finished speaking, Arnulf lingered. He was ignored and finally left, shooed away by the pack members.

The camp was set up, everyone turning to his appointed task. The Saxon found them puzzling but refreshing. No one gave orders. The occasional outsider who did so was totally ignored. Tents were pitched, fires were lit. Matrona and Gavin found fresh reeds to floor the tents and bed ground, rather the way rushes were used in more permanent dwellings.

The horses were fed and lined up on the edges of the encampment, forming a buffer zone between them and their more unpleasant neighbors. Audovald presided over the picketing and distribution of food, an unusual but efficient arrangement, since he knew where each animal preferred to sleep, and no one was ever hobbled or tied. None ever strayed, either.

The horses found security in being draft animals. Since those at the mountain stronghold who did not care for the work were allowed to fend for themselves, food was the wage and the horses earned it.

In spite of Matrona's pronouncement, no one cooked. Regeane unpacked a cold meal of fruit, sliced meat, cheese, and wine. The Saxon, Regeane, and the rest of the women shared it.

Gavin vanished as soon as it was dark, and the rest, including the powerful Silvia, followed.

Matrona chafed at the confinement.

"You could go," Regeane said.

"No, I won't leave you here alone."

"Thank you," Barbara said.

"Barbara, don't take offense," Matrona said. "Nor you—whatever your name is," she said to the Saxon. "You know what I mean. I told him to stay clear of these royal quarrels. They are almost always motivated by greed, a greed we don't share."

"He didn't feel he could," Regeane said. "He was afraid for the rest of you, don't you see that?" she appealed to Matrona.

"No," Matrona said, looking away from the candles on the table into the night. "Many wars as I have seen—and I've seen a mort of them in my lifetime—except for one or two when the people involved acted clearly in self-defense, nearly every one began in folly and ended in grief for all the participants."

"And how many have you seen?" the Saxon asked.

"The first was too many," Matrona said. The candle nearest her guttered, burned blue, and the night stalker's mirrored gaze looked back at him. "War is said to be the sport of kings, and I cannot think their appetite for it will ever abate."

"Get more candles and light them," Barbara told the Saxon. "If anyone came now and saw the eyes on the two of you, we would likely all be killed."

There was a shout and then a scream from outside.

The Saxon hurried to the door of the tent and pushed the flap aside. Arnulf was standing there with four of his troopers; one was writhing on the ground.

"I'll have compensation for this. Your horse kicked my man."

"Horses kick," said Regeane. "What was he doing near the part that kicks?"

"They are not even picketed," Arnulf shouted. "He wasn't near the horse. It walked over, wheeled around, and kicked him."

One of the mares, Matrona's mount, was standing near the fallen man, who was still moaning and gasping. Her hooves had caught him in the abdomen. She looked as if butter wouldn't melt in her mouth.

"What were you doing here where you could be kicked?" the Saxon asked.

"We came to call on the ladies," Arnulf said. "To assure ourselves of their safety. None of the men seemed to be about." His eyes raked the almost empty camp.

"They are in the tents, asleep," the Saxon replied. "As all the just and virtuous should be at this hour."

"It is late and the ladies are not receiving," Regeane said. "Now, go away. See to it," she told the Saxon curtly, then closed the tent flap.

The Saxon stood quietly and folded his arms.

Arnulf tried to stare him down. It didn't work. The Saxon was six feet, two inches tall in his socks, two hundred and thirty-five pounds stark naked, carried a long sword with a one-handed grip that most men would have had to swing two-handed, and the expression on his face suggested he was spoiling for a fight. No one wanted to challenge him. Arnulf and his companions took the wounded man and beat an ignominious retreat.

Maeniel and Antonius were taken to a tent near the main pavilion and placed in irons. Antonius protested volubly in Latin; Frankish, the Germanic version of Latin; Gaelic, a spoken Latin similar to Italian Latin; and other less recognizable dialects. When Maeniel tried to open his mouth, Antonius cut him off.

"Retain the demeanor of a great nobleman. I am here to complain for you. This is what chamberlains, seneschals, and the like do."

Maeniel shrugged. "I can get out of these any time I want," he said.

"I know," Antonius replied. "But don't, please don't."

"No," Maeniel agreed. "One thing I found out early on in my association with humanity is a maxim I keep in the forefront of my mind at all times."

"What?"

"Nothing is ever as simple as it ought to be or that I anticipate it will be."

"I wonder what happened?" Antonius muttered to himself.

"I cannot imagine." Maeniel spoke in a resigned fashion.

"My lords." A young man entered the tent. "I am Arbeo of Sens. My apologies to you, sirs, but what I have done is at the orders of my lord, the king." Servants entered the room with a folding camp table and a bench. "Please be seated, and I will send for bread, cheese, and wine that you may refresh yourselves."

"I understand," Maeniel answered courteously.

It took Antonius about three seconds to take the young man's measure. He wore an undecorated cuirass of boiled leather and the sword he carried was old with a plain, wire-wrapped pommel. *Poor,* Antonius thought, *and therefore, if courteously treated, susceptible.*

They seated themselves at the table; the young man left to procure the refreshments.

"You may understand, but I don't," Antonius said. "I don't," he repeated. "Not nearly enough. Give me one of your rings."

On Antonius's advice, they had all dressed to the teeth. Maeniel wore a ring on each finger. He unscrewed one and handed it to Antonius, a priceless creation of heavy gold set with a beautifully carved head of one of the Roman emperors, he didn't know which one. But the stone was a large Indian ruby.

"My," Antonius said. "The things you come up with. Where did you get that?"

"I forget," Maeniel said. He hadn't, but he wasn't about to tell Antonius the story.

Arbeo returned, followed by a servant with a platter of bread, wine, and cheese. The servant placed it on the table. Then, at a signal from Arbeo, he retired. Just to be sure, Antonius checked Arbeo's boots. Bad, very bad. They were overlarge, so worn and scuffed as to be almost shapeless. He'd wrapped his legs in linen strips to keep out the cold; they were visible through the holes in the boots.

"Sir," Antonius addressed Arbeo.

Obviously surprised to be so addressed, Arbeo developed an owlish look on his face. "Yes?"

"My lord," Antonius said, "wishes to be sure that you suffer no deprivation because of your courtesy. He instructs me to give you this," and he offered the ring to Arbeo.

The youngster took it gingerly and stared at it in wonder. "This is too much."

Antonius opened his mouth, but Maeniel spoke. "Not if you tell us what's going on. Why are we being treated this way?"

Arbeo weighed the ring in his hand, then, with a look of regret, he placed it on the table. "Sir, I was specifically forbidden to discuss anything about your arrest with you."

Maeniel fumbled in his scrip and found some silver. "Then take this. I still don't want you to have to pay for our supper. And take the ring, if you care to. The lady who gave it to me would have liked you."

Arbeo half drew his sword, unscrewed the top of the pommel, and placed the ring in the hollow.

"Won't it rattle?" Antonius asked.

"Can you tell me if my wife is safe?" Maeniel asked.

"Oh, yes, sir, I can tell you that. She is. The lady is, after all, a relative of the king."

"Is Count Otho here?"

"Yes." The boy looked mystified.

"Good. Can you take a message to my wife?"

"The lady Regeane? Yes, sir! I would be honored."

"Fine. Tell her to roust that fat—"

Antonius gave him a hard look.

Maeniel took a deep breath and began again. "Ask her to call on Count Otho and . . . and . . . ask for his protection and . . . assistance."

When the boy was gone, Antonius spoke. "You handled that well. For a moment I had my doubts, but you came through at the end. By the way, who did give you that ring?"

"Never mind," Maeniel said. "I paid that snake's prick, Otho, enough that he should be willing to do me some favors. Quite a few in fact."

"Do snakes have pricks?"

"Assuming they are male, yes."

"I have never known anyone who has seen one," Antonius said.

"They are retractable."

"My," Antonius said. "I imagine that's necessary, given their method of locomotion. You watched a pair in the act of sexual congress?"

"Yes, one long, boring afternoon, I did."

"Indeed." Antonius nodded and stroked his chin. "Indeed."

ARBEO DELIVERED THE MESSAGE.

"Otho! I should have thought," she said, and gave the young man some gold. Then she set out, with Arbeo as a guide, in search of Otho's tent. Barbara, Matrona, and the Saxon accompanied her.

She did need protection.

The great king's army was in a mood for revelry. There were lines in front of the tavern and brothel wagons. Some whores accommodated customers publicly, lying on the baggage in the back of the ox carts while men lined up in front of them. Regeane took in the sights as well as she could with her veil and mantle pulled up over her mouth, but Matrona and Barbara strolled along, looking around insouciantly.

The higher-paid ladies of the professional *friedelehe*, those who preferred longer associations—courtesans, in other words—presided over loud and occasionally violent parties. One man, naked, ran past. He was bleeding and being pursued by two others carrying weapons. Screams erupted from another tent, sounds indicative of a battle royal in progress, punctuated by shrill female cries. When Matrona wanted to investigate, she was hustled along by the Saxon and Arbeo. She allowed herself to be urged to greater speed by the men, but bestowed a heavy-lidded look of disgust on them both.

"It's not proper for a lady to be exposed to such scenes of debauchery," Arbeo said.

"Why? Are you afraid one or more of us just might want to join in the fun?"

Arbeo looked horrified.

Regeane sucked in her cheeks to keep from laughing out loud and saw the Saxon was struggling with his own attempts to suppress mirth.

"Fear not, I'm too old," Barbara said.

"Speak for yourself," Matrona told her. "I'm not, but I am busy right now. Come visit me," she purred at the young man, "some day when I am at leisure, and I will instruct you in the art of creative and civilized debauchery."

Arbeo's look of absolute, frozen shock nearly destroyed Regeane's composure completely.

Just then one of the working girls at the edge of the path spit at a customer. The man pulled a knife. The girl's pimp tried to intervene and caught a nasty gash across the chest for his trouble.

Matrona rather casually grabbed the soldier's wrist, jerked it up between his shoulder blades, and took the knife away from him. Then she kicked the legs out from under him, and when he went down on his face, whacked him hard just behind the ear on the sensitive mastoid process. The soldier lay twitching, semiconscious and paralyzed by pain.

The girl in the cart sat up. She cursed her pimp for being so inept as to let her trick wound him, then the soldier for being a stinking louse-ridden pervert.

Matrona asked, "Why?"

"He wanted a blow job. I don't suck. I work strictly on my back."

"We are looking for one Count Otho," Matrona said.

"I am, too," the girl said. "He set me up with this . . ." She jerked a thumb at the pimp. "I haven't seen him in four days. This shithead—" She jerked a thumb at the pimp again. "—he takes too big a cut. And as for protection." The girl rolled her eyes. "Well, you saw—"

"Otho has women?"

"A whole string." The girl shook her head for emphasis. "Plenty of women. The king's men are hot as a fuck in a haystack. Fatso's losing money all over the place."

"Doesn't sound like Otho to neglect business," Regeane said.

"True," Barbara said. "I'm not certain that lord has a heart, but if he does, money is the dearest thing to it."

The girl nodded. "We're talking about the same guy, for sure. When I went to his tent, nothing. Old woman there wouldn't let me in."

"Where is his tent?" Matrona asked.

"Near the king," the girl answered.

The camp was formed roughly like a set of rings, with the king's pavilion in the center. Around it were grouped those of the great nobles; beyond them, the *scarae*; and beyond, in outer darkness, the rabble of peasants, foot soldiers, camp followers, whores, tavern carts, and the shadow classes: cutthroats, brigands, beggars, and professional thieves looking for loot in the case of victory. But equally happy with defeat, as they would be able to despoil the wounded and the dead on the battlefield.

This was where they were now.

The Saxon offered her some silver, two or three nights' wages for a prostitute of her class. "Show us to his tent," he said.

She snatched the money and jumped off the back of the wagon. "Right away," she said. "You have to watch for the horsemen. They patrol at night and don't want any of us to sneak in."

It was late, and once away from the revelry among the infantry, the camp grew more quiet. The shelters occupied by the wealthy were larger and farther apart. Servants were quartered there. Most had a rubbish heap and a latrine. The girl pointed to a large tent. Three rooms at least, on the outer edge of the enclave belonging to the highborn. It was set rather far away from the rest. A torch burned in front of the tent closest to it, but otherwise, it was completely dark.

"Maybe he's asleep," Arbeo suggested. "Maybe we should come back in the morning." He sounded apprehensive.

"No," Regeane said. "If he's asleep, we're going to wake him up."

"He's not asleep," Matrona said. "Something's wrong."

"Is it?" the Saxon asked.

"Yes," Matrona said. "Regeane, the wind is at our backs. We must circle, but don't draw any closer."

Regeane nodded and the two women began to ease around the tent next to Otho's.

"Put out your torch," Matrona told the Saxon.

He did, dunking it in a ditch filled with dubious liquid. Some of it rose as steam and there was no further doubt as to its identity.

"Phueeee," the girl said.

The Saxon turned to the girl and Arbeo. "Go." He pointed back the way they had come.

They both voiced objections.

"The ladies may need my protection," Arbeo said.

"I'm not a *girl*, I'm Gilas," the girl said. "And I need to know about Otho. If something's happened to him, I must get another protector."

"Stop wrangling," Regeane ordered. "You, Gilas, may stay. Arbeo, escort Barbara back to our camp."

Barbara smiled, took a very unhappy-looking Arbeo's arm, and towed him away.

"Gilas, you remain here," Regeane said.

"No, I want to see," Gilas insisted stubbornly.

"All right," the Saxon said in a dangerous tone of voice. "But be silent. If you make one sound, I will drive you into the ground like a nail."

"I promise, I promise. I'll be silent as a stone." She jumped up and down.

"All right, then shut up."

Matrona led the party, weaving in and out between the tents until she felt the almost-still air push against her face. "Here," she said.

The air was thick with wood smoke, human effluvia, cooking food, and the thick aroma of stagnant water from the lake. The Saxon declined to sniff. He decided he probably couldn't smell his upper lip, but Regeane did.

"Oh, my God," she whispered to Matrona. "I've not encountered anything like this since Rome."

"You knew him as Otho there?" Matrona asked.

"Yes. Living or dead, I can't say, but he is here."

Gilas opened her mouth to ask what they were doing, but she caught the Saxon's eye and closed it immediately. The Saxon lifted the sword quietly from his sheath. Regeane drew her sax, and Matrona pulled a nine-inch knife from her full sleeve.

"The back!" the Saxon whispered.

The rest nodded and moved as silently as possible. They approached the rear of the tent.

OTHO WAS STILL ALIVE, THOUGH HE WAS CERTAIN not for long. At this point he was almost beginning to wish the creature who'd captured him would kill him. His whole body was a furnace of pain. Knives driven through his wrists and ankles pinned him to his once spacious and comfortable bed. He'd been given no food in four days, and no water in the last two, but he still clung to life. He was gagged, but the gag was so soaked with blood from his lips and cheeks and occasional bouts of vomit from his belly that it no longer functioned. Still, that didn't matter, because his mouth and throat were so swollen he could no longer utter a sound. Mercifully, he had begun to drift in and out of consciousness a few days ago.

Yet he still clung to life. Otho was corrupt to the marrow of his bones. He had decided as a young man that money was the only thing worth having in life, and he'd sought wealth with a single-minded energy and diligence that totally surpassed the rather feeble and sporadic efforts of those who were drawn by a desire for other, more mundane forms of gratification, such as sex, drink, food, or the more complex considerations of love, family, professional or even artistic endeavor. In a surprisingly short time he'd found himself very, very rich. It wasn't enough. Too much is not enough for any spirit motivated solely by avarice. In fact, adding to his bodily torments was the knowledge that his own greed had landed him in his present situation.

When the stranger had come to his tent a few days ago, Otho had initially refused to see him, but the present of a heavy gold bracelet, an almost pure gold bracelet, changed his mind. He had agreed to admit the stranger and made the fatal choice. He took the stranger's money, a lot of money, making the sums he'd extorted from Maeniel seem paltry by comparison. He had listened to the stranger's accusations. He went to visit the king, repeating the stranger's accusations into his ear.

When he had returned to his tent in the king's encampment, Otho had tried to dismiss the man, if indeed man it was. When the creature merely laughed and refused to leave, Otho ordered his servants to throw him out . . .

They had failed; hardened gang of mercenaries that they were, they had failed. Oh, how they had failed. In fact, their remaining intact weapons were what pinned Otho to the bed. The only reason he still lived was that it wanted him to suffer. Otherwise, it was content. Prowling the tent night and day in one horrific form or another, it waited. For what, he couldn't guess.

So Otho tried to wait, struggling against death because late in life he had added another passion to the desire for wealth that ruled his life, and this passion was fully as overwhelmingly strong as the first. The second was absolute loyalty to the king. Charles, whom men were already beginning to call the Great, was the central love of his life. And Otho was convinced that in talebearing for this creature, he had somehow betrayed him.

ABOUT THE SAME TIME, ANTONIUS AND MAENIEL were led before the king. He was surrounded by a dozen other nobles. The gray wolf had heard that Charles did not wear elaborate or distinctive clothing. In fact, he was often surrounded by men who made a more ostentatious display of wealth than he did, but Maeniel knew him as soon as the man entered the room; knew who and what he was. Only once before had he ever seen an individual with that look in his eyes, and without even asking Antonius to point him out, Maeniel went to one knee.

Charles was not the best dressed nor the eldest or even the most impressive man present. He was like Maeniel, thickset, muscular, with dark hair, and he wore a short beard—possibly in deference to his wife Hildegarde's wishes that he not present himself close-shaven to the Langobards who were, after all, famous for their facial hair, being called Long Beards. She wanted him to show he was man enough to cover his chin with hair also.

He stretched out two strong, callused hands and raised both Maeniel and Antonius to their feet. "Please, no ceremony. If the tales that have been brought to me are found to be false, then I should embrace you both as brothers. If not, then . . . we will have to see what measures must be taken."

So saying, he seated himself in a folding camp chair. The nobility of the Frankish court clustered around him. "I will be brief. Information has been brought to me that you and Antonius conspired in the murder of your wife's uncle Gundabald and his son Hugo. And that, further, you robbed the monastery at the foot of the pass guarded by your stronghold, murdered the inhabitants, and then burned the buildings, including the church."

Antonius opened his mouth.

"No," the king said. "Let him speak for himself."

Maeniel nodded.

"First Gundabald and Hugo."

"They were men of somewhat licentious habits," Antonius began.

"Antonius," Charles said. "Are you having problems with your memory? I told you, let him answer for himself."

Antonius raised his arms, and the chains clinked.

"Antonius, you can make bad sound like good, day sound like night, morning sound like afternoon, and, in short, by your circumlocutions, thoroughly confuse an army of lawyers, judges, and scribes and bury major crimes in such obfuscating legalese that even a hardworking king and his equally hardworking scholars cannot sort it out. As I said, let him answer for himself."

Antonius sighed deeply.

"Very well," Maeniel said. "I will be brief. To be blunt, Gundabald was a wastrel and a sot. His son was an apprentice wastrel and sot. So unpleasant a pair were they that his holiness saw fit to remove my wife from their company and place her among holy nuns until we were married.

"Though they were not the most charming company in the world, I respected them as my wife's kin. I settled a large sum of money on them at the time of our wedding.

"The results of my generosity were entirely predictable. Within days after the wedding, they both vanished without a trace and were never seen again. His holiness Pope Hadrian did me the courtesy of looking into the matter himself, but neither one could be found. Antonius here will attest, as he was privy to the matter. Probably their throats were cut and then their purses, or vice versa. Likely their bodies wound up in the Tiber, as it's done duty as a Roman cemetery since the city was seven hills of farmland.

"Now as far as the monastery is concerned, it had its own rather considerable demesne, and those lands do not touch mine in any place. While my wife and I journeyed here, an avalanche occurred. It wiped out a long stretch of the road the Romans built over the pass. We were obliged to take a detour and saw smoke. We investigated and—"

Someone screamed, "Fire! Fire!"

The king ran to the door and pushed the flap aside. Fire painted the low clouds of the night sky. Antonius turned toward Maeniel. Chains were lying on the floor. The gray wolf was gone.

THE SAXON CUT A LONG SLIT IN THE CANVAS. FORtunately the tent had something of a list to it, and the fabric was loose. The first thing he saw was a cocked and loaded crossbow pointed at the entrance to the tent. The second, third, and fourth things he saw were corpses.

One looked as if it had been butchered. The second was neatly decapitated. The third was the reason the tent pole was loose: it had been pulled out and driven through the man's body, back into the ground.

Then he saw the figure on the bed. It moved. The Saxon stepped through the slit into the tent and looked down at Otho. The open, staring eyes looked up at him and blinked. The Saxon reached out and jerked the two knives out of Otho's arms and the two swords out of his legs.

Somehow Otho managed not to scream. He could have screamed in that extremity, even though his throat and tongue were so swollen they almost blocked his air passages. The pain was so dreadful that he could have screamed. But he managed to supress any sound as he lost consciousness.

As he was pushing Otho's legs through the tent slit, the Saxon sensed the thing behind him. He turned, sword upraised. The shape was a bear this time, but no living bear was ever this big.

It swung one set of hooked claws at the Saxon's face, and he parried with the sword, chopping deep into a foreleg. The thing gave a scream of sheer fury, but the sword couldn't stop the forward motion of the blow. The paw caught the Saxon on the side of the head, sending him spinning.

But Regeane was wolf and into the tent, a streak of dull silver in the half-light. The thing was partially turned, recovering from the blow it struck the Saxon. She slashed at the thigh, going for the deep arteries, but failed, though she inflicted a respectable wound to the muscles of the upper leg. Blood sprayed everywhere.

It roared again in fury and went after the silver wolf on all fours, crowding her toward one corner of the tent where the powerful clawed forelegs could literally rip her to shreds.

Matrona, a black wolf, landed on its back. The neck was too thick and powerful for her to bite, so she went for one massive shoulder and felt her canines grate on bone.

This time the thing screamed in agony. It spun around, trying to reach the black wolf. Failing that, it began twisting from side to side in an attempt to throw her off.

Whap. The black wolf's body was snapped almost like a whip. Matrona wondered if her back would break, but hung on, her teeth buried to the gums in the giant bear's shoulder.

The silver wolf got her feet under her and charged again, this time going for the lower leg. If she could snap a bone, the battle would be over for good and all—or so she thought.

Behind the knee. It would take a few seconds for it to get to her. She lunged and connected perfectly. Another scream as her canines severed tendons and sank into the gristle of the knee capsule itself. But both female wolves had forgotten what they were fighting.

Abruptly it changed tactics and snatched up the crossbow. The silver wolf couldn't disengage quickly enough. She'd just managed to get her jaws open when the crossbow bolt tore through her body.

Death! and everything stopped. The world became a pall of silence. The woman stood over the dying wolf; she was birth naked. She'd split herself once before when she went into the other world to obtain healing for Antonius. She looked into the bear creature's eyes and felt the pull of its loneliness. The long, solitary, aching ages of silence and despair. She was in both places at once, trapped in her dying body, struggling for breath as the bolt tore her lungs to fragments and destroyed her living heart, clutching at consciousness as it fled down the darkening corridors of her brain. And woman, aware of the thing and its endless wailing, sobbing sorrow over what had been and would never be again. Feeling her form of flesh—arms, legs, hands, stomach, breasts, legs, and even the soles of her feet— pressed against the dusty cloth floor of the tent, and she saw the gray, his jaws closing on the wrist of the thing's forepaw in a desperate attempt to deflect its aim. *Oh, my love,* she thought. *That I should leave thee thus . . .*

Something slapped into her outstretched hand. She knew the shape and feel of it and remembered always she who carried it. A blackthorn stick.

She struck out with it. Not to kill, because she pitied the thing for all its monstrous darkness. *Banish it. I will banish it. Begone,* she cried, but only in her mind.

Now I die, she thought. *As my father died at the hands of Gundabald and my mother.*

Then she fell, folding into the wolf shape below her, became a woman, conscious now that the wall of the tent was a sheet of flame. Looked down in shock at her own nude but unwounded and intact body. Became wolf again as the flames raced over the dry canvas roof above. Then, scrabbling desperately, she was on her feet, fleeing into the wild commotion and confusion in the night beyond.

MAENIEL AND REGEANE SAT IN THEIR TENT AND talked things over later that night. She was wearing the silk nightgown, but he wanted to talk and found her too distracting in silk, so he made her put on one of his long woolen nightshirts.

She also sometimes wore his ordinary linen shirts, but she was even more distracting in those since she didn't wear anything under them. Sex is fun when one is young and in love, and she was. He wasn't young any longer but it was fun for him, too, and always had been.

"Why didn't you kill him?"

"I don't know that I could," she answered. "If Hildegard hadn't come, he'd have killed me. But somehow she made time stop and then handed me her blackthorn stick. I knew it must be powerful; everything connected with Hildegard is. I chose to use it to banish him."

"I don't like it," he said. "Hildegard belongs to Christ. We don't. I salute Christ—so do you, I notice—but we don't belong to him."

Regeane shrugged. She was sitting in a camp chair across from him. She pulled the nightgown up, baring her legs.

"Stop that." He looked away.

She grinned, then became serious. "I don't know who people like Hildegard belong to. The first time we met, she defended me against a ghost—"

"And the second time she got you thrown out of the convent where you were living."

"No," Regeane said. "I left of my own accord. I had things to do. She came to warn me and the nuns that the pork roast was poisoned. I already knew. I could smell it, but they didn't and some of them might have eaten it. Hildegard is good. She's almost the definition of what goodness is. I didn't want to kill even so evil a thing as he is, not with anything of Hildegard's."

"I don't know how you can be sure about Hildegard. In heaven's name, the woman was dead when you first met her."

"Yes," Regeane said. "She was."

For a short space they were both silent.

"I almost lost you tonight," he finally said. "It wasn't one of my happier moments."

"Did you think you were alone there?" she asked. "The worst part of the whole thing for me was knowing that in dying I would leave you, perhaps forever. I'm sure the dead don't perish, but I'm not sure of anything else about the worlds beyond death. I have reason to believe death is a far more complex journey than any of the living understand, and who knows if we reach the places where our loved ones dwell or simply must wander on throughout eternity? Happiness in this life takes a lot of luck. Happiness in the next may also. I do know one thing—I don't want to talk about it any longer." She rose and walked to the curtain that separated their room from the rest of the tent.

Maeniel had equipped himself with a pavilion at least as large as any owned by the nobles. The front room held a dining and reception room. The entire household was gathered at a long table, all eating and drinking. Lacking anything better to do when they became wolves, they went hunting and had bagged two deer and numerous small game. They were feasting, at present, though the feast was winding down.

"Hungry?" Maeniel asked his bride.

"No, worried," she said. "Antonius said you left the royal dwelling at high speed."

"Antonius removed his own chains and made mine look as if they'd been forced," Maeniel said. "Trust Antonius to cover all our asses."

"I'd rather not," Regeane said. "If you perform any miracles in front of Charles, I hope you have a good, solid explanation for them. Do you think anybody noticed anything?"

"No, I don't, and if they did, they don't believe their eyes anyway. Some seventeen tents burned. The entire camp was up in arms, thinking Desiderius somehow sneaked over the mountains and attacked the army by night. Charles almost had a rout on his hands before he ever managed to fight a battle. It took hours for him and his nobles to get them all calmed down. There were numerous minor injuries, burns, scalds; some people managed to stab themselves with their own weapons or almost suffocate themselves dragging their possessions out of the burning tents. So no, I don't think anyone noticed a few dogs running around in all the confusion."

"Otho?" she asked.

"He's badly hurt but Matrona thinks he will live, and she's not only usually right, she's always right. At least about that. He's in great bodily pain and also in great agony of mind because he believes he betrayed me and the king by listening to whatever that was—the creature who accused me of crimes."

"You did kill Gundabald," she said softly.

"Please! Are you sorry?"

She let the curtain drop closed. "No, no. Lucilla and Antonius were right. It had to be done. How about Hugo?"

"We never found out where he went. All the money Gundabald had was gone. Hadrian was convinced he fled, taking only what he could carry. We looked into the matter before you and I left Rome."

"You didn't tell me," she said.

"You'd been through a dreadful ordeal. I didn't want to worry you, but as far as I know, Hugo is running yet."

Regeane nodded, but she still looked troubled.

"Tomorrow Otho is going to talk to the king," Maeniel continued. "Charles saw him, and it was obvious he'd been brutally assaulted. Otho said enough to Charles to clear my name completely."

"Where is he?" she asked.

"In the next room with Matrona and . . . Gilas. They're looking after him."

"She's a sweet child."

"She's a whore," Maeniel said.

"Who are you to be judgmental?" Regeane asked.

He nodded. "Your point is well taken, but I wouldn't call her a sweet child. And for that matter, I've often wondered about your affection for Silvie. Setting her up with her own business, a stand-up wine bar in Rome, was a little ridiculous. She did her very best to get you burned at the stake. Why not let her go on selling what she's been selling all her life?"

"Silvie sells her body," Regeane said quietly, "because it's the only thing she has to sell. All I did was give her a place of refuge where she can make a little money, be comfortable, and sleep alone if she wants to. Gundabald used to beat her. He used to beat me, too."

"Yes," Maeniel said quietly. "I know."

"No," Regeane said. "I'm not in the least sorry you killed him. I'm just glad I didn't have to do it myself. What I'm worried about is . . . well, you said he and Hugo disappeared?"

"Yes, they did. And so . . ."

"Who ate him?" she asked.

He frowned. "Probably . . . probably . . . Certainly not Matrona. She's fastidious; even Silvia is too picky. Probably Gavin. He'll eat anything."

"You mean Gavin is Gundabald's tomb?"

"Yes, I think so. I never broached the matter to him, but yes, presumably he is. Does that make you unhappy?"

"No. It's just so staggeringly appropriate, that's all. So completely and devastatingly appropriate that Gundabald should end as dinner for Gavin, that's all."

I N THE NEXT ROOM, OTHO WOKE AND ASKED FOR water. Matrona, who was napping in a chair by the bed, fetched it for him. He was pale and, while heavy, no one would call him fat any longer. He was wearing a clean dalmatic, one of Maeniel's, his own having been lost in the fire.

"Are you in pain?" Matrona asked.

"No," he said. "I'm wondering what to tell the king tomorrow."

Matrona did not suggest he tell the truth. "Do you love the king?" she asked.

"Yes."

"Then find a way to explain your actions to him in a plausible manner—one that he will believe—while clearing the lord Maeniel and lady Regeane of all wrongdoing. My lord is loyal to Charles and can be of great help to him in his present endeavor, but only if he is free to do so."

"Yes," Otho answered. "Will I recover?"

"Yes," Matrona said. "If you do as I tell you. Possibly even if you don't, but it would be much better for your health if you did, in the sense that I am an accomplished healer and you would not want to lose my services prematurely."

"Oh, no. Definitely not. I fully understand your concerns and share them. Oh, yes, dear lady, you will never find me ungrateful for your services. You and your mistress saved my life and at no little cost to yourselves. I saw the fight, at least some of it. Of course, my mind and senses were somewhat disordered, so I can't be sure about everything I saw but, trust me, I am not only willing but eager to be of service to your lord and lady. And I am more than willing to believe you can be of great assistance to the king."

"Just so," Matrona said. "So pull yourself together and get your story ready for when the king arrives in the morning."

Out in the common room, Antonius, Barbara, and the Saxon were playing chess, or rather, Antonius and Barbara were playing and the Saxon was watching.

"Mate in three moves," Barbara told Antonius.

He studied her position for two minutes, then picked up the board and turned it over.

Barbara began laughing.

"This makes the third game," the Saxon said. "Why don't you try something else? Knucklebones, dice . . . something she doesn't know as much about. Here, have some beer."

Antonius walked over to a side table that held wine, fruit, and cheese. "No! Lord deliver me from that German pig piss. And as for knowing the game, I . . . I taught her."

Barbara laughed even louder and elbowed the Saxon in the ribs. "Sore loser. You can give me some beer. I won't complain."

The Saxon filled a cup and pushed it over to her. Antonius poured a cup of wine for himself, then returned and began to pick up the ivory chess pieces and replace them in their box.

Satisfied she would hear Otho if he called her, Matrona strolled in and joined the players. "Where are they?" she asked.

"All in there." The Saxon inclined his head to indicate Maeniel and Regeane's room.

Matrona took a cup of wine also. Then she walked over and pushed aside the curtain and peered in. "Oh, my heavens," she said. "And here, of all places."

"What are they doing?" Barbara asked. "We didn't look. We wanted to, but knowing too much about some things that go on . . ." Her voice trailed off. She took another sip of the Saxon's beer, a dark brew, malty and rich. "I like this," she said to the Saxon.

He nodded, grunted. "It makes you piss a lot. More than wine. It's healthier." He looked virtuous. "Flushes your drains."

"I think that's the first time I've heard it put that way," Barbara said.

"What are they doing?" Antonius asked Matrona.

"Just sleeping together," she answered.

Antonius looked aghast.

"Sleeping. Just sleeping." Matrona repeated. "If you like, go look."

"No. I'm tired. It must be near morning. I think I'll turn in. There are many things I don't know and a still greater number of things I don't want to know and this is one of them." As a high-ranking court official, he had his own tent on a wagon.

The Saxon rose, wiped his mouth, went and pushed the curtain aside. The room was full of wolves. They were piled up on the bed, on the floor, and over the Persian carpets that covered the floor. As leader, the gray wolf was nearest to a brazier filled with coals. The silver wolf was nestled in the curve of his body, her muzzle resting on his neck. Gavin was pressed against his back. As the Saxon watched, he whined deep in his dreams, his paws twitching. The Saxon was able to recognize most of them even this way: Joseph; Gordo, a stray from the Spanish mountains; Silvia, fat as a woman and massive as a wolf. All sleeping deeply together as a pack. He let the curtain drop closed.

"Together as a pack," he said, repeating his thought.

"Yes," Matrona said. "They must remember that from time to time."

Antonius and Barbara were gone. All the ladies had their own wagons.

"We honor them," the Saxon said. "The wolf is a trustworthy friend, a bad enemy, faithful to his kind. Gentle with his woman, devoted father to his children, chaste, and attentive in his duties to his pack. What man could ask to be more virtuous?

"So it is said. So I believe. The gods placed the wolf here for our instruction, that we would know how to behave. Then they gave us a talisman, a mark of our covenant with them, that they care for us, as we care for them."

Matrona went to the table and blew out the lamp.

"Then our way of life troubles you not at all?"

"No," he answered. "I feel as if, after a long journey, I have come home."

Then he got his bearskin, rolled up in it, and went to sleep on the floor.

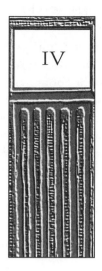

IV

SILVIE HAD BEEN UP ONLY A FEW HOURS. SHE peered through the shutters that sealed her wineshop, wondering if it was worthwhile to open so early. Most of her clientele didn't begin to show up until after dark, and most of them were furtive even then, preferring shadows and dimly lighted eating and drinking places.

Silvie catered to them, keeping the lights low, the wine measures honest, and the food she served cheap, plentiful, and always fresh. To everyone's absolute and utter shock, she was a very successful businesswoman. Though tavern keepers even in the most rundown sections of the eternal city wouldn't have welcomed her customers, she accepted them for what they were and she prospered.

None were even remotely honest, so she only took cash. Most were thieves, with a sprinkling of assassins, bravos who fought for pay covertly, and a more open group of killer mercenaries who hired out to the quarreling nobles and any other splinter group in all of sundered Italy. They welcomed a quiet place to eat, drink, and transact business before beginning their nightly rounds. Silvie provided this.

And, in return, her grateful if violent clients kept the peace in her wineshop. Although there were quite a few killings in the immediate area around the shop, none could be traced to its now very respectable proprietress.

It was no more than the seventh hour, late afternoon. The only creature that could be seen was her neighbor's calico cat, and all the cat was doing was sleeping in the sun, its white belly up, paws in the air, the picture of complete and utter relaxation.

Silvie yawned and thought about going back to bed. She might still be able to catch a short nap before nightfall. She was turning away when a man appeared and rapped on the shutters softly, so softly. The cat on the doorstep across the street didn't even stir.

She thought about going upstairs and returning to bed and ignoring him, but she was pretty sure he was one of her regulars. Few others went hooded and cloaked on warm afternoons. So she pulled the bolt and folded one of the shutters back.

The man slipped in.

Silvie went behind the counter. "I don't have any food cooked yet, but—"

Then she got a clear look at his face.

Hugo!

The slap knocked her down. He dropped to one knee and pressed a knife to her throat. "Where is your money? I know you own this place and it's prosperous. Now, where's the money?"

Silvie tried to pull away from him using her elbows. She was flat on her back on the floor, but Hugo grabbed her hair with one hand and pressed the knife closer to her carotid artery.

She hadn't been afraid of Hugo before; he had been utterly domi-nated by his father, Gundabald. But she was afraid of this Hugo. He was thinner, looked much older, and was already beginning to lose his teeth, but he had a savage, feral cast to his features that he hadn't had when he was a younger man. He looked as if he'd had to struggle to survive, and it hadn't improved either his judgment or his temper.

"Silvie." The knife tip drew blood.

"Yes, yes, Hugo," she whispered. "Money. It's upstairs in the bedroom. Let me up, just let me up. I'll go get it."

Another man entered the shop, followed by a third. They looked, if possible, older and more battered than Hugo. One's ears were cropped and the third lacked a hand.

"Wedo, go get it," Hugo ordered the crop-eared one.

Wedo hurried past them to climb the stairs at the back of the shop. The third man watched the street anxiously.

Silvie used the momentary distraction to get to her feet and try to put as much distance between herself and Hugo as she could.

"Go ahead. Go ahead," the one-handed man urged Hugo. "She told you where it is. Finish it, you fool. Finish it."

Hugo bared his teeth and lunged at Silvie. He stepped on the cat.

The cat wasn't hurt—this was ascertained upon later investigation—but the resulting ghastly screech probably awakened everyone on the entire block from their siestas, and Silvie went over the bar. She wasn't sure afterward if she high jumped, broad jumped, or just took wing and flew, but in one second she was over the bar and running down the street, letting fly with long, loud, wailing screams sufficient to end the siesta of anyone who managed to sleep through the cat's cry of anguish.

A half hour later, she was sitting in Lucilla's peristyle garden with Lucilla's maids applying restoratives while the redoubtable Lucilla tried to get a coherent story out of her.

"You're sure it was him?"

Silvie stopped her coughing and sobbing long enough to say, in high indignation, "Of course I'm sure it was him. He was going to killlll meeeee."

"You're beginning to make me wish he'd succeeded," Lucilla snapped. "Get some control of yourself, woman, and answer my questions properly."

Dulcinia, the singer, was with Lucilla, as she often was these days. Silvie had first run to Dulcinia, in terror that Lucilla might kill her. Hugo was, at best, a hunted man. Lucilla, the pope, and even just possibly the Lombard duke Desiderius would like to have a chat with him. The sort of chat one has in a room where racks, branding irons, and thumbscrews are the most prominent furnishings. Lucilla might believe—perish the thought—that Silvie gave him money of her own accord, or cherished some secret tenderness for him in her heart.

Dulcinia, seeing Silvie's emotional condition, understood this was manifestly not the case and conducted her at once to Lucilla. She promised to intercede with Lucilla if the lady became testy.

"Please, Silvie," Dulcinia pleaded. "Gain some control over yourself and try to tell our illustrious patroness what happened."

Dulcinia wrung out a cloth in a basin of water and pressed it with her long-fingered hands to Silvie's forehead and eyes, then handed her a clean handkerchief. "Now blow your nose, girl, and try to make some sense."

Silvie blew, then took a deep breath. In the darkness, where she didn't have to look at Lucilla's disapproving face, she felt better.

"There now," Dulcinia cooed. "That's a good girl."

"I really don't know anything except that it was Hugo," Silvie said. "He tapped on my shutters. He was cloaked and hooded, so I couldn't tell who it was, so I thought . . . I thought—"

"We're not interested in what you thought," Lucilla said in a terrible voice.

Silvie burst into tears again.

Dulcinia ran out of patience. "Now, stop. Both of you. Silvie, stop yowling like an alley cat in heat, and you, Lucilla, stop frightening her.

"She thought it was one of her regular patrons. We all know what kind of people frequent Silvie's establishment."

Silvie gulped. "Yes, that's what I thought. But it wasn't. It was Hugo. I was on the floor and Hugo had a knife to my throat, and he said he wanted money. I told him where to find it."

"There were others with him?" Lucilla asked.

"Yes, two. Outlaws."

"Outlaws?" Lucilla asked.

"One had cropped ears; the other had only one hand. Hugo called the crop-eared one Wedo. He didn't say a name for the other, the one-hand man. Anyway—" Silvie's eyes were wide with terror. "That one told Hugo to finish it! He came after me and he stepped on the cat—"

"Who came after you? And what has the cat to do with anything?" Lucilla asked.

"Hugo came after me, and he stepped on the cat. The cat is a yellow, black, and white one. She belongs to my neighbor across the street and sometimes comes into my shop. To get scraps. I feed her because she catches mice for everyone, not only her owner, and besides—"

"I'm getting to know this cat entirely too well," Lucilla interrupted. "Now, Silvie, take a deep breath and tell me what Hugo did after he stepped on the cat."

"I don't know, because when the cat screamed, everyone jumped, and I ran and I ran and I ran . . . until I got to Dulcinia's villa. And . . ." Silvie began sobbing again.

"I don't think there's a bit of doubt. It's Hugo," Dulcinia said.

Lucilla rose and went to call her guards.

"Don't worry," Dulcinia told Silvie. "You have friends now, powerful friends. We will protect you. I'll send one of my men to the shop with you tonight, and then we can meet again in the morning and decide what to do. Now, calm yourself and go lie down. Lucilla's physician will see you."

"I don't need any physician. There's nothing wrong with me," Silvie added.

"Yes, you do, my dear. You may not have noticed it yet, but you have a very ugly black eye. Now, go with the servants and do as they tell you," Dulcinia said as Lucilla's maids shepherded Silvie away.

Dulcinia spent a quiet time alone until Lucilla returned. She wasn't lonely, however. Music played at all times inside Dulcinia's mind. She was famous for her singing and sometimes composed her own melodies for poems she set to music. Now she tried to find a theme to express the beauty of Lucilla's gardens at dusk. The beauty of the fountains' endless chime, the subtle aromas of the herbs and flowers growing along the paths and borders. A rose was blooming nearby, mixing its fragrance with white thyme and sage bearing soft blue flowers. Something—jasmine, perhaps—brushed her from time to time with its ravishing scent.

A wormwood with silvery foliage and downy yellow flowers glowed pale in the first moonlight. Lucilla returned and sat down beside Dulcinia.

"Thank you for bringing her here. This really is an important piece of information. I'm sorry I was so impatient with Silvie, but I find her histrionics maddening."

"Yes, but you are irritable today. I think if I had the same experience Silvie had, I'd be hysterical, too."

"Nonsense," Lucilla said. "Never in all your life, not even as a child, did you behave as badly as Silvie at her best. When Regeane asked me to supervise that one's 'business venture,' I was wild. But of course I didn't show that to Regeane. I agreed. Regeane had done too much for me, for Hadrian, for everyone, for me to deny her that rather modest request. When I think of what that girl went through at the hands of her repulsive relatives, of the Lombard party, of all the squabbling factions here in Rome, it chills my blood. Tied to a stake, watching her champion fight for her life. Do you know they actually—"

"Lit the fire," Dulcinia finished. "Yes, I was there. So was everyone else in Rome above the age of two and below ninety. And now one of those selfsame relatives is back. Ready to cause the child more trouble."

"Not if I get my hands on him," Lucilla said. "I alerted Hadrian, the papal guard, and sent my own people out to scour the city, but I don't think we'll find Hugo. Even that nasty little son of a bitch isn't that stupid.

"Moreover, someone is with Silvie, and they will watch her shop day and night. I detest Silvie sometimes, certainly. I haven't forgiven her for speaking out against Regeane, when the girl was only trying to save Silvie's louse-ridden hide. Regeane forgave her and then even managed to put Silvie under my protection. And anyone under my protection is to be kept safe at all costs. My reputation demands it. What I'm doing now is trying to think of some way to discredit Hugo to Desiderius.

"Because depend on it, my love, it is to the Lombard duke that Hugo is going. No one wants to harbor the little rat any more than they want a large collection of leeches, bedbugs, or any other sort of vermin."

"You're sure?" Dulcinia asked.

"Certain. Hugo is probably destitute. They fooled us royally when they forsook Regeane and transferred their loyalties to the Lombard party here in Rome.

"Maeniel is a good-natured man and would probably have paid them to stay away, but when they tried to get Regeane judicially murdered, it was too much for even his stomach. Regeane had tried to get me to refrain from having their throats cut, and if they had remained in the background, I might have acceded to her wishes.

"But those bastards thought they could make a big score and get even with Regeane for crossing them. They failed. Gundabald is dead."

"You're sure?"

"Yes," Lucilla said. "I'm sure. But none of us—not me, Hadrian, or Maeniel—could ever find hide nor hair of Hugo, and believe me, love, we all have different but highly efficient methods of searching. My guess is Gundabald told Hugo he was going to tell Maeniel what sort of wife he'd married. Maeniel knew already and the information was, shall we say, redundant."

"This troubles me," said Dulcinia. "I met Regeane. I liked her. But you and Silvie sometimes speak of her as if she weren't quite human."

"Yes, yes . . . ," Lucilla answered. "But sometimes ignorance is a great deal safer than certain types of knowledge. So please don't trouble yourself about it, my love.

"In any case, when Gundabald didn't return, Hugo's guts promptly turned to water. After he got off the pot, he probably ran as fast as he could. Between one thing and another, Gundabald had amassed quite a lot of money, so it took Hugo some time to run through it.

"Pity, I'd hoped someone would cut the little weasel's throat for his ill-gotten gains, but it appears they didn't. Now he's come back to sell the only thing he has that's worth anything—information."

Dulcinia was pleased. She hadn't seen Lucilla this animated in months. She was beginning to think her beloved was ready to succumb to old age, but now she seemed revitalized. Yes, Dulcinia realized Lucilla was simply bored. In her youth, Lucilla had been absorbed in a brutal struggle to survive. Then she'd been drawn into politics through her association with Hadrian and spent her middle years battling the Lombard party, who were determined to gain control of the papacy.

Now the Lombards were defeated, at least in their designs on the papacy. Hadrian was pope. Lucilla's children were grown: her son Antonius was with Regeane, her daughter Augusta had married into one of the wealthiest and most socially prominent families in Rome. Lucilla was rich, secure, and in most quarters highly respected, but bored and lonely.

Regeane and Antonius were gone. Hadrian and Lucilla were still lovers, but he was more and more involved in administrative matters both secular and sacred. Fifteen minutes of Augusta's conversation was sufficient to induce either a coma or rage, depending on whether she saw fit to instruct her mother on politics or society. Augusta knew nothing about the former and too much about the latter. In any event, Lucilla found herself alone with very little to do.

But now! Hugo's return brought some new and interesting troubles into Lucilla's life.

Dulcinia smiled.

"This is no laughing matter," Lucilla said.

"To be sure, but it's late and I believe, if I remember correctly, you invited me to supper this evening. I haven't had a bite since this morning. I skipped lunch, and then Silvie broke in and—"

"Oh, good Lord." Lucilla slapped her forehead. "I had forgotten. I received a shipment of artichokes and a barrel of oysters, and the cook promised to do artichokes in Sicilian style with a wild boar stuffing made with olive oil, cheese, and bread crumbs. And the oysters raw with a tart citron butter sauce. Not only that, but I have a wonderful amphora of six-year-old Falernum from my own estate."

"What a feast," Dulcinia cried. "Just us two?"

"Yes, but I greatly fear I'll make you sing for your supper."

"It's always a pleasure to sing for you, my love."

And the two women went off together, arm in arm.

HUGO AND HIS FRIENDS HAD TAKEN SHELTER IN A tomb far outside the city gates along the road to Lombardy. The tomb wasn't Roman or even an Etruscan tomb of the earlier period when the wealth yielded by iron and Greek trade made a civilization bloom in Etruria, but a still older one of the bronze age, when the dead were not separated from the family but returned to their kin as bones to be buried under the house floors, and were the recipients of sacrifices as revered ancestors. So it was a strangely vacant place, peaceful yet empty, made of dressed but unmortared stone in the shape of a beehive with a basin near the door to hold the lustral water and, at times, the sacred fire—both fire and water used to sanctify the burial rites.

It would soon be evening. Hugo and his cohorts were gobbling down some bread and a little cheese they'd managed to steal from Silvie's wineshop. Hugo had given his friends only a few silver coins and kept the rest for himself. "After all, she's my wife. I own the shop, and I can make her sell it, and—"

"If you do, you'll be a fool," the crop-eared man named Wedo said.

"Why? I've been thinking it over, and she is my wife. We were married before I left home, and—"

"If Rome is like every other city I've been in," Wedo whispered, "a woman or, for that matter, a man alone couldn't own any business—not without the protection of higher-ups."

"Silvie's a slut. She doesn't have any highborn friends."

"She does now," Wedo said. "Depend on it. From what you told me, Silvie earned at the most a few coppers a night selling herself to drunks in the back room of taverns. I saw that shop. A counter with wine wells, tables, chairs . . . And upstairs was nicer. A bed with curtains around it, linen sheets, wool blankets, and three dresses and even more than three aprons, all hanging from nails on the wall. That woman of yours, she's got friends, all right.

"If Gimp and you hadn't been such fools and scared her, we might have gotten even more."

Gimp ducked his head and tried to look invisible.

"No, you go back there, boy," said Wedo, "and the next thing this Silvie cooks is your goose.

"Now, how about a decent split on what we got from your woman? Then we can all go our separate ways in peace."

Hugo finished eating, stood up, brushed the grease and crumbs off his hands, then went and urinated in the basin that once held the water for the sacrificial rites.

No, he thought as his stream hit the meander that once marked the path the dead must take to paradise. No, he didn't want to give any more of Silvie's money to either the man called Gimp or to Wedo. He needed every copper of it if he was to gain an audience with any of Desiderius's servants.

Regretfully he admitted to himself that Wedo was right. There was no way a girl like Silvie could have earned enough, even from a generous protector, to have paid for such an establishment. The only person he could think of with enough compassion to help Silvie was Regeane.

Hugo was afraid of Regeane, but the thought of Lucilla or Maeniel made the blood congeal in his veins. Compared to either of them, Regeane was a gentle person. Maeniel would certainly kill him on sight, and Lucilla would do worse: have him tortured until she was sure he had no more to tell her, then put him to death in the most painful way possible. She'd promised him just that. He'd been present when Lucilla was tortured by the Lombard duke's men.

He finished urinating, then turned back to where his companions were eating. Hesitation. Hesitation had cost him his opportunity to kill Silvie. So he didn't hesitate. He grabbed Wedo by the hair, jerked his head back, and slit his throat.

Gimp raised his head, looking shocked, but a second later Hugo's boot toe caught him on the point of the chin. He never felt the blow when Hugo's knife pierced his throat from the front and severed his spine at the back.

The tomb was suddenly quiet. Hugo had killed men before, his first in a tavern brawl not long after Gundabald died. But usually it was more difficult than this had been, and far more complications followed. He sensed, however, that it wouldn't be prudent to linger, so he cleaned his knife on Wedo's shirt, then searched both corpses, noting as he did that blood was still flowing from Gimp's throat in a dark stream.

Predictably, Gimp had nothing. But Wedo yielded two gold coins he must have held back from the money in Silvie's strongbox.

Hugo congratulated himself on taking the sensible approach to the problem of dealing with his two companions. He had needed to rid himself of them both. They would certainly have proven an embarrassment at the Lombard court. And the two gold coins would go far to helping him put on the show necessary to gain Desiderius's ear.

Then he rose and left the tomb.

The brightness of late afternoon stung Hugo's eyes for a second. He glanced around furtively, but he was absolutely alone. The only sound came from insects singing in the tall new grass, and the only moving thing in sight was a dust devil whirling along the stones of the ancient Roman road to Lombardy.

He set out walking, trying to put as much distance as possible between himself and the corpses he'd left behind.

Inside the tomb, Gimp began moving; the dark blood from his jugular vein flowed faster as he began returning to consciousness.

On the road outside the tomb, the evening breeze dropped and the dust devil vanished, melting into the still air like a wisp of smoke. The consciousness riding it hung motionless, indifferent to movement or stillness. It remembered a sort of grim malice but not much else. It was fading; without human energies to feed on, it would soon dissipate the way even thick fog does in sunlight, fading into tenuous filaments until at last it is gone.

The tomb guardians were only shadows now. The last processions they could remember were over two thousand years ago. They lay and dreamed of a vanished people who came with offerings of wheat, fruit, and flowers to feast the dead before they were burned on a pyre. Thus the spirits might begin the journey to the distant land of the dead. The people they had known were gone, the world so changed that their intercession was no longer deemed to be necessary. The only reason they lingered was because some few farmers hereabouts came and made offerings of oil and wine, believing such offerings brought good luck.

They had always done so. Time out of mind.

The guardians slept even when shepherds used the ancient tomb as a refuge in bad weather for themselves and for their sheep. Because the shepherds, no fools, made such offerings as they could, and these spirits understood the eternal needs of those who struggle to gain a living from the dusty, hot soil near the sea. Understood them, in fact, far better than their later counterparts and were both more tolerant and kind.

But Hugo had awakened them, first with his desecration of the ancient bowl and then by shedding the blood of his companions. They would have done but little to avenge his vandalism—could have done but little, they were now so weak and shadowy—but they sensed both the stronger presence in the road and Gimp's weakening struggle for life. So they invited it in.

ANTONIUS WAS UP FIRST. HE LEFT HIS WAGON IN the campground and picked out a tent, one of those used by Maeniel's people, and cleared it of furniture. Joseph arrived about then. He'd wanted to take a leak, but after he'd poked his nose out of Maeniel's tent, he realized doing it against a tree as a wolf might entail complications. There were what seemed to him an uncomfortable number of humans wandering around. He became human, dressed, and was able to find a trench nearby. Then he ambled—Joseph never moved any faster than an amble—back to the tent he shared with Gavin.

"What are you doing?" he asked Antonius, who was drawing lines and circles in the sandy floor of the tent.

"Ah, good, someone is up. I need rocks, all sizes, small and large; at least four or five buckets of dirt; and some green branches."

Joseph, who had no affection for work, looked at Antonius in disbelief. "Why?"

"Never mind why. Just get them. I'm busy."

Joseph considered asking Maeniel if he should obey Antonius, but was smart enough to know his leader would say yes, and if he was wolf would probably follow the yes with a nip on the shoulder. So he shambled out, followed by Antonius's order "And be quick about it."

An hour later, Antonius had built a pretty good model of the mountains on the floor of Joseph's tent. He used the dirt for the lower hills, the greenery for forest, and the rocks for the higher peaks. True, it was schematic, not to scale, and ignored a number of features, but it was clear enough to Maeniel, who had lived in the Alpine vastness for a greater number of years than Antonius cared to think about.

Not long after he and Regeane had joined the others in the mountain fastness, Antonius had plied Gavin with wine one evening and gotten him into a state of deep drunkenness. Gavin babbled about a number of things: Caesar—the first Caesar, the one who gave his name to all the rest; Britain; a powerful sorceress; Romans—imperial Romans who, according to Gavin, Maeniel had known well; and all manner of oddities. Antonius didn't believe even the half of what Gavin told him, but if any—even a tenth—of it was true, Maeniel was a far stranger and more powerful man than he'd ever imagined.

In any case, he submitted his model to Maeniel for approval.

He received it. Maeniel made some changes, not very big ones, and pronounced it true.

About this time, Arbeo arrived to inform them that the king was breakfasting with his nobles and would arrive shortly. Regeane retired to her room, leaving the rest of the women to greet the king.

She lay on the bed and closed her eyes.

Barbara and Matrona entered. "What's wrong?" Barbara asked.

"I have a headache," Regeane answered.

Barbara placed her hands on her hips. "You never have headaches."

Matrona looked at Regeane speculatively.

"I have one now," Regeane said shortly.

Barbara looked at Matrona. She felt at a loss, but Matrona simply studied Regeane, looking at her with opaque, dark eyes. "I think I have something for this headache," she said, left, and returned with her Etruscan mirror. She handed it to Regeane.

"Oh, it's that sort of headache," Barbara said.

"Yes," Matrona answered.

"I don't want to look," Regeane insisted.

"No?" Matrona asked. "Why not?"

"I am afraid of what I will see. In Rome I looked before the trial and saw myself burning."

"I know," Matrona said, "and you couldn't know that a second later they would extinguish the fire. But you went forward courageously, and you will do the same now."

Barbara walked over to one of the camp chairs and sat. These people were prescient, Barbara knew that much. She did not consider them fortunate. Foreknowledge was a disturbing gift, far more apt to be painful than not.

For a second, Regeane held the mirror in her hand, pressed flat against her supine body.

Matrona walked over to the brazier in the corner intended to warm the room on cold winter nights. The coals were almost burned out. Only a small cluster in the center covered with white ash still glowed, the rest were black and dead. Matrona threw something on the coals.

Regeane found herself sitting in a forest populated with numberless high, tall trees. The trunks rose like the pillars of a great church, limbless until they reached a great height. There they harvested the sunlight, leaving the ground below in deep shadow, thick with the discards of a thousand winters that formed a soft, springy carpet. The forest floor was dappled by sunlight only when the wind moved the giant treetops in a slough of whispers, eternal sound wedded somehow to eternal silence.

In the bed, Regeane felt a flash of panic. She was here, and yet not here, as she had been in the tent when she faced the dark one. She could see Matrona and Barbara, the room and its furniture, but somehow the incredibly ancient forest seemed more real to her than the shadows of people and things surrounding her, so she sat up and looked into the mirror.

Wind moved through the forest, a dazzle of sunlight came and went. Then it vanished, fading the way mist does before sunlight.

"Well?" Matrona asked.

"That was an anticlimax," Regeane said.

"What did you see?"

Regeane's lips curled in disgust. "Hugo!"

Matrona chuckled. "Is that all?"

"Well," Regeane said, "he looked frightened."

HUGO WAS FRIGHTENED.
Gimp had caught up to him.
Hugo bought bread and cheese from a farmhouse not far away. He'd seen no men, but the place was fortified and the women suspicious. But when he'd offered silver, they chained their dogs and sold him an onion bread mixed with black olives, and soft, white cheese in a pottery jar. It had the sharp tang of goat cheese. It was heavy, salted, and had a thick, pale crust on it, but the inner part beyond the rind was rich with cream and had a good taste.

The level countryside here was deserted and the Roman road dwindled to a dust trace, at times only indicated by the cypresses the Roman engineers planted along its borders. Here and there he saw the tumbled stones of a farmhouse long ago abandoned, weeds growing tall in the courtyard.

Once he saw what had been a big villa and he almost turned to seek hospitality for the night, but he'd gone only a few steps when he realized the still-closed shutters on the windows were fire blackened, the fields and pastures around it were thick with weeds. The empty building, which must have harbored human beings until not too long ago, gave him a particular sense of disquiet. He felt as if eyes watched him through crevices in the charred shutters, and something wandered through the empty roofless rooms behind them.

He hurried on. These plains, which were subject to raids from the sea and quarrels between the Lombard states and the pope, had been depopulated centuries ago. Only a few strongpoints stood. Now these were falling, as internal and external disorders spread.

He began to be fearful he could not find a safe place to spend the night when he saw the remains of a village just ahead. Like almost every structure now, it was located on the highest point for miles around.

Just then the old Roman road vanished, gone, washed away by winter floods that had formed a shallow ravine reaching down to the sea. At the edge of the road, Hugo saw that if he turned and followed the dry ravine, it would lead him to the town in the distance.

When he reached it, he realized that, far from being a town, it had been a small city, but most of it was gone, broken up and washed away by the torrents that created the ravine. Whether its abandonment had been caused by the destruction wrought by the flood, or it had been abandoned long ago and then destroyed, was impossible to ascertain.

So Hugo climbed the slope of the ravine and found himself in the forum. The ruins of a temple loomed over him on one side, and a colonnade on the other that must have held shops now stood looking out on the empty ravine and the beach beyond. The cobbles flooring the ancient town were almost buried by windblown beach sand. There were plenty of tracks in the sand. Birds, mice, rabbits, and, here and there, wild cat prints could be seen, but no human footprints.

Hugo shivered. This was the most desolate place he'd ever been in. He climbed the steep steps up to the temple that had been set on a high platform overlooking the sea. He found the temple platform cold; the wind from the ocean, earlier a refreshing breeze, now had a bite to it, and the sun was not far above the horizon's rim.

From his perch, he could see the surrounding countryside. There was no sight of any human dwelling anywhere. Night was coming on and Hugo didn't want to be caught in the open.

He found shelter in a pit near the temple. It must once have been a shop that looked into the forum, but the floor had rotted or burned when the town was abandoned and it left only this shallow cellar. There were plenty of deadfalls in the ravine leading to the sea, enough to build a fire, and the walls of the cellar were high enough to shield it from any prying eyes.

By nightfall he had a good blaze, not too high—he didn't want it to be seen by others adrift in the war-ruined countryside—but sufficient to keep him warm. He had a little wine left. He drank that and ate the bread, but hugely enjoyed the cheese until a voice asked, "I wish you'd save a little of that for me."

Hugo looked up and saw Gimp sitting across from him. The hole in his throat was still open but no longer bleeding.

Hugo began to scream.

ONE OF THE PAPAL GUARD, A CAPTAIN, AWAKENED
Lucilla the next morning. He looked pleased with himself.

"I think we found one of the men you're looking for, my lady."

He was carrying a sack. He set it down, picked up the end, and
Wedo's head rolled out.

"You killed him?" Lucilla said accusingly.

"No," the captain said. "We know better than that. He was dead
when we found him. Somebody slit his throat. His head kept trying
to fall off, so we sawed it off the rest of him and left the carcass for the
crows and wild dogs. Seemed a lot simpler that way."

Lucilla nodded. "I was hoping to get one or more of them alive."

"Wish we could accommodate you, my lady, but this is all we
have. Some shepherds found it on the via Aurelia. They were in an
old cave or tomb. It's still cold out. They sheltered there for the
night. Found him. Lot of blood on the floor, though. Might have
been some wounds. Little falling out among thieves?"

Lucilla nodded. "On the road to Lombardy."

Silvie was fetched. She hung back until the soldiers told her the
man was dead. Looking at corpses didn't bother her.

"It's not Hugo," she said.

"I know that," Lucilla said between her teeth. "But is it one of
them?"

"He looks different." She rolled the head faceup with one foot.
"Yes," she said. "That's the one Hugo called Wedo. He stole my
money."

"Yes," Lucilla said.

"Did they get it back?" Silvie asked disconsolately.

"Of course not," Lucilla answered. "But don't worry, I'll make
it up to you. Not that I give a rat's ass one way or the other, but
Regeane would want me to."

"I'll need it," Silvie said. "I'm pregnant."

V

REGEANE ELECTED NOT TO PRESENT HERSELF AT
what could only have been a council of war.
Charles arrived. He was accompanied by his horsemen
companions, the *scarae*. Today Arbeo was among them, bursting with
pride.

The king met Maeniel, would not let him bow or kneel, and
clasped his hand. Charles said to Arbeo, "He spoke well of you; that's
why you're here today."

"Thank you, sir," Arbeo stammered.

"How is Otho?" the king asked.

"Doing better. A lady of my household, Matrona, is caring for
him. She is a skilled physician. Otho could not be in better hands."

When it came to sickroom visits, Charles left his escorts outside.
Matrona was relaxing in the same camp chair she'd been in the day
before. Though she wouldn't have admitted it, she'd dressed for
the king in an impossibly beautiful dalmatic patterned like two bird
wings overlapping, with full sleeves, and under it a severe long-
sleeved shift of white silk. Her jewelry, a choker with a hundred
golden chains dangling from it. When Charles entered, she rose and
went to one knee, bowing her head.

The silk clung to every voluptuous curve of her body. Charles
was impressed and indicated for her to rise, which she did with an
almost inhuman grace.

Otho, lying in bed, was smiling a wicked smile.

"I must thank you for giving my friend such excellent care that he is now recovering from his injuries."

"I find it pleasurable to exercise my skills for such a good cause. I will, with your permission, now withdraw and allow you to speak privately with your servant."

He nodded, getting a good eyeful as the patterned silk drifted against her body as she glided away.

She entered the next room where Regeane and the Saxon were standing. The soft murmur of voices drifted through the canvas wall.

The Saxon said nothing because, though he could hear only a muttering sound, Regeane and Matrona were obviously listening. Once or twice their eyes met. Matrona nodded and then so did Regeane. After a time, even the Saxon could hear Otho weep and the king comfort him.

"Genuine tears," Matrona whispered. "He loves the king."

Regeane's eyes filled. "Matrona," Regeane asked, "what was that thing?" She placed her hand on the Saxon's shoulder. "We fought it at the monastery, but before, I met it near Rome at a tomb. I fought it then. It tried to take me or Silvie. I think it wanted me most, but I think it would have taken Silvie if it could have gotten her. But she ran. I told her to run. Then I fought it. In the end, after nearly paralyzing me with horror, it fled. That was why Silvie believed me a witch and testified at my trial. She told the truth, but no one thanked her for it, least of all Gundabald and Hugo."

"Silvie told the truth as she saw it," Matrona said. "Remember that. Silvie's mind is limited, at best, and she was never able to comprehend what she encountered in either it or—" She paused and raised a finger. "—you."

"Yes." Regeane nodded thoughtfully.

Maeniel entered just then. "My lady." He extended a hand to Regeane. "Come be presented to your kinsman, the king."

Regeane was dressed for the occasion also, but not as Matrona was. Magnificently, but with a Byzantine stiffness that concealed as much as it beautified. Shift, fine Egyptian linen; long-sleeved overgown of silk shot with gold thread; and over that a dalmatic of stiff gold brocade. The ensemble was finished with a white lace veil that covered a stiff gold wimple, starched and held in place, covering her hair, by long gold pins.

Maeniel led her forth proudly.

The Saxon turned to Matrona. "She might as well be a nun."

He'd seen some in Lombardy. They wore long blue or black dresses with white headcloths. Someone told him they were the Christian God's women, but if they were, the god never seemed interested in them, since they had no children. Another Christian among the slaves said that was as it should be. He'd answered somewhat nastily, asking of what use is a woman if you do not get her with child? But the other slave was apparently not that convinced a Christian, since he had answered, "Don't know. It puzzles me, too."

It hadn't been a long conversation. They were both exhausted, having been condemned to pull a plow that spring. The Saxon had broken the jaw of one of the drivers. He didn't know what his companion had done, and he never found out because after three days of brutal labor in the hot sun, his companion died.

His owner had considered it a loss and so the Saxon was returned to the work gang. Only this time they never took off the chains.

"That's the idea. She chose to avoid trouble," Matrona replied. "The man has an eye for the ladies. A whole procession of women has passed through his bed. Regeane doesn't want to be among them. It's a complication we don't need."

"Her husband needn't know."

"Don't be a fool," Matrona replied. "He knows everything. He'd know exactly what happened the moment he drew near her. How long, how often, who the man was, and whether it was voluntary or involuntary on her part. Don't ever *think* to hide anything from him. Desire, even thwarted desire, is as plain as Charlemagne's dragon standard to any of us."

"Then he knows that I am in love with her," the Saxon said.

"Yes," Matrona answered, "and so do I. But so long as she doesn't respond to you, he won't care. As far as the king is concerned, we plan a diversion. Otho told the king I was accessible."

The Saxon's eyebrows rose.

"I would like that," Matrona said, with an evil smile, "and so would the king."

"Where did you get—" The Saxon pointed to the necklace.

"From a man called Priam at a place called Troy."

The Saxon shook his head. "Never heard of the city or the man," he said.

REGEANE RETURNED TO THE PRIVACY OF THE BED-room, and Maeniel and Charles went to see Antonius's model. All the young men crowded around, very interested, though both Maeniel and Antonius had some doubt as to how well they compre-hended its meaning. They jostled each other, showing off for the young king. At least they were trying to say intelligent things about it.

"This is meant to be Geneva, where we are camped." Antonius pointed to a piece of blue cloth at the edge of the table. From here he traced with his finger one of the routes Charles would take over the mountains.

"See," Charles said to the youngsters of the *scarae*. "I won't say it's easy, but it won't be impossible either. Not with such friends as these."

He indicated Maeniel and Antonius with a sweep of his arm. The youngsters cheered. Antonius smiled urbanely, as if the whole thing were a quiet walk through a garden.

There were shouts and screams as a fight broke out in one of the mobile taverns outside.

"How did you manage to end up in this wretched spot?" Charles asked.

"We were conducted here, or at least my wife and friends were, after—not long after—our arrival."

"Indeed," Charles said. "No doubt in error."

Charles turned to the *scarae*. "Friends, I'm sure there are better campsites. Please see to it that my lord Maeniel finds one. But don't—" He turned to Antonius's model. "—don't disturb this."

"It's portable," Antonius said.

Charles nodded. "I think the two of you are going to be no end of help in my endeavors.

"We will talk of this later. Now, boys," he spoke to the *scarae*. "Help our friends break camp and move."

THE NEW CAMPSITE WAS MUCH QUIETER. ON THE edge of a forest, it was shaded by trees and cool by day. By night it was even more appealing, at least to them.

Barbara and Matrona combined to make a feast: wild boar with sage, apples, wild onions, beans with sausage, and some of last autumn's salt-smoked ham. Wild greens that Regeane and Silvia collected near a stream, dressed with oil and wine. Breads, a dozen kinds. Matrona was an expert baker, and what she didn't get around to, Barbara did.

As usual, people got up from the table, stepped out into the night, and vanished. When dinner was over, Regeane, Maeniel, Antonius, Barbara, and the Saxon sat in the tent around the model, discussing it.

Antonius had formed the landslide, showing how it destroyed the road. "Do you think he understood?" Antonius asked Maeniel.

Maeniel appeared distracted. "Someone is coming," he said. Of all of them, his senses were the most acute.

The Saxon took the candelabra and lit four more candles. Nobody wanted their eyes to do any shining.

"I think," Maeniel said, "the king and possibly three others."

Regeane rose. She'd been seen in cloth of gold, and that was the only way she wanted Charles to see her. But he was in the tent before she could withdraw. His eyes raked over the company.

"I see you are not so formal with your intimates." He smiled at Regeane.

She was wearing only a long-sleeved linen shift covered by a brown gown embroidered with gold at the neck and hem. She'd put aside her veil and mantle. "With your permission." She curtseyed and eased toward the door.

"Tell me," Charles asked, "would you leave if I were not here?"

"No."

"An honest girl," the king said.

"Sometimes too honest," Antonius said with a sigh.

"In this instance, I don't think so. I wondered if she would be comfortable with this marriage. I knew neither one of you before I approved it. It was, in fact, Otho's idea."

"I'm rich; she's beautiful," Maeniel said. "How would we not get along well?"

Regeane flushed.

"Now I'm happy," Maeniel said. "And she's spoiled."

Regeane turned redder and began to laugh. "It's true. He denies me nothing."

He took her hand and raised it to his lips and kissed it. "Certainly not my company," Maeniel said.

"I'm afraid I may do that," Charles said.

"How so?" Maeniel asked.

"I have several maps of the region we are to cross," the king said, examining the model again. "But I cannot believe they are very accurate."

"Maps, yes," Antonius said. "Maps are a problem. There are few good ones. But my lord Maeniel has lived among these mountains all his life and has pointed out two good routes you may take."

"As for a safe passage," Maeniel said, "buy what provender you want and pay for it. The people living in the high valleys aren't warlike; once maybe, in the time of the Romans, they were, but not now. What they want is to be left alone. Life is not easy there, and they must struggle. The Romans garrisoned the passes and harried them, but I don't think they were ever really conquered. They have learned the benefits of accommodation with large armed parties; however, I warn you, do not promise what you are not willing to perform.

"There are a great many rabble in your train. Dismiss them before you leave. Take only fighting men."

Charles nodded as he listened. "Sage advice! Hadrian was not mistaken in you. He sent letters saying you were a man of ability. But my arrival then is predictable in both time and place."

"Yes," Maeniel answered.

"Then Desiderius will be waiting for me. If he isn't, he's a bigger fool than I think he is. Because if I knew he were coming, I would be waiting for him."

Antonius walked to the model and pointed out two or three places.

"But I won't know which one, will I?"

"Not unless someone finds out for you," Maeniel said.

"Yes," Charles said.

"Oh," Regeane said.

"I know the people, I know the route. I have crossed these mountains many times," Maeniel said. "I will ride tonight. If—if I have your word that my wife and friends will remain under your protection."

"Yes," Charles said. "You have my word."

HUGO FLED BUT FOUND HE COULDN'T RUN FAR. The front of the cellar hole was low, but the back was high, and enough of the roof remained to prevent his climbing the wall.

Gimp laughed. Or rather, the thing inhabiting him laughed. "Come," it said. "Build up the fire. The creature I'm riding is cold. Or would you like to be caught alone in the dark with me?"

No, Hugo thought. That would be impossibly horrible. Almost gibbering with fear, he edged back and set more fuel on the blaze.

"You're not Gimp," Hugo whimpered. "You don't even sound like him."

"No. I'm a lot smarter than little Gimp here. So don't try any of your tricks on me."

"Where are you?" Hugo asked, glancing around wildly.

The thing that had been Gimp bared its teeth at him. "Here. Right here. Inside him. You mightily offended the keepers of the tomb where you left him, so they sent for me. I happened to be nearby.

"I can confer life on the dying. The other of your victims was dead, too dead, for my attentions. But poor little Gimp here was still struggling—paralyzed and dying to be sure, but with the spark of life still in him. He admitted me to his mind without argument when I promised him life. You see, he, like you, enjoys life. And so do I."

Hugo was sick with fear, but he was not what Gimp had been. Hugo had a lot more intelligence. True, he'd been dominated by Gundabald while he was alive, but since his father died he had had to make his own way and he'd found it by no means easy.

Now this thing, something from darkest nightmares, expressed a desire to possess him. And in a sick, dark way, Hugo found himself attracted by the idea. But he wasn't going to sell out as cheaply as Gimp. No. He would become this thing's possession only if it would promise to provide those things he most wanted.

He flashed his teeth at the thing across the fire in nothing like a smile. "I can be bought."

Gimp's companion considered the purchase. He had seduced the abbot. Others he terrorized, bullied, as he'd done to Otho. But he'd never outright bought. Now this creature, only marginally more capable than the one he was inhabiting, offered itself for sale.

It considered the pros and cons. Force and terror were of only limited use in dealing with the best of them. But its practice had always been to overcome with force first, because the mind would then weaken and cave. In Rome he'd seen Regeane as a creature of great power, so he'd tried to take her, but she had fought him off with a resolution and success he had not heretofore encountered, defending not only herself but Silvie also.

And even Otho beat him back when he'd tried to rule Otho's mind. He was sure he could turn this thing into a puppet if he exerted all his strength, but why exert all his strength in trying to dominate? Like the cringing creature before him, he was also finite. The battle with the wolves had almost drained him into nonexistence. Why work any harder than he had to?

But the price. It all depended on the price.

"What would be asked?"

W HEN REGEANE WALKED IN, MATRONA AND THE Saxon were washing Gilas, the girl who'd guided them to Otho's tent. Every so often she let out a soft, high, shrill scream like a bird in deep distress.

Outbursts of emotion did not sit well with the Saxon.

Matrona was washing her body, the Saxon her hair. He'd told Matrona he found this less disturbing.

"Why are you making noises like a sick chicken?" he asked the girl sternly.

"I'm wet all over."

"That is not a reason for complaint," he answered rather flatly.

"I'm wet. All over." She screamed. "The priests say—" That was all she got out. The Saxon, who had hold of her hair, dunked her at the word *priests*.

She sat up screaming. "At least let me get my mouth closed."

He seized her hair again. "If you hadn't opened it in the first place, the water wouldn't have gotten in," he said grimly. "One more word about priests and I will drown you."

Gilas gurgled, then shut up.

"What did she say?" he asked Matrona.

"I don't know. Something about sin," Matrona said. "Girl, you sell yourself from the back of a wagon. What do you care for the maunderings of priests?"

"It's my business, my trade," Gilas answered in a tone both defiant and aggrieved. "I don't enjoy it, so it's no sin."

"What is sin?" the Saxon asked.

"The concept is unclear to me also," Matrona said. "Though when the Christian religion began to make noise in the world, I betook myself to a Christian community and studied the philosophy. I was never able to make any headway with certain of their ideas. Sin is one of them."

The Saxon grunted and hauled Gilas out of the tub. Matrona wrapped her in clean linen sheets.

The Saxon built up the fire in the brazier, and Matrona began combing Gilas's hair with a fine-tooth comb.

"Do you know," Gilas said, as if making a remarkable discovery, "I think that feels good. If I become Otho's maidservant, how often will I have to do it?"

"Only about once a month," Matrona said. "But you may get to like it. Otho is rich. He has a villa with its own baths, like the Romans had.

"She is rising in the world, as Otho is grateful for her loyalty and wants her to find another profession," Matrona explained to Regeane. "He feels that without her help, he would soon have died."

"He's probably right," the Saxon said. "Until his eyes moved, I thought he was dead."

"Gilas?" Regeane asked. "Have you any other name? Besides Gilas, I mean."

"No," Gilas answered. "My mother followed the army, and her mother, too. And that's as far back as anyone can remember. During the campaigning season we usually made enough to keep us for the winter. Sometimes we could find an officer who would pay us to wash his clothes and look after his things, but they all wanted plenty of hard work for a few coppers. She could always do better in the back of a wagon. The same with me. Otho promises good wages. I'll just see," she said darkly. "I'll just see. I'll just have to see," she repeated as Matrona led her away.

The Saxon tipped the bathtub, sending the water into the weeds outside. "Did you want me, my lady?" he asked Regeane politely.

"No. I really came to talk to Matrona."

He nodded while he was swabbing the remaining water out of the bathtub with a sponge and drying it. The thing was leather, boiled leather, and was stored in one of the wagons.

He'd inserted himself expertly into their lives on the way from the mountains. He was quiet, never intrusive, always willing to turn his hand to any task that presented itself. He made himself useful to everyone, and his tremendous strength made him an invaluable presence in any and all difficulties, from facing down Otho's tormentor to freeing a wagon stuck in the mud.

"Why do you remain with us?" she asked.

"Because of you."

"There's no future in that."

"Are you asking me to leave?"

"No, no. I do love you, but not . . . not in—"

"Yes," he said. "I know. I feel much the same way as you do. I am possibly more drawn to you in the way of passion than you are to me, but perhaps that's only the man in me. I equate one with the other."

"He's leaving," Regeane said. She studied the tip of one of her riding boots as if it had suddenly become very important. "I don't want him to go alone."

"Then go with him."

"I don't know if he will take me."

"Then don't ask."

"I'm his wife."

"Don't make me laugh. You are no more a conventional wife than he is a conventional husband."

"There's a problem."

"What?" He lifted the tub from the floor and leaned it against one of the tent poles. Empty, it was very light.

"He is a wolf who is sometimes a man. I'm a woman who is sometimes a wolf. I'm not shape strong by day, not as much as he is."

The Saxon nodded. "Then I will follow with a sumpter mule and carry clothing for both of you."

"I don't like this business of being a wife. The king made me feel unnecessary."

Matrona entered behind Regeane. "Women are weak," she intoned in a religious manner.

"You should be ashamed of yourself," the Saxon said.

MONEY," HUGO SAID. "WHAT IS MONEY? GOLD, silver, precious stones, silks, velvet, and other fine clothing. Money."

The thing withdrew. Gimp sat with his mouth open, a vacant look in his eyes. Finally he blinked and seemed to regain his consciousness, then said, "Let me have some cheese."

Hugo's eyes darted around the ruin. Was the thing gone? He handed Gimp the pot and watched as he began eating with his fingers. When he had finished, Gimp gobbled the few remaining bread crusts. Then he sighed, lay down on his side, and began to look as if he were about to go to sleep.

Hugo watched him, wondering if it would do any good to sneak off in the darkness. Suddenly Gimp sat bolt upright and said, "Go to the left-hand corner of this cellar hole and dig in the spot where I tell you."

"I'll need light."

Gimp picked up one of the burning branches and walked over to the back corner near the wall. Hugo followed.

Curious in spite of himself, Hugo dug.

He'd made a hole only about six inches deep when he began to tire. He paused, panting.

"Dig," the thing in Gimp commanded.

"I'm working as fast as I can."

"I know," the thing in Gimp said. "You mortal creatures are the worst I've seen about abusing yourselves. He is drunken and lazy and stupid, and you are drunken and lazy. But he has more damage than you do, so I prefer you."

"Damage? You mean sticking my knife in him?"

"No. His mother was sick too long before he was born. Dig," he roared.

Hugo found the strength to scrape away a few more inches of soil and found himself staring at a small terra-cotta pot. He forgot his fatigue. He scraped away the soil around it; he jerked it out of the hole, breaking it. Gold coins spilled everywhere.

Hands trembling, Hugo began counting them. They were golden aurei, the currency of the ancient empire and a fabled source of wealth—a type of coin uncirculated for hundreds of years.

Hugo knew he was rich when he tried one of the coins with his teeth and it bent. Pure and heavy gold. He had no idea what they were worth, but he needn't worry about that right away because along with the gold, there was a lot of silver—also in the form of coins and broken jewelry.

"I take it our partnership is worth the price?"

The words brought Hugo down to earth with a thud.

The wind from the sea was beginning to rise. It fanned Hugo's fire, burning near the ruined forum. It flared, casting yellow flickering light throughout the old cellar hole.

Hugo's fists clenched and unclenched on the metal in his hands. "I have what I want," he said, his voice trembling. "But is there more?"

"What do you think I am?" the thing in Gimp asked. "A cheap conjurer? A mountebank, a charlatan who performs for pay? You have seen not a tithe of what I can do."

Gimp screamed as his clothing caught fire, and he was outlined in flames. Then, as quickly as it had come, the fire was gone. Hugo crouched, quivering, against the earth, the coins scattered unregarded around him. As Gimp knelt with the rags of charred cloth hanging from his body, Hugo quietly sobbed. Then Gimp spoke.

"Speak. I am tired of bargaining with you, fool. Say yea or nay, and be done with it."

"Yes." Hugo whimpered, his teeth chattering, his whole body shivering. "Yes, yes."

Something dark as a storm cloud seemed to hang over Hugo, then fell like drenching rain or a breaking sea. For a second Hugo feared he'd be crushed. But then the weight, the shadow, passed through him, into him, the way water enters dry soil and vanishes.

Hugo rose to his feet, trembling, weak with absolute and uncontrollable physical and emotional exhaustion. His mantle lay beside the fire. He staggered over to it, lay down, and sank at once into deep unconsciousness.

IN THE WEEKS TO COME, HUGO SHOWED AN ENERGY that anyone who had known him in the past would have found most uncharacteristic. In truth, he was afraid to disobey his "guest."

He awoke, or rather his brain awoke, staring out at the sun just beginning to rise over the sea. The surf was quiet and the wind in his face cool. "What?"

"Be quiet, fool. I'm watching the sun rise."

"It does that every day," Hugo complained.

"Yes, a miracle that you and your kind cannot comprehend."

Hugo managed to drift off to sleep again while the thing was using his body—somewhat to the amusement, the very secret amusement, of his guest.

When he was awakened again, his guest took him in search of more coin hoards. There were two neither as rich as the first, but enough to give him a good start in the first town he reached after his walk along the coast.

Gimp followed, walking along silently. He could talk, but apparently his voice had been affected by the stabbing, and besides, the spirit ordered him to be silent.

The money enabled Hugo to buy horses and clothes and to sojourn at the best lodgings available for travelers. The best were none too good. On the third night, they were sleeping at an inn in a tiny place called Corvo. For the first time since their agreement, his guest had let him drink himself into a fog, and he and Gimp staggered up to bed. He was awakened in the small hours of the morning by his guest, conscious that he had a dull, throbbing headache and a raging thirst.

Hugo tried to moan, but his guest warned him to be silent. There was a sound and movement in the darkened room. There shouldn't have been either one. Hugo had not been so drunk that he had left the door unbolted, and the windows were both narrow and covered by iron grills. "Sit up," his guest commanded him. "Strike a light."

Hugo did. In the first flare of the wax light, he saw the innkeeper coming across the floor at him, upraised ax in hand. Hugo tried to scream, but couldn't because his guest gave vent to a roar of laughter.

The chamber pot rose into the air and discharged its rather considerable contents directly into the innkeeper's face. Piss stings when it lands in eyes, and the man was both blinded and infuriated. He reached forward and swung the ax at Hugo—or rather at the bed where Hugo was sitting.

This time Hugo did scream and he jumped away, swearing frantically. His guest laughed again and threw Gimp's body at the innkeeper's knees. The innkeeper toppled over Gimp's back, but the ax continued its downward progress. Instead of embedding itself in the straw tick, it swept clear and came down to cut off two of the innkeeper's toes.

The innkeeper gave a scream of agony and fell writhing to the floor.

The wax light flew out of Hugo's hand and landed on the mattress. It took a few seconds for the cloth covering to scorch through, but then it burst into flames.

"Run," Hugo's guest ordered. "He's bound to have friends. This is his town."

Hugo gathered up what few possessions weren't already in his saddle bags and followed Gimp, who had reached the courtyard near the stable. They found the horses saddled and waiting—a fact that gave Hugo pause. He had not known his guest could function so efficiently without him, but he didn't spend more than a split second considering the matter because the whole town was buzzing like a hornet's nest. Men were shouting, women screaming; and flames had already spread from the window of his room to the dry, thatched roof. Hugo put spurs to his horse and, headache or not, he fled.

By dawn they were miles away and already turning off the coast, hugging via Aurelia inland toward Florence. Hugo was allowed to pause by a mountain stream to get a drink of water and wash his face.

"You shouldn't drink so much," his guest said. "Especially the rotgut they serve in taverns like the last. Fool, he was trying to drug you."

"Fine time to tell me," Hugo muttered.

A powerful kick in the rear sprawled Hugo facedown in the stream. "That will clear your head," his guest said.

Hugo rose, sputtering. The water was icy.

No one could have kicked him. Gimp was standing near the horses, wide-eyed and ten feet away.

"How do you do things like that?" Hugo asked, bewildered.

"I don't know. How do you see blue?"

"You mean you can't?"

"Only when I borrow your eyes."

Hugo staggered over to the horses and leaned against his saddle. "How do I get some peace?"

"Make me a god, Hugo. Make me a god," his guest said. "I once was one, you know."

"A god?" Hugo muttered. "You aren't a god, you're a ghost."

The subsequent kick lifted Hugo an inch off the ground. "Ever met a ghost who could do that?"

"No. Ow." Hugo crawled into the saddle, where he felt at least his backside would be protected. "If you were a god," he sniveled, "you'd know how I see blue and you wouldn't need to kick people."

"You're probably right. I hate to admit it, but you are probably right."

Just then something—his guest, Hugo was sure—slapped the horse's rump and it took off at a gallop.

R EGEANE SAT BESIDE THE TRAIL IN THE MISTY half-light of dawn when Maeniel passed by. He'd slipped out of his bed before dawn and felt sure he'd left her sleeping.

He *had* left her beside him.

He stopped and gave her a long, thoughtful look—one she'd seen before. He had directed it at Gavin when his worthy captain was found gnawing a big meaty elk thighbone on one of Maeniel's fine Persian carpets. It began a chase that had ended when Gavin took refuge behind Regeane and began whimpering piteously.

Regeane, who had been in human form, had said, "Please, my dear—" And Maeniel had turned human.

"Get out," he had ordered Gavin. "Get out before I fetch my horsewhip."

"You own a horsewhip?" she had asked.

Gavin took off like a crossbow bolt.

Maeniel had thrown on his robe, grinned, and said, "No, but Gavin doesn't know that."

However, Regeane now thought, *I am not Gavin.* She threw Maeniel a haughty look and continued to sit by the trail, her nose slightly elevated.

The stare between them continued.

Regeane refused to be intimidated.

Finally Maeniel resumed the traveling wolf's bicycling gait and made no objection when she fell in beside him.

The sun never troubled them, and Regeane was surprised; as a young and inexperienced shape-changer in Rome, she'd believed day and night limited her access to the wolf. Yes, light tugged at the woman, and sometimes she felt dizzy, as if her human half wanted to take charge and made a strong push to do so, but at those times she sought the deep coverts, heavy with thick brush and tall trees, and avoided the open where the sun might catch her; soon the wolf was able to reassert herself strongly.

Maeniel broke trail for both of them, leading her along paths she was sure no human foot had ever trodden. Along Roman roads and outposts, winter was only just losing its grip on the heights, so he kept to the valleys now. They were warmer; flowers had begun to bloom, yellow and white daisies, and the trees were leafing out green-gold and green. Higher, the evergreen spruce, fir, pine, and even the few remaining cedar perfumed the air. The grass, new and emerald green, was filled with violets, purple and white, and even yellow clusters.

They came to the lake in the later afternoon. His first impression was that it was smaller now. Had it really been that long? Reaching back into his memory, he knew it had been.

The rock where she used to rest after her bath was on dry land now, where, long ago, it had projected out into the water. The waterfall remained, but now it appeared that much less water ran down the black basalt steps, and even from where he stood, he could tell the lake above was much smaller, and saplings from the encroaching forest surrounded it.

The lake beneath the falls was silting up. Greenery from the shallow margins extended far out into the water. Hemlock, with its innocent-appearing white flowers; pickerel weed, with its spikes of indigo blue; tall cattails overlooking beds of sweet, sharp, yellow-flowered cress. Beyond the cress some vagrant thing with fuzzy white flowers and long spear-shaped leaves; and toward the center, wild lotus and water lily opened perfect cups of white, yellow, mauve, and pink, and round olive green pads floated on the surface.

Both wolves slipped into the lake; sunlight shimmered on the ripples their bodies made in the still water, sunlight that would have blinded any watcher. Suddenly they were both human.

"It's beautiful," Regeane whispered, not wishing to disturb the afternoon's silence.

"Yes," he said. "Even after all these years and so much grief."

"You've been here before?"

"Oh, yes, many, many times—but that was a long time ago."

"I've seen it."

"When?"

"On the night we were married. You were making love to me, I think, right here."

He held quiet, listening.

"Do you hear something? Someone?"

"No. Only wind in the forest, the music of the waterfall, and the sound of your heart beating."

"You can't," she said softly.

"I can. I do." He embraced her then and kissed her.

When they broke to breathe, he spoke. "Let's make your prophetic vision come true."

"Yes." It was a sigh as much as a word.

HUGO WAS QUIET FOR THE NEXT FEW DAYS. TO his guest's and Gimp's surprise, he didn't drink to excess at the taverns and inns where they stopped. He watered his wine and ate well, going to bed replete, his stomach full, and waking without a headache in the morning.

He said little to his guest, only asking one question when he was about to go to bed the second night.

Gimp was gone, relieving himself behind the inn on a brushy hillside.

"How does Gimp fit in with your plans?" Hugo asked rather acidly.

"I promised him life. I keep my promises even when my priests are madmen and my adherents from the gallows."

Hugo nodded.

"You will not abandon him."

This Hugo clearly recognized as an order.

Hugo had spent most of his adult life in an alcoholic fog— adulthood being recognized as occurring at age twelve. But he had a brain, and when dried out it worked fairly well. He remembered Gundabald's life before their descent into abject poverty: good food; warm, soft, comfortable clothing; the finest wines; servants to pick up after him; and at least passably attractive women at his father's beck and call. And when Hugo grew old enough, at his also. He and his father had been treated with respect by tradesmen and even the lesser nobility. But Gundabald had courted disaster by trying to buy his way into the inner circle of great magnates surrounding the king. He was overly ambitious. His estates were simply not large enough, and the amount of land and money able to keep all of them in comfort went to gild a rathole created by the promises of the outer fringes, the impecunious hangers-on, at the royal court. But to the end of his life, Gundabald believed the golden prize of royal preferment dangled just out of his reach. The lion's share of loot from the Frankish king's conquests went to line the coffers of the greatest of his courtiers. To be among his intimates was to be rich beyond even Gundabald's dreams of avarice.

Forcibly sobered, then voluntarily sober, Hugo considered all of these things. As a man he'd never liked his father, and thinking over his ambitions, he came to the realization that Gundabald had been a fool. The man had abused and terrorized Regeane by his insistence that she fall in with his plans for murdering her husband. Gundabald had driven her at last to rebellion, all so he could gather more money to further gild the rathole.

No, Hugo thought. That road was not for him. Thanks to his father, he was a hunted man, cut off forever from the world of the Frankish aristocracy he'd been brought up in. But now, now there was a chance to recoup his fortunes. Sober, he began quietly to consider how to do so.

His chance came on the road to Florence.

His guest had directed him to the site of an abandoned villa. Or perhaps it had once been a town; the site was so ruined, it was impossible to tell. This trove was very rich in silver. His guest directed him to pry a brick from one of the walls. The box behind it had been a fine one. The jewelry inside had been carefully wrapped in silk and, though dark, was still in good condition, as were the silver coins— probably hoarded over a lifetime—in the bottom.

On his way back to the road, he saw the brigands. He was looking down on them because they'd hidden themselves in a cut-rock ditch overgrown with wild roses. The hiding place was a good one because the rose canes were so thick it was easy to overlook the fact that the ditch was even there.

"Why?" he asked his guest.

"A caravan of merchants is coming."

"This is our chance."

"Chance to do what?"

"Start you on the road to becoming a god," Hugo said, feeling superior for once. "Tell that fool Gimp to become mute from now on."

The brigands' plan was very simple: to burst from the thicket of rose canes, snatch a laden mule from the merchants, escape into the rocky thickets of scrub oak and broom. The caravan was escorted by a party of mercenaries. They and the merchants would be mounted and could not take their horses into the rocks on the hillside, at least not quickly enough to keep the thieves from stripping the laden mule and vanishing without a trace into what was now a wilderness of broken ground, stunted trees, weeds, and thick briars.

The brigands were unarmed or poorly armed. All Hugo had to do when they snatched the mule was ride in front of them and shout. One, more stubborn than the rest, kept hold of the mule's bridle. The rest scattered.

Hugo drew his sword but a well-thrown rock cracked into the side of the man's head.

The mule brayed, reared, and kicked. The last holdout panicked and ran off with the rest. Hugo took the mule's dangling rein and led it back to the road.

At that point the squad of escorting mercenaries rode up. Hugo had a brief, unsettling moment when it looked as if they might mistake him for the thieves. But he was able to put an end to the misunderstanding at once by pointing out the direction in which the brigands fled. They gave chase.

"I'm afraid it's pointless," Hugo said to the merchant.

Already the mercenaries had pulled up. The ground was treacherous and no one wanted to lose a valuable animal.

"Yes," the merchant replied. "But thank you for saving our property. I am Armine Welborn of Florence."

"Hugo of Bayonne." Hugo bowed. Hugo had never been near Bayonne, but it had a good sound.

"You don't know what a great service you've done me. Every animal here is precious. We carry nothing but silk this trip. Gauzes, damasks, tapestry, woven hangings from the east, all intended for the king's court in Pavia. The loss of even one of these mules might have ruined me."

"Not at all," Hugo said, bowing again. "Delighted to be of service. If you are a native of the city of flowers, perhaps you might tell me where I can find safe lodging for the night."

Hugo felt the merchant's eyes on him, shrewdly assessing his worth. His clothing was wrinkled and travel stained, but he was wearing a heavy silver ring on one hand and gold one on the other. He and the silent Gimp were both riding very good horses.

"Why, at my house, of course," Armine said. "You have done me a great service. The very best lodgings in the city are, I'm sad to say, squalid, without the amenities a gentleman like yourself takes for granted."

Hugo managed a sanctimonious smile. "I have indeed endured many hardships on this trip, but if I can accomplish my objectives, I will feel well rewarded."

"My goodness," Armine said. "What can those objectives be?"

"I have," Hugo said, "both sad and unpleasant family business to settle."

The tip of Armine's nose twitched. "My," he exclaimed. "In Florence?"

"No, not at that fair city, but farther on, in Pavia."

"Armine," someone shouted. "Come on, we must reach the city before dark unless you really want to lose those precious things of yours. Get moving."

Hugo and Gimp fell in with the merchant caravan, and they started off. A few hours later, they were crossing the Arno and entering Florence.

HUGO FOUND FLORENCE DEPRESSING, A PLACE OF high walls, narrow streets, and almost constant fear among the powerless. The city was now in the hands of perhaps a dozen powerful families, each with its own fortified residence, each claiming a segment of the populace as adherents.

With the decay of Roman government, the small holder, the independent entrepreneur, disappeared. The only way the small tradesman or farmer survived here was to accept the patronage of these few leading families and pay homage to them. Street violence between these contending families was almost constant and no night passed without a savage brawl between one family's adherents and another's.

Armine's residence was comfortable but frighteningly well fortified with double gates—one of wood, the next of iron—and high walls fronted the street, guarded by iron spikes at the top. Hired mercenaries patrolled the walls both night and day.

Inside, there was an attractive garden surrounded by a colonnade. This, Hugo discovered, was for the ladies, who seldom if ever left the compound. In fact, Armine's daughters had never been outside of the house, and they were both in their early teens.

On arrival, Hugo made his first visit to the bathhouse and then, clean and fresh-smelling, he was shown to a forbidding suite of rooms. All of the windows were covered by iron gratings; the walls and floor were of stone.

Gimp said only, "Looks like prison."

"You're mute," Hugo reminded him.

"Still looks like prison."

Hugo was going to hit him, but his guest stopped him. "He will stay mute when necessary. Let him be. How is this nonsense going to make me a god?"

"Watch and see," Hugo said truculently.

His guest growled. "You're upsetting me."

Hugo stretched out on the bed. "What do you want?" he muttered.

"An explanation."

"I have no explanation," Hugo said. "I'm going to have to improvise."

Just then there was a knock on the door. A servant entered with a tray. It held a silver wine pitcher and a cup, among other things.

"My lord told me to tell you that supper will be late this evening," the servant said. "So you don't go hungry, he felt you might need refreshment."

Hugo wasn't interested in the other objects on the tray. A few days of sobriety were enough for him. With some alacrity he rose and grabbed the wine pitcher and poured a large cup, while Gimp helped himself to the fruit, bread, and cheese on the tray. Hugo got only one cup down, the second was slapped out of his hand.

"I don't trust improvisations when you're sober; how do you

think I feel about them when you're drunk?" his guest said in a thick, grating voice.

But the wine on an empty stomach had done its work and Hugo fell asleep on the bed.

He was awakened much later by a servant. He'd had a nightmare about Gundabald. All Hugo's nightmares were about Gundabald. He felt as if he hadn't slept at all, but considering what he was about to do, he felt he'd better look a little haggard. So his appearance was all to the good. He dressed himself with care, choosing his darkest clothing, and went for pale and interesting.

From the hoard amassed by his guest, he chose presents for the girls and an exquisite chain for their father.

Gimp sat on the floor in the corner and stared at him.

"Well, what do you think?" he asked his guest and Gimp.

"You look like you had the squirts for about a week," Gimp said.

"How the hell should I know?" his guest said. "One human looks almost like another to me. You're all skinny and ugly. Get downstairs and put this magnificent plan you're being so secretive about into action. And stop bothering me. If you must know, you look like someone with a wasting disease. There, does that satisfy you?"

Then Hugo was spun around, the door opened, and he was pushed out into the corridor.

Dinner was stately and the food was good. Hugo thought it was as gloomy a meal as he had ever attended. Madonna Helen and her two daughters were in attendance. They all looked rather like prisoners broken on the rack and then allowed to live out their days in the care of their families.

The girls were both blondes and outdid Hugo in paleness, and this wasn't helped along by the fact that current fashions in Florence called for liberal applications of white lead to protect the complexion from even the slightest ray of sunshine. Considering the way they hung on Hugo's every word, both were starved for company.

Three boys, younger than their sisters, tried to enliven the proceedings with a food fight and were marched off to bed early in the company of twelve attendants.

To Hugo, not an imaginative man by any means, they looked like prisoners being escorted to the gallows.

Madonna Helen, their mother—a slender blond woman—was in what was politely known as a decline. The physicians had bled her copiously and prescribed all sorts of expensive nostrums containing poisons like mercury, alum, and opium. This was complicated by the fact that she must eat a special diet consisting only of boiled vegetables. This treatment had brought her several times to the edge of death and had reduced her to such a state of wraithlike emaciation that Hugo had trouble believing he was looking at a living woman.

After the boys left, the conversation lagged until the merchant began asking Hugo about his travels.

"How was Rome?"

"I was there for only a few days," Hugo replied.

"A few hours is more like it," Hugo's guest said to him silently.

Hugo plowed on, "The present pope is a foe of the Lombards and, though I tried to enlist his help with my family problems, he threatened he'd have me driven from the city if I did not leave quickly. I am alone now—but for my poor, mute servant—so I fled."

"How terrible," the older of Armine's daughters said. Her name was Chiara; her sister's, Phyllis.

"My life has been sad since my father was killed," Hugo said.

"How horrible for you," Phyllis said, and sighed.

"Terrible in the deed," Hugo said, "and terrible in the way it was done; but I fear 'tis not a tale for the ears of gentle ladies."

"Oh, I'm quite liberal with my daughters," Armine said.

"I approve," Hugo said. "For this story is one that should improve the hearts of women, teaching them to respect the greater wisdom of their menfolk, and the folly that can result when their desires of the heart overrule the head. A fine moral lesson."

"You see," Armine said to his daughters. "Listen and learn."

"It began," Hugo said, "when my aunt Gisela was betrothed to a wild pagan Saxon named Wolfstan. My father—" Hugo raised his eyes to heaven. "—God rest his soul, a saintly man if there ever was one . . . In any case, my father, Gundabald, objected to the match, seeing that this Saxon refused to become a Christian, bow his neck to Christ's sweet yoke, and be washed in the water of rebirth and eternal life.

"But Gisela would hear none of the warnings given by her

brother or any of the objections of the many priests he called to support his position that Christian and pagan flesh should not commingle in the marriage bed. For this Saxon was both handsome and rich, and Gisela was wildly in love with him. The fortunes of our family were in decline then, and Gisela, while not poor, was not nearly as rich as she wished to be, and I think she might possibly have been in love with the fine life he could give her.

"And, indeed, for the first year they seemed to be happy and the match a fortunate one. He allowed her to have her own chaplain and receive the sacraments, but she did say that he would not observe the many occasions during which the church enjoins chastity upon even those joined in wedded bliss."

Both Armine and his wife seemed a little uncomfortable as Hugo began to recite the list. "All Sundays, all holy days, the entire period of Advent and Lent, and quite a few more."

"There do seem to be a lot of them," Armine said, with a side glance at his wife. "Not all churchmen are as strict—"

"But my father felt Gisela should be doing more to advance the cause of Christianity with her husband, rather than allowing herself to be won over to his ways. So he rebuked her strongly, leaving her in tears and angering this Wolfstan greatly.

"A few days later he set out with some of Wolfstan's Saxons on a hunting party. Somehow they contrived to lead my poor father into the deep woods and abandoned him there. Whereupon he was set on by a gigantic wolf. At this point, he despaired of his life, fell to his knees before the ravening beast, and seized the cross of Christ that he wore always around his neck. To his utter astonishment, the vicious creature recoiled before the sacred object.

"Seizing his opportunity, my father snatched up a crossbow, called down God's blessing on the bolt, and fired at the wolf. The beast went down, gasping, in its last agony. To my father's horror, a great wind swept through the forest, and the sky darkened as if it presaged a dreadful storm. This lasted for only a few moments, but . . . but . . ."

They were all openmouthed, hanging on Hugo's every word.

"But when the wind ceased, the sky cleared, and the birds began to sing again, my father saw—where the wolf had been lying—the body of Wolfstan, his sister's husband."

This revelation called for a bracer for the men and honey cakes and sweet wine for the women. Hugo could see he had achieved instant popularity in Armine's household.

"How dreadful!" Phyllis pressed her hand to her breast. "I cannot see how he survived the shock of such an experience."

"My father was a strong man," Hugo said. "But alas, that is not all, only the beginning."

"Really?" Chiara said.

Hugo thought he detected some mockery in her tone, but the rest were staring at him in openmouthed credulity. So he ignored her and pressed on.

"As you so aptly observed, my father's shock was great. But that did not prevent him from seizing Gisela and returning home with her. Nor did he rest until she was married to a good—Christian—man, named Firminious.

"But he forgot the contumacy and obstinacy of some women. On her return home, shortly after her second marriage, she was found to be pregnant. We urged her to be . . . rid of the child, tainted as it would be by evil, but she refused."

"She refused to kill her child," Chiara said.

Armine shot her a reproving look, and her face became expressionless. *I am not winning this one over,* Hugo thought. *But then, it's the father I want.*

"We meant the child no harm," Hugo said, "but we felt it would be best oblated, that is, sent to an establishment of holy nuns and brought up in, shall we say, seclusion. But Gisela defended her child vigorously and was supported in her stubborn, misplaced affection for Regeane by Firminious."

"Regeane was the little one's name?" Chiara asked.

"Yes. But early, very early in life, Regeane began to display affection for the black arts, as her father had. Alas, Firminious died while Gisela was a young woman, and she would no longer yield to the strong male guidance supplied by my father, Gundabald. In vain she brought the child from shrine to shrine, churches devoted to the worship of Christ, his holy mother, and many saints, trying at all costs to quell Regeane's turbulent spirit and bring submission to her rebellious soul.

"But she failed, and we were in Rome seeking the blessing of the pope himself when Gisela, worn out by so many sorrows and tribulations, went at last to her eternal rest. Not long after she died, we received news that Charles, king of the Franks, had arranged for a marriage for Regeane.

"Naturally, we were horrified."

"Naturally." Chiara lifted one eyebrow and echoed Hugo ironically.

Hugo ignored her. "But the pope, the new pope Hadrian, interfered with our attempts to obstruct the marriage. He removed Regeane from our care and saw to it that she was wed like poor Gisela to an outright barbarian and scoundrel. Needless to say, this scoundrel was delighted with her."

"I take it his affection for Regeane is in very bad taste?" Chiara asked.

Again Hugo ignored her. "We are a great family, though fallen on evil times, and are related to the house of the Arnulfings, the Frankish kings. A lowborn commoner like this Maeniel would have thought her a great prize, even had she been a hunchback half-wit with only one tooth in her head. But the pope was deaf to my father's warnings.

"So Gundabald and I contacted the Lombard party in Rome. The pope himself was brought to book, and Regeane was tried as a witch."

Chiara frowned, but everyone else at the table gasped.

"She determined trial by combat, and this Maeniel championed her. It was a long, bitter battle, but—I can hardly credit it, for the Lombard champion was so puissant, bold, fair, and honest a warrior—but he met defeat at the hands of this Maeniel.

"I believe he and Regeane must have compacted in the black arts to destroy God's champion."

"Don't lay it on too thick," Hugo's guest warned him, "but keep going, you're doing fine so far."

He was and he knew it. All but Chiara were staring at him in openmouthed admiration. "But that is not the worst."

"No?" Armine gasped.

"No. My father felt this Maeniel was hopefully not too far under Regeane's spell as to be immune to all good counsel, so he went to try one more time. He found them at their wedding feast. I know; I followed him. I was deeply worried about his safety, and I had good cause. For when he began to remonstrate with this Maeniel, he and Regeane forsook their borrowed human shapes. In the semblance of a wolf, as her father had been, she fell on my saintly father and—joined by her besotted lover, he also in wolf form—they rent him limb from limb.

"It happened so quickly! I could do nothing. When I saw that if I tried to bring them to book for this ghastly crime, my own life would quickly be ended, I fled away, determined to avenge my father and then retire to a monastery to live out the balance of my life in prayer, self-mortification, good works, and holy penitence. But before I go, I must warn the Lombard duke of this Maeniel and Regeane, who now serve the Frankish king and hope to aid him in his war against the rightful ruler of Lombardy, Duke Desiderius.

"That's quite a story," Chiara said.

"Oh, dreadful day that Christ's anointed lord, his excellency the ruler of the Lombards, should be attacked by black sorcery," Armine said. "But what can he do against this pair, pray tell me?"

Hugo smiled. His remaining teeth were impressive, a little scummed by green but still good. "Tell him to include wolfhounds among his war dogs, because, depend on it, Maeniel and Regeane will try to bring intelligence about his movements and plans back to Charles, the Frankish king. If the Lombard can destroy them, he will deprive the Franks of one of their most useful weapons."

Armine frowned. "I was to send letters to the King Desiderius tonight. This tale is so fantastical . . . I can hardly credit it. But all know the strongholds of paganism constantly threaten those who receive Christ, so I will warn him that this vile pair have bent their malice on him—and to include the finest of his wolfhounds among the dogs of war."

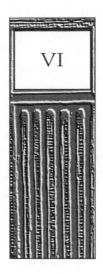

VI

WHEN THEY WERE FINISHED WITH THEIR LOVE-making, they swam out to the falls in the center of the lake and rested on the black basalt platform carved by the water over the centuries. The nights in the mountains were cold still—sometimes cold even in high summer—but the afternoon sun was warm on their bodies and the water was, to Regeane's surprise, almost hot.

"There's a warm spring hereabouts," Maeniel explained. "It fills the pool above. Once it was called the Lady's Mirror."

"The Lady?" Regeane asked.

"Yes," Maeniel said. "She is only the Lady. Matrona said they called her that in Greece two thousand years ago."

Regeane smiled. "Matrona remembers?"

"Yes." Maeniel did not smile. "Matrona remembers."

Regeane was resting on her back on the stone, her head in his lap, letting the warm water flow over her. It was, with the air around them still bearing a bit of winter chill, a sensuous delight. She reached up and touched his face.

"We have made love as man and woman often, but we have never loved, not in our other form."

She looked a bit apprehensive.

He bent over and kissed the tip of her nose. "You weren't old enough. As a woman, you are full-grown, but a she-wolf avoids desire until she is at the height of her powers. You have not reached yours yet, but know, if you are thinking it is like dogs, it is not."

"No?"

"No. When the time comes and you are ready, I will guide you. Until then, be content."

She reached up, wound her fingers in his hair, and pulled his face down to hers for a kiss. The sun was warm, his body was warm. The sunlight was a dazzle on the water and the very air around them was redolent of springtime. When they broke off the kiss, she found she was no longer resting against his body. He was on top of her, and she was in his embrace.

"Again?" she asked in mock annoyance.

"Yes."

"Well," she said. "I don't mind if I do. Or rather, I don't mind if you do."

"I will," he said, "do."

She gave a little start. "I think you have."

"I'm only just beginning."

"If that's the beginning, what is the end like?"

"Concentrate—and I'll make sure you find out."

After that, neither of them was interested in words any longer.

When they were finished, she fell asleep in his arms. He was too much the wolf to sleep. He lay there and held her. The sun sank lower in the sky. All he heard was birdsong and the sweet rushing sound of falling water. Sometimes the wind muttered as it ruffled the treetops and changed the aspens bordering the lake from green to silver with its breath. Far away, a wolf howled. And he wondered if the pack still gathered at the pool above before the hunt; but then the wolf cry turned what had been pleasant languor into discomfort.

She awoke, opening her eyes. He slid into the lake near the falls, and she followed.

"There's a pack hereabouts, and we'd best be going. To them, all we are is other wolves. They won't want us in their territory."

She nodded and turned to swim to shore, but he caught her arm. "Quiet." He put his finger to his lips. The wolf song was beginning again, and he wanted to listen. "They are talking about a human camped not far away."

They were resting together in the water, their arms on the basalt platform near the falls. He looked at her.

"Oh," Regeane said. "The Saxon. I forgot to mention him. He came with me, just in case."

"What is this?" Maeniel said. "A state procession? Who will pop out of the bushes next? Matrona? Gavin? Antonius? Barbara?"

"Gavin," she said. "He hasn't really been seen since we made camp with the king."

"Naturally," Maeniel replied. "His opportunities for debauchery are limited in the mountains. When he discovered the 'refreshment' wagons accompanying the king, he probably went wild."

Regeane dove, turned, and began to swim toward shore.

Maeniel followed.

A few hours later, they came upon the Saxon's camp. He was hunched morosely over a fire. The two wolves emerged from the timber, ghosted down silently toward a tent pitched near the forest. When they entered and found it empty, they changed form and dressed in human clothing, then came out to greet the Saxon.

He'd set snares and they all had a fine dinner of rabbit stew, accompanied by bread, a flat bread he had made by simply heating a rock and throwing the dough on it. It had been a long time since Maeniel had seen anyone make bread that way.

They spent the night in comfort. Regeane and Maeniel took the tent; the Saxon rolled up in his bearskin and slept beneath the stars.

The quarrel erupted before dawn.

"You have had a fine day in the forest," Maeniel told Regeane. "Now you're slowing me down and keeping me from my real work."

It was not yet even dawn and a silver mist flowed through the forest, feeling its way among the trees with long, wispy tendrils. It had begun to fall from the peaks just after sunset until it filled the hollows and valleys lower down and shone like mother-of-pearl in the lambent moonlight.

Then, just at daybreak, before the sun reawakened in the notch beyond the pass, it had seemed to hold the whole world in its soft thrall.

It had entered the tent then, so softly, silently, that even Maeniel, the gray wolf, didn't sense or feel it. But Regeane waked, swam up out of the depths of the dark water that rests at the bottom of consciousness. Perhaps it haunted the silver wolf—as it haunts us all—because that is where the first ancestor, neither plant nor animal, coalesced out of nothingness and crossed the infinite, unknowable barrier between animate and inanimate, and life was born. Life knows water before anything else. It fills our lungs in the womb as a reminder of what we came from and who we are; it rests as a pool beneath consciousness and farther down below dreams; and in the deepest sleep, the mind-brain rests in it and is renewed so that it may attain consciousness when it awakens.

And from that deepest pool, the well beyond the world, from the mist, the voice had called to Regeane, *If you love him, don't let him go alone.* Then the voice was torn to tatters by the winds of time as the mist faded in the dawn wind, and she sank down into sleep and didn't remember.

Maeniel now kissed her on the forehead and pushed her toward the Saxon. "Go home," he commanded. "From now on I must travel fast—in the shadows by day and the darkness by night. I've no mind to worry if you cannot hold your shape, or defend you from other wolf packs, or teach you how to live in the wilderness, snap down whatever you can catch, and avoid leaving traces for other wolves or men. You don't know enough to follow at my heels, and it will be many years before you do. This is not a daytrip on my land or a hunt organized for your amusement, and I haven't time to tutor you in the skills you will need to survive. A mistake on your part might get me killed in the best case, or us both in the worst. This is war—and war is no place for fools.

"And as for you." He turned to the Saxon. "I can charge you with the task of getting her home safely. In all the time you've been with us, you have never really seen me angry, but if I find you've aided and abetted her folly any longer, you will feel my wrath. That I promise. And you will suffer it for a long, long time.

"Possibly you think your Lombard masters were hard, but what they did to you is nothing compared to what I can do. I will track you down wherever you might flee and exact my due, and if any-thing happens to her—" He broke off.

"Regeane," he said. "His life is in your hands. Do you under-stand?" Tears were pouring down her cheeks. "There is no earthly force that could ever bring me to touch one hair of your head, but I can't say the same for him. Do you understand?"

"Y-y-yes," she stammered.

"Good."

For a second a fleeting gray shadow was visible in the morning mist and then was gone.

LUCILLA AND DULCINIA MET A FEW DAYS AFTER Silvie imparted her big news.

"How in the hell did Silvie get pregnant?" Dulcinia asked.

Both women were in Lucilla's garden resting after dinner. Neither one felt like moving too much. Lucilla simply rolled her eyes toward Dulcinia.

"Either I've completely neglected your education or—"

"I know, I know, but half of Rome has marched over Silvie's body. If she didn't get pregnant then, why in God's name now?"

"She may have," Lucilla said, "and taken a potion or lost it. Remember, she endured a great deal of privation before Regeane took her in hand. Now she has plentiful meals at regular intervals, and she's stopped drinking that godawful stuff she used to."

"Now she serves it to her customers," Dulcinia said.

Lucilla shook her head. "What they serve in the lowest grade of taverns is a lot worse than the stuff she sells. I won't say the potions she hands out over the counter are good for your health, but she's oddly honest in that way. The whole neighborhood resorts to her for drink, and she treats a lot of illnesses with her mixtures."

Dulcinia looked surprised.

"The poor often go to the tavern when they are sick. She has potions for the ague, recurring fevers, sickly children, and even colicky babies. Little can help the falling sickness, but a few herbs mixed with wine can somewhat limit the effects. And then, of course, the woman whose period hasn't come, and whose husband is out of town—mayhap she's just late but . . ."

"Ahh, yes," Dulcinia said.

"And then there are those with the wasting disease of the lungs, not to mention others simply old and troubled with aches in their bones."

"What she doesn't know," Dulcinia said, "Simona probably does. She advises Silvie frequently."

"Simona?" Lucilla asked.

"Posthumus's mother," Dulcinia said. "It was to her Silvie ran first after she escaped Hugo. Simona sent her to me and then . . ."

"You brought her to me," Lucilla said.

"What about the child?"

Lucilla took a deep breath in through her nose. "Well, she wants it; otherwise, with her skills, she wouldn't be carrying it. So I sent her home with Susana, my maid, and gave her strict orders to do everything Susana says."

"The father?"

"She hasn't the slightest idea."

"Probably just as well. Given the nature of Silvie's friends, if she knew, it might only cause trouble."

Lucilla nodded. "Likely when she begins to show, her customers will all be looking at each other."

"Yes, and they will probably all have good reason to do so."

"Not a doubt of that."

A FEW DAYS AFTER HUGO'S STORY TO ARMINE, CHIara was foolish enough to let him catch her alone in the garden. She'd done her best to avoid him since she'd heard the tale, even going so far as to take a tray in her room when the family dined with him, but the garden had to be tended. This was simply a practical matter. True, the courtyard garden was one place to take the air and receive visitors, but it extended around the back of the fortified house and contained a small orchard of fruit trees: quince, peach, pear, and pomegranate. A large herb garden supplied seasonings and greens for the household, not to mention medicines for Madonna, who was—much to Chiara's sorrow—not doing well at all. The physician had bled her again, but her lady mother was so frail, Chiara had been appalled by the cruelty of the procedure.

The physician had reeked of drink that day and cut her in a half dozen places before he found a vein to his liking. When at last her mother's arm was extended over the basin, the blood kept clotting, and the physician had to keep reopening the wound until, at last, Chiara drove him from the room in a fury and consoled her mother. While she lay weeping in Chiara's arms, Chiara promised she would get rid of the man, no matter what her father said.

Chiara was in the garden collecting herbs for her mother's medicine cabinet and considering how to accomplish this feat. There were, she knew, several things growing right here . . .

Then Hugo had her in his arms and was breathing in her face. His breath stank like swamp water. Chiara twisted away in pure revulsion and clawed at his eyes and came rather close to blinding him. This roused his guest, who slammed him back, hard, into an iron arbor used to grow table grapes.

"Leave her alone or I'll knock the shit out of you."

Chiara backed away from the reeling Hugo, her face perfectly white. Both the guest and Hugo knew she'd heard him speak.

"Idiot," the guest roared. He clipped Hugo on the ear. Hugo fell to the ground. "You'll ruin everything, you stupid lecher. In a city full of courtesans, you have to pick on a respectable girl. How big a fool can you manage to be?"

"No," Chiara said. "Don't hit him again. You might kill him."

"Does that worry you?" Hugo's guest asked.

"Not in the least," she said, "but I'd never be able to explain it to my father."

"True." Hugo's guest laughed, an unpleasant peal of mirth.

Chiara's skin crawled. "What are you? A daemon?"

"Probably. I'm surprised."

"At what?"

"That you can hear me at all. Most can't."

"Yes, it's a gift," Chiara said. "When Aunt Stella died, I saw her climbing the stair to my mother's room. I didn't know she had died. I thought she'd simply come for a visit, but when I asked my mother about it she burst into tears and told me Stella was dead. But don't worry about me telling. I won't. I . . . I . . . I think I understand better what's going on—that strange story. Did he sell his soul to you?"

"What would I want with his rotten, filthy little soul? His body is bad enough. No, I just want use of him for a time."

Hugo was sitting up, holding his head.

"I wonder if you could help me with a problem of my own?" said the guest.

Hugo started to rise.

"Sit," his guest said. "Stay."

Hugo sat.

"What would you want?" she asked tremulously.

"Your influence with your father. Has he written the king?"

"Yes. As soon as he heard the story he—" She pointed to Hugo. "—told. But I persuaded him not to be too credulous."

"Try to get him to write and sing dear Hugo's praises."

"Yes," she said, and nodded as if to reinforce her words. "Yes, I certainly will."

"Now, what's *your* problem?"

"I want to get rid of the physician treating Mother. I think he's killing her."

"He is," Hugo's guest said nastily. "Pour his medicines out and replace them with cordials. They're poison." Then he shouted, "And for God's sake, feed the woman."

Chiara backed away, blinking. "I will. I will. I was going to take her some capon and soup."

"That's good for a start. Now get moving."

Chiara fled.

R EGEANE MARCHED BACK TO THE TENT WITH HER head up and her fists clenched. Once inside, she really broke down and wept. Tears were equally balanced by rage. There wasn't a lot to smash in the tent—a cooking pot or two, that was all—but she smashed them. And then she attacked the heavy canvas walls with her knife and shredded them.

"I will leave him. I will. He can't hold me back. At least that's what Matrona says. I will go. I will stay—stay just to punish him. I'll never speak to him again."

The Saxon shrugged and went to shave by the creek, a short walk downhill. When he returned, he sat on a rock and waited. When the noises from the tent ceased, he rose and began to mix bread for breakfast. After a time, Regeane emerged. She was calmer, but her eyes and nose were red. She sat on a log near the fire.

The Saxon made bread on a hot stone, paired it with cheese, and handed it to her.

"He knows me very well," she said. "I might risk myself, but I couldn't bear it if anything happened to you." She tore savagely into the bread with her teeth.

"A man," the Saxon said, "any man, finds something he loves to distraction, and he will protect that person or thing. If necessary, protect it to death."

"Yes, but what do I do?" The tears began to slip down her cheeks again.

"Eat your breakfast," the Saxon said. "We will think of something."

They tossed ideas about for several hours but couldn't come up with anything either one believed would be workable. Then, discouraged, they walked the few miles up to the lake and stood looking out over the water.

"He brought me here yesterday. He behaved as if he knew the spot," Regeane said, "but it's far from the fortress."

The Saxon shivered, and gooseflesh rose on his arms.

"It's not cold."

"This place," he said, rubbing his arms. "Can't you feel it?"

"I suppose."

"Near . . . near the tree it was like this."

"What tree?" she asked.

"Do you know of the Irmunsul? The sacred tree, the one Charles felled?"

"I don't know."

"He came to our land; it wasn't long ago. When I was captured, we—my family—were keepers of the tree. I rode out and spread the alarm, but this Charles is a very good soldier. He had taken us by surprise, and my mother and I were the only members of our family present."

The Saxon stood quietly, seemingly lost in his memories. "Charles came to the sanctuary for the gold, booty we buried in the field. But he needn't have felled the tree for that.

"My mother was in the sanctuary. It was bounded by three rings, berms made of earth, and the tree stood in the center on a mound, all alone. We met there and held our assemblies four times a year. My mother met the Franks alone. They killed her.

"It is said that before she died, she told Charles that everything he did would turn to ashes in the end. She said he would conquer an empire but his sons would not rule long, they would lose it; and the person he most loved would betray him, and others would reap what he had sown."

"I think," Regeane said, "that he dreams of remaking the world as the Romans did and extending his rule even farther than theirs, but he thinks that to do so he must receive God's blessing. It seems as if the great tree was his first offering to the Christian god.

"He accused my husband of burning the monastery. Maeniel said he didn't seem very concerned about Gundabald, my uncle, but mostly about the insults to the church."

"Ah, well," the Saxon said. "We did that. And a good job it was, too."

"I cannot regret it," she said. "And neither would Charles, if he knew the full truth."

"What happened to this Gundabald?"

"He was not a very pleasant individual."

"No, I gathered that."

"He murdered my father."

"Wolfstan?"

"Yes. They called it a hunting accident, but Gundabald murdered him. My father was—"

"Like you. I know. Your father was greatly loved. We are related—distantly, but we are blood kin. That is why it is my honor to serve you."

"Oh," Regeane said quietly. "Now I see. I didn't realize that. But you must know my father's people?"

"Not so well," the Saxon said. "Remember, I was sold into slavery to the Lombards. I haven't been home in a long time. Besides, you have obligations here."

"Yes, and . . ." She broke off and pointed to the top of the falls. "He called that place the Lady's Mirror."

"Then let us go look into it."

S O THEY CLIMBED TO THE TOP. Yes, the pool was a still one. It appeared no one went there anymore, not even the wolf pack that frequented the region. Mountain ash, the rowan, grew thickly around the water, and wild rose canes covered with sweet dog rose blossoms dipped down to the pool. The blossoms of this rose were larger than any the Saxon had ever seen, and more brightly colored. A deep pink, almost mauve at the edges, shaded into the white surrounding the bright gold cluster of stamens at the center. The perfume of the flowers hung heavy in the still air, but the long, thorny rose stems twining around the slender rowan seemed to form an almost impenetrable barrier to anyone wanting to look into the pool.

"I don't know if we can get by," the Saxon said. "At least not without cutting our way through." He started to draw the sword he wore in the old-fashioned way, slung over his back.

"No," Regeane said. "Not here." She stretched out her hand, and the Saxon felt gooseflesh rise on his arms as the briar rose stems parted at her touch, opening a way to let them both through.

A second later, they stood at the edge of the pool. The rocks were covered with moss that yielded like a soft carpet under their feet.

"Nothing comes here, not even the animals," Regeane said.

"You mean nothing is allowed to come here, don't you?"

Regeane looked into the water; so did the Saxon.

"Only a forest," he said.

"Yes, but not this forest."

And it was true what she said, because the forest was another one and they were looking upslope at a cloud-capped mountain whose sides were high ridges and deep ravines. The trees were giants, bigger around than any tree Regeane and the Saxon had ever seen.

As they watched, the sky blackened and the massive forest filled with greenish light, and a magnificent thunderbolt struck at a tree. It burst into flame and cast a lurid golden light against the low rolling clouds, and the rain hit and the landscape hazed with its sinuous curtains. The pool blurred and the forest vanished in dozens of concentric circles, the way clear glass clouds when rain strikes it.

On impulse, Regeane thrust one hand into the water. It vanished, simply vanished. She should have been able to see her fingers just below the surface, but she didn't.

The Saxon grabbed her arm and pulled her away. "No," he shouted.

"It seems," Regeane said, "there is more than one way for me to travel."

THEY WERE AT DINNER WHEN HUGO'S GUEST GOT rid of the physician.

When the physician came down to dinner, he was unsteady on his legs. Chiara gave him a glance of pure hostility. The man had gone to her father to complain of Chiara's interference. It had given him a good chance to warn Armine that Madonna Helen, his wife, might not live long.

Armine had been gravely stricken with the news. He had been an up-and-coming merchant when he had married Madonna. He had never seen her before the wedding day, and on that day she'd been a disappointment. Far too thin, quiet, reserved, and shy, her pale blond, almost colorless looks didn't intrigue him. After the marriage he'd never really gotten to know her. She became pregnant within the first month of marriage, and he left her bed until it was time to lie with her again. Once again she became pregnant at once. After the birth of their second daughter, his wife's health failed for a time and matters of business required that he travel. When he returned she was in blooming health and they resumed relations. He was somewhat troubled by the fact that his two eldest children were girls.

Though Chiara was learning the business and was a help to him, he'd relied on his wife to help him with things having to do with both keeping accounts and investing the considerable profits of his business. At least in part because of his wife, he was one of the richest and most important men in the city.

He was stricken with fear; he didn't know what he was going to do without his wife. He was also filled with guilt that he had never even bothered to know someone so important in his life.

The look of sheer, fatuous self-satisfaction on the physician's face enraged Chiara, who, if she could have found a way, would have murdered him on the spot. She was wondering if Hugo's friend was going to keep his promise when he did exactly that.

The physician was working on the soup, beans with salt pork and rice in the broth. He was slurping loudly when he broke off to let out a screech and jumped about a foot.

"What ails you, man?" Armine asked.

"No-no-nothing," the physician stammered.

"Nothing? What is this? Nothing?" Chiara heard Hugo's guest say. She heard the words so clearly, she was sure everyone at the table heard them, too. She glanced around and saw only blank faces.

This time the unfortunate man made a sound reminiscent of a whole pack of hounds on the scent. It began on a bass note and rose higher and higher until it ended in an almost feminine note. At the same moment, he clutched at his groin and jumped onto the seat of his chair.

"Ah, that's better," Hugo's guest said, and turned over the chair.

The physician gave a terrible scream and landed hard. For the next minute or so, the man engaged in the most extraordinary acrobatics Chiara had ever seen. Rolling over and over around the room as if trying to escape a pair of invisible hands that followed, prodding and punching, poking and, yes, goosing him. At one point he lay on his back kicking, turning around and around in a circle, while letting fly with scream after scream at the top of his lungs.

All this, to Chiara's ears at least, was accompanied by peal after peal of raucous laughter. Armine leaped to his feet.

"Good God, man. Are you daemon possessed?"

The physician didn't even slow down. "Oh. Ow. Sno-o-o-o-o, oh-o-o-o-o. No! No! No!" He was on his knees by now, crawling toward the door.

The laughter stopped. Instead she heard the voice shout, "Faster, faster. Faster, mule," and Chiara realized the unfortunate man was being ridden.

She rose, ran to the door, and pulled it open.

"Thank you," someone said.

The physician exited the dining room precipitously. There were two brass standing lamps containing oil, one on either side of the doors. Oil fountained from both lamps, leaping into the air, catching fire as it flew. The physician ran screaming.

Chiara followed him to the door. Fire or no fire, she wanted to see him in the street.

The man reached the entrance. The door opened by itself—or rather without the assistance of any human agency—and the physician exited as if propelled forward by a good, hard kick. He cleared the steps and landed on his nose in the street, followed by a shower of golden coins. The man got to his knees and began snatching them up as quickly as possible.

"What?" Chiara asked.

"His fees," Hugo's guest answered. "Gold is a powerful motivating force with you humans. His stay with your family has been a lucrative one. I thought I'd best send the money with him. You don't want him back."

"Yes," Chiara said. "I mean no."

The man heard her voice and looked up to where she was standing. Chiara met his eyes with her own stare. It burned into his brain. "Go," she said. "Go. And never return."

The man had collected all the gold and was on his feet, departing at a dead run, before she got the door closed. She dropped the bar into the socket and turned around. "Thank you," she said.

"Nothing to it," was the reply.

When she returned to the dining room, servants were cleaning up the spilled oil. Her sister, Phyllis, and the boys were vastly entertained. Her father was shaken, her mother looked relieved.

Chiara returned to her seat.

"What happened?" her father asked.

"He drinks too much. He's seeing snakes," Chiara told him. "They tell me it wears off in time."

"Too bad," her father said. "Now I'll have to find another—"

"No, you won't," his wife said.

Armine looked shocked. In the entire time they'd been married, she'd never contradicted anything he'd ever said.

"Never again will I allow anyone to treat any illness of mine. I cannot describe the torments I endured at the hands of that miserable, drunken fool. I may live or I may die, but whatever I do, I will have my own way about it. Chiara is perfectly capable of caring for any of my needs, and she is the only physician who will attend me.

"One more day of that fool and I would have hired an assassin. Is that clear?"

"Yes, my dear," Armine said.

A few days later Hugo left Florence on the road to Pavia, accompanied by Chiara and Armine, to be presented to the Lombard's ruler Desiderius.

Armine's wife was much improved and recovering nicely.

M AENIEL MOVED FORWARD THROUGH THE MOUNtains, as he told Regeane he would. Traveling largely by night and hunting at dawn and dusk, he managed to feed himself sparingly, until at last he reached the opening of the final pass and looked down from the lower slopes of the mountain on the well-watered river valleys of the Po.

The river valleys at the mountain's foot were the gateway into Italy. The Romans had garrisoned the two river towns that offered the easiest passage. This country route was not simply the best passage, but in many ways the road through the two river valleys was the only one. Defensive positions had been taken in the gorges of both Ivrea and Susa. Not only taken but fortified, and the Lombard king had committed enough troops to hold both strongly.

From his perch on the mountain slope, Maeniel looked at the earthworks stretching across the narrow neck of the gorge and thought this Desiderius was no fool. This was, of all places in the mountains, probably the best place to stop Charles.

The gray wolf lay down, resting his head on his paws, to wait until nightfall. He had already inspected Ivrea and felt that it was the worst place to challenge Desiderius. Even if Charles could force the neck of the earthworks across the gorge, there were two or three excellent fallback positions for Desiderius's force. Attacking there would be like running a gauntlet. *But here, here,* the wolf thought, *there were possibilities.*

He was careless that night. He was dealing with humans and was used to having his way. The wind was at his back and there was still a lot of daylight left when he started down. In fact, it wasn't even sunset yet but the sun was behind the cliffs overlooking the valley. The river and the road lay in deep shadow, and the wind from the mountains at his back was turning cold.

Yes, there were the ancient Roman ramparts overlooking the river, the trace no more than a rocky footpath that ran down to the river's edge and followed the water below the stone-built towers. An army trying to get past would have to march almost single file between high cliffs next to a river that, now fed by snowmelt from the heights, was a raging torrent. But unlike the fortress, the road only narrowed for a short distance before it widened out again. The river tumbled over rapids past the Roman fort; and then beyond the fort, a town stood. Not a very large one, it was the sort of place that grows up near army depots, offering the services both desirable and necessary for military men.

The town was fortified also. It clung to a spur of rock jutting out into the river. It consisted of a clump of limestone buildings with red tile roofs, a stout wall, and a heavy gate to the landward side that protected it from any marauders. The position of the remaining buildings, surrounded by a raging ice-cold river, was in and of itself enough to discourage anyone bold or foolish enough to try to break in.

Beyond the town the valley widened and continued downward toward a pleasant-looking fertile plain. The wolf, however careless he was, wasn't foolish enough to use the road. He eased along next to it, through the thick growth of brush, tall weeds, and trees that bordered the narrow track, until he got so close to the fortress that he realized he was in danger of being seen. So he turned and began to climb the slope behind the walls.

Yes, he thought. *This one can be flanked.* The place must have been unassailable in the time of the Romans. The fortifications dominated the first point in the valley, the town the second, but during the years the high walls between the fortress and the town had begun to erode.

A landslide had come and created a steep ramp precisely between the town and the fortifications where once only sheer walls had stood on either side. An attacking force could circle the fortress and come down behind the defenders. The town as it stood would offer few problems to a determined group of warriors. Yes, it would be almost impossible to get into, but then its defenders would have no easy way out, either. Simply seal the gates while Charles's main army passed and leave a small garrison, and within a week or two the people inside with no way to provision themselves would surrender.

Charles would be coming from two directions, Mons Jovis and Mont Cenis. The part of the army bypassing Mons Jovis, Maeniel's alpine stronghold, could feign to be frustrated by the defenders at Susa, while the rest circled and flanked the Roman fortification.

Something like this, he was sure, had been in Charles's mind when he determined to split his army, sending one by Mons Jovis and the other at Cenis. The overall strategy was mapped out in Charles's mind already, but Maeniel or someone else familiar with the terrain would need to suggest tactical approaches to him.

Maeniel paused on the almost impossibly steep slope overlooking the fortifications closing the neck of the gorge. Here he could climb no higher, but he was able to reconnoiter inside the Roman walls.

Yes, they were not closed from the rear, though the parts facing into the valley had been improved. New wooden scaffoldings had been added behind the battlements, and fresh earthworks had been thrown up in front of the walls. These earthworks had been armed with sharpened stakes to repel a cavalry charge, if necessary.

The earthworks on either side of the river extended beyond the walls all the way down to the river. From the front it looked formidable enough, and in a way even more so from the rear because it was obvious from the number of horses Maeniel saw grazing in the open valley that a considerable reserve force was present to hold the line should the attackers fail to give up easily.

The light was going now, the sun setting beyond the western peaks. Maeniel fluffed his fur. It was still cold at this altitude after sundown. He sat, head resting on his front paws, waiting for darkness, and enumerated the things he still needed to do before he could rejoin the king: draw close to the curtain wall and inform himself about how many troops held the strongpoint; make sure the town didn't contain any nasty surprises for the king; map out a path that would allow the second part of Charles's force to flank this fortress.

He felt a sharp pang of guilt about Regeane, but no doubt at all about his decision. It was sufficient to allow himself to be put in danger; if something happened to him, well and good. He could deal with it. He'd had a good, long life and had experienced many joys and sorrows; but to put a period to the prospects of one as young as she was would be intolerable. Deep in his heart, he knew the wish to protect her was as much selfish as loving. He was certain, in the deepest and most secret part of his soul, that once having possessed her, he would simply not ever be able to live without her and that her loss would destroy him as surely as death. And so the determination to prevent her from accompanying him on this dangerous journey was a forgone conclusion.

She would forgive him. In the time they'd lived together, he'd found her loving, kind, and anxious to please him. She was not one to cherish a grudge. So he would make peace as soon as possible. Then he sighed, wishing this business, even more foreign to his nature than to hers, was finished so he could go home and revel in the company of his beautiful wife and good friends without interference or interruption. His eyes closed, and in true wolf fashion, he napped while waiting for nightfall.

HUGO WAS A BIG HIT AT THE LOMBARD COURT IN Pavia. He'd picked the right person to help. Armine was the king's representative in the cloth trade. Kings have to eat. The Lombard ruler was supposed to supply himself financially from his estates, but the market for the wine and oil those estates produced was hit or miss at best. Most food was consumed within a few miles of its production.

Times were too unsettled for shipping; bulk items such as agricultural produce yielded little more than sporadic profit. The cloth trade was another matter. Despite poverty, church teaching, war, and civil disorder, the appetite for ostentatious apparel had only grown among the new barbarian aristocracy. There were few other ways to make a splash and show off how successful a man was than to dress to the teeth, and everyone who possibly could did.

The silk that arrived from Constantinople at the already rising port cities on the Adriatic Sea flowed through Pavia, over the Alps, into Europe. Desiderius took his cut and Armine managed his supply routes.

Hugo was introduced as a man of ancient wisdom with much knowledge of the arts for which the ancients were renowned: a polite way to put the fact that he was learned in divination and sorcery. And while the Lombard court wasn't deficient in so-called wise men, Hugo's guest made sure that his predictions were correct and his occasional minor miracles, such as identifying hidden objects and reading messages concealed by envelopes, were genuine.

His guest did not trust Hugo with all the information he gathered. Some of it he imparted to Chiara in the garden.

"The king is not faithful."

"I don't think they are expected to be," Chiara answered. "Kings, I understand, are very much a law unto themselves, at least where women are concerned. Everyone will either pretend not to see or, if there is an acknowledgeable issue, congratulate him."

"Ahhh," Hugo's guest said.

"Where is Hugo?"

Hugo's guest began to laugh.

Chiara shivered. "I wish you wouldn't do that. It gives me chills."

"Why?"

"I'm not sure. I will have to examine my feelings about it."

"Hmmm, how odd. I didn't think your species was at all analytical."

Chiara frowned, bent over, and pretended to be smelling a rose. "You talk as if you are not of our species."

"I'm not. You, yourself, called me a daemon."

"I know," Chiara whispered. "But I thought daemons were only damned souls who worked for the devil."

Again a peal of raucous laughter rang out, at least to Chiara's ears.

"I know nothing of the devil, daemons, and such, though a late priest of mine was fond of driveling on and on about such things. He, too, believed I was a daemon, especially since I allowed him to indulge his taste for cruelty and a perverse desire for sexual congress with the dead."

"God!" Chiara whispered. "I wish you would talk of something else."

"I know nothing of God, either," Hugo's guest replied. "And yes, you are right, I came to believe that particular servant of mine was a madman. In the end he wrought his own death because he challenged one who was strong enough to face his attacks, turn them back on him, and kill him.

"But mad or not, I kept faith with him and even with that half-wit Gimp and that pig Hugo. And also, my fine persnickety lady, I kept faith with you. When you asked for help, I gave it. When you had no other help, I was there."

"Peace, peace. It's true. You did. And I owe you more than I can ever repay, and I thank you. And I do believe you are faithful to your friends. But have you never thought about a higher good?"

"No." The reply was a rather resounding one. "Nor do I believe such a thing exists. No. Not since my people were destroyed and *you*, of all creatures, were allowed to take their place. No, the universe is simply the result of random forces set in motion by some unknowable cause, and I look to my own survival and the prosperity of those who serve me, and if you're smart, you will do the same."

Then he was gone.

Chiara didn't know how she knew when the creature vanished, but as she sensed his presence, she also felt his absence and was surprised by the emotional response his angry departure roused in her heart.

She realized she liked him. This slightly horrified her, but his conversation intrigued her and she could say anything she liked to him. For instance, she'd asked him about her mother's illness, and been told, "She bleeds too much when she has her women's courses."

"Is that all?" Chiara had asked.

"Probably. It's a thing I've noticed when women have several children, and she has borne five. Sometimes they have an increased flow."

She didn't ask him how he came by this knowledge, because his answers were almost invariably truthful and sometimes very disconcerting. She wondered where he had gone.

H UGO'S GUEST WAS WITH HUGO, WATCHING HIS futile attempts to persuade one of the older ladies of the court to yield up her virtue. He felt sheer disgust, at least in part because he knew this particular lady was considered to be a pushover by most of the nobility, but she was something of a connoisseur where male seduction was concerned, and Hugo's absolute lack of technique rather appalled her.

"You are," his guest told Hugo, "a complete fool."

Hugo broke off his attack—because that was pretty much what his attempts at seduction amounted to. He'd managed to corner Ilease in a window embrasure, and she was straight-arming him.

Hugo stalked over to a table and poured himself some wine. "I'd like to see you do any better," he muttered under his breath to his guest.

His guest exerted all his strength, and Hugo found himself a spectator at what followed. Hugo's guest never heard that "liquor is quicker," but he knew it. Liquor and other blandishments offered to the lady Ilease persuaded her to accompany him to Hugo's chamber, where he gave Hugo a comprehensive lesson in lovemaking with Ilease as the subject. Hugo had not known that a woman could be pleased and penetrated in so many ways, so many times. It was almost dark when Ilease staggered away from Hugo's door. She was exhausted, sore, scandalized by her own behavior, and black and blue in a few places. None of which could be attributed to Hugo's guest, but to her own rather overenthusiastic acrobatics. She was wearing a silver bracelet and a gold broach and felt profoundly satisfied.

After she left, Hugo—who hated to part with anything of value—began to whine about his guest's generosity.

"Shut up. I can find things like that anytime I want. When you need some more, I'll get it for you, but in the meantime, shut up."

Hugo staggered out of bed. He was nude. "What have you done to me?" he whimpered. "I can barely walk."

His guest stopped him at the window.

Hugo moaned. "It's cold, my teeth are chattering . . ."

"Hold still," his guest commanded. "You're lucky I'm in a good mood."

Hugo's window looked out over the half-ruined Roman city toward the pass at Susa. "Keep complaining," his guest snarled, "and I might toss you out. Want to risk it?"

Hugo was silenced. He wasn't sure if the spirit could accomplish this feat, but he remembered the kicks after the debacle at the inn and the physician's exit from the dining room in Florence. He wasn't sure and didn't care to push his luck.

"I'm leaving now," his guest said. Then he kicked Hugo's legs out from under him.

Hugo landed on the floor with a screech and a crash.

"Get the wine. Take the flagon to bed with you and don't—don't—get into any mischief until I return. Is that clear?"

"Y-yesss." Hugo moaned, but his guest noticed he was already crawling toward the flagon on the table.

THE WOLF WOKE BEFORE THE MOON ROSE OVER the peaks above him. He drifted like a shadow down toward the riverbank in the valley. Brown dairy cows gorged in the open between copses of trees. Predator or not, they ignored him except to raise their heads from time to time and keep track of his progress.

Though the moon wasn't shining into the valley, its light silvered the sky above and he could see almost as well as he could by day. Keeping to the shadows, he crossed the earthworks thrown up near the river, then approached the town. As far as he was concerned, the going was easy, though the rockfall above had left its debris all across what had been clear pasture at one time, and trees had taken root in the rocky rubble. The cover it gave him compensated for any inconvenience.

He was able to make his way to the town and draw very close to its walls without being seen. It was bigger than it looked from high up in the valley. It was walled and the gates were closed. The wolf paused in the brush along the river. Something about it didn't feel right. Had Regeane been there, she might have warned him. She herself had taken shelter along the Appian Way in a tomb that wasn't there . . . but then, she hadn't noticed anything wrong at the time, and he could see nothing overtly wrong here.

A pour-off that cut through the remnants of the rock slide ran past the town into the thick half-drowned brush on the riverbank. It seemed to have undermined the walls at the bottom near the water. The wolf eased down into the brush. Yes, there was a crack in the wall just before it joined the first house. Over the water the walls were unnecessary and the houses themselves presented blank walls to the stream. He looked through the crack and saw the cobbles of a square. He began to dig with a view to enlarging the hole.

A HALF MILE AWAY IN A CAVE, GIMP WOKE TO THE triumphant shout of Hugo's guest. "He's sprung my trap. Get down to the river and man the nets."

THE DIGGING WAS EASY, MAENIEL THOUGHT. ALmost too easy. *I'll be through in a minute,* he thought, and plunged headfirst into the river.

The wolf was a strong swimmer but the river, fed by snowmelt from the glaciers at the top of the pass, was freezing. Shock rendered him temporarily helpless. He was dragged along by the swift-moving current into the rapids, white water spreading, swirling over a stony bed.

A creature less tough than he might have been killed. Maeniel was rolled over and dragged along the rocks that floored the riverbed. As it fell toward the valleys beyond, the stream widened abruptly, and for a second the wolf was stranded in a shallow spot. He got his legs under him, then he was dragged down into the current again and sucked into a boiling maelstrom that spit him over a falls and into a millrace at the bottom, and then slammed him into the meshes of a steel net. For a second he was trapped underwater. He struggled frantically against drowning, and was pulled to the surface. Aware he was in human shape, he felt the metal cut into his skin as the collar closed around his neck.

IN HER TENT OVER A HUNDRED MILES AWAY, REgeane sat up in her bed, clutching her throat. *A dream,* she thought. *It was a dream,* she tried to tell herself. She had just dreamed about the time Gundabald had chained her up, and about the second time when he'd *tried* to chain her up . . . but her fears wouldn't quiet themselves.

A few seconds later, the Saxon was looking into the tent. A torch flared in his hands. The light blinded her. The coiling flames cast an eerie glow around her face.

Regeane was hardly immodest; she was wearing a woolen shift and a white lawn overgown trimmed with lace. "He . . . he . . . has met with—I don't know—I can't . . ."

"Are you sure?" the Saxon asked.

"No! Yes, yes . . . I am."

A second later he was looking at a wolf. The shift and gown were on the floor. He felt her thick ruff as she surged past him. Then she was gone. As wolf she ran through the forest toward the pool. When she reached it, she saw the moon was full and its reflection was mirrored in the still surface.

The silver wolf paused, and the fair, pale light glowed on the long guard hairs on her coat. Once again she felt the odd strength the light brought her, as she had on that long-ago night in Rome after her mother died, when she found herself alone on a dark and dangerous road.

Since then she had been a bold adventuress, friend to a pope, and shared the favors of his lover, Lucilla, then wife to the lord Maeniel— the spoiled wife of the lord Maeniel. Did the gray wolf think his protection had changed her essential nature? If he did, the more fool he for believing such a ridiculous thing. She was the same Regeane who had adventured across the campagna and into worlds beyond to save Antonius's life. The selfsame woman who had not hesitated to risk the stake and death by fire to help her friends. And the more fool she for letting him shake her hard-won confidence in the abilities conferred by her double state and push her into allowing him to journey alone into danger: an act of folly on both their parts.

Had he been captured? Was he dead?

She didn't know. Whatever happened, she must act in the belief that something could be done to save him.

She turned, trotted along the lake's edge, and began to climb up to the Lady's Mirror. Again, as before, the rose and blackberry canes parted at her touch, but she was disappointed when she reached the pool to see the same sky and moon reflected in this water as in the pond lower down. If there was a gate here, it was closed. The woman was fearful. *What will I do? How will I reach him?* The ever-practical wolf said simply, *You are thirsty, might as well have a drink of water.*

Her muzzle dropped to the pool. But when her nose touched the water, she found she was looking into a moonless world just at the instant of first light, when the sky is a band of fire opal across the eastern horizon and there is breathless hush, all still, and the outlines of the world's garden are suffused by the jewel-like light of the first sunrise.

Regeane didn't hesitate. She dove forward.

The water closed around her soundlessly. An observer would have been disconcerted by the lack of a splash. The pool shimmered for a moment and then the moon's light returned to the water, a disc bright enough to dim even the farthest stars.

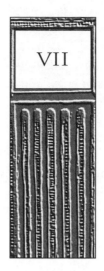

VII

THE SILVER WOLF'S HEAD EMERGED FROM THE
water. Daybreak was graying the trees around this lake into
visibility. She swam toward the shore. The tree roots
reached the water and ran down below the surface and felt like slimy
ridges under her paws as she scrambled toward the edge of the lake.

She pulled herself up on the bank and shook the water out of her
coat. The world of the trees was foggy and dim. It was silent except
for a faraway cry too distant to put a name to. Above her the trunks
rose up and up until they vanished into a low fog bank. Not one side
branch could she see.

She knew the sun was rising because the light grew brighter and
brighter. She'd never seen trees like this. They left no spot of bare
ground between the trunks and roots. They covered the earth the
way scale mail formed the cuirass of a warrior, the roots and the
trunks spreading out over the ground until they touched the roots of
another tree, where they formed knuckles and turned down into the
earth.

Things did grow here in the region of perpetual shadow. Soil
trapped in the nooks and crannies of the twisting roots supported a
magnificent variety of ferns and other odd plants the like of which
Regeane had never seen before. Something that rooted itself in bark
dropped long trailing stems covered by leaves so tiny and numerous
that they looked like fur and were just as soft as fur when she stroked
them, except that they were green, cool, and ever so slightly moist.

Others were like the ferns she was used to, but many were larger, filling the holes between tree trunks with a dazzling array of green lattice and lacework. But however bewitched they were, none disguised the fact that the trees created an almost impossible surface over which something like a wolf would not be able to travel.

As a human she might be able to find passage between the massive trunks, but she suspected that one wandering among them might do so forever or until starvation and despair claimed him—or her. In the growing light, she saw the lake emerge from a cave or overhang not far from where she surfaced.

Regeane forsook the wolf and turned human. She dove back into the lake and swam toward the cave. As she approached more closely, she saw it was no cave but a gorge thickly overgrown by the gigantic trees. Their roots from above hung down into the water, forming a vast network as impassable as the bars of a giant cage. The trees drank as the water pulsed between these big, spongy roots and flowed an unguessable distance down a stair of rocks only just faintly visible through the mesh of roots.

No, Regeane thought. She had been placed on a road and it led in only one direction. She was about to turn and swim back into the lake when she saw it. It was all red feathers, ruby scales, and teeth.

It fell on her neck with a screech and sank claws into her shoulder. She was wolf in one jarring, protective reflex and her jaws closed over the thing and ate it. But before she could think, it was gone.

Then the wolf turned and swam toward the outlet from the lake into a river. By the time she reached it, the light was much brighter. Clouds rolled above, moving swiftly as if driven by high winds aloft. The low mist that greeted the morning was gone, but the surrounding trees were so tall the clouds moved among them. Like mountains, they caught the ever-changing maelstrom of vapor. They admitted long shafts of light that tracked hither and yon over the fern forest growing in the embraces of giant trees.

Regeane the silver wolf followed the river. It led her in a winding course over heavy cobbles. It wasn't deep and most of the time covered only the wolf's paws. To Regeane there was no sight or smell other than that of damp air and a pleasant almost-rain smell that she associated with green, growing plants. She regretted that she'd eaten the red thing. That was a problem. But it had attacked her and the wolf was hungry. She wondered if it might poison her, but after a few hours of her trek, she decided that if it hadn't bothered her by now, it probably wouldn't. The only other animal life she'd run across had been small creatures that let out a small, bell-like sound when disturbed, then flew off, vanishing into the misty aisles of the fern forest that stretched out from the river for an unknown distance on either side.

Near what she surmised was noon, the river widened and expanded into another marshy lake. It was lined with water plants. Some she knew: the large, purple-pink Egyptian lotus, flowers borne high above the water; the blue spires of pickerelweed blooming in massive clusters near the giant tree trunks. Yellow cress abounded, and Regeane turned human for a few moments to make a meal of some.

She found a tree festooned with the long creeping plant covered with small, soft leaves. She took hold of one of the vines and discovered that at the terminal of each long furry stem, there were fruits. She tried one. The taste exploded in her mouth. Rich, tangy, and then sweet. She knew she would never be able to describe this to anyone. As with most things, they tasted of themselves alone.

She noticed while she was making a meal of cress and fruit—the sort of meal the wolf was ill adapted to make—that the clouds had begun to thicken menacingly. She let go of the vine and let herself drop back into the water. Wind moved over the surface of the water, ruffling it slightly. Reeds and sedges began clicking their stems. Regeane noticed they were bent, as shore grasses often are, molded by the prevailing winds. So this rain must come often. High above, lightning zigzagged across the sky.

Using the ferns as stepping stones, Regeane climbed back up the tree. The epiphytal plants grew everywhere on the deeply fissured bark, and the long soft stems of this particular plant, the one that grew the fruits, were stronger than they looked.

Higher up than the drooping creeper grew a giant fan-shaped fern with big, lacy leaves. It looked as if it lived on rain. A broad, leafy holdfast tied it to the tree, and the fronds spread out from its center.

When she reached a spot among the ferns, she looked down and found she could see through the clear water to the lake bottom. It, too, was covered by the massive roots that formed the forest floor.

The life in this place seemed to be a gift of the great trees. They were quite literally everywhere.

The water plants that didn't drift on the surface were rooted among the trees, and she saw the long shapes of some sort of fish sculling along the drowned tree trunks. The sky was almost black now; the whole world as far as she could see was wrapped in the green gloom that presages a rainstorm. Above, lightning flashed and a terrific thunderclap shook the water forest. Not far away one of the giant trees burst into flame. Then the wind hit and the rain battered her body. She was blinded for a second when the wind forced a mixture of smoke, steam, embers, and smoldering bark toward her, engulfing her body in the debris of the burned tree.

Regeane closed her eyes and ducked her head against the lace fern to shelter herself from the wind-driven rain. Only a few hundred yards away, in spite of the rain, the giant tree burned like a torch, hissing and spitting as the fire consumed the resin-filled heartwood.

It seemed to Regeane that some dark tower burned, because the tree was tall enough to carry the fire into the dark, rolling clouds high above. All around Regeane heard a rising cry of grief, a moaning shout of bottomless sorrow. *The wind,* she tried to tell herself. *The wind. It must be the storm wind.* But then the wind ended, the rain pounded straight down, extinguishing the fiery tree, and Regeane was surprised to find she was looking out at the world through an enclosure of fern fronds. She was wrapped in the soft fronds of the fern she rested against.

For a second she was frightened but then realized the fern fronds offered no more resistance than a fine lace dress. In fact, they covered her like a piece of clothing, warming her against the chilling rain. For a time she rested, dozing against the fern's supporting clasp until the sky cleared and the overcast broke up into puffy, white shapes.

The fern released her, spreading its fronds to catch the intermittent sunlight. Regeane jumped down. Her momentum carried her to the bottom of the lake where she pushed off from the silt-covered roots. Just before she broke the surface, a school of fish swam by, their bright scales a flash of mirrored light in clear water. She felt a sudden knifelike chill, and when her head broke the surface she found herself wolf in the shallows of the river that ran out of the mountains past a fort and its town. The air was cold and the sun was going down.

BEFORE DAWN HUGO WAS PULLED OUT OF BED. HE landed on the floor.

"I have him," his guest shouted in his ear.

"Who?" Hugo asked.

"The wolf," his guest shouted again. "Maeniel, the gray wolf."

"No," Hugo said, clutching his head.

"Yes!" His guest was jubilant.

"Did you kill him?"

"No. Why would I do a stupid thing like that?"

"Because he's dangerous," Hugo snarled. "Big, strong, and very dangerous. There was at least some truth in the tale I told Armine. I know. I saw him."

"I don't care who or what he's killed, I want him. And besides, he will make your reputation at this court in Pavia. No small matter. Don't worry. I will tame him."

"Don't worry," Hugo muttered, beginning to dress. "That's just what Gundabald said before he visited them the last time. They killed him and then one of them probably ate him."

"Yes, the two women nearly got me," Hugo's guest said. Hugo's face froze. "You met them?"

His guest laughed.

"Oh, yes, we met. They killed my votary. She—the bitch—and a friend. I almost got her again, but that time she came with another woman. They took the cringing human that I was torturing away from me.

"Now I want my revenge. She will certainly come looking for him, but I will possess the lord Maeniel—and her in the bargain. Wait, see if I don't."

"No," Hugo said. "Kill him. Or he'll find a way to kill you."

"Pig." Hugo's guest exerted all his strength again, but this time he failed. He'd wasted much too much of his energy on last night's sexual encounter, and besides, Hugo was in mortal terror of Maeniel. That lent him strength he had no idea he possessed.

They began wrecking the room.

Hugo's guest started hurling everything he could lift at Hugo. Hugo's contribution to the brawl was to run madly from place to place, tripping over the furniture and yelling at the top of his lungs.

His guest snatched up the bedclothes and made a credible attempt to smother Hugo with them. Hugo escaped by crawling under the table. His guest then dropped the linens, snatched up the wine pitcher, and tried to dash the contents into Hugo's face. He needn't have bothered: it was empty. But the same could not be said of the chamber pot . . .

Hugo stood up and gave vent to a howl of fury and disgust that rattled the rafters, then he seized the table and threw it in the general direction of his guest's voice and actions. At this point in the proceedings, Chiara opened the door.

"Are you both out of your minds?" she shouted. "My father is in terror, as is everyone else within earshot. I'm sure someone has called the watch."

There was a sound of feet pounding, and a few seconds later a half dozen armed men dashed past Chiara into the room. Hugo had managed to get himself quartered in the palace and did not want to lose his place at the center of the action. He attempted to fob off the captain of Desiderius's personal guard with a story about getting out of bed and falling over the chamber pot.

It was a story the grim-faced old soldier did not believe, and he gave a stern warning that the king kept an orderly house and to please minimize such disturbances in the future.

Chiara told the captain that she had heard the noises and ran to see what was the matter. This he did believe, since she was dressed in the four layers of clothing required by her virginal status and the very cold mountain nights. However, he did accompany Chiara back to her rooms and saw her safely inside. She ducked back out as soon as he was gone.

Hugo reeked of stale urine and his guest was still furious. "You cowardly bastard. You whimpering, sniveling excuse for a human being. You cock-sucking louse. You—"

"Stop," Chiara whispered. "Abusing him won't get you anywhere. Well, at least nowhere you want to go. If you rouse that old iron-pants martinet again, you can both look forward to spending the night in the street."

This was true. Both creatures subsided.

"God!" Chiara whispered to Hugo, "You stink. Go bathe and remember you took—" She glanced around. "—*his* money and you made some promises." She stamped one small foot. "Don't tell me you aren't prepared to keep them."

"He'd better be," Hugo's guest said.

"Well," Chiara said to Hugo. "What have you to say for yourself?"

"He—he—he's captured that thing."

"What thing?"

"The man-wolf," Hugo said, and spat. "And he won't kill it."

Chiara looked taken aback. "Why not?"

"Because he, the lord Maeniel, has great powers, and I want control of him . . . and them."

"And of his beautiful wife the lady Regeane," Hugo supplied.

"Yes, there's that," Hugo's guest stated flatly. "I fought her in Rome over a silly, sullen drab. Then again with my priest. She killed him, she and her kinsman, a Saxon lord. Though she doesn't know him, he is her kinsman. And then in Charles's camp, I was nearly bested—extinguished, I suppose you would put it."

"Killed?" Chiara asked.

"Yes. I do not die, at least not the way you do, but I can be destroyed. And she and her woman Matrona nearly succeeded.

"Now . . . now I have him and want her." He shook Hugo the way a dog shakes a rat.

Chiara stepped back because he splattered a little. There had been a lot of pee in the pot, and Hugo's hair and clothes were wet.

"Wash yourself, pig."

"I think you better do as he says," Chiara told him.

Hugo whispered something really vile under his breath.

"Shut your filthy mouth," Hugo's guest said.

"You're both against me," Hugo moaned.

"No, I'm not," Chiara said. "I, too, think it might be wiser to do away with this creature Maeniel, as you call him, but, but . . . you and I have accepted his favor and so bound ourselves. As I see it, we have no choice in the matter."

Hugo received a shove, a hard shove, in the direction of the baths. "Go, wash yourself."

Cursing the whole world and everything in it, Hugo staggered away.

He was still there. Chiara knew she was not alone.

"Is this wise?" she asked. She was surprised at the reply. It was thoughtful, even judicious.

"Yes, I do believe so. In the first place, creatures such as Maeniel are very difficult to kill and have resources even they are unaware of. If I tried and failed, he might win his freedom and, once free, he would be a terrible enemy. I can, as you have seen, do *some* things, but I am not as strong as this man-wolf is. Hugo . . ."

"Don't bother," she said. "I wouldn't trust him to go to the market and buy onions. I see, or I believe I see."

"Good," was the reply.

"By the by," she said, her eyebrows lifting. "Do you have . . . Hugo accused you of wanting this Maeniel's beautiful wife."

"Go back to bed," Hugo's guest said sharply. "And don't trouble me with any more questions."

GIMP WASN'T A BAD MAN, AND IN HIS OWN WAY— because he was used to doing as he'd been told—he was more efficient than Hugo. He'd been told to fish this stranger out of the river and chain him up. And Hugo's guest told Gimp exactly how to chain Maeniel up, and Gimp did it, being afraid to disobey. He went in mortal terror of Hugo and his guest, only hoping to somehow be free of them both. The one had killed him and the other had in some incomprehensible way saved his life.

He chained Maeniel to a staple on the wall of the cave, put another pair of fetters on his hands, and then a separate set on his feet. And since he was not cruel, he gave the prisoner an old tunic and covered him with a blanket.

Maeniel held off the change. He didn't dare. It didn't take him long to figure out that Gimp was only slightly smarter than the average tree stump, and he didn't want to unsettle his captor's mind. Minds. Actually there were two or three others, but they were, if possible, even slower than Gimp.

They sat looking like owls lined up on a log, watching him, appearing very much as if they expected him to turn not into a wolf but at least a dragon. He decided he'd best disappoint them. So he vomited water, twice, and then somehow fell asleep.

Near dawn the sound of Hugo's arrival woke him. Gimp,

accompanied by the rest, got up and went outside. A very loud argument ensued and Gimp returned, as it appeared, alone.

"You can tell Hugo to come in," Maeniel said. "I heard him, and I can smell him. I know he's here. He has a rather distinctive aroma even when he's as freshly bathed as he is now."

There wasn't much light outside. Gimp pushed another log into the fire at the cave entrance, and Maeniel saw him more clearly for the moment and knew this wasn't Gimp. He would have been hard put to tell someone not endowed, as he was, with wolf as well as human senses how he knew, but he did.

"Who are you?" he asked. Even chained as he was, he managed to sit up and set his back against the stone wall.

"The bear," came the answer. "I am the bear." Then Gimp-not-Gimp laughed. It was a distinctly unpleasant one.

"We fought," Maeniel said.

"Probably more than once," the bear answered. "If you have the same kind of memories that I do."

"I do," Maeniel said, "but more recently."

"Yes. I was the bear then and, as always, in the past. I am the bear, and once we contended for the world."

"Yes," Maeniel said. "But I was the wolf then and not part of the fight."

"Oh, yes," Gimp-not-Gimp said. "You even then were part of their bands, though you followed them through the snow and begged scraps from their feasts. They relied on you and you were welcomed at their fires."

"I suppose that's true," Maeniel replied slowly. Then he said, "The bear, all the bear, remember you, though they will not admit it. They remember when you hunted almost as equals and they felt honored to take your name.

"Even these Romans," Maeniel continued, "called themselves sons of the wolf, suckled at a bitch wolf's teats. They, the sons of the wolf, left their tracks across the world, and these wild barbarians still take names from you and, sometimes yet, challenge you.

"Yes," Maeniel said. "If you say you are the bear, then your people are long gone, forgotten. The trees, the grass, the wide starry sky know them no more."

"Yes," Gimp-not-Gimp said. "And I will never be done mourning them. Even if I alone am left to remember, I will always yield them the tribute of my everlasting sorrow. But this is more difficult than I thought, because you seem to understand."

"I cannot say I am without understanding," Maeniel answered. "But what is it that you want from me?"

"You, yourself. I wish to join you, join you the way I have possessed Hugo and others."

"Possess? One possesses a slave. I am no one's possession."

"My choice of expression was poor," Gimp-not-Gimp protested. "For once, after all the ages of preying on these gibbering half-apes who replaced my own kind, I would have an equal partner, one who could share my mind, my will. We could brush aside these quarreling kings and rule the world. Rule it our way. Return it to what it once was: forests without end, savannas where a million wild beasts roamed, deserts bejeweled with flowers that leap from the stems by day and starlit skies by night, oceans that caress clean, white beaches, snowfields that flare with a thousand colors when the northern lights glow in the heavens.

"Remember, wolf, remember when your ancestors roamed free in packs that numbered hundreds and ruled without rivals the long winter night?"

"Yes, I remember," Maeniel said. "And I remember when the others came, bearers of fire at first, then stone and steel. We struggled then as we do now sometimes, but it was never war. Not as you propose it."

"Well, look around you. War is the only thing they understand. Look at these kings, ready and willing to spend how many lives— even their own—to control what? I ask you, what? An iron crown made from a nail used to crucify a man who would have despised them both."

"Yes, I think you may be right," Maeniel said. "But it is also said, 'What does it profit a man if he gains the whole world and loses his soul?' Is it my soul you want?"

"Yes. What could withstand us, joined together?"

"I must think on this."

"Fine. I will see you this evening. This—" He gestured toward Gimp's body. "—servant of mine will feed you. I await your decision."

Gimp sat down and slumped against the wall, his face void of expression. A few minutes later he awoke, scratched his head, rose, and stumbled toward the fire at the mouth of the cave.

When Gimp came out of the cave, Hugo was gone. Hugo's guest had brought clothing for Maeniel, so Gimp brought it into the cave. There wasn't much of a way for Maeniel to dress, but a mantle was included among the clothing and Maeniel wrapped it around himself and made a meal of the bread and dried meat Gimp brought him.

Hugo's guest wished a large number of unpleasant fates on Hugo and then departed to search the pass at Susa for Regeane.

The soldiers arrived at midday. They arrested Gimp and put Maeniel on a horse and rode for the Lombard capital at Pavia. Someone Maeniel knew had double-crossed someone else. He didn't know how or why this had happened. Maeniel's bet was on Hugo. The scrawny little rat was most likely ready to piss his britches at the thought of facing Maeniel, and he had probably run right to Desiderius as soon as he found out his enemy had been captured. How he'd managed to evade his guest, Maeniel had no idea, but somehow he'd done so, and now Maeniel was on his way to Pavia in chains.

That fact that he'd changed captors was no consolation to Maeniel. The Lombard soldiers made sure he remained as thoroughly fettered as Gimp had, and Desiderius was much more likely to kill him.

HUGO'S GUEST DID NOT FIND REGEANE. AS WOLF, she had already gone beyond Susa. When the silver wolf climbed out of the river, she had no difficulty in locating the spot where Maeniel went in. Then as she cast about downstream, she also found the spot where Gimp and his men pulled him out.

The illusion was still present. The spirit seemed to have no trouble producing these things, but she was not fooled by this one. A town, any town, always had some movement about it. There would have been at the very least smoke, and given the early spring chill, one or more fires would have been burning in a real town. Besides, there would have been noise—people coming and going even late at night. None of this was present.

She saw instantly how he'd been trapped and then, after finding where he'd been chained by his captors, she set out on their trail. She found the cave but reached it after Desiderius's men had set off for Pavia, taking Maeniel with them. After investigating the traces they left around the cave's mouth, she sat down in the dim coolness near the entrance to consider matters.

She was afraid to shadow a large party of armed men by day. The countryside was open, and she could only too easily be spotted, driven into a corner by horsemen, and killed. Besides, they would stop at villages along the way, and such were always guarded by fierce mastiffs. Where would they go? Turin possibly, but the Lombard capital Pavia was the likely place. Yes, the Dora Riparia would join the Po downstream, and Pavia was located near the confluence of the Ticino and the Po.

The woman nodded to herself.

The wolf was satisfied also.

For a moment they confronted each other.

What if in the river valley we meet other wolves?

We will have to deal with that, she answered to her dark companion, *if it happens.*

THEY SPENT THE NIGHT AT A FORTIFIED VILLA BE-longing to the king. Maeniel was allowed to bathe. Four Lombard soldiers watched him, and since the baths at the villa had gone downhill since Roman times, there was only one—none too clean—plunge served by a nearby spring. But the ancient hypocaust was fired and the water was warm. The building was native limestone. The roof was cement with big glass plugs that let in light. Only one door served the baths as an entrance and exit.

The four Lombard soldiers, by their weapons and regalia palace guard, stood at the door watching him the way eagles watch a chicken yard. Maeniel heard one mutter to another, "He is said to be a powerful sorcerer and able to change his shape."

"Are you serious?" one of the others answered with a smile.

"Yes," the captain answered. "And don't any of you take any chances with him. Whatever else he may be, the brigands hereabouts give his duchy a wide berth. He has a reputation as a fearsome warrior, and when I was in Rome I watched him slowly cut to pieces the most dangerous swordsman the Lombard party could send against him. Take any chances with him and he'll likely cut your throat—and if he doesn't and somehow escapes, I will. Got that?"

Maeniel noticed the other soldiers seemed impressed. When he was finished bathing, they gave him fresh clothing and no less than ten stood by while he was fettered again. They took shifts and he was always watched by at least two men and chained to a staple in the wall in the cubicle where he slept.

They gave him a heavy, dark mantle. It was welcome. So near the mountains, the nights were always cold. But it had a strange, powerful odor that gagged him when he got his nose too close to the cloth and sometimes made him sneeze.

None of his guards got drunk, either—something of a surprise since nightly drunkenness was common among soldiers. Given the efficiency of his captors, Maeniel decided that he would make no attempt to escape now. He was sorry to fail in his task, but he hoped a commander as able as Charles would have more than one string to his bow, and he would find someone else to reconnoiter. Possibly all was not lost, and Maeniel could make arrangements to ransom himself. It all depended upon how much Desiderius believed of Hugo's story; Maeniel didn't remember Hugo as an impressive individual. Best for him to play the injured innocent and offer a heavy bribe to Desiderius or whoever was making the decisions at the Lombard court. He had, he was confident, the resources to buy his freedom if necessary.

With that, he yawned, made himself as comfortable as possible considering the number of heavy chains on his body, and went to sleep.

EARLY IN THE MORNING, CHIARA WAS WAKENED BY hideous noises in the corridor. Her father slept in an inner room; thankfully, his door was closed. She cracked her door and saw Hugo running back and forth in the corridor. He was bare-assed naked and being flogged by someone or some thing. The hideous noises were his screams, muffled because he had a pewter chamber pot firmly fixed over his head. Between cracks with the switch that she saw swinging at his buttocks and thighs, he was tugging, trying to pull it off. However, the metal was bent in such a way as to make this impossible.

"Oh, no," she whispered. "Oh, please . . . please."

"Get back in your room," Hugo's guest said. "I am not finished."

Hugo screamed, "Blearee, melfph."

Which Chiara translated as "Chiara, help."

"Melfph! Melfph! Melfph," Hugo howled.

"You betrayed me," his guest screeched. "You dared to betray me. You . . ." Then his guest lapsed into several other languages, none of which Chiara understood.

Chiara closed the door firmly behind her and stood in the doorway with her back against the planks. "Stop! You just stop," she told Hugo's guest.

He did, but not before fetching Hugo an incapacitating kick in the groin.

Chiara brought Hugo a mantle and called for the blacksmith. He arrived carrying a metal saw and a large, dangerous looking metal clipper.

"Thank heavens it's pewter," the smith told her. "Any stronger metal and we'd never get it off. But, begging your lady's pardon, what I can't understand is how he got it on there so tight in the first place."

For a second Chiara was at a loss for words. She finally managed, "It was an accident."

"I see," the smith said calmly. "Men of his age are sometimes prone to such accidents, but a young woman of your tender years . . . to be involved in such high jinks as this . . ."

"Oh . . . my . . . God!" Chiara whispered, her face turning scarlet, her ears feeling on fire. "I . . . I . . . didn't, I mean—I couldn't—I wouldn't. Oh, God. I just heard noises in the hall . . . and found him . . ."

She alone could hear Hugo's guest give vent to a roar of salacious merriment. "Serves you right for interfering with my little amusements."

Chiara fled.

T HE COUNTRYSIDE WAS REVERTING TO WILDER-ness. Smallholders couldn't maintain themselves any longer. The Lombards had kept the big Roman estates and ran them as the Romans had with slave gangs. Regeane saw such estates at a distance.

Crops were seldom planted close to the river, though it was clear some water was being diverted by means of canals for irrigation, but the sometimes steep, rocky banks and thick growth of trees discouraged any settlement too close to the water. Once she did run into wolves. A small pack of no more than six individuals, they were feeding on the somewhat well-aged carcass of a bullock who looked as if he'd fallen down a bank and broken his neck.

She gave them and the remains of the bullock a wide berth. She still had many human leanings, and to the woman the meat had an appalling stench. When she came into view, they raised their heads and watched her as she passed.

She didn't think any of the them would pay any more attention to her, but one came after her. She heard the faint sounds of pads in the soft mud.

The woman felt a thrill of pure fear, but the she-wolf was angry. Wolves do have some laws. She was not interfering with them. She had not threatened any of them or killed in their territory. They should have let her pass unmolested, but here was this fool coming up behind her. Matrona had told her what to do. The woman hoped it would work.

At the last second she wheeled and slammed her shoulder into the oncoming wolf. The silver wolf was half again as big as the other. She—it was one of the females—went over, rolling in the shallows.

The silver wolf stood her ground, snarling.

The other jumped to her feet and showed no desire to continue the attack. She stood on the bank and shook herself dry.

It had worked, the silver wolf thought, a little bit triumphantly, so she almost didn't see the other two screened by the cattails and brush who were moving up alongside her. In fact, she never knew what warned her, but one second they weren't there, the next they were.

She was standing next to a fallen tree, and they came over it, ready to land on her back or rather, she knew—her memories told her—one of them would land on her back, go for her spine, and the other would try to tear out her throat.

Don't run, Matrona had told her. *Don't even think about running. If you do, they'll have you.*

She didn't. She turned and met them in midair. She flanked them. The first one went down on top of number two, and her jaws closed on his throat. The woman willed her to hesitate but the wolf sank her fangs in to the gums.

Her adversary pulled free with as near to a scream as she'd ever heard a wolf give, and when she turned, ready for further battle, she realized they were all in flight. The speed of their disappearance was amazing. They seemed to melt into the brush on the riverbank. All vanishing except for the bullock, flies still buzzing around it, and a pool of blood beside the log half sunken in the mud.

Shaken, Regeane—the woman was now firmly in charge—bolted and didn't stop running until she was winded and several more miles downstream. She hoped she didn't meet any more of her brethren. They had, however, exceeded her expectations, being devious, intelligent, and fierce. She understood better now why Maeniel had been reluctant to take her with him. She didn't possess nearly enough of those qualities herself. Certainly not enough to impress such as he. She was determined to cultivate them in her own personality.

She dove into the river to clean her fur, shook herself, and continued on, realizing she had a dismaying prospect ahead of her. Last night didn't count. She'd spent it hot on the trail of the men who'd captured Maeniel. She hadn't had a chance to rest. She must sleep. Now.

How do I find a den? she asked herself. *A safe den?*

She had no idea.

HADRIAN CAME TO SEE LUCILLA. HE, LUCILLA, AND Dulcinia had supper just before dark. Dulcinia kissed Lucilla good-bye and went home. Hadrian and Lucilla walked in the garden.

"He is coming via Lake Geneva through the Alps," he told Lucilla. "This is, of course, not for public consumption.

"Desiderius has blockaded some of the passes into Lombardy. Where and what the dispositions of his forces are isn't known."

Lucilla nodded. "You want my help in finding out?"

"No," Hadrian said. "I believe that's already taken care of. We—Charles and I—have a more pressing problem."

"What?" Lucilla asked, then she sighed. "My dear, I'm growing old." She sat down on a bench.

The garden was dark but her servants had set torches on the walls of the triclinium bordering the garden and near the fountain, so there was light. It had rained earlier in the day and the air was cool and moist.

"I'm not sure I want to hear about this," Lucilla said.

"No?"

Lucilla looked down at her hands. "You are pope. It's what we both wanted and I am weary."

He lifted her hand. It was scarred by her torture at the hands of the Lombards, and the nails were thick and crooked. She remembered the pain as they were jerked out one by one. She'd screamed. She remembered how she'd screamed and felt terrible shame that she could be brought so low. The hand clenched into a fist, and she pulled away.

"They jerked out my nails and when that didn't work . . . It was working, though they just didn't know it. I didn't know if I could bear another one. But they brought out the hot irons."

"Shush." He kissed her on the lips, then drew back. "Can't you forget?"

"No." She shook her head. "I can't. I'll never let you see my body again."

She hadn't. Not since she was tortured. Not since he got her back from the Lombards.

"You are avenged," he said bleakly. "Basil the Lombard agent is dead. Gundabald . . . I don't know. But this Maeniel who married Regeane told me before they left Rome that I needn't concern myself about him."

"Believe it," Lucilla whispered. "Regeane told me what happened, and you don't want to know. I am indeed avenged."

"But," he said, "that little turd Hugo somehow has found his way to Pavia and become a respected member of the court there."

Lucilla gave out a hiss of pure fury. "Tell me what you need done," she said.

"No," Hadrian said. "Not tonight. I came," he said quietly, "to repair this estrangement between us."

"No," Lucilla whispered. "Take a younger mistress. Give me a few weeks and I . . ." She was rising to her feet as she spoke. "I will find you a clean, not too intelligent girl, one so lowborn she will not come burdened with a tribe of relations—"

"Stop it." He rose also and caught her by the upper arms. Lucilla closed her eyes and in the torchlight he saw two tears trickle from beneath her lids and make their way down her cheeks.

"When I go to my home—the house where I was born—to visit my brothers and sisters, I know the house is old, the frescoes peeling; the very flagstones in the courtyard and on the stair to the roof are worn by the passage of many feet.

"But also I know that there my ancestors sacrificed to the lares and penates belonging to my family and later celebrated the eucharistic sacrifice in the triclinium after they heard Christ's words and accepted him as the center of their lives. I would not exchange that building for Nero's famous golden house. I touch my lips to the lintel of the doorway when I enter; and, my very dear, a house is only a thing of stone, brick, and mortar. How much more do I love the one who brought joy to my youth, the mother of my children and my life's companion.

"There is no other woman in my life and what's more, my dear, my soul, there never will be. Our love was never about the lust of the flesh. Remember when we met?"

She did, and the sun seemed to shine on her, hot on her neck. She had been pregnant, four months, and had walked a long way from the mountains that ran like a spine down the center of Italy to Rome. Lucilla had gold, but she was afraid to spend it. A gold coin in the hands of a lone woman without kin to protect her was simply an invitation to thieves. The gold was sewn into her shift and in a belt around her waist.

She wore black and had told those she met she was a widow. She had, in fact, dyed the dress and veil with oak galls in the mountains. She paused at a fountain near the entrance to the city. She knew the women would gather there before sunrise to get water for their families to prepare the morning meal before the day's heat set in.

The women had directed her to a community of women, widows themselves, who kept safe lodgings for the multitude of lone female pilgrims who thronged to the holy city. They rented her a room up a narrow stair on the third floor of a bakery near the ruins of the forum. She couldn't spend the gold and she had to eat, so they told her to apply to the church at the Lateran Palace where daily bread, wine, and meat were distributed to the poor.

"There is a colonnade," one of the oldest widows told her, "where you may rest, shaded from the sun, and across the street a stair and a portico surrounded by a painting of Christ and his saints giving alms to the poor. Tell your name to the priest who cares for the needy, and he will help you."

"Do you know," Hadrian said, "when I fell in love with you?"

"No."

"When I saw you standing with the other women who had come to receive alms."

"How strange. I didn't know you noticed me that day."

"I did. The veil fell from your head, back on your shoulders, and your face and golden hair were like a flower blooming against the black of your gown. A flower looking up at me. I wanted to kiss you then, but I was so shy it was all I could do to take your name. But every day I waited in agony for you to appear. I knew you were pregnant."

"Did you?" She was surprised. "I thought I had everyone fooled."

"No," he said. "I may not have known a lot about women, but I certainly had seen enough of them in my work among the poor. I can tell when the lady is breeding. I could tell the lady something else, too. No scar will ever make you ugly to me."

Lucilla would have argued but she found she was being kissed, and in a few moments she wasn't disposed to argue any longer.

Later, in her bedroom, she made him look at her breast.

"God," he whispered. "The pain."

"It doesn't matter now," she said. "But I confessed," she said. "There are certain things—"

"No," he said. "No more—not tonight." He took the lamp from her hand and blew out the flame.

"For that, I will see to it Charles wears the iron crown. Wait, my love, wait and see if I don't.

"You are my only love and when we part, however we part, you may be assured you will be my last—as you were the first. Forever."

Near dawn she woke him. "I will help you find Gerberga."

"I had determined not to ask you," he said.

"No, the late Carolman's wife and her two sons are the crux of the matter. Those boys are legitimate heirs to the throne of Francia. Even if Charles unseats Desiderius, all his skill in statecraft and his might in battle may well come to nothing. Time is on Gerberga's side and well she knows it. If she can evade Charles, she will not only keep the Lombard cause alive, but she and her sons will become a focus for every unhappy magnate in Francia. All who hope to unseat Charles or even cause difficulties for him will turn to her. And it doesn't help matters that she has more claim to be the legitimate ruler of Francia than Charles himself."

"I don't know," Hadrian said. "The boys are children yet, and these barbarian kingdoms won't accept a child as a ruler."

"Why not?" Lucilla asked. "They did once. The lady Fregundis got the support of the king's nobles and brought the sons of Clovis to power in Francia, and they were only children."

"Gerberga is not another Fregundis," Hadrian said. "She has neither that redoubtable lady's intelligence nor, for that matter, the trust of the notables who decide matters for the Frankish realm."

"No, I quite agree. She can only cause trouble. She will do that. She already has, a lot of trouble. And each day those sons of hers grow older and in no long time will be excellent candidates for king-ship. Charles himself was only sixteen when he succeeded Pepin le Bref as king. No, my dear, I have been investigating on my own. She has slipped away from Pavia to . . . no one knows where. Probably with Desiderius's son Adalgisus; he is said to be her lover, and certain it is that he hopes to advance her cause.

"Scheming bitch," Lucilla whispered. "He is blinded by the thought of not only wearing the iron crown of Lombardy but being the de facto king of Francia when she sits on the throne ruling in the name of her two sons. My love, men aren't the only ones who can whisper false promises to achieve their ends."

Hadrian chuckled softly. "I won't deny that. You will be my only love."

"Forever?" Lucilla asked.

"That is true. And sometimes I wish it were not so, but it is," he answered sadly.

"Oh, my love, whatever my fate, live your life and love again. You taught me how to love; teach someone else, when I am gone.

"For I will not help you find Gerberga out of devotion to you, but because I have been a player in this game of power for too long to rise and yield up my place at the table to another. It is entirely fitting that a peasant girl would traffic in the sport of kings."

A S EVENING APPROACHED, REGEANE FOUND HER-
self in a wilderness. She was becoming very weary. She'd been
on her feet for the better part of two days and nights. She had used up
a lot of her physical resources: not all by any means, but a lot.

The Po valley was one of the richest parts of Italia. But though
productive, much of it had succumbed to the pervasive depopulation
and neglect that haunted the remnants of the once-great empire.

What had been wrong with them, this people of gaudy magnificence, that their accomplishments had turned to chaos so quickly?
Such an analysis was beyond a hungry, weary wolf.

Because she was hungry now, very hungry, the carrion consumed by her confederates upstream was beginning to seem attractive
in hindsight. If not to the fastidious woman, then to her sister of
moonlight.

The land around the river was turning quickly into fen and marsh
as the river continued its snakelike course through the wetlands. The
silver wolf found herself swimming as often as walking. She was
sighting a lot of ruins. They were slowly being engulfed by the
marsh. Most were only tumbled stone overgrown by willow, water
oak, giant reed, and cattails, but from time to time a roofless house,
the inside filled with green weeds, would stare at her with eyeless
windows from the other bank.

In the distance the sun was sinking into a ledge of smoky clouds
riding just above the horizon. The air was warm now in the valley of
the Po, and occasionally she was troubled by a mosquito. The pools
were filled with waterfowl, ducks and geese of all kinds, but the
hungry wolf had no idea how to hunt them.

The woman, however, was able to admire them as they took
wing at the mere sight of her. She was wondering if she had another
hungry night ahead of her and metaphorically shaking her head over
the deficiencies in her wolfish education, when she saw the town.

The ruins spread out on both sides of the river. Broken stones,
solitary columns, fragments of a forum with its shattered temples long
robbed of anything of even the slightest use to anyone—a melan-
choly sight in the slanting golden light of the late afternoon. The
woman sighed. The wolf tested the air.

For brigands, she told her companion. Ruins were not charming but sinister places, often unpleasantly populated after dark. The more dangerous outcasts of her world often found shelter in them.

The wolf, still in the shadows of the overgrown riverbank, tested the air again. No, nothing, but this place bothered her. Why? She had no idea.

She pushed into and among the shattered stone blocks that once housed the town. No, nothing human could live here. All that remained of the town was part of the marsh already. She found herself leaping from one small stone island to another. She paused on one, wider and fatter than the others, to get her breath and look down into the water. A big fish rested in its shadow, slowly moving its fins to hold its position in the sluggish stream. Regeane had learned fishing after the manner of wolves from Matrona. Within moments, she'd caught, killed, and consumed her dinner and was relaxing on the big stone block, basking in the warmth of the late afternoon sun.

Now, a den.

The Romans had bridged the river here. The arches were still standing. Roman engineering being what it was, they were probably good for another thousand years. The river hadn't destroyed the bridge but spread around it, engulfing the town. Where the bridge once terminated near the forum, it passed under an arch topped with what once must have been a guard post overlooking the drowned forum. A few leaps from block to block and a short swim brought her to the guard post.

The guard post had been reached by a narrow stone stair that now began in water and went up the top of the arch onto a platform. The wolf couldn't climb the stair, but the woman could—and did. It was difficult and the stones were slippery and damp, but when she reached the top she found she could survey the countryside for miles around. She was also dressed in webwork of white, flowered waterweed.

Well, the woman thought, *not so strange.* She'd been covered by fern on her journey through the other world. The waterweed was equally fresh smelling and beautiful.

The sun was touching the edge of the horizon and slightly obscured by the sooty clouds, but their shadow was more than compensated for by the metallic purple, red, and gold reflections thrown back by what she could see from here were wide wetlands, both open and forested, inhabited by a rich variety of birds, fish, and no doubt deer, wild boar, and other magnificent game. And far away in the distance, downstream, she saw the distinct towers of what she knew must be Pavia, faintly picked out against the blazing colors of the sunset by a few pinpricks of light.

Regeane lifted her robe of waterweed from over her shoulder and let it fall back into the tarn below; became wolf; turned once, twice, three times, then four; lay down, dropped her brush over her face, and slept.

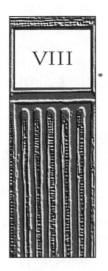

VIII

PAVIA WAS THE BREADBASKET OF THE LOMBARD kingdom. Here, on estates where slaves toiled raising crops on reclaimed wetlands, most of the wealth of this rich kingdom was concentrated. The Romans had adorned the city with the best of their manufacturers. Most of the people who lived in this jewel set in a countryside of magnificent abundance were either wealthy or slaves here to tend the needs of the wealthy or care for their property when they were absent. The city showed this, being a collection of magnificent villas, expensive public municipal buildings, and recreational establishments.

No one fortunate enough to enjoy amenities such as the racetrack, the arena, or the extensive and comfortable baths worried in the least about the ring of respectable but poor timber, stucco, and brick homes and shops that ranged the city, clustering on the inside and outside of the walls. The streets here were narrow, the houses were not spacious villas, and the people who lived in them worked for a living and were not in a position to enjoy the theater, the arena, and the baths.

The Lombards were of course not Romans, but when they took the town, they decided that living the way the departed Roman inhabitants had was a suitable prize for the conquerors. But by now the system was beginning to fray at the edges. Slaves were more expensive. The poorer class of the town were proving more difficult to control—much more demanding about their legal rights, for instance—than the rather cowed humiliores of Roman times. But the direct presence of the king and court were to some extent holding things together.

The hypocaust in the baths was still fired. Gladiators rarely fought in the arena, and the bishop kicked up a terrific fuss when one of them happened to get killed. Not because he sympathized with the poor man but because it should not be entertaining to watch blood be shed. But so long as they stuck to pagans, the elderly prelate didn't get in too much of a snit. And if all else failed, there were always public executions and runaway slaves to be punished, so the Lombards had been able so far to preserve some aspects of Roman culture. And since slaves could still be purchased to be worked to death on the vast estates, and the crops still brought in a good price, the Lombards felt they were doing their best to preserve classical society.

Maeniel was brought into the forum at the center of the city. He was still in chains. The cold-eyed commander of the king's guard was taking no chances. Maeniel had never seen Desiderius before, but he was immediately sure the tall, graying man looking at him from the steps of a converted temple of the goddess Roma must be the Lombard king.

The concept of the goddess Roma was a late classical invention. By then the entire empire had been a jackdaw's nest of odd religions, including not a few cults of quite human deified emperors. Someone, it is not recorded who, swept the whole mess together and decided that if there were disputes about how state worship was to be conducted, the best and safest thing to do would be to throw a few sacrifices and a lot of incense at a personification of the Roman state apparatus from time to time; thus, if questions arose as to where the loyalties of individuals or groups lay, they could cover themselves by saying they paid homage to the goddess Roma.

She was a sort of generic stand-in for antique gods, dead emperors, the whole gang from Olympus, local spirits evil and good, fairies, trolls, kobolds, incubi, succubi, gnomes, dwarves, tommy-knockers, and anything and everything that happened to go bump in the night, whose propitiatory rites might have gotten somehow neglected, overlooked, ignored, or just plain forgotten. The temples looked good and the votary wasn't worshiping anything or anyone who ever could have existed, and only those really crazy Christians could possibly object to tossing a little incense on the coals.

This particular temple was now a Christian cathedral. The goddess, cosmopolitan that she was, probably never turned a hair. But the new bell tower looked awkward near the fine, late Roman concrete, marble, and brick basilican edifice.

Maeniel sighed and dismounted. The chains dragged.

Twelve rather steep marble steps led up to the large double bronze doors. The captain of the king's guard poked the business end of a spear at the small of Maeniel's back and said, "Move."

Maeniel, not wanting any closer acquaintance with the spear, *moved,* up the steps, across a narrow porch, and through the bronze doors. The bishop, or someone dressed impressively enough to be a bishop, aspersed him with holy water and blessed him as he passed. Since Maeniel didn't give off sulfur fumes, burst into flames, or vanish in a cloud of smoke, both the bishop and the king decided it was safe enough to follow him up the aisle into the church.

The king took a seat on one side of the altar and the bishop on the other. Maeniel looked at each one of them. The look was wolfish, but they apparently didn't take it as such. Behind him, Maeniel heard the sounds of people crowding into the church.

The Lombard lords and ladies had priority. They and their servants—carrying fans, chairs, stools, smelling salts, nosegays of herbs against contagion, and last but certainly not least, food and drink—got all the best seats near the altar. Behind them the townspeople pushed their way into the spaces left clear by the nobility until every nook and cranny of the building was packed full.

Maeniel waited. In the interim, he bowed his knee to Christ, saluting him as the most powerful of all gods and paying his respects. Then he rose to his feet. The chains clanked when he went down and again when he rose; otherwise the church was silent.

The king chose to speak first. "My lord Maeniel, what are you doing in my kingdom?"

Maeniel answered truthfully, largely because he'd spent a lot of time trying to come up with a convincing story to explain his activities to the king and hadn't, even after a good many hours of serious effort, been able to think up an even halfway believable story.

"Your majesty, I was endeavoring to spy out the disposition and number of your troops in order to bring the intelligence to the Frankish king Charles."

"This is not a secret," Desiderius replied. "I have reinforced Ivrea and Susa. He must come by one route or the other. I will be waiting for him."

"So I saw," Maeniel said.

The king nodded. He was older than Charles by some years, his dark hair was threaded with gray, and an air of weariness and doubt hung about him.

He will lose, Maeniel thought. *I can see it in his face. He doesn't have the self-assurance he should have to defeat the Frankish king. He doesn't have the self-assurance any king must, to maintain his position. I have chosen the right side. Whatever my fate, this man is doomed.*

"An honest answer," Desiderius said.

"I know," Maeniel said. "I couldn't think of a good lie."

A soft titter of laughter swept the church.

"Very well," Desiderius continued. "What then am I to think of the other stories told of you?"

"Oh," Maeniel said. "What stories?" He tried to sound guileless. He didn't quite succeed.

"That you are a powerful sorcerer in league with the devil, able to change your shape at will from man to beast and back again, and have come not to gain knowledge of my military plans, but to take my life," the king said.

Maeniel took a deep breath and answered as well as he could. "My lord king, I have no designs on your life. I am a soldier, not a paid assassin. And I know nothing of the devil. Nor, if such a being exists, am I in his debt."

Someone laughed.

Maeniel recognized Hugo. "Oh, well," he said. "I thought you'd be here, Hugo. Why don't you step out where I can see you?"

Hugo laughed again. "I think not."

"You're smart," Maeniel said. "Because if I ever get my hands on you—"

"Be silent," Desiderius said. "A clever answer, my lord Maeniel, but only a partial one. If you please—answer the whole question."

"I am not a sorcerer," Maeniel said. "And you may place what trust you like in the tales this deluded fool tells, but I would not lay a wager on the veracity of any statement coming from his lips."

"Very well," the king said. "Then you deny his charge?"

Maeniel felt the blood turn cold in his veins. The king lowered his eyes and wouldn't meet his gaze. *A trap,* Maeniel thought. *A trap.* He was wearing the mantle they'd given him last night. Naptha. At a touch of the wax light in Hugo's hand, it burst into flame.

The wolf took him with the full strength of mindless mortal terror as his clothing burst into flame. Maeniel's fetters and flaming clothing landed in a heap on the church floor, and the gray wolf was restrained only by the iron collar around his neck.

The chain brought him up short and at midleap, and the captain of the king's guard brought the butt of his spear down hard on the wolf's skull. Hard enough to kill, but there was enough life left in the wolf's body to bring him through the change and leave him lying on the church floor in the human shape, bleeding from both the nose and mouth and deeply unconscious.

THE SILVER WOLF WOKE TO THE TRAMP OF FEET ON the bridge and then remembered there were no human feet within fifty miles, and yes, there were arches but no bridge. *The dead,* she thought. *This ruin is a place of the dead, as Cumae was.* She rose up woman without willing it and found herself looking at the dark world.

She could see the bridge as it once stood and, when she turned, the city forum with its marble square was intact, but all except the city was black. She could see no moon or stars but only the Roman cohort on the bridge: their commander and the men who followed. She was deeply puzzled by their appearance. They must be Roman, the temples and the forum all proclaimed a Roman place, but the armor and weapons they carried were archaic. Triple-ring breastplates, spears, single-edged chopping swords, long laminated wooden shields—the exteriors were painted but there were no colors in this world—helms with thick cheekpieces and feather crests. A wolf's head bared its fangs at her from each shield. The centurion, the leader, carried no shield but wore three feather crests.

"I am," Regeane asked, "with the dead?"

"Dead and forgotten," the centurion said. He sounded proud of the fact.

"I am not dressed," she said.

"I am not alive," the centurion answered. "But I will lend you my mantle." He pulled it off and tossed it up to her.

Regeane wrapped herself in the all-purpose garment and descended the steps. They led her to a guard room—unattended, to Regeane's relief—and she turned through the door and walked out to the bridge that wasn't there.

The centurion stood with his men. Looking at him, Regeane couldn't repress a shudder. He was an eyeless, lipless mummy, the dried skin stretched tight across his bones. His men were no better. They each wore their death wounds: part of one's face was simply missing, another had a terrible wound that nearly amputated his leg and a cut throat. Regeane tried not to look too closely at the rest.

"We held the bridge," the centurion said, "while our commander and his son retreated. They avenged us on the Carthaginian. We are content, we are honored to keep the bridge. We struck away the wedge that held the rock that crushed our enemies. Rome became great. Had we not fallen, the west and all subsequent time would have been different. But we were asked and were willing to pay the price."

"It's dark here, though." Regeane glanced away into what was, but for the bone white buildings of the bridge and town, an impenetrable darkness surrounding her and the soldiers. "Dark," she repeated, "and so cold. Where are the moon and the stars, the wind, the midnight shapes of trees, the soft rush of water, and the silken feel of grass? You were men and you remember the sun."

"Yes," came the answer. "I remember the sun when it was not cruel."

Regeane saw a vineyard sloping down to a lake that caught the colors of sunrise over misty rows of vines bejeweled with clusters of moonstone, amethyst, and sapphire fruit. Then the vision changed, and she saw a man dying in the sun on an X-shaped cross: the centurion. His eyes were gone and the boiling heat tightened the skin on his bones.

"I was the last. I cut the throats of the wounded, but the Carthaginian was angry that the Roman commander got away and I died as you saw. But my spirit lives on, a thing to ponder—and you summoned it. Sometimes we must build with boundless sorrow."

"I can't believe that," Regeane whispered, but the Roman and his men were gone and the wolf sank into a deeper sleep. When she awoke she found herself looking out across the marshland's open water at the rising sun. She was lying on one of the blocks that had floored the town forum and was wrapped in the stained, tattered remnants of a scarlet cloak.

THIS MUST ONCE HAVE BEEN A CISTERN, MAENIEL was thinking, like the prison in Rome. He'd seen it long ago on one of his journeys there. Seen it and smelled it: a hole in the ground. The prisoner stepped off into the pit. The executioner waited below. No executioner here this time, but he didn't think the king would show any mercy. He sat up. His head ached, he was naked, there was dried blood on his face and chest.

He was wary, though. Still a little dizzy from the blow, he checked his immediate environment carefully with all his senses, wolf and human. He could just see.

The prison was in the form of a flat-bottomed bottle; high above, a round cover, about three feet across, was the only entrance he could see. The sides of the bottle widened, sloping outward from the entrance at the neck, and formed a round space about ten feet across at the bottom. It was covered with sand. Very soft sand. And then he saw something else that made his skin crawl. There were gratings, heavy ones, set into the walls on either side of the cell.

No, it hadn't been a cistern. It was a cistern.

He rose to his knees. A voice on the other side of the grating asked, "Are you comfortable?"

He recognized the king's voice. "Hardly," Maeniel said. "It's cold, I'm naked, and I could use a little wine and something to eat."

"Too bad," Desiderius said. "But you will just have to make do. At least unless you teach me how to do that trick."

"What trick?"

"Oh, for heaven's sake. Please, don't play the fool. The trick I saw you do—not only I, but half the town and the entire court. We all saw you change yourself into a wolf."

Maeniel didn't answer. He was silent.

"Amazing," the king continued. "You won't admit it."

"No."

"Man, the fact that you are alive now is a tribute only to my insatiable curiosity."

"Indeed."

"Certainly," Desiderius answered. "The bishop can't wait to burn you. The captain of my guard wants to have you strangled. Your friend Hugo made some suggestions; rather imaginative ones, I might add."

"Predictable."

"Yes, and equally lethal as the other suggestions, though somewhat more painful. After all, you strangled his father."

"Yes, yes, I did; probably one of my more useful and virtuous actions. I cannot regret it." Then he laughed. "I doubt if Hugo does either. I think he was more pleased than not to be rid of his bad-tempered, drunken, scheming sire. He was probably overjoyed to snatch up whatever wealth the vile old scoundrel was hoarding and flee the city. If you must know, the pope and I looked high and low for him, and he could by no means be found. He probably only discovered his bereavement when he woke up sober one morning and realized he had no more money. By all means, keep him near you. I would rather caress a viper."

The king chuckled. "You are indeed a master of dissimulation. He warned me about that. But I, as you, digress. What is the trick of it? How do you become the wolf?"

"I do not—as you say—become the wolf. I am the wolf, only sometimes I seem to be a man. And in the interest of both truth and brevity, I will say now I cannot teach you how to skin turn because I don't know how I do it myself. I simply do, and she who gave me my name and power didn't provide an explanation."

"It is from the demonic then? This power of yours?" The king sounded eager to have Maeniel incriminate himself.

"I know nothing of daemons. I have never met one. Nor do I quite know what you Christians mean by the word. I do say that if you label everything you don't understand demonic, the world you see will be filled with evil."

"You are not a Christian, then?"

"No."

"Would you accept baptism, if given the opportunity?"

Maeniel was about to reply with a snarl of fury when his human side reined him in sharply. This chance was too good to miss. He'd already concluded there was no good way out of this cell. If he could persuade this king to believe he might be converted, the process of instruction and baptism might offer an opportunity to escape. Once without chains and in the open . . .

"Why?" he replied.

"To save your soul, of course."

No, he didn't like this, and he didn't trust the king's intentions. He'd been tricked once. This had the overripe odor of another trick. "Don't make me laugh," he said. "My head is still sore and it hurts my nose. The best you will get from me is a ransom, your majesty. I have a lot of money; content yourself with that. When Charles crosses the Alps, you will need it."

He heard an indrawn breath from beyond the iron screen.

"You reject my offer of an opportunity for salvation? What contumacious obstinacy! Consider your eternal soul."

"It's not my soul I'm worried about," Maeniel said.

Beyond the screen he heard a door slam, and then the slow creaking of a gate being raised. Maeniel called the wolf but only for a few moments. The beast offered strength and resignation. A look into the eternal dark that held no human terrors, no heaven, no hell. Long ago he had simply seen himself as part of the world, his behavior for good or ill determined by what he was and not by any code imposed by others, and he found strength in this knowledge.

The man would struggle. The man didn't know how not to struggle. But the wolf would center him with the knowledge and confidence of the night hunter's peace with the changing world and his eternal assurance of his place beneath the stars and among them.

I have lived as well as I can. I am content. Then he abandoned the wolf because water cold as death was pouring in through the grating and beginning to fill the cell.

REGEANE PULLED THE TATTERED MANTLE FROM around her body and became wolf. The Roman said she'd summoned him. She was not sure what that meant. Once before she'd traveled in the land of death and another man had left her a token. So she became woman again and folded the mantle carefully, pushed it into a deep crack in the stone.

She looked out over the water and took a deep breath. The air was fresh and cool, too cool. She rubbed her arms uncomfortably. They were broken out in gooseflesh, but she clung to the woman shape for a few moments longer, drinking in the beauty the dream had denied her. How terrible to be sealed forever in darkness.

The water mirrored the changing morning sky, gold at the sun-struck center, then green and blue at last at the edges. Reeds, brush, cattails, and willow were black silhouettes against the burgeoning light.

Sometimes we must build with boundless sorrow.

Remingus—that was his name. She knew but didn't know how she knew; that's what Remingus had said. The phrase haunted her. He had spoken to her across the surely impenetrable barriers of time and death.

If you call me, I will come.

The whisper was so soft she could barely hear it. Paper rustling against paper, or a serpent's scales moving over rock. She looked toward Pavia. Against the violet red and purple of the dawn, those few pinpricks of light still glowed, already almost extinguished by the breaking day.

Then she was wolf, warm coat glowing, burnished by the new light. Within a few moments she had found a fish, breakfasted, and was already on her journey. She spoke to Maeniel. *Be alive. Wait for me.* She tried to will it as she hurried on.

IN ROME LUCILLA BREAKFASTED WITH DULCINIA. A buttermilk cream cheese with fruit and boiled eggs in a pepper and onion sauce; a well-watered white wine accompanied it.

"You're being very unpleasant, sister mine," Dulcinia told her gently after a few moments' conversation about the weather, spring vegetables appearing in the market, and those families still able to withdraw to country estates to escape the oncoming hot months.

"How so?" Lucilla contrived to look surprised.

"Don't you dare!" Dulcinia said. "Half of Rome knows. No, not half—all of Rome not senile, below the age of two, or severely brain sick knows that he visited you and where he spent the night. What happened?"

Lucilla stirred in her seat, looking away from Dulcinia and out over the morning green. They were just inside, and the folding doors to the triclinium had been pushed back. Sudden tears appeared in her eyes.

Dulcinia drew in a deep breath. She'd known Lucilla a long time and loved her. "No. Don't tell me he behaved . . . badly."

"No. He didn't. He said he loved me, would always love me, and then I'd say from the amount of ardor he brought to our lovemaking, he proved that nothing that happened made the slightest bit of difference to him."

"Yes, at the Lateran Palace they said he'd returned all smiles and seemed very happy."

"Yes, my dear, and so am I. But he did acquaint me with one disturbing fact. Gerberga has vanished."

"Politics again." Dulcinia sighed.

"When I met him," Lucilla said, "politics was one of his chief interests, and I quickly became enamored of the game. If I hadn't, I don't think our relationship would have prospered. Even then the pro-Frankish party was beginning to groom him for high office, and I could see any woman who wanted to gain his love and keep it must take her place at the table. We rose together.

"And I cannot say I regret my ambition, when I remember my father's farmhouse with its endless work, filth, screaming children, half-starved livestock. My mother died of overwork and childbearing before she reached your age, Dulcinia.

"The minute one of us girls' hips began to spread and her breasts started pushing out the front of her dress, my father began looking to sell her to the highest bidder even if it were to the slave dealers from Ravenna. My sister went that way, and . . . and . . . yes: so, my dear, did I. And considering what I saw of those leering friends of my father's—" Lucilla broke off. Her eyes had taken on a hardness that frightened Dulcinia. Her fists were clenched. She looked down at her hands, relaxed her fingers. In a few places her nails had bitten into her palms and drawn blood. "I must find Gerberga and that son of Desiderius, Adalgisus."

"All I can see is that you are betting heavily on Charles doing some very difficult things . . . Bringing an army across the Alps, for instance. Even under the Romans, that wasn't child's play," Dulcinia said.

"Yes, well, he has his part and we have ours. I prefer to concentrate on what I can control than on what I can't. Are you still in demand among all these barbarians?"

Dulcinia threw up her hands. "Yes, but—"

"No buts. I've already spoken to Rufus—"

"Lucilla, I can't help but be spotted as your agent. Our relationship is so well known no one even bothers to gossip about it any longer. I won't hear any news about Gerberga and her lover. No one will tell me anything."

"Yes, yes, yes, but your tiring woman, my dear, that's another matter. Oh, these women from every town and village will be dying to know what's new and all the rage at the courts in Constantinople and Rome. They will flock to have their hair done the way the Empress Irene does hers and find out what combination of oil of violets, myrrh, with a touch of rose, is current among the Greek ladies of easy virtue; and are stays made best of yew or hardened sinew, and how are they best sewn into silk to give minimum discomfort and maximum lift. Very complex, this business of being a woman, my dear, very complex.

"And credit me with being an expert in these matters of hair dressing, the uses and occasional exquisite abuses of face painting, and the lesser art of embellishment where paint does not belong. And I have a hundred recipes for perfumes, powders, and fragrant oils. I can even value jewelry, tell if it is silver, silver gilt, or gold—pure or alloyed—and have an excellent eye for stones, both precious and semiprecious. I can weigh a broach in my hand and say whether it is silver, gold, or plated pewter or even that impostor of impostors, gilt lead. I do believe I'm going to enjoy myself very much indeed."

"Yes," Dulcinia sighed. "Again this adventure is made for you. Did you say the lord Rufus is to accompany us?"

"Oh, no, Cecelia wouldn't let him out of her sight. Do you know he's made her a mask with a silver nose? And she wears it all the time.

"But he will lend us an escort of twenty-five stalwart soldiers, all tied to him by oath and holding lands in return for service. A bit better quality men than paid mercenaries. I didn't wish to take any chances with the safety of your person, either on the roads or in the cities."

Dulcinia nodded. "I'll go home and speak to my secretary about what invitations I've received and what inducements I've been offered to travel to the Lombard kingdom."

Lucilla's plan was fraught with danger for Lucilla. Dulcinia didn't like to think about what might happen if she were recognized or caught, but she had seen Lucilla move around Rome incognito and arouse little interest. Women's dress lent itself to disguise.

A woman wearing silk, gold, and expensive perfume was assumed to be one sort of person, while the same woman wearing a worn dress, a dark veil, and mantle was assumed to be another. People rarely questioned those assumptions.

Clothing was used to indicate social position, degree of wealth, and rank. It would be considered mad for someone not to use it for this purpose.

Women for hire, prostitutes, wore their own distinctive dress and painted their faces. They advertised their profession. As would the tiring women and personal maid to an artist like Dulcinia. She would find herself in almost as great a demand as her mistress, and Lucilla, with her skill and familiarity with all classes of people, would have no difficulty in passing herself off as such a woman.

She was going gray now, and Dulcinia knew if she put aside the vanity of hair coloring, expensive perfume, makeup, and corsets, Lucilla would seem almost another person.

Every city had its court notables and ruling family, and the women among them starved for gossip, fashion advice, news of the barbarian kingdoms and the Greek east; they would talk freely in front of her tiring woman. And they would tell her everything they knew. Oh, God, would they ever.

If her tiring woman couldn't find out where Gerberga was, no one could. And that was probably why Hadrian had given Lucilla the job of finding her. It wasn't the first time he was in a pinch and didn't care to let the right hand know what the left was doing.

Lucilla broke in on her thoughts. "My, what a disappointed face you're wearing."

"One thing we haven't talked about," Dulcinia said as she rose, "is what we are going to do about the queen of Francia if we do find her."

"Don't borrow trouble," Lucilla commanded. "Charles, as you astutely pointed out, has got to cross the Alps. We will have to make that decision when the time comes."

CHIARA WOKE WITH HER BED BEING VIOLENTLY shaken. "Help me, damnation on it. You must help me. They are killing him."

"Who? What? What him? Who is being killed?"

"The wolf."

Chiara recognized Hugo's guest, and she had been in the church with Hugo when Maeniel was tricked into revealing himself. "I'm not sure I want to save that creature," she began.

That was as far as she got. Hugo's guest flipped the bed on its side, dumping her on the floor. Chiara stifled a shriek. Her maid, as usual, was sleeping in an alcove nearby and her father was in the next room. She scrambled to her feet and began pulling on her shoes, soft leather things, almost sandals. Something took her by the hair and began to drag her through the door into the darkened corridor.

She got a good grip on the doorpost and spoke through her teeth. "You stop that. Now."

He did. She knew he had limitations on his strength. She wasn't sure what would happen if she set her will against his, but she didn't really want to find out—at least not now.

"Yes," she said. "Yes, I'll help you, only you've got to behave decently."

"I will, but you'd best come quickly because he won't last much longer."

Chiara snatched up her mantle and wrapped herself in it. "Where is Hugo?"

"In his bedroom gibbering with fear, a broken man. He is sure the wolf will kill him. That was why he arranged that filthy trick to get the creature to declare himself. I have news for that piece of dung. If the wolf doesn't kill him, I will," Hugo's guest raged.

"You don't want to do that," Chiara said as she ran quickly down the stairs, trying to be as quiet as she could. "You must need him for something, as well as the rest of us, otherwise you wouldn't restrain yourself. Where is Gimp?"

"Drunk in a taverna near the river. Just when I need him most."

In a few seconds they were out of the building. Chiara paused for a moment. The street was dark and deserted.

"My heavens, what is the hour?"

"Late," came the reply. "Hurry. I cannot comprehend what you silly humans do to time, which is after all more like a river than a segmented—"

"Don't lecture me. Where? Where do you want me to go?"

"To the forum. Run!"

Chiara ran.

Pavia was not a big city. A few moments later she was approaching the cathedral. "What if we meet the watch?" she gasped out.

"That will be his misfortune," Hugo's guest said grimly, "but we won't. He's at the same taverna with Gimp, also drunk."

She flew up the cathedral steps. The big bronze doors were closed and locked. "What now?"

"I go inside, lift the bar, and let you in." In less than a second he had done so. The bar was on a pivot. Once inside, Chiara let it fall back into the socket. Then she turned and faced the large, dark, empty church. "Oh, oooohhhh," Chiara said.

"As far as I can tell, we are alone," Hugo's guest said.

"Are you sure?"

"No, but if you see something, you will no doubt complain—as is your wont—and whether it be living or dead, I can chase it away. Hurry."

She was pushed forward. She hurried past the altar. Only one faint light burned there, a flickering sanctuary lamp. Hugo's guest snatched it up. An impressive feat, since it was suspended by chains from the vaulted ceiling. It seemed to fly down toward where Chiara was standing, then go before her, leading down into the crypt where the Lombard kings were buried.

Various gates and doors barred her way, but they all opened before her. She scurried across the crypt, a fairly dull place. The people of these times didn't go in for effigies or even exciting sarcophagi, as the Romans had. The Lombard lords and ladies were encased in plain stone boxes, all tastefully engraved with the name and rank of their occupants.

Chiara rolled her eyes a time or two, but the members of the Lombard nobility stayed put. When they reached the back of the crypt, another stair led down deeper into the ground. It was damp here. Damp and cold.

The sanctuary lamp hovered in the air before her, about five feet in front of her face. "Put it lower," she said. "You're blinding me. I have to see where to put my feet."

"Plague take all women," Hugo's guest said, but the lamp dropped down a few feet.

The steps were very narrow and seemed to be carved from the high rock that supported the cathedral. Chiara negotiated them cautiously, helped along by the fact that things grew brighter as she neared the bottom.

T HE GATE WASN'T VERY BIG, SO WATER DIDN'T FILL the chamber quickly. The river by rights ran through the cell rather than into it; the other grating was connected to a passage that returned the water from whence it came. But Maeniel soon saw the nature of the trap. Because the main hole that sealed the cell shut at the top was open, the swirling water rising moment by moment would bring him to the top, and when the water reached the top it would enter a short wellhead, a tube that led to the basement above, and rise almost but not quite to floor level. It would rise up and out of the cell but he wouldn't because it was covered at the top with an iron grating. The water would rise past the grating, and he would be trapped beneath it. And he would drown.

He had a few moments yet, riding the swirl of rising water, until he reached the grating. A few moments to contemplate his fate and wonder in passing who constructed this vicious trap. It allowed an observer above to watch the struggles of the individuals below the grating, watch them drown. He was calculating rather coolly that it wouldn't take long when he found himself looking up at the face of a girl staring down at him.

She was on her knees near the opening of the cistern. She knelt for a second, trying to find a way to release the grating, and quickly realized there was no way. It was latched; the bolt that opened it extended up the wellhead and was secured at ground level with a stout lock and chain. She pulled at it vigorously.

"No," Hugo's guest shouted at her. He forcibly turned her head to the right.

The gate that opened and closed the pipe that allowed the river to fill the cistern was raised by a simple pulley arrangement attached to a lever on the wall. Down, it lifted the iron plug that shut the pipe. Up, the heavy plug fell back of its own weight and sealed the pipe.

A simple, elegant arrangement, the fill pipe was high, the drainage pipe was low. Lift the iron plug, the river flowed in. It took two men to lift it. Release the lever from the down position, the iron plug dropped back in place and the chamber drained. Not as quickly as it filled, but it drained. And though it took two men to lift it, a child might drop it back.

Whatever this man might be, Chiara didn't want him to meet such a horrible end. She began to scramble to her feet.

Hugo's guest pushed her back down. "No," he said. To Maeniel, he said, "Can you hear me?"

"Yes," Maeniel answered. He was floating in the rising water just below the grating. He reached up and clamped his fingers around the bars. He was looking up at Chiara's face.

"I want," Hugo's guest said, "full power over your body including the change from man to wolf. I want to possess you as I do Hugo."

"You let him trick me."

"I did. I did," Hugo's guest howled. "But I didn't think they'd kill you this quickly. Now give me what I want, and I'll get you out—let you live."

"As your slave—"

"No. No, we will be partners. We will destroy these monkey things, these creatures of folly and cruelty, and the world will be as it was—at peace. Each with his own kind. And my people will return and worship me again."

"No," Maeniel said.

"No?" Hugo's guest sounded unbelieving. "No?" he echoed. "You will drown."

"Then I will drown," Maeniel said. "I would rather drown than have my life ruled by another. The life of a slave is to me no life at all."

"Die," Hugo's guest screamed. "Die in your stubborn stupidity. Die like the fool you are, wolf."

But he wasn't paying any attention to Chiara. She wrenched free of the grip he had on her shoulder. Hugo's guest screamed, a bear roar of rage and terrifying fury, but she was at the wall. The lever was secured in the down position by an iron pin set in a hole above the shaft. In one motion, she jerked the pin out and sent it clattering away across the floor.

The lever hung, quivering, as the swift water battered the heavy metal stopper. For a second, it looked like the plug might not fall.

But then it did, jerking the lever into an upright position. Maeniel found himself battering the grating as Chiara began to scream.

T HE CLOSER REGEANE GOT TO THE CITY, THE MORE settlement she found around the riverbank. It seemed plowed land more and more often encroached on the forest and marsh that surrounded the stream. She found herself traveling through the day, listening to her sister of moonlight. *Be cautious, don't be seen or heard unnecessarily.* So she drifted quietly, easing among the willows and water oak, close to the shore. She avoided soft soil that would take a footprint—or pawprint as the case might be. So silent was she that waterfowl feeding close to the banks paddled undisturbed in the shallows. Once, spurred by the woman, she paused to admire a mother wood duck with a flock of ducklings swimming near a deadfall close to shore. When they saw her, the mother's cry of alarm froze the babies into immobility and near invisibility among the reeds. Regeane moved on. She knew in neither shape would she have been welcome company, but she did feel they were less fearful of her as a wolf than they would have been as a human. *We know too many tricks,* she thought.

The wind was behind her—a thing she knew Maeniel would never allow—so she didn't sense what lay ahead of her until she blundered into it. The girl lay on the riverbank. She was naked, her body half in and half out of the water. The flies were already at work.

The wolf wanted to bolt. When Regeane questioned her dark companion, the wolf stated on general principles—or as close to a statement as the wordless creature could manage: *Let's get out of here!*

"No," the woman replied.

She began to search the riverbank.

The family was just ahead, two men and a boy, near a flat-bottom boat grounded in the shallows. They were all dead; except for knives and staves they all seemed to have been unarmed.

Death has stink. Regeane knew that, and it was polluting the warm spring air. Blood, feces, urine, the miasmic odors of the killers and the slain. Fear, rage, sex, the odors of spilled semen and thick, clotted blood. The wolf didn't have to be instructed about the motives of murderers.

Farther along the river, she found the second woman, older than the girl but still attractive. The girl's throat had been slashed, the ground soaked with blood near her head. The one farther along probably had been her mother. She had been surprised while washing clothes on a shallow rocky spot. The daggers that had pinned her still-living body to the riverbank while she was used were gone, and her blood had been washed away by the clear water. She lay in the shallows just below the surface, her face calm and eyes closed, no less than five stab wounds in her chest.

Just beyond where the woman lay, the silver wolf saw a road. The family must have kept the ford here, ferrying travelers across when the water was deep. Soldiers? Yes, there was iron in the complex of odors along the riverbank. Soldiers must have come to cross.

She trotted back and checked each corpse. Yes, five of them. Five signatures of men not dead. Signature odors; footprints, shod—these peasants had all been barefoot—and here and there a wisp of cloth, a thread caught on the new-flowering briars that flourished at the edge of the forest. They went the same way she was going, toward Pavia.

The wolf sat down and considered.

She needed clothing, but didn't want to get it this way. Still, a dress was a dress and the two women she'd seen wouldn't miss them. The woman had finished her laundry and it was drying on bushes near where her body lay. Regeane found a shift, skirt, and blouse, and improvised undergarments from a torn-up old shift that seemed to have been used as a nightgown.

She used the rest of the garments to cover the corpses. She pulled the two women's bodies out of the water and tried to arrange them decently, but since rigor was beginning to set in, there was little she could do. She finally settled for covering them all, including the men.

She found the house they had come from on higher ground overlooking the ford. It was empty. She looked inside only long enough to be sure there were no children who might have hidden nearby, and then walked on toward Pavia.

She'd braided her hair back and covered it with a veil. She knew the killers had gone the same road and she was afraid of coming upon them, but she didn't. They were mounted and must have been in a hurry to reach the city, because once finished with their murderous work at the ford, they had spurred their horses to a gallop and were long gone.

Mercenaries. Yes. The woman smiled bleakly. Desiderius would be hiring.

The sun was hot on her back but the walk wasn't a long one. When she reached the top of the hill, she saw that the city crowned the next rise. It was nested into the river curve just ahead, surrounded by orchards, croplands, vineyards, and gray-green olive groves, all basking in the fair spring sunlight.

She crossed a footbridge over a creek that flowed into the river. People were out and about, women in their yards, sweeping, shelling peas, even kneading bread in troughs near their doors. Men were busy, involved in cultivating fields and gardens and among the vines. Her passing caused no comment but she got a few long stares. Women alone were an unusual sight, but her veil, braided hair, and long over-dress proclaimed her a respectable girl on some private errand.

Regeane knew the rules: her eyes were downcast, and she avoided all of the masculine stares fixed on her, pretending, as was proper, that they didn't exist. The road quickly began turning into a street. Houses of timber and wattle and daub crowded on both sides. These weren't so public as she had seen in the countryside: they all had heavy wooden doors and few windows fronting the road. But she could still see a curtain or two move as she walked past. Just ahead loomed the gray stones of a Roman gate.

She hurried, uneasy with the almost squalid dwellings around her. She was regretting the river and the forest, the wilderness she'd left behind her. She was entering another wilderness now—a much more dangerous one.

She saw five men loitering in front of a tavern just outside the gates. The wolf knew them before the woman did, and the woman felt the hair stir at the back of her neck. Those were the ones. One muscular soldier had scratches on his face. The women must have put up a fight. Two others; nondescript, sandy haired, but their eyes gave her chills, empty and dead. One had a fresh, bloody bandage around his hand. And two not much more than boys, but with faces that said they'd left childhood behind a long time ago.

They studied her with calculating interest as she came closer and closer to the gate. She didn't think they'd try anything. There were too many people about. The tavern keeper was standing in his doorway, a clay cup in his hand. It was late now. The sun was high overhead but the jumble of houses was so high, two and three stories, that the streets were shady.

Regeane passed them, breathed a sigh of relief, and entered the gate. Two doors bound in iron stood open. There were no guards or any other signs of official presence. The houses on the sloping street inside were even taller than those on the outside and were even more inward facing, as in Rome. Only barred doors and high stone walls faced the street.

Regeane found herself climbing; the street canted up. From time to time she saw women looking down at her from second-floor balconies, but when she looked directly at them or paused as if to call out a greeting, they vanished back into their dwellings.

Regeane kept on walking, growing more and more uncertain as she did so. She'd given a fair amount of thought to reaching Pavia but not much to what she would do when she got there. She knew no one in the city. She had no money. A wolf perforce must travel light. She'd hoped to find a fountain. Women tended to congregate when they drew water. She might ask after the king and what prisoners had been brought to the city and where they were kept. But unlike Rome with its endless piazzas and fountains, this city seemed to have no public spaces. Unless you counted the tavern she'd passed, and she didn't care, as a woman alone, to approach that. And yes, as she hurried along, the wolf told her there were footsteps behind her.

The five at the tavern?

The wind was blowing up the street. Yes, they were distinctive. The wolf's mind could pick apart the sensory data the way the human hand sorts change. Two were together, the two youngest ones ahead of the rest. Yes, they had the most energy. They were the soberest. The other three were about half drunk.

Regeane lifted her skirts and began to run. They continued at the same pace. Her feet were bare. When she reached the top of the hill, she saw why they had been in no hurry. The street dead-ended into a small plaza. It was surrounded by houses all turning a blank face to the street and one small church of the kind the poor visit, with a simple, pillared porch and a low roof. On one wall beside the porch was a fountain, a pipe set in the wall that emptied into a stone basin.

Remingus stood beside it. He was no longer the corpse reclaimed from the cross where the Carthaginian had left him. No, he looked like a man. As she watched, he pulled off the old-fashioned legionary helmet. He was wearing a leather cap under it. He pulled off the cap and ran his fingers through perspiration-soaked hair. He reminded her a little of Maeniel, thickset with dark damp curls.

"At noon," she said, "under the sun." Yes, he was a being of awesome power.

"We are allowed to do this," he said.

"Allowed by whom?"

Remingus laughed. "They are coming." He pointed down the shady street. The square was filled with sunlight.

"I know," Regeane said. "I will have to kill them."

Remingus rinsed his helmet in the fountain, filled it at the pipe, and offered Regeane a drink. She drank. She hadn't known her thirst was so great.

He pointed to a narrow passage next to the church. She hadn't seen it because it was almost lost in shadow. "Where does it go?" she asked.

"To a small garden in back of the church. It's quiet there. No one can see you. All of the houses around it turn blank walls to the space."

Regeane drank again and nodded.

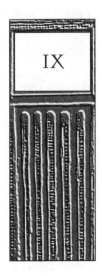

IX

I 'M NOT SURE I CAN KILL FIVE MEN," REGEANE SAID.
Remingus just laughed and said, "Catch them as they come
out of the alley. You can take them by surprise."

The first two entered the square. They made no bones about
their intentions and ran toward her. Regeane turned and ran down
the alley. It was rather long, stretching the length of the church. She
never reached the end because a door opened, then someone grabbed
her arm and pulled her inside.

Regeane, nonplussed, found herself standing in a small kitchen
with a tall, lean, grim-faced woman. She'd opened the door only
long enough to pull Regeane inside. She slammed it shut and threw a
big bolt.

From the outside, one of the men threw his shoulder against the
door. The woman snatched up a heavy iron frying pan and shouted.
"Son of a degenerate pig, go away or I'll brain you." She slammed
the frying pan against the heavy door.

Regeane could hear the men talking outside. One of the older
ones was remonstrating with them. "Don't be a fool. You have no
idea how many people might be in that house. Let it be, goddamn it.
Let it be. I don't plan to get killed here. Not over a woman."

Someone slammed a fist or a shoulder against the locked door.
This was followed by a cry of pain. "I told you, let it be."

There was another cry of pain and a string of curses. "I'm
bleeding, I'm bleeding."

"Try that again and you'll find that's only a scratch, you stupid bastard."

"I'll kick your ass so hard . . ." The voices trailed off as the men moved away.

"Sounds like they're leaving," Regeane whispered.

The old woman snorted. "I wouldn't be too sure. They probably just went back to the square."

The room was warm. Regeane found herself perspiring. There was a fire in one corner of the room. The smoke was vented by the Roman precursor of the chimney, a double wall with a vent near the fire that allowed heat and smoke to rise and exit outside of the building.

There were stone counters on the other three walls. Bread dough rose in a wooden trough in the center of a counter. It was very dim, but the room did have a window, so small Regeane hadn't seen it from the outside, just a narrow slit near the door with a grating over it.

"Fool girl," the woman said. "What did you think they were going to do when they got you alone in the priest's garden? Why didn't you go into the church?"

"They came upon me so quickly . . ."

"Yes . . . ," the woman answered. She sounded suspicious. "Well and good, but what are you doing wearing Mona's dress?"

L IKE MANY ANOTHER WOMAN WITH NO GOOD EX-planation for her behavior, Chiara took refuge in hysterics when the watchman found her in the forum in front of the cathedral. The watchman called the captain of the guard. He could do no more with Chiara than the watchman could. He called the king.

Desiderius arrived. He'd been up late drinking with his cronies, so at least two-thirds of the court mustered out trying to find out what all the excitement was about.

Chiara found herself just where she didn't want to be: the center of attention.

"Call her father," Desiderius said. "She's Armine's daughter."

Chiara was sobbing now in terror, not of Hugo's guest—he had, it transpired, done very little—but in complete despair of thinking up a really good explanation for her presence in the forum in her nightclothes.

Armine arrived. He gave Chiara short shrift. "You stop that right now, my girl. You never were a screamer; don't try to convince me you've started to come all undone at this late date."

Chiara calmed herself. "I must have been sleepwalking. Mother always said I was given to it as a toddler and—"

"Sleepwalking," Armine said. "And no, I never knew your mother to say any such thing. Sleepwalking . . . what are you? Angelina, the upstairs maid? She sleepwalked herself into becoming the mother of twins."

Chiara's face flamed. "I am not in the least like Angelina."

The bishop had just arrived in time to hear Armine's last statement and Chiara's angry denial.

"What have you done?" he shouted angrily at the captain of the guard. "Awakened me from my warm bed over a simple case of fornication?"

Chiara didn't know what fornication was, but she wanted nothing to do with it. "I don't know anything about forn—forn—whatever that was he said. The watchman woke me. He stank of wine. He frightened me. He began shouting at me. Everyone is shouting at me and saying I forn—forn—whatever that is. I didn't. I didn't do it—whatever it is."

Chiara was upset, really upset by now. Besides the uproar around her, she could hear the almost Homeric laughter of Hugo's guest. Peal after peal rang out over the noise of the crowd.

The bishop was an old man and was wearing a woolen gown and a nightcap. "I told you," he said waspishly to Desiderius, "not to entertain that sorcerer Hugo at your palace. Now look what he's done. Debauched the innocent daughter of one of your most faithful men. The blacksmith said he found that madman wearing the piss pot on his head yesterday. This silly besotted girl—" The bishop pointed at Chiara. "—rescued him from his own folly. Further, he carries on conversations with the empty air. All night long this necromancer consorts with daemons. The woman who lives beneath him says she fears for her soul's salvation, so loud are the sounds, the moans of the damned souls he commands. His own servant, Gimp, fears him like death."

The archbishop became so vehement that his nightcap fell off. Reaching for it, he lost his balance and only the captain of the guard's strong arm saved him from dashing his brains out on the stone floor.

The captain got little thanks for his pains. The archbishop cursed him roundly and called for his staff and chair. Both were fetched by his servants.

"Is this true?" Armine seemed thunderstruck. "Are you in love with this Hugo?" he asked Chiara.

"What?" Chiara screamed. "Hugo? You think Hugo and I are . . . Hugo? Hugo!" His outrage was nothing to Chiara's. "I'd rather make the beast with two backs with—with—a sick goat than with *Hugo*."

Hugo's guest sounded as if he was going to die.

"And you," Chiara said. Her eyes roamed around. No one was quite sure whom she was addressing. "You! You just stop it." Chiara tried to say something else, but all that emerged from her throat was a harsh croak. The captain of the guard gave her a cup of wine.

Desiderius was deeply annoyed; he wanted to get back to his drinking. Chiara was thirsty, and besides, she was certain she'd managed to make a complete fool of herself.

Hugo's guest told her, "I can't remember when I have been so entertained."

"I wish you weren't dead," she muttered into the wine cup between clenched teeth. "I'd like to kill you, too."

Hugo arrived, being supported by two members of the king's guard. It was clear even by torchlight that someone had beaten the snot out of Hugo. One eye was closed, the other barely open. His upper lip was swollen, his lower split. It was impossible to count his bruises and those were only the visible ones not hidden by his clothing. Hugo seemed only about half conscious, and he was rubber legged.

"Did you drown him?" Hugo asked Desiderius.

"Drown?" the Archbishop screeched. "Drown who?"

Desiderius looked dismayed.

"The wolf," Hugo said, spitting blood between his broken teeth.

The archbishop was on his feet, moving like a much younger man. He aimed a swing at the king's head that would probably have split his skull if the captain of the guard hadn't deflected it with his shield. The staff was sheathed in silver and had a lead weight in the handle.

Again the captain got little thanks for his pains. The bishop fetched him a whack with his staff and cursed him again. "You hell-bound pagan!" the bishop yelled. "I'll have you know my church is consecrated ground. I told you if I caught you drowning any more of your enemies in the basement of my church, I'd excommunicate . . . I'll deny the sacraments, I'll see you in hell. In hell—" The archbishop tottered toward the church.

Desiderius and the rest followed Hugo, carried along by the watch.

"I apologize," Armine told Chiara. "He couldn't possibly—I mean the man is in such a condition that . . . How? Why?"

When the crowd reached the subbasement, it was apparent no one was going to be drowning anyone for some time. The watchman peered down into the gloom where the stopper was fixed into the pipe that filled the cell. The chain that connected it to the lever was snapped off near the top of the handle. It dangled from the stopper into darkness.

The watchman made the sign of the cross and told the bishop, "When we tried to fish for the end of the chain with a pole, someone—some thing—began laughing."

The bishop called down into the cistern. "Is anyone there?"

"Yes," Maeniel answered. "Would you send down a bit of food and water? I'm hungry and thirsty."

"No," Hugo muttered.

"Daemons, daemons," the bishop muttered.

M ONA'S DRESS?" REGEANE REPEATED. "Mona's dress," the woman said.

"Her name was Mona?"

"Was?" the woman asked.

"She's dead," Regeane answered.

"Dead? She can't be dead. She's betrothed to my son." The woman grabbed Regeane by the shoulder. Regeane felt her nails bite. "Dead?"

"They're all dead," Regeane said. "I found them at the river. She, the older woman—"

"Itta."

"Yes," Regeane continued. "Itta had been washing clothes. I think her daughter—"

"Mona."

Regeane nodded. "I think her daughter was with her. The five men who followed me up the street—"

"Five? I saw only three."

"I think the others were behind them," Regeane said, "but they came across the river. I think they wanted the two women, but the men—I mean Itta's husband—"

"Alberic?"

"Yes," Regeane said, "and another man and boy—"

"Avitus and Alan, his brother and his brother's son."

"Yes," Regeane said. "It helps to give them names, I suppose . . . But in any case, when I got there they were all dead."

"No!" the woman shouted. "You're lying. You have to be."

Regeane heard a creaking at the back of the room. A stair was descending from the upper floor; as soon as it hit the ground a young man hurried down.

"All dead? Woman, what are you saying?" he shouted.

"My son," the older woman said. "My son, Robert."

"Dead," Regeane repeated. "All of them."

The boy ran out.

"No," the woman yelled after him, but he slammed the door in her face, saying, "Stay here, Mother."

"No, no, no," the woman whispered stubbornly.

"I think," Regeane continued, "they wanted the women. Their menfolk defended them, but they were no match for well-armed mercenaries, and—"

"It can't be. I was talking to Itta only yesterday at the fountain about the marriage. My son worried about them living at the ford, since it seems the Frankish king Charles will soon carry war across the mountains. He has some quarrel with Desiderius."

"Yes," Regeane said.

One narrow shaft of light entered through the window slit, creating a bar of gold on the trough filled with bread dough. "By now it's finished its first rise. It needs to be punched down and the pans filled. I can't waste the fire in the oven."

"Here, let me braid the dough," Regeane said. She followed the woman's directions, braiding as Matrona had taught her. That's what the loaves were: long braids heavy with olives, eggs, and oil. Regeane saw some like them hanging from wires near the fire grate.

"They keep a long time," the woman said, "and are good work bread. The men take loaves to the field with them. I braid so there will no quarrels about who got the largest share. I'm a baker; it's my business to sell bread."

And then unaccountably she staggered over to a stool in the corner and began to weep into her apron.

"Oh, no." Regeane went over and embraced her. "I wish I could have brought you better news. I'm so sorry. So very, very sorry."

After only a few moments, the woman dried her eyes, then pulled off the apron and went to get a clean one from a stack on the counter near the door. "Itta washed them," she said. "I bake, she did laundry." And then she began weeping again. Whispering over and over, "I can't stop. I just can't seem to stop. She was my best friend."

At the woman's direction, Regeane put on the apron and loaded the ramekins and two or three pots of stew into the oven.

"They leave them here to make use of the heat while I bake," the woman explained.

Regeane nodded, then closed and locked the door to the oven. When she was finished and washed her hands in a bucket, the woman spoke.

"You're a noblewoman."

"How do you know?"

The woman seemed annoyed. "No peasant girl has hands like yours."

Regeane studied her hands for a moment. "Yes," she said.

"Why are you here?"

"Desiderius imprisoned my husband, the lord Maeniel."

"Well then, you may soon have grief of your own. He is in the bottle."

"The bottle?" Regeane repeated.

"The cistern under the church. Prisoners seem to drown there."

Regeane rose, pressed her hand to her breast, and closed her eyes. "No."

"Yes."

"How?"

The woman explained the workings of the bottle to her. " 'Tis said the Romans built it to assure the city would have a good water supply if attacked, but no one will drink from it now. Too many who crossed the lord Desiderius have died there. There was a disturbance in the square last night, and it is said Lord Maeniel still lives. But who knows for how long?"

"Yes," Regeane whispered. "I have to get him out. Would the king hear a plea for mercy?"

"The storm from the mountains roaring over the valley knows more about mercy than that man. I will not say his name and never will again because if what you say is true, he killed my friend. He will never see any wrong his soldiers do. Never. We of the town have complained of their depredations in vain. We're supposed to be protected by laws. We insisted on our own laws when we conquered here and settled this valley, but he knows them not."

She spat on the floor and rubbed it in with her foot. "We are less than this to him.

"My great-grandfather raised his great-grandfather on his shield. We fought for him. We made him king. And he—he denies us. Beningus the law speaker will be here tonight. We have a meeting of our . . . burial society. We will see what he says about this.

"What is your name?"

"Regeane, daughter of the Saxon lord Wolfstan."

"Yes, I have heard of you. No bad things; only good. I am Dorcas, baker of Pavia. I follow the trade my father and husband did before me. We are not well met, but I am glad to know you."

HUGO'S GUEST VISITED MAENIEL. MAENIEL WAS furred against the cold; the underground cell was chilly.

"What do you want?" he asked Hugo's guest rather unceremoniously, once he'd turned human; it wasn't comfortable. "I hope you didn't hurt the girl."

"No," the bear howled. "She's one of the few humans I rather like. Tell me, can you see me?"

"Yes, I see a sort of bear shadow, and if you'll excuse me, I will call the wolf." He did and sat, his tail curled respectfully around his body, listening to what the bear said next.

"Let me in, I ask you one more time. I think I can probably still save you, but you must offer me the use of your body."

The wolf rose and turned his back on the bear, curled up, dropped his tail over his nose to keep it warm, and went to sleep.

"They will burn you," the bear shouted. "Even if I am able to keep them from repairing the pipe, they will find another way. I am the only thing that is keeping them away."

The wolf opened his eyes, looked past his rather large brush at the bear.

The bear stormed out, rattling the grating over the cell, all the pipes, and anything loose in the chamber above.

The guard, the watchman Sextus, was above, sitting on the basement steps. He was, as usual, about half drunk, but he sobered immediately at the bear's bellow of rage and made the sign of the cross. His hand grabbed for the wine jug but the bear got it first, lifted it, and hurled it full force at the wall next to Sextus. To the watchman's eyes, the wine jug seemed to leap into the air and explode, drenching him with clay fragments and wine.

The bear stormed out of the church, flinging open the doors before him. Seeming and sounding like a destructive wind gust.

Sextus fled screaming.

REGEANE HELPED DORCAS PREPARE FOR THE MEET-ing. It would take place here in Dorcas's shop. A table was placed on trestles, and Dorcas and Regeane carried benches down from above. The stair was constructed so that it could be pulled up and the top part of the house cut off from the basement.

Regeane found the upper living quarters comfortable and attractive. Windows in the back of the room looked down on a courtyard with a fountain and a garden where herbs and vegetables grew, or at least had been spaded up and were ready for planting. Rosemary, thyme, borage, garlic, and other winter crops filled the herb garden.

The side walls had no windows, as the house shared them with the buildings on either side. The other set of windows overlooked the street. Regeane noticed these had heavier shutters than the inside windows. This floor had benches and a rather fine table and folding chairs, and even a few books on a shelf against the wall.

Dorcas pointed to a stair, a rather steep one rising along the wall. "Sleep rooms up there. If you won't mind sharing my bed tonight, I offer you the hospitality of the house."

"Thank you," Regeane said. All the walls were hung with tapestries of Dorcas's own making and in the corner there stood a large loom. "Do you know, I never learned how to use one."

"A noblewoman like you?" Dorcas sounded surprised.

"They are expensive, and my uncle and his son spent all the money," Regeane said.

"I hate to see a smart woman sacrificed to worthless men."

"I think that's what happened to my mother, but then she listened to my uncle, and . . ."

"And what?"

Regeane found herself in a corner. She certainly didn't want to tell the story of how her father died. "She repudiated her first husband. Folly! He was rich and my uncle hoped to get some of his money. I suppose he succeeded to some extent, but it never came to any good."

"Such schemes don't," Dorcas said. "Money is best earned. I know. I've worked all my life." Then she began weeping again.

Regeane tried to offer some comfort but Dorcas pulled away. "A lot of good it's done me, all that work. I had a bit saved and had mind to offer the money to Itta. She could have bought a house in town and set up as a washerwoman. She did well at it. She could have paid me back. Oh, why? Oh, why did I delay? My own grasping selfishness caused my best friend's death."

Regeane found herself crying in sympathy and embracing Dorcas. "Say rather cautious and afraid. The world is a cruel place. Don't blame yourself. How could you know such a dreadful thing as this would happen? You did your best. I'm sure she needed the work you gave her."

None of this seemed to help Dorcas much. Regeane thought of the people she loved, her women friends Lucilla, Barbara, Matrona. How would she feel if one of them were struck down in such a brutal, meaningless way? She didn't know how she could endure it either.

Then she saw Robert coming up the street. He was riding a mule. She and Dorcas went down to meet him.

CHIARA WENT WALKING IN THE PALACE GARDEN. It was, at present, near the end of winter, a rather bleak place, but some early flowers she didn't recognize were beginning to push their heads above the soil. A fine clump of some sort of white and purple mountain lilies was coming up at the base of trees. Quince and apple blossoms were swelling, readying themselves to open. The long catkins of the oak, ash, and willow decorated their branches with green chains of wind-pollinated flowers before the new leaves were ready to make an appearance. The air from the mountains that glowed almost like a mirage in the distance, lifting white and blue peaks against the warm azure sky, was cool and carried a hint of dampness from the river, a smell of growing things pushing themselves up from winter's new-mulched soil.

"It's beautiful," she whispered as she closed her eyes and let the sun warm her face.

"Yes," Hugo's guest answered.

She gave a snort. "You."

"Yes, again."

"Did you do those awful things to Hugo?" she asked sternly.

Hugo's guest chuckled.

"It's not funny."

"Yes, it is. Hugo is a piece of shit. Don't waste your sympathy on him. Hell, if I hadn't stopped him, the son of a bitch would have raped you in your own garden."

He was right. Hugo might not have been able to commit successful sexual assault—Chiara would have both fought and screamed—but he would have tried and might have injured her in the process. Chiara chewed at her lip. "You're right," she finally said, "but what happened?"

The bear growled.

"You stop that," Chiara said. "Now, what happened? Can't you see I don't think I'm special? I worry. What would you do to me if you got angry?"

"Nothing, and you know it. I couldn't have been more enraged than I was last night."

Chiara giggled.

"You stop that. I don't care to be laughed at. It's too demeaning."

"It tickled."

The bear swirled again. "Chiara, you creatures draw the energy you live on from the food you get. Plants somehow get it from the sun. If they are too long in darkness, as once happened to the earth, they die."

"Where did the sun go?" she asked, slightly horrified.

"Stop asking me to explain one thing while I'm trying to explain another." The bear, Hugo's guest, sounded waspish.

Chiara listened, all attention. "Please continue." She sounded so very sedate and adult, the bear found himself mollified and amused. He couldn't smile, but a soft ripple of laughter rolled over his being, and Chiara saw the shimmer.

"Very well." He continued, "I—I draw my energies. Specifically," he added because she still looked a bit horrified, "from my relationship with sentient beings. Without them I die."

"Die?"

"I'm not sure, Chiara, if death is the right word to apply to me. Perhaps I simply go dormant and then wake again . . . under certain conditions."

"Mysterious?"

"You are so young, Chiara. All life is a mystery. Born in poisoned air from the clash of lightning, wind, and rain above a raging sea."

"God made it?" Chiara asked breathlessly.

"I cannot say because I do not know. If God . . . The tools he used to make the universe are beyond mortal comprehension. Far more complex than these simpleminded priests would have you believe."

"I don't . . . understand."

"No, and you never will. I don't either, and I am a whole millennium older than you are."

"A millennium is a thousand years," Chiara said.

"Yes."

Chiara looked out over the river and toward the mountains. "A thousand years," she whispered to herself. "A thousand years? No wonder you think Hugo is a fool. What must you think of me?"

"I would think Hugo a fool if he lived a millennium of millennia. You? No—but only very, very young. And I envy you and your kind your engagement with the earth, with what to me is an alternative reality, even though it means you must die."

"Yes, I suppose that's true, but on a day such as this, death seems very far away."

"Is it very beautiful?" he asked almost wistfully.

"Can't you see it?"

"I perceive it, but that's not the same thing. Let me—Chiara?"

he asked. "Please let me, for a moment, look at it through your eyes?"

Chiara drew away from the faint movement she saw in the air nearby. "No." She sounded alarmed. "Is that how you got the terrible power you have over Hugo? Did you trick him into—"

This was as far as she got because a terrific wind gust roared at her out of nowhere, pulling her hair free of the fillet she'd used to bind it and whipping her skirts high as she turned her back to protect herself from the blast. And then quickly as it came it was ended, leaving her disheveled, frightened, and absolutely alone.

REGEANE WENT DOWNSTAIRS WITH DORCAS TO LET Robert in. He staggered into his mother's arms. He was gray and looked stricken. Dorcas embraced him. "Oh, my son."

He swallowed, and Regeane saw his chest heave as he gasped for air. "Mother, give me a moment. It's almost impossible for me to speak of what I have seen, but let me say one thing." He pointed to Regeane. "She told the truth, and they are all dead. I have another question to ask you." He stared at Regeane. "Did you have any part in their deaths?"

"No," Regeane said flatly.

"Did you travel alone?"

"Yes. I came following the river in hopes of rescuing my lord Maeniel."

"The clothing—"

"I needed a disguise."

"You picked a foolish one."

Regeane nodded. "I can see that now." She clenched and unclenched her fists.

"Your lord is known to the people hereabouts. He has the name of witch, and it is said he and his followers are not natural men but belong to the wild hunt that rides the clouds when the storms come sweeping down from the mountains in the autumn to flog the earth with bitter wind and cold. And at night when the summer heat draws cooling thunder from the clouds, and sheets of lightning bright as day dance over the wheat and rice cradled in the arms of giant rivers, you and your lord ride with the first hunter of all, among the tall cloud

tops on steeds born of thunderheads and revel in the caress of midnight rain."

"Yes," Regeane answered. "I suppose in a way that is true, but
remember the soil bears the fruit of the storm that embraces the earth
with rain. A thing may be terrible in its majesty but not evil. Neither
my lord nor I would harm the innocent or willingly cause them misfortune. I found what you saw, and I grieve with you at both the folly
and cruelty of such actions."

"It is true," he said. "No woman did or could do what was done
to Mona and Itta, and they were all killed by steel." With that he
began to weep. Dorcas tried to comfort him but broke down in
sorrow, and for a time they grieved together.

At length Robert regained his composure and spoke quietly to
Regeane and his mother. "When I rode to the river I took two
others along, Gannon and Sheiel. We found the bodies. Someone
had covered them and tried to compose their limbs decently."

Regeane nodded.

"Yes, we saw your footprints. When we had done all we could,
we washed them in the river and cleansed the marks of outrage and
murder on their flesh. Then we wrapped them in some clean linen
cloth Itta had at the house. We spoke among ourselves and came to
the conclusion that it would be best not to bring them publicly to the
city for fear the men who committed this brutal crime might flee. So
the corpses are shrouded and in their dwelling. Gannon sent for his
wife, and she and some of the other women and Sheiel remain at the
river.

"Then Gannon and I spoke with Johns. He keeps the taverna
where the soldiers are lodging. He and the rest of the men determined they are almost certainly the guilty ones. They left the taverna
at first light. When Johns asked where they were bound, they told
him, amid much laughter, that they were going hunting. We think
they planned to have their will of the two women while they were
doing the washing, as their habit is to wash in the cool of the
morning and dry the clothes in the sun when it is high. Mother, we
found a dozen of our aprons in a bundle near Itta. They seemed to
have seized her and Mona first, but Mona fought; indeed, one of
them has scratches on his face, and another is wounded. We think
Mona made the scratches. There was blood under her nails. She
reached her father, Alberic. He and his brother fought. We think

they wounded one of the attackers but they were taken by surprise and had no weapons. All three fell.

"Then, they . . . they—those human dogs—dragged Mona off." Robert was silent for a moment. "She was wearing my ring. They cut off her finger to take it. That's how I know, why I'm sure, they were the ones. Johns said when they returned from the 'hunt,' they paid him for another night's lodging. When one of them fumbled in his scrip for the money, Johns saw the ring. At the time he didn't think anything of it, believing it only a similar one, but when we told him what we found, he told us what he had seen."

Regeane whispered, "Her finger. But then, I didn't notice, there was so much blood."

"Mother, I want them dead," he continued almost calmly. "I want them all dead. I don't care if the king hangs them or I cut their throats myself, but I want them dead. And I will see them off to hell before another day passes.

"We will have the law. Lombard law gives us rights. We will demand justice of Desiderius. His men will not offer insult to his people without redress."

"So far," Dorcas said, "he has shown no willingness to listen to his people. Mona is not the first, my son. Lillas was accosted on her way to the fountain a few weeks ago. She is but a new bride. Of course, she won't tell what happened. God knows I wouldn't either. She won't bring disgrace to either her own family or her husband's, but she lost the child she was carrying. When her father and father-in-law confronted the king, he laughed in their faces, and two days later her husband was killed in the street almost at his own doorstep. And no one is brave enough to name the killers, though at least a dozen people saw who they were.

"Now Lillas sits in her house and mourns her husband and her child. My son, I would not sit in my house and mourn the last and the best of my children—you."

"Mother, I could not bear the name of man," Robert said softly, "if I suffered this to happen without seeking vengeance."

"Let me help," Regeane said quietly.

"How could you possibly be of any assistance to us?" Robert asked. "You are a small woman and weaponless."

"I have weapons you cannot see, I and my lord both. Let me be there when you take the king to task."

"We will have to put the matter to rest tonight," Robert said, "but I see no harm in it.

"We sent for Beningus. He will hear the case and tell us the law."

Someone knocked and Dorcas hurried to see who it was and admit them. Regeane continued to set the table, covering it with heavy cloth and placing spoons for the pottages that would begin the meal, while Robert helped Dorcas with the benches. The room began filling up with people who spoke softly to both Robert and Dorcas and then embraced them.

Everyone sat down together for the meal. Regeane and Dorcas brought bread and the four pottages to the table. Broad beans cooked with salt pork; chicken, a stewing hen with saffron and early spring greens; pork shoulder with cloves, apples, and wine; and lentils cooked with ham and thickened with eggs.

Beningus arrived and sat at one end of the table. Robert sat at the other. He had little appetite and, as still more people crowded into the room, he mobilized more benches and served them buffet style from the pots on the table.

It grew dark outside and candles, torches, and rushlights appeared among those gathered in the shop. Robert had set several torches on the walls. They were lit and they brightened the room immensely. When everyone was finished eating, the tables were taken down and more benches and chairs appeared from nearby dwellings. They were needed by now. Regeane was sure there must be over a hundred people squeezed into the room. Most were men but there was a sprinkling of women among them.

"Widows," Dorcas said. "Like myself, they are family heads. Many, again like myself, don't marry a second time. They fear to jeopardize their children's future. A second husband might lay waste the wealth garnered by the first."

Then Dorcas peered through the window slit. "It's dark," she said.

Robert joined her. "It's dark and there is no moon. Bring them now," she told him.

He nodded and left. Several other men accompanied him. They brought back the dead. They were wrapped in cloth, shrouded, all but their faces, which showed that last unearthly calm that even the violently murdered wear when the journey to dust has begun.

Dorcas wept over Itta and the men. Others from the crowd

joined in the grief, but Robert was silent. He stood next to Mona's shrouded form silently. From time to time he sighed, and once touched her cheek with the back of one work-roughened hand.

Regeane stood quietly among the general grief all around her. At length Robert raised his head. His eyes met hers and he beckoned her closer. Now the torches had burned down and were only rather dull, smoky lumps. The wax lights melted and the only lights in the room were the candles burning at the head and feet of each of the five corpses. They rested together on a hurdle stretched over the same supports that had held up the dinner table.

"Tell us what happened," he asked, "and tell us, if you can, who is guilty." Then he uncovered Mona's hand. Regeane saw the missing finger. He placed Mona's hand in hers.

Without hesitation, Regeane clasped the still, cold fingers in both of hers. She became aware the room had fallen silent behind her. Regeane tried to get Robert to meet her eyes but he avoided her glance.

"What do you expect her to do? Bleed?" Regeane asked. She was speaking of the belief that when a murderer touches the corpse of his victim, the body will begin to bleed, even though the person has been dead for some hours.

The stump where the finger had been remained raw flesh. No drop of blood showed on Regeane's fingers. "I had to know," he said.

Regeane replaced Mona's hand on her breast and stepped back. She didn't look at Robert or even the crowd gathered in the room, but only at Mona's still face.

"The five soldiers staying at the inn near the Roman gate closest to the river are guilty. And none is more guilty than the others. They planned it together. They all took part in the rape, in the murders. They came down the road from the city very early so they would not be seen, and they waited near the river for sunrise. If you look, you will find a clearing where they left their horses.

"Just at sunrise, Itta came down, accompanied by Mona, to wash a big bundle of clothing in the shallows. The men remained at the house, all but one who joined a party of charcoal burners and went to cut wood."

"How could you know?" asked Robert.

Regeane clenched her fists in the fabric of her skirt and said forcefully, "I know."

Dorcas said, "Avitus's brother is a charcoal burner. Robert, be quiet. She is not obliged to tell us how she knows. Go on, Regeane."

"Itta fought. She had a knife. She wounded one of the soldiers and badly scratched another one with her nails. The girl ran for help. Her father and his brother and nephew were near the boat, building a fire. They had no chance. The soldiers were upon them before they could seize such weapons as they had. Those were few and not very effective. They were killed, even the boy, out of hand.

"They dragged Mona away toward the river." Regeane paused. She knew what happened then but didn't want to tell it. Not to the man who had loved the girl who died so horribly.

"The rest were already dead," Robert said. "So there was no help for her."

"No." She remained silent.

"I wish I had been there," Robert said.

"Then they would have killed you, too," Regeane said. She spoke harshly. "Death hangs about them the way fog clings to water."

"Yes," Robert said, picking up Mona's hand. "I know." Then he, too, was silent.

Regeane stood with her head bowed next to him. When she raised her head, the candle's glow caught her eyes. They flashed like mirrored moons in the darkened room.

"They were following me," she said. "You shouldn't have stopped me. They weren't going to catch me alone. I was going to catch them." She lifted her hand in shadow; her long nails looked like claws.

The crowd gasped, but Robert strode over to the wall and lit a new torch with a guttering, spent one, and light filled the room. "Beningus, speak the law."

A tall, rather lean man stepped out of the crowd and faced the impromptu gathering. "I am," he said, "of your choosing. Long ago when words on paper were only foreign wonders to us, the men and women of our family committed laws to memory, and when we held our assemblies those who had disputes of sufficient importance to require the attention of our greatest men could call on us to tell them what was proper under the laws. We stood with and before our leaders and spoke of how disagreements and quarrels were settled in the past and how we felt they should be settled now, that the peace might be kept among us.

"To this end, I never learned to read and write. Because now kings turn to moldy books filled with symbols that but few understand, and they interpret the law to their own advantage. But I, and my kind, are living repositories of what has been and what should be and we are forbidden to twist the teachings we have received to our own advantage. We may accept no payment for our services. Our trade—we are stock merchants and tanners—sustains us. More than sustains us, actually. Last year I did quite well."

A gust of soft laughter swept the room.

Robert sighed and whispered to Regeane, "The honesty of Beningus's family is proverbial."

"Tell us what we must do, Beningus," Dorcas said.

"I have thought on it," he replied. "The laws of brigandage and outrage apply."

"Desire was present," a man in the crowd spoke up.

"Yes, but the laws of desire apply to marriage and property, not murder, and this was murder. The law protects women from outrage and men from secret murder. The women were both outraged and murdered. The men were secretly and silently murdered. The law of brigandage applies because these men are outsiders and not from among our people. But the law directs that the king or chief men of a place will protect the people against theft and bodily harm. So, soldiers of his or not, he may not shield them from answering the accusations brought against them. And should they prove guilty—why, then he must hang them.

"A king who does no justice is not fit to be a king. A king who cannot keep the peace is no king at all."

The room held a vast stillness. The silence was long and loud. Regeane knew something momentous was happening. She knew she'd been present at the birth of a change that would one day shake the world.

This was a humble gathering of a few sympathetic souls who came together to mourn some unimportant men and women who met their deaths by misadventure. She couldn't imagine why this very minor event would change all subsequent history or even make the very powerful Desiderius rest uneasy on his throne, but it would.

She knew because Remingus and his men were among the people crowded into this room.

She could see them everywhere, some as shadows superimposed on the faces and bodies of living men and women; others brought the absolute darkness of the grave with them, carving out niches in the shadows as the living instinctively avoided their domain. All were fully marked by the horror of their mortality and entrance into eternity, from Remingus, who had withered on a Carthaginian cross, to the rest who wore the wounds that had carved away their lives.

Honor, Regeane thought. *Honor and doom. They gave their moment under the eye of the sun to honor and to destruction, that their particular world might live. Knowing that life itself is not a profit-and-loss statement and cannot be totaled up like one. We are all more and less than the flesh we wear from birth to death, but we are never sure why or how much.*

CHIARA WOKE WHEN SHE SENSED THE PRESENCE OF Hugo's guest in the room. She was secretly relieved rather than otherwise. She'd been worried about him, since they hadn't parted friends at their last encounter. She was afraid he might stop speaking to her, and she found—much to her surprise—that she would miss him. Compared to the errant spirit, most humans she was allowed to meet were deadly dull. Like most girls of her age, she was virtually imprisoned; the preservation of what her family considered her innocence became of overriding importance as she approached the age when she would be married. So she'd found in the last few years that her human contacts were being sharply curtailed.

Her nighttime adventure frightened her father, though as it happened she survived with her reputation unscathed. A miracle, considering the circumstances, but the experience convinced Armine that his daughter needed protection from the hazards and temptations of the world. To this end, Chiara found herself moved to an inner room overlooking a pleasant garden.

Her new maid, a dour and grim old woman recruited from a community of anchorites vowed to the service of God's holy church, slept in the outer chamber. Since the building was four stories high and the only entrance to Chiara's bedroom was through the chamber where Bibo—the name of the formerly cloistered nun—slept, it was clear to Chiara she was going nowhere without paternal permission and supervision.

"Very nice. You got me into all kinds of trouble with my father, not to mention the bishop and the king, and then you not only don't apologize, you don't even drop by and talk to me. Some friend you are."

"Your father is a sweet innocent who understands everything about cloth and its manufacture and the difficulties of transporting whole bales of the stuff from one place to another, not to mention how to get the best price for his goods when he reaches his destination. But he's an absolute patsy for any personable soul who wishes to sell him a bridge over the Tiber near Rome."

Chiara thought this over for a second. "That being the pope."

"Exactly."

"Oh."

"Yes. Now get up. That hag in the next room is awake, on her knees, and trying to atone for some sins that even God has probably forgotten. She can hear one side of this conversation if not the other. She will judge you, at best, mad or, at worst, possessed if she hears you speaking to an empty room, and she probably gives regular reports to your father. And should you question her veracity to your devoted sire, he will believe her version of events rather than yours."

"I'm not dressed," Chiara objected.

"You are wearing undergarments, a linen shift, and a woolen nightgown. A nun could not equal your modesty at present. Get out on the balcony right now."

"You are high-handed," she said, but obeyed.

"You are in a right royal snit," the spirit told her. "But you are going to listen to what I have to say."

Chiara pushed the shutters aside, being very careful to make as little noise as possible. The night was clear. A sharp winter chill lingered in the air and the sky was crowded with what seemed like millions of stars. But there was no wind, and Chiara's bedgown and woolen socks were warm. She was about to exclaim, "How beautiful," but remembered the source of her last argument with the spirit and didn't want another, at least not so soon.

But he answered her unspoken comment anyway. "Yes, it is."

Chiara trusted herself to nod and she did. The spirit continued. "I didn't come here tonight to discuss the wonders of creation but to bring you a much more important message. A great deal of trouble is in the offing for both your father and the king."

"What's going on?"

"First and least important at the moment is that Charles, the Frankish king, is advancing through the Alps. Frankly, I must say I admire the perspicacity of the wolf in choosing to follow that particular ruler, who shows an unusually high degree of ability and intelligence for a human and above all for one nobly born. Most of that particular subspecies of human have roughly the intellectual capacity of nits; this one, Charles, seems to be a highly competent individual. Which, by the way, bodes ill for the cowardly and devious Lombard ruler."

Chiara said, "Huh?"

"Charles is smart and brave. Desiderius is stupid, cowardly, and inept. What do you think is going to happen?"

"Oh," Chiara said, "but there's many a slip between cup and lip."

"True," the being answered trenchantly. "But of more moment is the fact that the people of Pavia and the surrounding countryside are fed up with the depredations of the mercenary forces that your feckless king has hired to defend his domains. He doesn't trust his people or his nobility and with good reason. He has never taken steps to win the loyalty of either.

"Instead, he's made a state policy of scheming, backstabbing, and murder, and this policy is about to bear most unpleasant fruit. To put it very succinctly, tomorrow his chickens are coming home to roost, and he will find them very ugly fowl indeed. And you must warn your father that the square won't be a safe place to visit. Don't go there without protection, no matter what happens. Don't stir out of this room. I cannot emphasize this too strongly. Get a migraine, get a vile disease, fall into convulsions, but stay home."

"I was already planning to wake up with terrible cramps. They're going to try to burn the one you call the wolf."

"The bishop and king are going to call an assembly and try Maeniel for sorcery," Hugo's guest said. "But calling an assembly is a mistake."

"Why?"

"Because the people have the right at an assembly to introduce other business, and make no mistake about it, they will take advantage of this devious monarch's error and do so. As for burning the wolf . . . Well, his wife is here. Normally she might be stoned out of hand as a witch, but given the nasty temper of the citizenry at this moment, I find that against all odds they are listening to her—high-tempered bitch that she is—and she has plans that don't include her husband being burned alive."

"Good for her," Chiara whispered truculently.

"Ye gods, but you women stick together."

"Ha! I wish. Look at that dumb Bibo. Now I can't do anything without her finding out. I'm completely cornered by that old witch and my father."

"You're going to go to the square regardless of what I say, aren't you?"

"Yes," Chiara answered, and stamped her foot. "I wouldn't miss this for the world."

The spirit gave a hiss of fury that turned at last into a sigh of disgust. "You're going to get us all killed," the spirit snapped.

"All? Nobody can do anything to you—you're already dead."

"Yes, yes, they can," the spirit confessed. "If I expend all my energies in an act of violence, it can destroy me. That's why I didn't smash that repulsive little louse Hugo like a glass beaker."

"Then how did he get all those bruises?"

"He's a stinking sot. He got drunk to keep me from forcing him to help the wolf. Wandered out into the hall with, I think, some idea of forcing his way into your room. I pushed him down the stairs."

"I can't believe even a fall down the stairs would do that much damage."

"It didn't. The little pile of dog shit didn't seem to feel it, so when he crawled back to the top step, I pushed him back down again."

"You're terrible."

"Not as terrible as what he had in mind for you, my dear. I know. He was muttering about it all the way back up the stairs. You are an innocent and there are cruelties you don't even know exist. Cruelties a man like Hugo will commit without a second thought."

"Oh," Chiara whispered.

The spirit was pleased that she seemed much more subdued.

"I see . . ."

"No, no, you don't. And I would not have you do so. Now, will you stay home? Like a sensible woman?"

"No," Chiara stated flatly. "Can't you see I need to know what's going on? I have to at least try to protect my father, because even if I hide, he will go. Especially if the king calls an assembly. He will feel it is incumbent upon him to be there, and I won't let him go alone."

"Perdition on it," Hugo's guest roared.

Just then the door to the chamber where Bibo slept creaked open. "My lady, my lady," the old woman cried. "The danger . . . The night air carries the miasmic chill of the grave—death rides the night wind." She seized Chiara by the neck of the gown and one arm and made an effort to drag her back into the room.

"Stop." Chiara raised her arms, trying to fend her off and loosen the old woman's grip on the fabric at her neck. "Stop it right now. You're choking me," Chiara cried desperately. "I just wanted some air."

"A lover," the old woman cried. "That's it, you have a lover—a lover visiting you. He's in the garden." She twisted the narrow neck of the gown even tighter at Chiara's throat.

Chiara gasped and gagged. The gown was really strangling her. A fist exploded in Bibo's face, smacking her in the region of her right eye. With an ear-splitting shriek, she went down on her backside. At almost the same moment, Arminus charged through the outer door accompanied by two members of the king's guard, both armed cap-a-pie.

"He hit me. Her lover hit me," Bibo shouted.

"Take him alive," Armine roared. "If her honor is compromised, he must marry her. If not, I'll have his head on a pike! On a pike, I say, a pike."

"My God," Chiara whispered, and jumped back.

The first of the king's guard reached the balcony and wasn't able to slow his forward progress quickly enough to avoid slamming into the balustrade. Then he let out a truly unearthly yell as Armine, who was following him closely, crashed into his back and almost—almost, but not quite—shoved him over the rail; he was spared a fall of approximately fifty Roman feet to a flagstone courtyard at the center of the garden below.

Bibo wailed again, this time halfheartedly. "Her lover . . ."

Armine and the two guardsmen were no longer in danger of

falling, but since they all had their naked swords in hand, there was a real chance one of them might inflict a serious wound on another, completely by accident. Chiara was standing in an alcove protected on one side by the bed and on the other by a high, very elaborately carven solid oak chest.

"Her lover . . ." Bibo moaned.

"In God's name, haven't any of you a lick of sense?" Chiara screamed. "What is it? Are you are all maggot-brained madmen? How would I entertain a lover? We are four floors from the ground. The man would have to have wings."

"There is," Armine said, sounding astounded, "no one here. How can that be?"

"Her lover," Bibo whimpered.

One of the guardsmen reached down and set Bibo on her feet and then recoiled violently as she breathed on him. "Ya, she reeks of the tavern."

Armine leaned over and sniffed. "Drunk, by God." He turned to Chiara and shook a finger. "This is all your doing, my girl. Were it not for these midnight peregrinations of yours, we would—"

Chiara's fists clenched and a look of outrage began spreading across her features, but just then three things happened simultaneously.

Armine's feet were kicked out from under him, and he landed seated on the floor as Bibo had. The shutters to the balcony slammed violently shut, casting the room abruptly into complete darkness. And—

Chiara was suddenly but thoroughly kissed.

When one of the guardsman stumbled into the hall and returned with a torch, Armine gave a wild shout of surprise. Chiara drew in her breath sharply and pressed her fingers against her cheeks; her face felt incandescent. She followed the direction of her father's gaze and saw her bed was covered with white roses.

LOOKS LIKE NINE MILES OF BAD ROAD, LUCILLA thought. Rome was shadowed by its illustrious past, but here and there fragments of its former glory shone even among the ruins. Here, nothing remained. On their way into the city, they passed ruined villas and a decaying Roman town on the flatland below. Only a scattering of columns and tumbled stones remained of the forum and what once had been a large amphitheater. A few of the houses were inhabited by peasants who pastured flocks of sheep and goats on the rich grass that covered what once had been shops, streets, and dwellings. Beyond the city's ruins, the open fields were being plowed up by peasants living on the rocky promontory that towered over the valley.

Dulcinia pointed out the remains of the city and several villas to Lucilla as they made the ride up from the deserted coastal plain. "The lord of this place," she told Lucilla, "says the city was abandoned because it flooded during the spring rains. He said the villagers sometimes dig for treasure there, and even sometimes find it, but mostly they get pieces of broken glass, pottery, and from time to time a few fragments of marble. Shepherds pasture their flocks there because there is so much stone in the soil that it can't be plowed."

A nearby hill crowned by some sort of stonework was newly planted with a patchwork of olive trees and vines. Lucilla pointed to the tumbled stones. "I wonder what that was?"

Dulcinia shrugged. "Who can say, but it's a village now."

Lucilla looked more closely and saw the outline of huts and sheds grouped under the fire-blackened cupola of an ancient building. "Might have been baths or even a church," she said.

Dulcinia shrugged again. "I suppose so. I can't see that it matters. What will you do, my love, try to bring it all back? Not even you would want that."

Lucilla sighed, then chuckled. "It floods indeed. A pleasant, polite way of saying take care, the countryside is not safe here."

Dulcinia laughed softly, then looked back at their escort trailing along behind. The men rode negligently. Only a few wore their helmets and hauberks but most carried a businesslike assortment of weapons: swords, knives, and a powerful clubbed mace hung from every man's saddle. Even the two women carried knives, a pair each, one long—the ugly and dangerous single-edged sax—and the shorter a double-edged utility blade. Lucilla also had a vicious half moon–shaped ax sheathed in leather under her saddle blanket.

The day was warm and clear, the sky blue; a cool breeze was blowing, and birdsong filled the air as they rode past a small copse of trees bordering the road. The two women rode astride wearing tunics, leggings, and divided skirts.

"I thought we might have had to fight at that last river crossing,"

Dulcinia said. "I'm glad you're along. I don't know what I would have done alone."

Lucilla's face hardened. "Maybe we should have. He was one shifty-eyed bastard, and his threats may have been all a bluff. But I felt I couldn't take the chance.

"Likely we'd have won; almost certainly we'd have slaughtered that contingent of scum he had hanging about the ford. But he insisted he paid dues to the local authorities—whoever the hell they are in that godforsaken place—so the threat of a minor war was unsettling to say the least. That, and he reduced the amount we would have to pay ever so quickly when he got a good look at Rufus's men. Made me decide it wasn't worth the risk, not over a few coppers.

"But I'll bet his master, if he has one, sees damn little of whatever tolls he collects."

"There, you see," Dulcinia said. "I'd have paid the first price he asked. I'm not brave, my dear. Those outlaws he ran with terrified me."

"Bah," Lucilla said. "Parasites and scavengers all. He probably throws them his leavings. Not one decent scrap of armor or even one good sword among them. It's not my business to clean out that particular viper's nest, but I'll make damn sure both Hadrian and Rufus hear about them. One or the other might make it his business to see their leader winds up adorning a cross."

Just then they reached the rather steep road that led to the new town perched on the top of its rock. Quite a climb, but when they reached the top, both Lucilla and Dulcinia were heartened by what they saw. The town was still in the process of being built. The square was laid out in cobblestone, with a palace of sorts on one side, a church under construction on the other. At the end of the square was a stone balustrade where one could stand, take the air, be cooled by the spring breeze, and look out over the fertile and beautiful countryside beyond.

It was a market day and all manner of people were present buying and selling what was, considering the small size of the place, a variety of goods. Rabbits, chickens, geese, herbs, savory, garlic, thyme, mint, and small quantities of exotic spices such as cinnamon, cloves, saffron, and pepper. Mushrooms in abundance, onions, leeks, cabbage, artichokes scattered among bundles of fresh wild greens gathered by women before daybreak, their stems and roots in water to keep them fresh in the heat of the day.

The crowd in the square greeted Lucilla and Dulcinia with almost wild enthusiasm and escorted the two women and even their tough-looking male protectors to the steps of the palace. The local Lombard lord didn't rush out to greet her. He and some of his men were already out testing—just testing, mind you—a new batch of beer. He was hustled along with respect but no fear by the laughing townspeople, and only prevented by the press of people around the palace from breaking his neck because he couldn't see, he was so busy trying to pull a magnificent red velvet tunic down over a well-worn white shirt.

Lucilla thought he might as well have left his face covered up. One cheek was deeply scarred. He had a much-broken nose and part of one ear was missing. But his people cheered him and he bowed over Dulcinia's hand like a gentleman.

Lucilla curtseyed to him and he replied gravely. "Ladies, you are a joy to behold. I hope you had a safe journey."

"Tolerable," Dulcinia said, "except at the river."

The lord's face darkened. "What happened at the river?"

Dulcinia spoke of being stopped and a toll demanded.

"That is my demesne and . . . and it shouldn't have happened. That filthy little blackguard is back. I'd ride for the river now but—"

"He will certainly be gone, Father."

The speaker was a young man as handsome as his father was ugly. "I am Ansgar," the warrior said, "and this—" He gestured toward the young man. "—is my son Ludolf. When we came to this place, the filthy robber you encountered had his nest here. All the country-side around was waste, thanks to the fact that the people went in fear of him."

The young man laughed. "Father, you weren't married then, and I wasn't even born."

Ansgar looked a bit chagrined. "I'm sorry. I forget all this happened years ago. When my father died, my brothers and I divided his lands among ourselves. The eldest got the best. My other brother and I took the leavings." He gestured expansively toward the end of the square overlooking the valley. "But I believe I got the better of the bargain."

He was answered by cheers from the crowd in the square.

"But come, ladies. Come in. Sorry our housekeeping is a bit knockabout today, but my wife has a malaise she comes down with every spring and—"

"A song," someone shouted in the crowd. The rest took up the cry. "A song. A song."

The lord's face darkened but Lucilla saw Dulcinia's face flush with pleasure and a smile hovered on her lips. Ansgar looked ready to protest, but Dulcinia said, "No, no. Please, I would love to sing for them. Where?"

"The church porch." Ludolf pointed across the square.

Yes, the church had a colonnaded porch and walls, no roof yet, but the scaffolding was up and carpenters were on top setting the ceiling beams. Musicians appeared as if by magic out of the assembled people: a woman with a harp, two men with flutes, and several with different sorts of drums.

Dulcinia strolled across the square, smiling, greeting and being greeted by the townsfolk. She looked uplifted, Lucilla thought, by the prospect of performing for the people. *Yes,* Lucilla thought, and she remembered the day outside of the tavern when she'd first spoken to the eight-year-old child scrubbing pots almost as big as she was. The little girl was sad, filthy, and malnourished, but when Lucilla asked her to sing, the glow that suffused her face was magnificent, and then and there, before the child opened her mouth, Lucilla had decided she must be rescued from her brutal fate. No matter what her voice sounded like. Of course, once she sang . . . oh, that God-given, heavenly voice . . . Dulcinia had reached the church steps and she had a few moments to consult with the musicians.

Another man hurried up. He held a huge viol. They put their heads together for what seemed like a long time, the occasional squeak, ping, hoot, shout, gush of notes escaping from among them. Then Dulcinia and the rest stood on the church porch. Two of the drummers dropped out but one produced a horn and the other a strip of leather with bells. Dulcinia raised one hand and every voice in the square hushed as she began to sing.

It was a very simple lyric about a lover who compares his sweetheart to a rose, or rather a variety of roses, white, red, pink; even the supple canes and autumn rose hips were mentioned. A sprightly song, even just a little funny. It drew the analogy out a bit too far to be taken quite seriously and ended with a bit of vocal ornamentation that was rather pretty. This drew cheers from the crowd and cries for another song, but Ansgar clapped his hands and said, "Enough is enough. The ladies have come a long way and need to dine and refresh themselves."

One of the carpenters swung down from the church roof, donned a black velvet robe, and greeted them. He was, it transpired, Gerald, Ansgar's brother and the first bishop of the newly created diocese. Ansgar and his son conducted Lucilla and Dulcinia into the palace. Beyond the doors was a wide reception hall lit by glass plugs in the roof. Outside, standing in the sun, it had been warm, almost hot; here it was cool, even where the sun struck long shafts of light through the translucent but not transparent skylights.

"Here we dine," Ansgar said, "and receive visitors."

"State visitors?" Dulcinia asked.

Ansgar chuckled. "I believe you may be the first."

The hall ended at a double stair, one on either side leading up into the palace beyond. Someone, a woman, was descending, speaking as she came.

"Why didn't you tell me they were here, my love? You know—" This sounded very reproachful. "—you know I wanted so badly to meet the finest singer in all of Rome . . . and—"

"My wife," Ansgar said. "She suffers from a malady, seasonal in nature, that—"

"What he means to tell you is that every spring and fall I am a martyr to my damned nose. My eyes water, sting, and burn, and this nose runs like a damnable fountain, and I must—"

Just at that moment Dulcinia and Lucilla stepped into a pool of misty sunshine generated by the skylight above. The woman who had now reached the foot of the stairs paused, took a good, long careful look at them, and shrieked.

"Lucilla, as I live and breathe. Lucilla! What in God's name are you doing here?"

Ansgar's fist closed like a vise on Ludolf's arm. "Shut the door quickly," he snapped. "Now! And drop the bar. Now! Do you hear? Now," he repeated.

Ludolf was already moving, drawing his sword as he went.

Lucilla peered into the gloom near the stair. "Stella," she gasped. "How . . . ? What?"

"Ah, well," Dulcinia murmured. "So much for disguises."

REGEANE WAS DORCAS'S GUEST THE NIGHT AFTER the meeting. The two women repaired to the top of the tower house. Dorcas lent Regeane a woolen bedgown and a pair of socks. The room had four windows. One had glass and allowed a view of the courtyard below. The other windows bore curtains— embroidered white gauze—louvered shutters, and then heavy, solid oak shutters that could be bolted from the inside.

The room was lit by two candles, one on either side of the bed. The large bed was the centerpiece of the room, but around the walls, beneath the windows, were large chests for clothing and other linens. They did double duty as benches, as they were topped by soft, fragrant, downy cushions, very comfortable to sit on.

Dorcas lifted one and fluffed it for Regeane. "Itta helped me make these. She procured the goose down," Dorcas said, then stood for a time silent, her thoughts turned inward, looking as if she'd forgotten both Regeane and the room she stood in.

But then she came to herself with a start. "I'm sorry," she said, and placed the cushion on a bench for Regeane. "It's just that I cannot quite believe I will never see her again. But tell me," she asked, "are you one of those afraid of the night air?"

"No," Regeane answered, laughing a little despite her somber mood. "How could that be so?"

Dorcas nodded. "Yes." She gave a rather grim smile. "Are you not afraid of your . . . strange . . . lord?"

"No," Regeane said. "Nor he of me. In fact, if you knew him, you would find him more amiable and gentle than the majority of men."

"God, that's the truth. I can remember a time or two when we were first married that I bore the marks of my man's displeasure."

"He struck you?"

"Once. Once I complained to my father and mother but they laughed at me."

"What did you do?"

"The second time he did it, I told him he'd best not sleep in this house, so he left. There was a terrible to-do." Dorcas laughed. "My parents visited me, then the priest who quoted scripture. I told him I never saw it in the scriptures where a man had a right to give his wife a black eye.

"The town was without bread, but my husband returned and said he would do me no more violence and gave me his word. I took it and we lived together in peace and joy until he died. You see, I could not see wherein I had earned his displeasure. I was doing my best and working hard. He simply didn't care for his supper. I had not cooked the meat long enough. I told him, my mother and father, and the priest I would not live with a cruel tyrant. I would rather die or take myself off to the roads and earn my bread begging at church doors or spreading my legs for all comers with the price."

Regeane nodded. "A victory. By such victories women make their lives tolerable."

"Itta never saw it that way," Dorcas said. "She let her husband rule her in all things. That's why I didn't lend her the money to set up shop here in the town. I wouldn't put my hard-earned cash into his hand. He'd just as likely have frittered it away on nonsense, drinking, gambling in the taverns, trying to impress his friends. So all I have now are my regrets for what I have lost: my closest friend and Robert's future wife."

She began weeping again and Regeane did what she could to comfort her. "Don't blame yourself so," Regeane whispered. "How . . . oh, how could you know? Besides, those men are the ones responsible."

Dorcas dried her tears. "They're dead men."

"You're sure?"

"Yes," Dorcas answered quietly.

"How will they go about it?"

"Tonight the tavern keeper will drug their wine, then Robert and some of the other men will bind them and take them to yonder church." She pointed across the alley.

Regeane turned and looked through a crack in the shutters. The church appeared dark and empty, but the wolf's ears heard movement in the alley and inside the building.

"They will remain there until the king calls the assembly to deal with your husband the wolf. Then we will give Desiderius one more chance to be a king to us. But one way or another, these men will die. They will fall either to private vengeance or to the king's justice. Robert and the other men are determined upon it."

"My husband?" Regeane asked.

Dorcas looked away and would not meet her eyes. "He will have his chance to speak in his own defense. The law guarantees him that. More than that I cannot promise."

The cold night wind fanned Regeane's cheek through the shutters. "I see," she said.

"No, no, you don't," Dorcas said. "I have procured a quiet night's sleep for you, but that is all." This time she met Regeane's eyes directly. "Should you try to escape this room, well, Robert and some of the other men will be just below us. There is a sentinel present now.

"You and your husband come to aid our enemies. Yes, the men here are loath to kill a woman, especially one only trying to do her duty to her wedded lord—whatever he may be. But should you cause a disturbance or try to escape, they will do what they must. Understand?"

"Understood," Regeane said.

"Now, let us sleep," Dorcas said. "If we can. If I can. Blow out the candle."

Regeane extinguished the candle on her side of the bed. Regeane settled herself into the bed with its down mattresses and comforters. Soft, softer even than her bed in her chamber in the mountains. She was asleep almost the moment her head touched the pillow.

But Remingus and his dead legionaries walked with her through her dreams, and together they spoke of many, many things—about life, death, desperate loss, and the rise and fall of empires, cities, and men. Regeane remembered the night as one long conversation, but when she was awakened by the cold gray predawn light creeping past the shutters, she could remember nothing of what was said.

"My thoughts are with you," she whispered. *My only love. I must try. Forgive me, but I must try.* Then she rose and, donning Mona's clothing, began to braid her hair, readying herself for this important day.

Dorcas was already up and gone. Regeane descended the ladders down to Dorcas's bake shop. The woman was waiting. Time for a bit of breakfast.

Regeane didn't feel like eating, but another of Matrona's lessons was that she needed more nourishment than most humans commonly require to fuel the energies that allowed her to change from wolf to woman and back. And she might need all her strength today. Sops of bread and wine, a pottage of beans with snails and garlic.

Then Dorcas lent her a heavy brown veil. "With luck they will not know who you are," she said as Regeane wound it around her head and shoulders. "Now I must bring food to the men in the church." She lifted a basket in the corner and left, going to the alley at the back of the church.

Regeane stood alone. Dorcas hadn't shut the door behind her— an open invitation to flee, Regeane thought. *I will not leave him to his fate. He would not leave me to mine.* She turned and saw Remingus standing in a corner, finishing the last of the pottage. "You are here," she said.

"I am here," he answered. "For you."

He was no longer the empty-eyed ghost that had first confronted her, but the man she'd seen yesterday. She remembered sharing a drink from his helmet. "You are dust," she said.

"Not so anyone would notice," he replied. "We will go together to the square. I will accompany you and Dorcas—she will see me."

"What will happen?"

"I don't know." He tipped the pot and swallowed the liquid in the bottom. "Very good. Dorcas is an excellent cook; the snails were a nice touch. You see, my magnificent hunter, death does not confer omniscience." He was swathed from head to foot in a dark burgundy and brown mantle.

Dorcas returned and was surprised to see him. "Who is this?" she asked.

"A friend," Regeane said.

She stared fixedly at Remingus. "I didn't know you had any friends in the city."

"I don't," Regeane replied. "Remingus is from somewhat farther away. He lived near a lake in the wine country near Rome."

"Yes," Remingus replied. "I did. Yes, once long ago. But let us be on our way. The sun is up and burns away the morning mist. Soon the king will be in the forum."

He was right. When the three reached the ancient forum, they found it already crowded and more people arriving every moment.

The sellers of fried bread and vegetables and others with wineskins and beer loaded on muleback were already doing a brisk business at the outskirts of the crowd. All one needed was a cup and a few coppers.

The morning coolness was fading in the bright sunlight, and the people were imbibing freely of the refreshments offered by the food and wine vendors. Regeane felt uneasy. This was, despite the party atmosphere, not a happy gathering. Too many men were drinking heavily, too much, too early. A significant number of men clad in heavy mantles weren't drinking anything at all.

Regeane felt the hair rise on her neck as the wolf informed her almost every adult male was armed, and not a few of the women also. Dorcas had two heavy, long, carving knives in her belt. They were, as with most of the rest, concealed by her mantle. Most folk were milling around, greeting old acquaintances and passing the time of day. Regeane knew almost no one here, so she and Remingus drifted toward the outskirts of the crowd. The forum was surrounded by colonnades on all four sides. Two colonnades were the porches of shops and warehouses where the rich produce of the countryside was stored and business was transacted. The third was the portico of the king's palace, and the fourth the entrance to the sometime temple of Roma, now a Christian cathedral. Its high steps and massive portico towered above the rest.

"He is there," Regeane said.

Remingus had no need to reply. The wolf found traces of Maeniel on the stones, the steps, and on a gust of unaccountable wind that lifted her veil and tugged at her braided hair. A terrible bottomless sense of loss tore through her entire being, even as the wind lifted dust from the cobbles under her feet and set the clothing of what was now a mob to flapping and snapping in the blast.

"They are going to riot," she whispered.

"I think so," Remingus answered. He steered her between the shops across from the church to the edge of the forum. The wind died, and the air was oddly still.

When they reached the end of the alley between the warehouses, Regeane found she could look out over the rooftops of the town and the countryside beyond. She sniffed the wind. In the darkness of her deepest mind, the wolf rose.

Go, her nightmare sister whispered. *Go. He was mad to have involved himself in the doings of these foolish kings. He will pay the forfeit. Run! Smell the rain carried by the wind. They will burn nothing today. Change. Leap out. The tile roofs and stone walls will bear your weight easily.*

Regeane's hair shifted on her head. The braid unraveled itself, and her hair fell unconfined to her shoulders. Then there was a shout from the forum.

"The king. The king is coming."

The veil slid away from her face to her shoulders. "No," the woman whispered. "Whatever happens, whatever fate he meets, he will not journey forth alone. In life or death, I vow I will be at his side."

"The horizon is darkening," Remingus said.

"The air is still," Regeane answered.

There was another louder shout, "The king."

In the church the bishop, servants, and the captain of Desiderius's guard threw a rope ladder into the pit.

Maeniel came up.

They had ten crossbows trained on him. One wrong move, and he would be a sieve. He calculated the wolf's chances of survival under those circumstances and found them nil. He was ordered to kneel, and chains were fastened at his wrists, ankles, and neck. He was still nude, but the captain of the guard took pity on him to the extent of cutting a hole in a worn-out blanket and dropping it over his head. Then he was prodded along at spearpoint up the stairs, through the church, and past the door until he stood on the portico.

The square was filled by now. Most were gathered near the church as the trial had been announced. He was the most celebrated prisoner and enemy of the Lombard kingdom the king had ever taken. His warrior prowess was legendary even over and above his reputation for sorcery.

Maeniel stared, with the feral gaze of an absolute wolf, at the people pushing and shoving for a good look at him. His face held the defiance that is at the same time indifference, as if to say, You are lucky I am chained but it doesn't matter because you cannot frighten me with fire or the sword. I know who and what I am, and in life or death I am free: the absolute self-assurance of the beast that is absolute innocence and cannot be forced into guilt or regret as lesser human creatures can.

He studied their eyes and then looked out toward the haze of the horizon's rim. He saw the building storm, felt the heat, saw dust rise over the newly plowed fields of the royal estates near the city. Then his guards prodded him down the steps and across the square toward the king, who was sitting along with the bishops and other Lombard notables in the shade of the palace portico overlooking both his prisoner and the throng.

Regeane pushed in with the rest toward Maeniel. She hadn't thought how the sight of him would affect her, so close and yet a world away. But she was practical, too. In this situation, he would need all his strength and confidence to save his life. So she must not unman him. He must not guess her presence among the crowd.

In a half-frozen forest in the upper reaches of his wild domain, he would have known if she drew within a dozen miles of him, but here among the press of perspiring humans, her presence was masked by the thousand odors generated by men and women and all the items of commerce in the shops and warehouses around the forum, compounded by the bellicose mood of the males in the crowd.

To the wolf their raw fury and aggression was a strangling reek. Left to himself in this atmosphere, the wolf would have tucked his tail between his legs and fled at as fast a run as he could manage and, moreover, not stopped until he reached a much cleaner place. The man thought darkly that someone was in for a lot of trouble today. Was it himself?

No. No. His guards were able to shove the throng aside easily, and when the males, the most dangerous ones, looked at Maeniel, all the wolf saw in their faces was mild curiosity. He was being properly humbled, barefoot, wearing an old blanket as a tunic. His hair a rat's nest, his body smeared with silt from the stone floor of his damp cell, he wearing a steel collar around his neck and chains dangling from every limb.

If anything, he seemed to arouse pity in the hearts of the women; the men were indifferent. He sensed they were preoccupied by other urgent concerns.

Just ahead he saw the king sitting comfortably in the shade of the palace portico. This time Desiderius didn't allow the bishop to present himself almost as an equal, as the prelate had in the church. The king was seated in the center of the porch, his court standing around him. The bishop, in deference to his age, had also been given a chair but lower and to one side of the king, whose throne was placed on a dais.

Maeniel suppressed a smile as his guards reached the foot of the three steps leading to the portico. He was thrust to his knees by the captain of the guard, while the mercenaries rather brutally cleared an open space before the king.

Chiara was standing near the throne, just to one side, next to her father and Hugo. Maeniel's eyes rested on her for what was to her a truly frightening moment, but he gave no sign of recognition. Well, the church was dimly lit and perhaps he hadn't got a good look. *Don't be an idiot,* she told herself. *He knows who you are, but he also knows better than to make a fuss, here of all places.* She gave a sigh of relief.

The bear was present. He was riding Gimp; Hugo and the bear were on the outs at the moment. They'd wound up throwing things at each other after the bear visited Chiara. The commotion roused the palace guard and Hugo was almost ejected forthwith. Chiara again intervened and persuaded the bear to leave. He found the tavern where Gimp was getting sozzled and, in a serious snit, took up residence with his more amiable disciple. Gimp was a more comfortable residence than Hugo at present, since he was a quiet drunk. After a certain amount of any intoxicating beverage was consumed, he went to sleep; he was, in fact, dozing at present. The bear had taken over more of his body functions than he did with any of his other hosts, even down to telling Gimp when to scratch, piss, and shit. Gimp didn't mind. He was happy. He was drunk most of the time now, and he had more than enough to eat. His guest could never get him very clean, and he hadn't even the intelligence and skill to dig up the occasional coin hoards the bear showed Hugo. Though he was not particularly useful to the bear, he was at least restful and cooperative—more, much more, than could be said of Hugo.

There was one thing the bear didn't realize. His possession of Gimp showed on Gimp's face. Chiara was uneasily aware of his presence and so was Maeniel when he got a good look at Gimp.

The bear, studying Maeniel kneeling in the dust, couldn't forgo the pleasure of gloating. "You should have listened to me in the first place," the bear told Maeniel. "You know what they're going to do to you, don't you—well, don't you?" he asked gleefully.

Maeniel looked up at Desiderius, Gimp, and Chiara.

"They're going to burn you, burn you alive!"

Chiara gave a gasp of horror. Then, equally horrified by her reaction, she clapped her hand over her mouth.

The bear roared, laughing. "I'm going to enjoy this."

In the crowd, Regeane, standing next to Remingus, heard him also. "That evil thing is here," she whispered.

"Yes," Remingus answered quietly. "Be careful. I do not think he has yet sensed your presence. I saw him from afar the night we met. He summoned me from silence and darkness, back, back from peace, from the waters of Lethe where I could drift and dream the dreams of joy and sorrow abandoned by the living on those misty shores. Back to the searing light of being and belonging, love, hate, and pain. I came to you. I live."

Regeane shuddered as she felt his hand on her arm. Then she froze, because the king was speaking.

"This man," he said, and pointed at the kneeling Maeniel, "is an enemy of our people and a servant of the Frankish king Charles. He has openly admitted his guilt. I think there is not more to say before—"

"May I speak?" Maeniel asked.

"No," Desiderius answered. "Silence him," he ordered the captain of the guard, who then smacked Maeniel on the side of the head with his mace.

The blow made Maeniel's ears ring and opened a gash on his cheekbone; blood ran scarlet down his face.

Regeane cried out. In fact, quite a few women in the crowd shouted or spoke, "No. For shame. He is bound."

The king glared at them over the heads of his mercenaries. "Be silent," he roared. "I'll flog the next who creates a disturbance and hang any who think to join in the disorder. I will have no riots in this, my royal city. As for this—" Desiderious rose and pointed to Maeniel. "—take this offal out and hang him, then burn his corpse so he will not walk the night, vile sorcerer that he is."

The roar that rose from the mob frightened even Maeniel.

Desiderius quailed back.

The mercenaries suddenly decided they would much rather not have their backs to the citizens they'd been pushing around so cavalierly, and they rushed up the palace steps and turned toward the crowd in the square, spears and crossbows at the ready.

Maeniel was on his feet, but the captain was an iron man and he held Maeniel where he was at spearpoint—the small change being that he was now facing his prisoner instead of behind him.

Regeane for the first time understood the temper of the towns-people. She knew, as did Maeniel, that they were ready to rush the guards and kill everyone they could get their hands on, and even the thickheaded Desiderius saw he'd gone too far. From Maeniel's side, someone spoke to the king.

"Majesty, I believe it is our custom to allow the accused an opportunity to defend himself before sentence is pronounced."

She recognized the voice as Robert's.

"Y-yes," Desiderius stammered, then pointed to Maeniel. "Speak . . . speak."

"I have little to say," Maeniel said. "Yes, I am Charles's man. Yes, I came to spy out your defenses, but I was captured before I could accomplish my mission and so was unable to do any harm to you, the city, or its people. I believe my actions were honorable. I never made a pretense of being your friend, and I believe it is your custom to allow a captured prisoner to ransom himself."

A distraction was what Desiderius needed, and this was a good one. "What are you offering?" he asked bluntly.

"For you, two pounds of gold."

"That is a large sum."

Maeniel could see the wheels turning. "And further, one half pound for the bishop. Ten gold pieces for each of the gentlemen of your court and one for every family head in your city."

This was a truly staggering sum, but Regeane had seen Maeniel's coffers, and she didn't doubt that he could pay that and more. His duchy was awash in prosperity, and his people were not such as to desire much in the way of possessions. For a moment, the ill humor of the people departed. The courtiers murmured among themselves and even the mercenaries did some mental arithmetic, as some were in arrears as to their wages. For a short time, everyone was immersed in the pleasant task of spending imaginary money.

But Hugo proved a spoilsport. "What?" he screeched. "What? Are you going to let him go? And on what? His word alone? Who? Who, I ask you? Who will be his surety?"

"Hugo," Maeniel shot back. "Hugo, many things have been said of me, both good and evil, but none have ever been so base as to question my honesty. What I promise, I will perform. I kept faith even with you and that vile father of yours."

"You killed him." Hugo was almost frothing at the mouth. "I saw you kill him."

"So you were there? Well, if you were watching, then you know he tried to murder my wife, Regeane. Regeane, who begged mercy for you both. Enough." The chains on Maeniel's wrists and ankles clattered. "Oh, you're lucky, you piece of dung, that I am fettered. Any man who calls himself a man would defend the woman joined to him by law and love."

The answering shout from the crowd was deafening.

"They know what happened by the river," Regeane whispered.

"Did you think they didn't?" Remingus asked.

Desiderius looked frustrated. Hugo stepped forward. He looked both frustrated and infuriated. He shouted at the king, "What? Will you let this sorcerer, this stinking murderer, buy his liberty with nothing more than promises?"

"Yes." Desiderius frowned. "There is the matter of sureties. What manner of guarantee will you give me that you will keep your word?"

Regeane stepped forward, pushing back her veil as she did so. "Your majesty," she spoke in a loud, clear voice that carried to the edges of the crowd. "I will undertake to be surety for my lord and husband."

Chains or not, Maeniel spun around. "Regeane? You? Here? How?"

The color drained from his face. He reached out one hand, chained at the wrist, toward her. Regeane took the outstretched hand and stepped up beside him.

"I will be my lord's security," she repeated. "He does not lie. I know this well. He will pay the ransom down to the last copper, but set him free and I will remain—prisoner or your guest, the choice is yours—until he returns with payment."

"No," Maeniel said.

"Yes," Regeane said, and looked directly into his eyes. "Yes, I will. You need have no fear he will default." She pressed his hand. "My love," she whispered. "Don't deny me this opportunity to save you."

In spite of the crowd and the courtiers peering down from the porch at them, the two seemed alone together. He stretched out his other hand and rested it against her cheek. Then, gently, kissed her on the lips.

"So fair a victor, how can I help but be conquered. It will be as you wish, my love," he said.

Women in the crowd were weeping; Chiara was weeping, tears pouring down her face.

The bishop studied them both, then said to Desiderius, "Better it is to settle quarrels with money than blood. Release him."

"Very well," the king said.

He was cheered. He looked uncomfortable. Desiderius wasn't used to being popular. Maeniel said the same thing to Regeane when he whispered to her, "The king is not used to the affection of his people."

"Don't worry," she replied in an even softer voice. "He won't have it long."

Maeniel pulled her closer to his side, then looked up at the sky. It was noon or only a little later. The sun beat down on the crowd. Only the porch, where the king had his mercenaries, courtiers, and other notables, was in shade. Not a breath of air was stirring.

"Do you feel it?" she whispered to Maeniel.

"Yes—since this morning. Even in that horrible hole they call the bottle. Even before dawn I knew."

"Very well," Desiderius said, and clapped his hands. "This business is settled." He gave Maeniel an oblique glance. "And settled, I hope, to the satisfaction of all."

Regeane felt Maeniel's hand tighten on hers.

He's lying, she thought. *Maeniel knows it; I know it; he doesn't mean to keep his bargain.*

"He's lying," the bear's voice spoke from his residence in Gimp. "He doesn't mean to let you go." Both Regeane and Maeniel heard the bear's words, as did Chiara and Hugo. "I'll wager," the bear continued, "that you will both be dead by nightfall."

"Yes," Maeniel answered bleakly. "I wouldn't take that bet. You might not ever be able to collect, but you'd win."

"I want one of you. I have the power. This enraged mob is like a fountain of life to me. Chose. Let me have one of you. Give me the woman-wolf, Maeniel, and I will get you out of the city into the forest. Or, if you like, yield yourself to me, and I will get her safely away. Otherwise you will both perish."

Maeniel pulled Regeane even closer. She felt the comforting warmth and strength of his body against hers, but they never got a chance to answer. Robert spoke up.

"Our business is not concluded," he said loudly.

Desiderius was turning to leave. "I will hear no more cases today," he snapped irritably.

"Oh, yes, you will," Robert roared. "You will hear this one."

Robert stood among the crowd of men within the larger throng. These were the ones Regeane had noticed earlier who drank no spirits and were somewhat more heavily clothed and didn't seem to feel the heat as much as others.

The bishop's eyes scanned them. He was still seated. "My lord," he said to Desiderius. "My lord, I think the matter is urgent and you should hear this one."

Something like the snarl of a giant animal rose from the mob.

The king paused.

His courtiers, even the mercenaries of his guard, looked frightened.

Robert's eyes were red from the long vigil in the church, and his face was ravaged by grief. To Regeane, he looked twenty years older than the boy Regeane had seen descending the stairs at his mother's house, alarm in his face. In time, Regeane knew, he would come to terms with his grief, but he would never be so young again.

There was a commotion at the edges of the square, and she saw some of Robert's friends escorting the five soldiers through the throng. The men had been disarmed, but otherwise, they seemed unharmed. The three older mercenaries were clearly frightened, but they had seen far too much violence to be completely intimidated by what they likely considered a few peasants. The two younger ones, not as hardened as the three older soldiers, looked terrified. The bodies of the ford keeper and his family, shrouded as they had been last night, were carried along behind them. She saw that one of the men accompanying the prisoners was Beningus, the law speaker.

A cloud covered the sun and a gentle breeze ruffled everyone's clothing. The smell of rain was strong on the wind. Down the alleyways between the warehouses, Regeane saw the sky darkening like a bruise all along the horizon. A storm, a big one, was coming from the mountains in the north.

The five corpses were rested, each on their biers, before the king. "These are?" Desiderius asked arrogantly.

Robert spoke their names beginning with the two men and then the boy and ending with the two women. "None died a natural death," he said. "Their wounds attest they were killed by steel."

Then the shrouds were removed and the wounds on each body revealed. Each body had a waxen yellow-white pallor, and the air was filled with the odor of spilled blood.

"I will agree," Desiderius said, his face tight with disgust, "they are, indeed, dead and they died as you have said. But what has this to do with me? Or—" He pointed toward the knot at one side near the throne. "—with the guardians of my person and my peace?"

"They are the killers," Robert said bluntly, and pointed to them.

"And have you some proof of this monstrous accusation?"

"Yes. The tavern keeper saw them leave early yesterday morning and return later with injuries. And when we searched their possessions, we found a ring belonging to my affianced wife; a pendant belonging to her mother, Itta; and two knives we recognized as belonging to the men of the household. Moreover," he said, and pointed to the oldest of the mercenaries, "the tavern keeper states this man's face was unmarked when he set out—as he said—to hunt, and the youngster had no wound on his arm. But when they returned, they were injured as you see."

"So," Desiderius said angrily. "I am to condemn faithful men of mine on the word of a drunken tavern keeper and the half-grown son of a widow who runs a house of ill repute?"

This last was a gratuitous insult. Everyone within earshot knew it. Dorcas was a model of propriety.

Robert went white with fury, but Beningus placed a hand on his shoulder and said, "Johns is a temperate and well-conducted merchant, and Dorcas sells bread for a living. Bread, I might add, that is eaten at your table. You may deny the accusation, my lord, but there is no need to insult those who bring it before you."

The crowd was silent.

Regeane noticed the wind was picking up.

"Very well," the king answered with ill grace. Then he pointed to the most hardened of the mercenaries, the man with scratches on his face. "Tell us," Desiderius ordered. "What happened?"

The man gave Robert a taunting, insolent look. "We went out, as it was said, to hunt, and those people attacked us at the ford. An ambush. They were not alone. Others were with them. We put up a fierce resistance to the cowardly assault by thieves, and the men were killed, the rest fled. As to the women—" He sniggered and elbowed the man nearest him. "—you can't blame us that we ran them down and collected some soldier's pay. They were not virgins and neither was really unwilling."

"Then why, I wonder," Beningus asked, "was it necessary to kill them?"

The large man looked uncomfortable. "We didn't do that. Must have been their menfolk when they came back and saw the ladies had been too accommodating." He gave a shaky laugh but no one, not even his comrades, joined him.

Desiderius snapped his fingers and pointed at the soldiers. "Release them forthwith."

Regeane felt nauseated. She could smell the scratched mercenary in a way no human possibly could. She knew what he'd done and knew Itta had inflicted the scratches, ugly ones, with her nails before she died.

No one moved.

The silence was thick now. Above, the sun was beginning to darken and the wind was blowing hard. The square was sheltered but occasional hard gusts lifted the dust into a cloud and whirlwinds danced like yellow wraiths over the humped cobbles. The men's mantles were fluttering, and women took a firmer grip on cloaks and veils.

Regeane saw, as did everyone else, that they were at an impasse. The armed mercenaries surrounding the king weren't about to jump down into the crowd and risk God knows what, and the men who'd captured the malefactors had no present or future intention of letting them go free.

Beningus tried to break the stalemate. "My lord," he said, addressing the king. "Perhaps before you act in such a hasty fashion, you should listen to Johns, the tavern keeper, and the men who accompanied Robert to retrieve the bodies. They will tell you that this family was caught unaware and unprepared. That there was no sign of any attack at the ford. Moreover the young girl, Mona, should be examined by the midwife to see if she was virgin before she was interfered with. You see, my lord, most possibly all the people here knew this family well, and they had a good name. None here consider them capable of an act of brigandage as is claimed by these soldiers."

Desiderius's face was flushed and his hands were shaking. He was, everyone knew, at the edge of an abyss. Robert was standing near Maeniel, who leaned over and spoke softly into his ear. No one but Regeane heard what he said.

"No, don't run mad. There are too many of them to keep a guilty secret. Put some pressure on one of the young ones. He will break."

Yes, Regeane thought.

The two youngest ones stood a little apart from the older three. One had his head bowed, seemingly drawn inside himself. He stared fearfully at nothing, eyes wide with shock. Robert picked him. He strode over to the soldiers and pulled him away from the rest. Holding the boy's shirt twisted tight in his fist, he roared, "All right, you tell me the girl I loved wasn't a virgin. You tell me she was a slut. Look me in the eye and tell me—tell me she wanted what was done to her."

The boy tried to turn aside.

"No, you stinking liar. Look. Look me in the eye and say it—"

"No." The boy broke as Maeniel said he would. "No, she didn't want us. She screamed and screamed. Oh, God, I can still hear her screaming in my head, even after I—" He paused, a look of horror frozen on his features.

"Even after you cut her throat?" Robert added in an unbelievably level tone.

"Yes," the boy answered in a strangled voice. "Yes, even then I could still hear her . . . screaming."

Robert stepped back and let go of the boy's shirt, wiping his hand on his tunic as if it were contaminated by something foul—as Regeane thought it had been. The boy sank to his knees on the stones, sobbing, moaning that he was damned.

Robert turned to Desiderius and pointed a finger at him. "You are no king. A king who will not administer his own laws and does not defend his people's lives is no king."

In the distance, lightning was flashing and thunder sounded a distant rumble.

Desiderius, in his turn, pointed at Robert. "Take that insolent little gutter rat out and hang him," he shouted at the soldiers gathered beneath the portico. "Do it and do it now."

Robert stood glaring at him defiantly.

The soldiers were afraid to move. The mob was a gigantic animal no one wanted to attack. Yes, there were about forty of them, well armed, in a position of command standing above the rabble on the porch, yet exclusive of women and children, there were at least several hundred able-bodied men among the citizens, and yes, these were men with families. So if the king and his mercenaries took a firm stand, they might run . . . But if they didn't, if they chose to fight back, the results could well prove disastrous for king, courtiers, and soldiers alike.

The bishop, old as he was, tried to save the situation. "My lord king," he spoke loudly into the tense silence. "My lord king, the boy's confession belies the first tale told. It is left to you to find the truth, and if these scoundrels deserve hanging, why, hang them.

"And you, young man," he spoke to Robert, "your sorrow and anger are understandable, but do not provoke your sovereign lord further. You have proven the truth is not in these—" He gestured toward the mercenaries. "—these hirelings. Be content, I beg you."

The boy ran toward the bishop and threw himself on his knees in front of the prelate. The bishop lifted his hand in absolution and made the sign of the cross.

"Am I damned?" the boy asked.

"No," the bishop replied. "I have, as well as any man can, implored forgiveness for your sins, but you must make confession."

The youngster pointed at Robert. "He speaks the truth. I and my friends are guilty of murder. No one attacked us. We saw the women, desired them, and planned to catch them alone by the stream and have our pleasure of them by force, but the women fought. The young one got away to her menfolk, so . . ."

"So," the bishop continued. "I know, there was no help for it. You must kill them all."

The bishop gave Desiderius a bleak look. "You are the king. Do justice." He looked up at the exposed braces of the colonnade, beams high up helping to hold the colonnade away from the building. He pointed. "They will do for a gallows."

A spatter of rain struck the square. Regeane felt a few drops brush her face. All around her Regeane heard people sigh. At the edges of the crowd the less interested members of the assembly, seeing the imminent arrival of the storm, began hurrying away to their homes. Regeane grabbed Maeniel's arm and moved him toward the bishop. She was hoping somehow to put both of them under his protection. Desiderius was a treacherous man. Maeniel was fettered still. Somehow, she had to get that collar from around his neck.

She saw the anger in the king's face and the fear in Hugo's when she pulled Maeniel toward the bishop. Rain was reaching the square as a wind-driven mist and under it the crowd was melting away. Regeane's clothing was drenched before she quite realized how it happened. Hugo bent over and spoke to the king in a low voice. Desiderius lifted his hand.

No, she thought. *No.*

Remingus the ghost, the terror, the mummified corpse, was beside her. His eye holes stared at Hugo.

The captain of the guard had a spear. Hugo snatched it and let it fly at Regeane. The spear took her in the body, low above her left hip. The pain of death ripped through her, and she fell back into the street. The change tried to take her the way a hawk takes a rabbit with a sudden pounce. She fended it off. She was still frightened of what the mob might do if she went wolf in the open day.

"Call the wolf," Maeniel roared. "Call the wolf, Regeane. Only the wolf can save you."

The full force of the storm hit then. Rain slashed at the crowd. The women fled toward the church, but the men didn't run. The world was fading. Maeniel went wolf as the lightning hit. The fetters fell away.

The chain, Regeane thought, still struggling in the street, *the chain.*

The collar was still around his neck and attached to the chain, but the end of the chain was no longer under the control of Desiderius's captain. A second later Maeniel was a man again, and the chain was a weapon.

The first of the mercenaries to try to take him died horribly. The chain swung around the man's neck. His face turned scarlet, then blue. Maeniel jerked; the links snapped into a tighter spiral and ripped the man's head off. The mercenaries on the porch fired into the mob. Led by Maeniel, Robert and his friends charged the porch.

Regeane felt her senses drenched by night as the wolf gained full control, and the silver wolf crouched on the cobbles. The nobles and functionaries of the Lombard court jammed the doorway into the palace in hysterical flight. Heedless of anyone's safety but the king's, the captain of the guard pulled his men in, made them into a wide wedge, and driving over and through the bodies of the terrified courtiers, he took the king into the palace. The silver wolf saw Hugo among the last few stragglers, clawing at the captain's back. He turned and, fixing Hugo with a malevolent glare, threw him at Maeniel who was leading the charge.

Maeniel simply elbowed him aside in his attempt to reach the king, but again, the captain of the guard prevailed. His mace slammed into Maeniel's shoulder and drove him to his knees. He was unable to really hurt the wolf but their struggling bodies blocked the entrance and gave the rest of the guard, now in mortal terror of the mob, time to swing the big doors outward.

"Back away," he told Maeniel. "We will slaughter those in the passage. Back away."

Maeniel and Robert both knew it was true. The narrow passage led directly into the palace courtyard and was constructed so as to be easily held by a few men. The door slammed shut and the sound was lost in the almost constant drumroll of thunder from above.

The bishop remained seated in his chair. The few stragglers who hadn't been able to escape with the king were crouched around him. These included Chiara, Armine—who embraced her protectively—a few elderly men, women, and Hugo, who had managed to elbow the weaker people aside and capture the position closest to the bishop.

Regeane saw that there was no sanity left in the faces of the mob.

Maeniel stepped deliberately between the bishop and the furious men, and coiled the chain around his arm. He said, "No. They are helpless and innocent. Robert, where are the killers?"

The bishop then demonstrated his acuity. "They fled," he said. "They could not get into the palace and the rest would not defend them." He pointed to the street leading to the cathedral, the only really good entrance to the square.

"No," Robert shouted. Sheets and sheets of blowing rain were flung across the square. "We'll never catch them in this."

"Speak for yourself," Maeniel shouted back. "And if I am too slow, my wife can."

Regeane spun around and charged across the square. Robert and the others followed into the rain. Lightning struck close to the porch, the bolt driving into one of the warehouses. Flames blossomed, filling the air with the harsh scent of burning hair and feathers, only to be extinguished by the driving rain.

Regeane, hard on the heels of the criminal band, faltered for a second, then ran on. The wind was in her face telling her they were ahead and frantic with fear.

Maeniel spared a moment for the bishop. "Get them into the church."

The bishop was already on his feet and gathering his little flock around him when Maeniel went wolf. The wolf glared for a moment at Hugo with savage yellow eyes. Hugo scrambled behind the bishop, pushing Armine and Chiara aside. Armine pushed back. The heel of his hand caught Hugo in the chest, sending him spinning into the rain.

The bishop glanced back at Maeniel. The wolf's lower jaw dropped, his tongue lolled, and for a moment the bishop would have sworn the animal was laughing. Then the wolf leaped from the porch and followed the rest, the chain snapping and dancing behind him, striking the cobbles as he ran and sending sparks flying.

Fire in the rain.

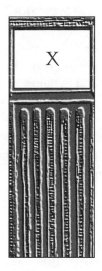

THE SAXON HEARD NOTHING, SAW NOTHING, but one moment she wasn't there and the next moment she was. He was stirring his low fire with a stick, wondering if he should bother to add more fuel, since he was about to roll himself up in the bearskin and sleep, when he felt eyes on him, looked up, and saw the black wolf. She was sitting on her haunches and staring at him from across the fire.

"Matrona?"

A second later she was a woman, the firelight's shifting patterns illuminating her voluptuous flesh. He averted his eyes and pulled off his mantle.

Matrona laughed. "You worry so about a little skin, you humans. Why not take a good look? What? Am I repulsive?"

"No!" he answered shortly. "Quite the reverse, but I would not be shamed or have my manhood show itself to no purpose."

Matrona gave a husky laugh. "How do you know it would be to no purpose?"

This time he blushed. "I wouldn't care to be caught with the king's mistress."

The woman—the black wolf—was wearing a necklace, a magnificent cloisonné dragon with scales of ruby, amber, topaz, and sapphire. Matrona gave a throaty laugh. She was wrapped in his best embroidered woolen mantle now, so he could look at her. She walked around the fire and stroked his rather bristly cheek with one long-fingered hand.

"Listen, you beautiful brute—and you are beautiful—I am no man's mistress and no man's, not even a king's, possession. I do what I like, with whom I like, and whenever I like. I always have and always will. Yes, I lay with Charles; the lord Maeniel requested it. The king enjoyed the experience and so showed me his favor. And he opened his mind to me. That's why I am here. Where are they? Charles is on the march across the mountains, but he entrusted the lord Maeniel with an important task. If he has failed, I am to undertake it, and if I fail, you are to finish."

"What?"

Matrona picked up a stick and drew a crude map. "Charles comes," she said, and made a line indicating one pass through the mountains. "His uncle Bernard follows another route. Here!"

"He split his force?"

"Yes, but so did Desiderius. One half is based at Ivrea, the other at Susa. If Charles attacks at either place, he feels sure Desiderius will pull his force from the other. Tell me the result. You have commanded men. You will see Charles's plan."

"Yes, I do," the Saxon answered. "When the attack comes, Desiderius will believe Charles's main force is there. For instance, if Charles attacks at Susa—because, were I Charles, that is where I would go—Desiderius will strip Ivrea of its strongest warriors. Then Charles's uncle, commanding the force at Ivrea, can attack the weakened garrison, punch through, and make a flank attack at Susa. Attacked from before and behind, Desiderius's forces will flee back toward Pavia. He dare not lose his army to Charles, but will hope to stand a siege."

Matrona nodded. "But," she said, "there are no maps of the land between Ivrea and Susa. When Charles's uncle reaches the garrison, the force at Ivrea must ride swiftly to Susa. The countryside is forested, wild, without clear roads or tracks. The wolf was to find the quickest way from Ivrea to a point at Desiderius's flank at Susa. Now I ask you, where are they? They both should be back by now."

"I don't know. They quarreled."

Matrona heaved a deep sigh. "He feared for her."

"Yes. But she followed, traveling in some way I cannot comprehend."

"The Lady's Mirror?"

"Yes. I promised to wait for her. As you see, I am here."

"Yes," Matrona said. "I know where it is. I traveled here with my people long ago, but it won't do me any good, at least not before morning. That place is dangerous by starlight."

The Saxon looked away from her into the dark forest. His imagination kept presenting him with a picture of what he'd seen before she'd wrapped herself in the mantle. All of a sudden he found he wasn't the least bit tired. But he did feel a need to get away from her before he made a complete fool of himself.

"I will conduct you there in the morning," he said. "The countryside hereabouts has changed over time, and I will continue to—"

Matrona stroked his cheek again. "Aren't you tired of waiting? How long has it been?"

"Since I got here?"

"No," Matrona said, and kissed him.

Lucilla was caught and she knew it. A second later Ansgar's son had the doors closed and his back against them.

"Stay there, Ludolf," Ansgar ordered, "until I find out what this is about. Lucilla?" he asked his wife.

She sneezed again. "Oh, God, yes, this is Lucilla. Pope Hadrian's . . . friend. Damn it, Lucilla, you tell me what you're doing here and don't stand there trying to look as if butter wouldn't melt in your mouth. I know you. And you wouldn't be here unless you were up to something."

"Lucilla?" Ansgar repeated. "The name is well known. And no, don't tell me what you're up to. I don't want to know. Stella," he addressed his wife, "no more questions."

Stella looked half-sick but outraged. "Just the same . . . husband, I tell you—"

"No, you have told me enough. Don't say any more. I don't want to be privy to some plot. I don't care to know of something that would require me to take drastic action. My lady Dulcinia, how could you allow yourself to be used in a way as to create such an embarrassing situation? I am a liege man of Desiderius, the Lombard king. I hold my lands according to his appointment as my father did before me, and I owe good faith and loyalty to my lord.

"Now, Lucilla," he continued sternly. "Are those men, the escort you brought with you, are they pledged to you?"

Lucilla gathered her wits. "No," she said. "No, they belong to Count Rufus of Nepi. Please, please, Ansgar, no bloodshed. Allow me to pay them for their services and dismiss them quietly."

"Very well, but no tricks. And nothing passes between you that my son cannot hear or see, and your friend, Dulcinia, remains here as surety for your good behavior while you go about this business. Son, accompany her, alert your uncle, but do nothing that will alarm the town."

Lucilla withdrew on Ludolf's arm.

"Dulcinia, you tell me what's going on," Stella said sternly.

"No, Dulcinia, don't, and Stella, you be quiet."

Stella sneezed three times and blew her nose in her handkerchief. "Oh, God, I feel awful and now this. Husband, she's up to something and you should find out now what—"

"Shush, dear," he said, embracing Stella. "Go back up. We will talk at supper. You're ill and need your rest now."

"My sweet," she said, "don't kiss me. You'll get whatever I have."

He shook his head. "No, I don't think so. Every spring like clockwork—and sometimes in the autumn—it comes upon you. Only Ludolf ever seems to suffer the way you do, though not so badly, thank heaven. And since he's your son, I can't think it's contagious. Now do as you always do, be an obedient and sensible wife. Go rest and we will talk later at dinner."

Stella climbed the stair, still muttering to herself. "Obedient and sensible, indeed." Ansgar could be so maddening. Lucilla's presence alarmed her and her darling husband didn't seem to have the slightest idea how upsetting this particular development was. *To tell the truth,* Stella thought, *I am afraid.* Instead of going to her own room, she turned into her husband's. It overlooked the square.

A group of servants were clustered at the window when she entered. All except her maid, Avernia, scattered. Avernia was a privileged character. She'd been with Stella since she took her first lover in Rome, at Lucilla's behest. Stella joined her at the window.

"Is that who I think it is?" Avernia asked.

"Yes," Stella snapped.

"As I live and breathe. Lucilla. Ah, well, you have nothing to fear. He knows all about you."

Stella gave her a withering look. "Any woman is a fool who lets any man know all about her.

"I told him when we met that I was practically a virgin—that Aldric was my first lover."

Avernia's eyes rolled. "No! You never said that."

"I was the star attraction in a brothel and, pregnant or not, he'd never have married me if he hadn't believed I was a wronged woman."

"What are you going to do?" Avernia looked frightened.

Stella licked her lips. "I don't know, but she can't stay here. Sooner or later she will pay me back for naming her to my husband by telling him all about my little adventures in Rome."

"He still won't repudiate you," Avernia said. "You are the mother of his children. Surely he wouldn't. No, it would be impossible—"

"Shut the door," Stella said between her teeth. "What, do you want to tell the whole household?"

Avernia ran, pulled the heavy oak door shut, and shot a big iron bolt.

Stella sat on the bed, clenching and unclenching her fists in her silk gown. "Damn Lucilla," she whispered. "Damn that scheming whore. What is she doing here? How dare she interfere in my life again. How dare she chance causing Ansgar trouble."

Avernia shrugged. "I can't think that what she's doing here matters. The problem is how to get rid of her."

"God," Stella whispered. "God. Ansgar is the best thing that ever happened to me. Why does she come here now and ruin everything? I'll kill her if she makes me look a common strumpet to him."

"Well, that's what you were."

The crack of the slap echoed in the room. Avernia shrieked so loudly that Stella was certain it had been heard in the street. Avernia burst into tears and began to run toward the door. Stella jumped up and threw her arms around Avernia. "No, no, don't. Don't run out there and create a scene. You have as much to lose by this as I have. You must stay here and help me think of a way out of this."

Avernia wanted to have hysterics, but there was so much truth in what Stella said that she brought her anger and hurt under control at once. She had a husband also, the town blacksmith. She'd borne him five children, all living and prospering in the new city. She couldn't afford scandal about her past, either. "All right, but don't slap people who are just telling you the truth. Put your mind to solving this. Losing your temper with me won't help."

"Yes, yes. Be quiet and let me think." Stella began to pace up and down. Her second circuit of the room brought her to the window. She looked down at Lucilla in the square below. She paused, then strode quickly over to her husband's desk against the far wall opposite the bed, sat down, found a wax tablet, and laboriously began to write.

"What are you doing?"

"I don't think Lucilla will want to interfere in my life if I give her a few problems of her own to worry about."

"How will you do that?"

Stella didn't answer but instead asked, "Are your sons still riding to Florence to purchase scrap iron?"

"Yes."

"Then they can carry a letter."

"They will if I tell them."

"You had best tell them, and not one word to Ansgar. Hear me? Not one word."

"I don't—"

"I do." Stella looked up. "You had best keep your mouth shut. Do it for both our sakes. Or that big, strong, bad-tempered husband of yours will find out how you earned your dowry."

Avernia gasped. "No." She made the sign of the cross. "I am silent as the grave, and so are my sons. I swear it."

SOMETIME JUST BEFORE DAWN THE SAXON ASKED Matrona, "How did you know I was not a peasant?"

She laughed. "What peasant knows how to clean the rust from mail, pick a fine warhorse and battle train him, sharpen a sword so expertly that it will shave a boar's bristles but leave the blade polished like a mirror? In the matter of the sword, I watched you with the weapon you picked up at that hideous place where you and Regeane tried to shelter. The thing had the look of a fire poker and, indeed, I believe someone probably used it for that purpose, but within a week you had it clean, sharp, and glowing like moonlight."

"Though mistreated, a fine weapon," the Saxon agreed. "I had to sacrifice some steel to clear the corrosion and rust from the blade, but since it was finely crafted in the first place, it was not harmed in the process. All sharpening takes steel from a blade; a good smith allows for that."

"Spoken like a true farmer," Matrona said. "They always worry a lot about their edged toys."

"In my country, sometimes they do," the Saxon replied. "I cannot be sorry for being taken for a son of the soil."

"Yes! Is that why you let them use you as a mule when you were sold across the mountains?"

"How did you know?"

He must have blushed; Matrona felt the heat in his skin. "Your body is marked by both the harness and the lash," she said. "Why didn't you let your kin ransom you?"

He was silent.

"Why?" she asked again.

"Am I sharing your bed or are you sharing mine?"

"We are in the forest, there are no beds," Matrona answered.

He absorbed this for a moment. "No promises between us."

"None. Mutual pleasure, that is all."

"I was too proud. My lady mother was dead. I would not have men point at me and say, there goes a man with a known price, and then hear women laugh. I would rather do the work of a mule."

Matrona sighed. "Men, the things they do in the name of honor."

"I think you cannot know. Many nights I confess I lay weeping in the vile cowshed where we were chained, wishing desperately for my home, my horses, hawks, and hounds. They would have killed me in some slow fashion had I been recaptured. I killed two men when I escaped, but better death than everlasting slavery, everlasting exile."

"Yes," Matrona answered.

"Even you?"

"Yes. Once, a time or two, I made the choice; but I'm falling asleep."

He replied by embracing her more tightly. He didn't know if he clung to her or she to him, but after so long alone, the feel of a woman's body was comforting.

He owed Regeane and her people everything. He dreamed of them, the wolves in the mist. Graceful, confident, moving down at nightfall ghostlike through the trees. Above, the sun was slipping into shadow as the clouds moved down from the mountains. He had been going down to his camp. Also, he was carrying a gutted deer carcass over his shoulders. He'd wondered if they would attack, try to take the deer from him. But they didn't.

One by one, they appeared, so like the patchy snow on the forest floor, gray white with glowing eyes, that he was not aware they were present until movement drew attention to them. He saluted them and watched them pass, the massive leader and his she the last. And he knew, without knowing how he knew, that they had been watching him, able to attack and kill him easily had he made any move against the rest, but they respected the coiled power they saw in him, as he in them. So they had a truce, one dangerous predator to another.

And when he was in the greatest danger of his life, they had come to offer protection and comfort, and they had sheltered him and set him free.

When she woke the sun was casting shafts of light between the pines. He was up; she smelled fresh bread. She rose, pushed the blankets aside. He averted his eyes and offered her his mantle. Matrona chuckled.

"What? You are not cured yet?"

"Looking at you makes me want to begin again."

"Make sure your wife is a warm-natured woman, otherwise I pity her. There is nothing better or worse than being constantly pursued about the house by a panting husband."

"Better or worse?" He got no reply and when he turned, she was gone.

The golden dragon lay among the folds of his mantle on the forest floor.

THE VIRGIN WOLF IS THE FASTEST OF ALL, THE most dangerous. The wind and driving rain were in Regeane's face, but the rain didn't bother her. The wolf is a wonderful bad-weather animal and the wind told her in which direction the killers were fleeing among the narrow, twisting streets of the town. The Roman grid pattern had long been superseded by the medieval mileage of tangled footways leading to miniature plazas.

The chase was complicated by the fact that in their terror, the fugitives ignored walls, fences, and even dwellings blocking their way to freedom. Led by the warrior with the scratched face, they kicked down the door of one house, exited into a walled garden, and jumped the wall—it was covered with spikes—when Regeane, hot on their heels, exited the house. She had two seconds to decide whether she would follow. Since she'd had no occasion to find out how high she could jump as a wolf, she was gratified to learn she could clear seven feet, but one of the spikes brushed her stomach, sending a chill of terror through her whole body. As soon as she landed in the stony street beyond, she understood why they had undertaken a maneuver hazardous even for a human. The dismay in their faces was almost comical. Almost. She could have been impaled on one of those spikes and killed.

The leader picked up a stone; thrown by a man's arm it was almost as dangerous as a crossbow bolt. She jerked, twisting to the left with the sinuous grace of a snake. But it caught her in the left chest, paralyzing her foreleg at the shoulder. She let out a cry of anguish, half howl, half scream, as she plowed into the stony street. But her legs were already moving, her claws catching at cracks in the paving. The pain—and she realized that the only injury was intense pain—receded and she got her legs under her.

The scratch-faced one was almost on top of her. Throat: too close. Groin: he was a soldier, too much chance he was wearing protection. The sensitive inside of the upper thigh: beautiful—it was his turn to scream. But he had a bigger rock. It grazed the side of her face, almost amputating one ear. She was forced to jump back, and he was on his feet and away but now he was leaving a trail of blood.

To a wolf it might as well have been a trail of burning pitch. She let out a cry, wolf speech, *The quarry is just ahead,* and heard and smelled rather than saw Maeniel and the rest at the end of the street. The chain striking the stones made a fearsome clatter. Then she took out after them again.

The street rose sharply and turned into a climbing stair. When she passed the bend, she saw the one she'd marked struggling in a welter of blood. She knew she must have nicked the big artery in his thigh. Almost she pitied him, but then she remembered Itta's eyes looking up at her, open, empty in death, through the clear water, and she knew he must have been the one to push the woman into the water, drive his knife through her ribs, holding her to the muddy bottom in the shallows until she drowned.

Her pity evaporated. She jumped, clearing his struggling body, and continued after the rest. By the nose she knew Maeniel, Robert, and his friends were behind her. That damned chain, what an ungodly racket. What would they do about that damned chain?

The street was a ramp now and curved outward, looking down on the city. The spear seemed almost leisurely as it arched above her. For a second she slowed and all her muscles jerked. She was thinking it might be aimed at her, but it wasn't, and she could see that clearly once it flashed overhead.

A beautiful throw. Beautiful. She and Maeniel hunted together after the human fashion and she knew how a spear should be handled. Of the four remaining criminals, the two older men were flagging now. The boys outpaced them.

The spear, at the highest point of its arc, broke, then fell, catching the slowest of the fugitives at the point where the shoulders joined the neck and shearing through the spinal cord. He fell, bonelessly dead even before he hit the ground. Three remained. Wolf kill, cat kill, they kill different ways. The wolf runs its prey into the ground. The cat is agile, the bite a death blow dispatching its victim instantly. But to the beast of mutable flesh and tangible moonlight, both ways were open.

Wolf kill, Regeane thought and loosed her last kick. Deadly, almost as fast as a cheetah, faster than most beasts of the hoof can run, she came, closing the gap between herself and the other straggler. He'd killed the boy and taken pleasure in the deed. The son had been, for all his weedy build, only a child and almost defenseless, an easy kill.

The broad, shallow-stepped street curved out over the town below with only a low safety wall between the street and a fall into the jumble of red-tiled roofs below. Behind, making the best pace he could, Maeniel felt his heart jump into his throat. He dropped back, ready to take out any man among Robert's friends who loosed another spear, but none among them even looked like trying it. They, as much as the wolf, scented blood and were ready to go hand to hand with the survivors.

Ahead, Regeane paced her chosen prey. He caught sight of her from the corner of his eye. He was running at the outer edge of the street, the safety rail no higher than his knee. He swerved toward it and his knee slammed painfully into the stone curb, but he might have saved himself if her shoulder and snapping jaws hadn't crowded his left side. He lost his balance and went over. The scream was terrible, chilling, but brief. His head contacted a terra-cotta roof tile. It snapped his neck and crushed his skull.

Regeane slowed for the final push. The street had reached the hilltop and the two ahead were counting on being faster than the wolves or Robert and his friends on the downslope. The rain had abated but the wolf warned Regeane that the storm had not ended, since it was growing darker by the moment. The light was failing and a greenish nightmare twilight hung over the city. Lightning flashed, striking close by, and the almost simultaneous explosion of thunder struck terror into the wolf. She almost escaped the woman's control. She slowed drastically. Her hair stood on end as static electricity danced like fire on her pelt, but the woman commanded the wolf. Inexorably, she shook off her fear, and her vision, dazzled by the flash, cleared. But when she was able to see ahead, she found the remaining pair of fugitives had vanished.

I N THE SQUARE, CHIARA WATCHED IN WIDE-EYED shock as the mob took up the chase.

"I warned you, dammit, I warned you," Hugo's guest roared.

For a moment Chiara didn't reply, then she said, "At least thank God they're gone."

"Don't bother to thank God. Thank the bishop. If he hadn't spoken up when he did—"

"We might well be dangling from the rafters. The mob was hot to hang someone, and they might have accepted substitutions."

The bishop was standing up. "No," he said to Chiara. "They are not all gone."

The weapons of Desiderius's guard had taken some effect. There were five sodden, bloody bundles left lying on the cobbles. At least three of them were still moving. Even though the sky was growing darker, the rain was abating; the bishop shrugged away his golden cope and robe. He was dressed in a worn linen tunic and trousers. He jumped a bit awkwardly from the porch and began to make the rounds of the wounded. Absolving as well as he could the sins of the living as well as the dead, he began to call out orders.

"You men go fetch litters. There are some in the church. The wounded must be moved to some safer spot. And take up the dead—" The corpses still lay where they had been placed earlier for the king's inspection. "Place them on the porch, sheltered from the rain until they can be given Christian burial."

Gimp, directed by Hugo's guest, and a couple of the other men helped in moving the bodies, while another party, some of them women, ran to the church.

Armine continued to hold a still-trembling Chiara. "Child," he said. "You have seen this day enough to unsettle the souls of grown men. Indeed, I shall not forget it."

The bishop returned to the palace porch. Armine gave him a hand up. His clothing was drenched, his sparse hair plastered to his scalp, but he looked oddly younger than he had when he had been weighed down with his ceremonial cope and golden robe.

"Two are beyond help. One, I don't know. Badly wounded. The remaining two will likely live if they are taken to shelter and given prompt attention."

Just then two men with a litter arrived. The bishop directed them in moving the wounded to the church. Chiara pulled free of Armine's grip and ran to the other end of the porch where the corpses now lay. The two youngest were together at the end of the row; they had been placed close to the palace door. Chiara looked down at Mona and her cousin. The skull-crushing wound in the boy's head had been washed by the rain and the mourners. It was a raw, red gash in his livid scalp and face. Mona's slit throat had been sewn together, but her hand showed the stump of a finger where the ring had been cut off.

"They are not more than children," Chiara whispered, reaching down to touch Mona's face.

"She was fourteen, he twelve," Hugo's guest told her.

"How did you know?"

"I heard it being discussed. I hear a lot of things. Now come away. I warned you."

Chiara ground her teeth. "You shut up, you . . . you . . . you . . ."

"What must I do next?" the spirit said, and laughed. "Teach you some mighty oaths?"

"I wish you had a face so I could slap it," Chiara said. "And by the way, what did you mean by that charade in my bedroom last night?"

Before he could answer, Armine arrived. "Dearest daughter, to whom are you speaking?"

Chiara looked around wildly. "Gimp," she more or less suggested.

"He is not here," her father said sternly.

"Hugo?" she said hopefully.

"He is in an absolute spasm of terror, clinging to the bishop's chair."

Down at the other end of the portico the bishop was trying to pry Hugo away from his chair and having little success in his endeavors. Most of the rest were crossing the square on their way to the cathedral. The rain slowed but the sky was black as night.

"Come, the weather is worsening. Come," Armine said in a tone that brooked no disobedience. He took her hand and began to pull her toward the edge of the porch.

"No," the spirit said. "Don't."

Chiara pulled free and spoke to the empty air in a way that frightened Armine more than the storm or the mob had.

"No," she repeated. "What's going to happen?"

"Be quiet," Hugo's guest said. "I'm listening. One."

Chiara glanced around, eyes dilated with terror.

"Two," Hugo's guest said. "Down, down, down," he shrieked. "On . . . three."

The lightning bolt hit. The whole forum was illuminated with an unearthly blue glow. The church tower, highest structure in the forum, crumbled, the heavy stones punching like nails through the leaded roof of the cathedral. The wooden framing crumbled and burst into flames.

Chiara saw the bishop flung away from Hugo as if by a push from a gigantic hand. Hugo was looking up at the sky, his mouth hanging open, and then a split second later, Chiara realized Hugo could see nothing. Only the whites of his eyes were showing, and then he collapsed like a rag doll.

Armine somehow stayed upright, clinging to his daughter tightly.

The bishop spun 'round and 'round until he, too, somehow ended up in Armine's arms. The explosion of thunder was simply deafening, the worst sound Armine had ever heard since the time he had only just barely escaped an avalanche in the Alps some years before. In fact, this sound was even worse.

The rain struck right behind the lightning, sheets and sheets of wild, wind-driven, blinding rain. Rain so thick that it was now impossible to see across the square. Rain that extinguished the fire in the belfry. Armine was a big, powerful man. He circled Chiara and the bishop in his arms and sheltered them against the blast until both wind and rain died down enough for them to flee the palace porch into the half-ruined cathedral. It was of Roman construction, stone and concrete, and, except for a few holes in the roof on one side, it remained hospitable, warm and dry.

A SECOND LATER, REGEANE REACHED THE HILLTOP herself. Both of the men she had been pursuing were gone. She had expected to see them on the downslope leading to the gate. The same blinding rain hit that had struck the square, slowing the wolf again.

Where? Where had they gone? One side of the street was a wall supporting a villa on a still-higher hill, but on the right side what had been a drop had become a tree-covered slope—steep to be sure, but climbable—that led down to a marshy swamp the river flooded every spring.

Regeane slowed, the wind and rain lashed her, soaking her fur and chilling her body. But her blood was up and she longed for the kill. The ancient dreams of females in wolf packs long ago commanded her, called out to her heart. *O little one, new one, for this you were born. When there were no humans, when we ruled and roamed the earth's hardest, most difficult places, glaciers, deserts of snow and ice, plains where grass dies in the scorching summer heat and fuels wildfires that darken the sky, forests, green forests where rain never stops, once in all of these we ruled and prospered. Strong and without fear. O most dangerous of mortals, drive your prey before you and strike it down.*

Yes, there they were! Forging their way down the slope through the brush. Weeds, blackberry, canes, wild roses, scrub pine, birch, and low-growing oak were making travel difficult. But if they could gain the river . . . She saw several small boats moored in the shallows; if they managed to get to one of those, they might escape. Once downstream they could lose themselves in the vast wetlands—only half tamed even in Roman times—of the Po valley.

Not even the wolves could trail them into the endless thickets of reeds, cattails, scattered islands, and tiny waterways formed by the river. Beyond lay the coast and ships that could take them away forever from any possible pursuit.

No, Regeane thought. *No.*

She leaped the low stone curb separating the street from the slope. Down she went, half running, half sliding through mud churned by freshets started by the teeming rain pouring down the slope. She half slid, half ran until the hill grew less steep, and she found better footing on grass and tall weeds, golden broom stitched with the thorny canes of wild roses.

The blow took her by surprise. One of them had turned and broken a heavy cudgel from a scrub oak. She staggered and he thrust the branch in her face, trying for her eyes. Enraged, she went for his throat, failed, and fell back as one of the sharp branches pierced her shoulder. She cried out in pain, trying to get her legs under her, but something that felt like the effective end of a battering ram slammed into her.

Maeniel, coming in hard, fast, and murderous. He hamstrung the man and tore out his throat.

Robert was hard on Maeniel's heels. He spared his foe's jerking body only a glance and closed on the last of the murderers, the boy who had confessed in the square.

He turned at bay, back to a thick, twisted willow trunk. Robert was upon him.

The two wolves simply watched. The mercenary had one last trick. He threw up his hands and said, "No!" as if in abject surrender. Then he went for Robert's eyes with two fingers of one hand and—somehow he had a knife—he went for Robert's belly, an underhand slash, with the other.

Robert, still coming down the slope, wasn't fooled for a moment. He tucked in his chin, half turned, and drove his own knife up through the diaphragm, through one lobe of the lung, and into the pericardium of his foe. In return, he took a wicked slash through the muscles of his left side below the ribs. But then his elbow snapped back, tearing the knife from the mercenary's hand, leaving him staring down at Robert's dagger protruding from just below his ribs. Robert backed away.

The two men's eyes met.

"It is mortal," the boy said, his hands clutching at Robert's knife.

"You will live until I pull it free," Robert told him.

"Have I killed you, too?" the boy asked.

For the first time Robert realized he was wounded. He explored the gash with the fingers of his right hand. "No, it is into the meat," he said.

"I'm glad," the boy said. "Enough has been done. I began it. I saw her when we crossed the river to take Desiderius's pay. I worked on the minds of the others. She smiled at me. She was beautiful. I hated you. I knew I would never have anything like that for my own. I don't know you; but I hated you."

Robert's hand reached forward and snapped shut around the hilt of his knife.

"Watch out."

Regeane heard the outcry from behind her and saw those remaining friends of Robert's were standing on the road looking down.

"I think not," Maeniel said. He was human and was trying to untangle his chain from a bush.

Robert placed his left arm like a bar across his foe's chest.

"Forgive me?" the boy asked.

"No," Robert said. "But I will let you ask God's forgiveness. I would not have you burn in hell. You have but a moment."

"I know," the boy said. "My heart stutters. My chest is filled with blood. Wait." He closed his eyes.

They waited, Robert, the men standing in the road, Regeane, and Maeniel. He was now wolf again. Then the boy's eyes opened. He grabbed Robert's wrist and jerked his hand back, pulling the knife free. It was followed by a terrible gush of blood.

The boy's eyes widened. A look of surprise spread over his features. "It doesn't hurt as much as I thought it would," he said, and then slumped down and died.

Robert staggered back a few paces, then sat down among the reeds in the muddy water and rested his forehead on his knees.

Regeane and Maeniel continued down the slope. Regeane was frightened for Maeniel. If he tried to swim the river with the chain around his neck, he might drown. But when they reached the bottom, Robert seized the collar around Maeniel's neck and tried to bend it open bare-handed. At first he had no success, but then suddenly, aided by a massive thrust of raw power, the collar twisted open in his hands. Robert didn't know how he'd done what he'd done, but Regeane and Maeniel both heard the bear's voice.

"Go ahead, run away, I can't stop you. And I certainly don't want you to drown. I want that fine body of yours undamaged—and your wife. I'll get her, too. Just you wait and see if I don't."

Maeniel vanished into the reeds and thick water plants at the river's edge. Robert hugged Regeane. For a moment, she rested her muzzle on his shoulder, then she, too, pulled away and was gone.

INSIDE THE CATHEDRAL THE BISHOP WAS OCCUPIED with the wounded. He was testy, cranky, and in very bad humor. Armine was helping him. This particular man was whining and moaning about an arrow sticking in his upper arm.

"It will mortify and I will die. The archers smear poison on them," the man cried. "Please, please, tell me I won't die."

"Shut up, Avold," the bishop snapped. "There's no poison on these arrows. The archers the king hires are too frightened of the stuff and too plain bone lazy to bother."

"You know a lot about this," Armine said.

"Yes," the bishop told him. "In my youth I was a notable warrior until the last king, the one preceding the present devious crook on the throne, decided he needed a bishop he was sure would not be a servant of the pope as head of this see."

At just this moment, the man the bishop was examining let out a blood-curdling scream. Not surprising, as the bishop had pushed the arrowhead through his shoulder and out the other side, then snapped the shaft, thus removing it all.

The bishop threw away the broken arrow, saying, "Now you're cured. Shut up."

When Armine tried to staunch the blood flowing from his patient's shoulder, the bishop snapped, "No, no. Let it stop of itself.

The blood will carry away any poison still left in the wound. Then put a clean bandage on him and send him home. There he can annoy his wife instead of me." Then the bishop moved on to the next casualty.

This one was quiet, pale, and very still. He seemed deeply unconscious. "Oh, God," the bishop whispered. "The only compensation I have had in my stint as the king's bishop is not to have to look at this sort of thing very often. He is gut shot and will almost surely die. All I can do is prepare opium and give it to his wife." The bishop shook his head and rose to his feet.

He turned toward the next but Armine pulled him aside. "My lord," Armine whispered. "I have reason to believe my daughter is . . ."

"Is what?" the bishop snarled. "Out with it, man, what? Pregnant?" His voice was loud.

"No. No. Shush. Be quiet. No, I don't think she's pregnant."

"Well, what then? In heaven's name, man, what?"

"Possessed."

"Possessed? In God's name—" The bishop spat. "In God's thrice holy name, what are you maundering about? Possessed, my ass—my horse's ass, my goat's ass. Possessed? In a pig's ass.

"Of course she's possessed. They're all possessed at that age. The boys, too. They are worse than the girls. At least girls are quiet about it. They are trapped in a mire of hot desire and fear of fulfillment. Yes, the boys, too. They have sex on the brain—all of them. Marry her off, you idiot. And see he is a man, you hear? A man, not a mincing fool. And she will be fine, and you will have grandchildren. You will both be happy. Fool, lack-wit, idiot. I am ridden by a plague of fools. Not the least of which is that treacherous royal sneak that occupies the throne. Ah, what I would give to have his father back . . . Yes, marry her off and not to that vicious little spider of a sorcerer Hugo."

"No," Armine said. "But I think no one need worry about Hugo any longer. I got a good look at his face before we ran to the cathedral. I think he's dead."

"Yes," the bishop said. "I agree. A fitting end for the drunken scoundrel. I, too, fear the lightning did its work well."

"Not well enough," someone said.

Armine, facing the bishop, saw his jaw drop. He spun around

and saw Hugo, standing in the archway leading from the vestibule of the cathedral, just stepping into the light of the candle's fitful illumination.

"I regret to say," Hugo told the bishop with a half-savage, half-triumphant grin, "I am still alive and not even badly injured."

Chiara, who was across the aisle helping some of the women tear a shift into linen bandages, looked up and gasped. She rose to her feet, seemingly transfixed, and then moved slowly toward Hugo. He smiled at her, the same savage grin he'd given Armine. His eyes sparkled with malice and intelligence, and he spoke in a low voice to Chiara who was, by now, only a few feet away.

Armine felt his mouth go dry. He swallowed a lump in his throat. No! Against all reason, against the evidence of his senses, he knew that what he was looking at—whatever he was looking at—it was not Hugo.

Only Chiara heard what it said to her, heard the words spoken by Hugo's mouth, tongue, and throat. "The way things are turning out is wonderful. Now, at last, I have a body of my own."

Chiara slumped to the floor in a faint, but did herself no injury because, with a look of utter longing and devotion, Hugo caught her and eased her to the marble tiles, ever so gently smoothing her hair back with one hand with great tenderness as he did so.

I WOULDN'T PUT ANYTHING PAST THAT GALLOPING bitch," Lucilla told Dulcinia. "Of all the bad luck, to be recognized on our first outing."

"Poor planning, I call it," Dulcinia said. "You should have known you were too prominent to escape detection."

"Well, we could have landed in worse places," Lucilla said.

This was true. Ansgar was not a cruel or violent man. Lucilla sent the men Rufus had lent her home to Nepi well compensated and carrying a rueful note to the pope admitting Ansgar had detected her intentions and would not assist her in further inquiries as to the location of the Frankish queen. Otherwise, Ansgar was the perfect host. It was spring. The countryside near the town was tranquil. Ansgar's brother, the bishop Gerald, was a devoted falconer. His hawks shared the church with his parishioners on Sunday, and after mass he rode out into the cool, fresh morning air accompanied by what Lucilla guessed was about half the town on horseback and on foot while he hunted with hawks and hounds.

His was a necessary contribution to the community. Migratory birds could and did devastate spring plantings. He and his fellow hunters reduced their flocks and frightened away a substantial number of the largest flights so that the crop could span the dangerous period of tender and succulent green youth to mature into bread wheat.

The daily harvest of woodcock, songbirds, rabbits, and the more slender, agile hare was prominently featured in the banquets that crowned almost every evening. Dulcinia sang at the banquets and, by popular and constant demand, at every other ceremony that offered even the slightest excuse for celebration of any kind: birthdays, weddings, christenings, saints' name days, all religious ceremonies, mass, te deums, benedictions, all the way down to humble funerals where the widow often found herself comforted by a magnificent rendition of "Stabat Mater" or "Panis Angelicus."

In fact, several die-hard pagans converted, simply because it gave them the opportunity to hear Dulcinia's voice during their baptismal ceremonies. Gerald, the bishop, was happy to have her sing before, during, and after mass. Next to his hawks, Dulcinia's art was his greatest pleasure. He would sit quietly while she sang, leaning back in his heavy, wooden throne at the altar, his eyes closed, with a great smile on his face.

One beautiful spring morning, Lucilla sat in the new cathedral, listening to her friend's voice soar and sharing the almost ecstatic peace the bishop and his congregation radiated during her friend's performance, wondering where it all came from. Although unfinished, the cathedral still managed to be beautiful. The walls were painted with important scenes from the life of Christ by a painter who had studied in, of all places, Athens. They were done in a fantastic, wind-blown style in light, bright colors on white stucco walls. The Marriage at Cana was celebrated with Christ as a beardless youth with dark, curly hair, seated with his mother among the wedding guests, crowned with laurel. On the other side of the church he was visiting in the temple, smiling, instructing his apparently astonished and delighted elders. Behind the altar he was the risen Christ, his wounds not relics of mortal pain and sorrow but the ornaments of a great conqueror rising victorious over evil and death.

Lucilla was an educated woman, to be sure, but she'd read the ancient historians and philosophers. They told of a people, self-denying, cruel, exploitative, madly militaristic, addicted to savage conquests, grinding their heels into the necks of every people within reach of their armies. A people who exterminated all who resisted their exactions and doomed the submissive to chattel slavery, enforced with the cruelest and most drastic punishments. A people whose idea of entertainment was the imaginatively savage slaughter of other human beings; a people who reveled in rivers of gold and rivers of blood.

And they had come to this: sitting in a church on a fair, cool spring morning, worshiping a God who preached innocence, forgiveness, and love. Listening to the voice of a girl who was an abandoned child, but who could outsing the lark rising up high and higher into the sunrise. *Even the simplest things are a puzzle,* Lucilla thought. *And the greatest of all gifts is to know how ignorant we are. To grasp the vast, dim outlines of what we do not and cannot possibly know.*

Then Dulcinia's song ended. She left the altar steps and genuflected to the everlasting presence. Gerald blessed her, saying the beauty of her art contributed to the greater glory of God. Lucilla came as close to prayer as she ever did—and just as well, because the next day the pleasant idyll ended and trouble visited the city.

Ansgar rode off at dawn. The brigand Trudo, who had forced Lucilla and Dulcinia to bribe him at the ford, was troubling merchants journeying to the city with imported goods for sale. Ansgar decided reluctantly that he could tolerate Trudo's depredations no longer. Among the goods the merchants carried to the city was salt, and Trudo was insisting on being paid in this valuable commodity. Ansgar's landlocked principality had no other source, and if Trudo continued to steal it, the citizens would be reduced to dire straits.

"He has to be cleaned out once and for all," Ansgar told Lucilla in the early predawn hours as he made ready to leave.

Stella created a scene. Weeping, scratching her face, rending her garments, throwing dust on her head.

Gerald, who'd exchanged his shepherd's staff for a sword and mail shirt without visible inconvenience, stood looking on indulgently while Stella had hysterics.

"Whatever else I may have thought of her," Lucilla said darkly, "I always believed Stella a level-headed person, but this—"

Gerald shrugged. "She's been like this since they met in Ravenna. I think she believes he will not think she loves him if she doesn't take on when he goes off to fight."

"I suppose . . . so," Dulcinia said, "but still . . . my heavens—"

Ludolf, roused from his sickbed by the commotion—he'd inherited Stella's tendency to the spring malaise—came down to help console his mother. Stella fainted into a convenient armchair, well furnished with large cushions. Ludolf held one hand, Dulcinia the other.

Stella cried out, "Thank God my son remains here. So that if you, my darling, the strength of my soul, the light of my eyes, perish, I will at least have him to console me in the brief time I linger like an unquiet spirit in the twilight of my sorrow in this vale of tears. Oh, woe. Woe. Woe."

Ansgar hurried his good-byes, urged on by Gerald. "Let's go now and she will quiet down. The longer you delay, the worse she carries one. Come," Gerald commanded.

Ansgar left with his wife's wailing ringing in his ears.

When he was past the door, Lucilla snapped, "Oh, shut up. Save your sympathy for that louse Trudo and that pack of cowardly, badly armed scavengers surrounding him. Your husband and his men will probably destroy them the way a blaze does kindling. Your husband is a competent and intelligent soldier, and Trudo is a lazy rapscallion who wants to live off the best efforts of others. He probably will never know what hit him."

Stella called Lucilla a name peculiar to the Roman argot that Ludolf didn't recognize, sat up, and demanded nourishment. Ludolf and Dulcinia hurried away to the big kitchens at the back of the house to find something for her.

Stella sat and stared spitefully at Lucilla. They were at the back of the rather imposing palace, in a small room adjoining an herb garden. The very expensive spices that seasoned the few state banquets Ansgar had to give were located here. Other herbs, medicinal and culinary, were prepared and stored. A short flight of steps led down to the wine cellar, a private place where Stella, the lady of the house, kept her accounts and oversaw the manifold and complex task of running the large household.

"What did you tell him about me?" Stella asked Lucilla.

"Nothing."

Stella sniffed. "I don't believe it."

"Stella, I'm not a fool, and don't take me for one. He is your husband. You are the mother of his son. I can't think he would be grateful to anyone stupid enough to bring anything discreditable in your past to his attention. I think you underestimate Ansgar. Yes, he's slow to quarrel, but once he does, I suspect he's extremely dangerous. I have no desire to earn his enmity. Certainly not by slandering his wife and certainly not while I'm a guest in his home, enjoying both his generosity and hospitality."

"I was afraid of you when you first came," Stella said abruptly.

"You have nothing to fear from me."

Stella frowned. "I wish I'd known that when you first came," Stella said. She avoided Lucilla's eyes.

A dreadful suspicion began to creep into Lucilla's mind. "Stella, what did you do?"

"I'm worried."

"Stella! You tell me right now—"

"I don't think he paid any attention—"

"Who?"

"Adalgisus," Stella said.

Lucilla's yell of sheer rage brought Dulcinia and Ludolf running. They found Stella vainly trying to keep the chair between herself and an infuriated Lucilla, but when spectators entered the room, both women stopped, straightened their clothing, and smiled.

"We were just having a little chat," Stella said, batting her eyelashes at Lucilla.

"It's quite all right," Lucilla said. "Pay us no mind. Our discussion, while somewhat animated, is basically friendly."

Both Ludolf and Dulcinia looked as if they didn't believe this, but left and went back to the kitchen.

"Lucilla, will you please be calm?"

"Yes, yes," Lucilla whispered. "Be calm. You knew this before you let Ansgar leave?"

Stella nodded. "I did, but I didn't think after the weeks you've been here that Adalgisus would take any notice. He is, after all, hiding out with his mistress in one of those fortified towns in the north."

"How close is the nearest town?"

"Not far. You can see the walls from the cathedral steps on a clear day."

"It's a clear day," Lucilla said. "Does it belong to the Lombards?"

"Yes, everything around here is part of the Lombard kingdom."

"Yes," Lucilla answered gravely.

"I'm tired of this nonsense. Tired and hungry," Stella snapped.

"Hysterics give you an appetite."

Stella opened her mouth but nothing came out. She drew in a deep breath. "Be grateful I'm a lady." she told Lucilla, "and don't care to call names."

"Something about a female dog? Was that on the tip of your tongue?" Lucilla asked.

"How very perceptive of you." Stella then swept out of the room.

They ate in the kitchen. Yes, Ansgar gave banquets and ate with the principal men of the city each night, and for this he used the large state dining room. But meals among the family were taken in the kitchen, a long room with the garden behind it on the east side of the house. The table was a simple plank affair set on trestles, with benches on either side. Because of the hearth fire on one end of the room, it was always warm. A double wall at the back with an inset grate carried away the smoke, and folding doors leading to the kitchen garden all along the back of the house were open in good weather for light and ventilation. A shallow porch with a colonnade protected the room in the summer from the worst of the day's heat and in the winter from the rains that drenched the countryside.

All in all, Lucilla thought, it was the most beautiful room in the house. She was looking out over the kitchen garden. Early greens, chicory, turnips, and carrots were waving their feathery foliage over the furrows; the last onions were in bloom and the garlic heading up. Hardy rosemary was covered with blue flowers, and thyme perfumed the walks between the vegetable beds. The flowers on the tiny, creeping plants—which ranged from white, purple, blue, to deep mauve— were drenching the still rather bare garden with early color and fragrance. The sage had not yet come into its own, but a few of the gray stems bore early violet flower spikes. Along the walls espaliered pomegranates were covered with the fiery orange buds that would open to begin the fine, tart, succulent crop of autumn.

Stella sat at one end of the long table in intense consultation with the cook over the night's menu and the future celebration when Ansgar should return. Dulcinia sat with Lucilla. They ate fresh cheese, bread, onions, and bacon.

"I need to talk to you, Lucilla," Dulcinia whispered. "Alone."

"We are about as alone as we will ever be," Lucilla said snappishly. "Stella's not paying a bit of attention. What's wrong?"

"Ludolf," Dulcinia whispered.

"I did notice he was sticking like a bad burr. Is he making himself obnoxious?"

"No," Dulcinia said, still speaking softly but sounding strained. "The reverse. Yes, the reverse is true."

Lucilla shrugged. "You're a serious artist. He's a handsome, young man. Have a fling. Because, make no mistake, that's what it would be—a fling."

Dulcinia shook her head. "That's what I thought at first, but—" She still sounded strained. "But, well, you see, I'm late . . . and . . . but—"

"Please, please be clear," Lucilla said between her teeth. "You know I have lived a harsh life. What? Are you afraid of shocking me? If you're pregnant, girl, there are medicines. If you care to bear the child, Ansgar will, no doubt, be happy even with a little by-blow. He can afford to support it and, by the by, so can you. Chrispus is very generous, and he won't give a tinker's damn who the father is."

Chrispus was Cardinal Chrispen Mantleck, collector of musical instruments and occasional musicians, Dulcinia being a case in point. "By the way, does he know about Chrispus? I hope you haven't been keeping a secret, too," she added under her breath.

"Oh, yes, he knows. He knows about my birth and parentage, or rather lack of known parentage, and even my early upbringing before you rescued me. I didn't keep any secrets from him. I do believe I'm pregnant, but that's not the problem."

"And so—" Lucilla spread her hands in a gesture of helplessness. "Tell me, what's wrong?"

"He's talking marriage," Dulcinia answered softly.

"My God, that is a problem. He can't—"

Dulcinia nodded. "I know."

"You won't—"

"Oh, yes, I would," Dulcinia said fervently.

"Oh, damn, you're—"

"In love," Dulcinia said softly. "Wildly, madly, and ever so hopelessly. Yes, I am in love."

"God, what a mess."

Then she became aware that Dulcinia was weeping open-eyed, silently, the tears running down her cheeks. And, as if from nowhere, it came to Lucilla that Dulcinia was as much her child as the two she'd carried in her womb, and she loved the singer perhaps more than those children of her own flesh and blood. And she was prepared to love Ludolf also. She knew little about the boy, except that he did have a fair face, and that when Dulcinia had confessed her pregnancy, he'd had the good taste to talk marriage. He seemed an honest young man.

"Where is he now?" Lucilla asked.

"He really feels bad," Dulcinia said. "He has the sniffles the way his mother did when we came here. I believe he has a fever. He went to his room but wants me to come up and read to him in a little while."

Lucilla rose. "Come."

They returned to the rooms on the upper floor. Now Lucilla was hurrying. She began pulling her divided riding skirt and boots from the cupboard.

"What's wrong?" Dulcinia asked. "What's the matter? You're acting as if something terrible is about to happen. What are you doing?"

"Something terrible is going to happen, but it needn't be terrible for you." Lucilla had the skirt on and was pushing her feet into the boots. "Where is Ludolf's room?"

"In the other wing. Over the garden. It's quiet there."

Lucilla grabbed Dulcinia's arm. "Go to his room." She had the two small bottles in her hand, one wrapped with gold wire. She pressed them into Dulcinia's palm. "The one with wire is opium, the other valerian. Go to his room, lock the door, stay there. Keep him occupied for the rest of the day."

"But what—"

Lucilla's fingernails dug into Dulcinia's flesh. "Do you love him?"

"Yes. Yes, but—"

"Then do as I say."

"Lucilla, you're frightening me."

"Be frightened. Sometimes it's very intelligent to be afraid. This is one of those times. Hear me?"

"Y-y-yes."

"Even if you have to drug him, keep him quiet for the rest of the day. Now, go."

Dulcinia fled.

Lucilla was dressed. She threw a leather bag over her shoulder then hurried to the stair. She saw Stella looking up at her from the foot of the steps. She heard the commotion in the street.

RAIN. THE RAIN WAS STILL BLINDING WHEN THE two wolves together swam the river beyond Pavia. It was swollen with snowmelt. *The spot where Mona and her family were murdered must be underwater now,* Regeane thought. She hoped the horror would be cleansed from the earth there, and the spirits of the dead would find peace. All the dead, not simply the victims.

Above, the sky was brightening as the worst of the storm passed over. Long shafts of sunlight were striking down through the meshwork of storm clouds, driving the shimmering wetlands they swam through into brilliance. They were gone, free. The town, its claustrophobic terror, behind them; imprisonment, death only a memory; and the fresh, clear water cleansing away sorrow, fear, the marks, the stink, and even dimming the memories of the pain.

He led. She followed, the old pattern reasserting itself, oddly comforting for both of them.

It seemed he hurried away. He hated the confinement of cities. She had been a little frightened by him after they had left Rome. Each night, even when she felt abominably weary, he had become the wolf and left, ranging out into the darkened and sometimes dangerous countryside. At first she'd accompanied him on these runs, but then the strain of days spent on horseback or riding in carts along roads that hadn't seen maintenance in several hundred years took its toll on her. That and the long terrors of her struggles with both the Lombards and her rapacious kin. Exhaustion began to set in and his rush to return to his stronghold seemed more and more senseless.

Matters had reached a crisis when, one evening, she'd climbed in beside him after a long blustery, rainy ride. She was chilled and so tired, she was almost without appetite for supper. She'd bitten her tongue all day to keep back complaints. She was almost desperately looking forward to the warmth of his arms and the muscular body that embraced her, made her feel safe, secure, and above all loved. A security that allowed her to spend the night in a profound restful sleep without dreams.

But instead of the man she felt the wolf, and he slid from the bed and drifted as silently as starlight toward the tent flap and the night outside. She sat up enraged, so enraged it frightened her. She began screaming and throwing things at him. When he turned human in astonishment and fright at seeing his formerly compliant wife turn into a shrieking virago, she'd dissolved into a storm of weeping.

In under a moment the tent was full of wolves. All of them blaming him for doing something terrible to her, or trying to comfort her and abate her hysterics. Matrona entered then, carrying a flagon. She persuaded Regeane to take a few sips. The stuff tasted dreadful but it warmed and soothed Regeane no end.

"What is it?" Regeane asked when she could speak again.

"A little something I picked up among the isles, back of the north wind."

No one said anything. No one knew where that was.

"It cuts the chill," Matrona said. "There they need it because it is always cold."

"What did you do to her?" Gavin asked Maeniel accusingly.

Most of them were human now because they wanted to talk, and wolf speech was far too laconic for the range of emotion flowing. Gavin was tastefully draped in a blanket, Gordo was wearing his mantle as a sarong, Matrona was clad in a shirt, one of Maeniel's. Silvia wore her skin only.

"He must have done something to her," Silvia said, "because I've never before heard her scream like that. What did you do?" She glared at a slightly bemused Maeniel, who had gone back to wolf.

"Yes, what did you do, my leader?" a somewhat horrified Gordo asked.

"It must have been something terrible," Silvia said. "Matrona, take her to your tent. I will stay with you. Have no fear, little one, we will protect you."

"Now wait a minute," Gavin said. "I've known him since I was thirteen years old and we met in that Irish forest and I've never known—"

Maeniel became human, and Matrona dropped a tunic over his head. "Be quiet," he commanded, and was obeyed.

Silence fell.

"Regeane, what's wrong?"

Regeane, now ashamed, opened her mouth to say, "Nothing," but Matrona caught her eye. "Tell him," she said.

"I'm so tired . . ." she whispered.

"Ah, I see," Matrona said. "Out. Everyone out. Leave the newlyweds alone to settle this."

Maeniel sat down next to her on the folding cot and took her in his arms. With a weary sigh, she rested her head on his shoulder.

"Next time," he said, his lips on her hair. "Next time don't try so hard to please me." She nodded, and as they both lay down, he said, "Promise?"

She was drifting off to sleep when she answered, "I promise."

Yes, she had promised, trusting him then as she must now. Tell him the truth.

She tested the depth of water around her by turning human and standing up. It was shallow, up to her waist. The forest of reeds around her murmured in the dying gusts of the storm winds. Odd, she stood not on mud but on stone.

Maeniel paused. He became human also, but his feet trod mud and he struggled toward her, landing his footing at last on the same platform her feet rested on.

"Where are we?" she asked.

"How you worry," he replied. "Somewhere in the Po valley."

"How should I not worry? I can't see dry land anywhere around. Nothing, not even a tree, only water plants, reeds, cattails, and long grass, grass with sharp edges," she said, looking down at a shallow cut she'd just gotten on the palm of her hand.

"Hush," he said, and put his arms around her.

She let him kiss her. As he did, a particularly hard gust of wind struck them, chilling her. In a second, her skin was covered with gooseflesh. She pushed him back.

"I'm cold. Night is coming on. We don't know where we are. We're lost and you want to—"

He kissed her again.

"You might at least apologize."

"Yes," he said. "I apologize."

"Apologize and mean it."

"No," he told her, and kissed her again. "I still think I was right. But you were lucky and so was I. Had the treacherous Lombard king not been a stubborn fool, we might both have perished, but we didn't, and so I will waste no more worry on something that almost happened. I did underestimate you, though. And you must be content with that admission and not ask for more."

Regeane gave a little cry of exasperation.

But then he kissed her again, and she found she was no longer cold. "Oh," she said. "It seems years since I saw you, but the water is too deep here."

"Too deep for what?" he asked.

"You stop. Stop teasing me."

"Shush. Look."

A cloud covered the sun for a moment, and to the west of them an abandoned villa emerged from the sparkling reflection of sun and the water.

"See," he said. "I knew something would turn up. It always does if only you relax."

"I don't like it," she said. "Remember the bear."

"What? Are you going to lose faith in your senses because they fooled you once?"

"Fooled you," she snapped, "not me."

"Yes," he said ruefully. "And in Rome, a certain tomb—"

"Point well taken," she said.

"Let's swim for it."

They did, threading their way among the hammocks of cattails and reeds until they reached a long, straight stretch of open water bounded by stone walls that had been a canal built to bring water to the fields from the river. The whole of the ground floor was underwater. Here and there what had been magnificent mosaics shone up through the water where they were not covered by streaks of silt. Two gladiators fought to the death in one panel, their names emblazoned beside each. A Mirmillo battled a Retiarius, and the portrait showed the Mirmillo entangled in the Retiarius's net while his sword was plunging deep into his opponent's body.

Regeane paused and looked at this one, thereby earning a disgusted look from Maeniel. Beyond, a peristyle garden looked up into the sky along with a blue pool filled with fish. The real trees and flowers of the garden long extinguished by flooding, their counterfeits shimmered on the drowned paving. Beyond, the rows of a kitchen garden—eggplant, onions, celery, parsley, cabbage, sage, and thyme—spoke of a joyous prosperity lost long ago to the river; fish picked at the tesserae that formed the images.

A few rooms on the second floor, mostly roofless with crumbling walls freestanding to only a few feet, offered the only shelter they had yet encountered. They dove in from the canal bank and swam to where the walls projected only a few feet above the water. Someone else must have taken shelter here long ago, because a substantial mound of dry straw covered the floor.

Regeane became human and a second later Maeniel stood beside her. "I see you met the bear," Regeane said. "What did he want with you?"

"The same as I think he wanted from you. Control."

"No," Regeane said.

"He has some dream of restoring the world to what it was before man, cities, farms, empires, and kingdoms fought among themselves and laid waste the land. To a world where there were only animals."

Regeane frowned. "Really?"

"Yes. He believes that with our powers combined, he might wipe out humanity. I believe him to be—if not deluded—at least, shall we say, overly ambitious. As far as I'm concerned? Ah, if it were only possible. But I've had a rather lengthy association with mankind, and I have found them a lot tougher than he believes."

"That would be a dreadful thing, to destroy one of the great kingdoms."

"Great kingdoms?" he asked.

"That's what Matrona calls them," she answered. "Birds, the kingdom of the air; fishes, the kingdom of the waters and the sea. Plants, the kingdom of silence."

He was standing behind her; the late afternoon sun shining down had warmed her, and he had his arms around her and was nuzzling her neck. "Will you stop?" she asked, half laughingly.

"It's all right. We're married. Everyone, even the church, approves."

"I doubt very much if the church would approve of anything about us."

"Still," he said. "The bishop shows the inability of even the most nonsensical institutions to silence the good-hearted. You just like him because he took my part about the ransom. But my love, the worst moment in my captivity came when you pushed back your veil and revealed who you were.

"Desiderius tried to drown me, Hugo tricked me into revealing myself before the high altar of the cathedral, and the bear threatened me with death if I didn't yield myself to him. But none of those ugly experiences frightened me the way the realization of your vulnerability did. I love you. If you met with some mischance, I do believe it would kill me. Yes, it's true. I underestimated your abilities, but you must remember the feelings of one who loves you to distraction when you take risks."

"Gundabald wanted to lock me in a cage with a collar and chain," Regeane shot back. "Is that what your love is, a collar and a chain?"

She turned in his arms and looked into his eyes, giving him the direct stare that he himself used so often on the others. The wolf stare, the evaluation of a creature that doesn't know how to lie. He found he had to look away, remembering that the mother of the pack is a leader in her own right, and not simply the leader's consort. Then Regeane was wolf. She leaped from their nest. Nearby, the tops of some columns that had once supported the peristyle porch protruded from the waters, little islands. She chose one and dropped into the stillness of a hunting wolf. *Fish,* he thought.

From her perch, she silently scanned the waters. The moment, when it came, was lightning fast. The fish flapped little, if at all. She'd snapped its spine with her fangs. She rested the body at her feet on the column's crest, and her look invited him to join her.

He did.

Later they returned to the nest and made love, man and wife. He told her of the experiences of his captivity; she narrated her journey.

"I met wolves, real wolves," she said. "But from what Matrona says, they shouldn't have attacked. I was mystified and angry. I thought there were rules."

He nodded. "There are, but likely the mother of the pack caught sight of you and sensed a strangeness. She feared you might become a rival. Like all rules, none are hard and fast, and some will break them if it suits their convenience."

Regeane digested this and said, "Somehow I can't see myself as the mother of a lowland pack, whelping cubs every year."

"You could be, if you wanted to," he said.

They were lying twined together comfortably. He saw her eyes widen in the reddish glow of the sunset light. "Really?"

"Yes, both lives are open to you, should you choose to exercise your gift in that manner."

"I simply can't imagine myself . . . The idea is frightening—yet somehow almost attractive. But I feel the same way about living as a wolf and only a wolf as I did when my mother described sex to me: I was sure I wouldn't want . . . that! But look at me now, and by the way, why don't I get pregnant? What is it now, almost eight months and . . . At first I didn't confide in you—"

"I know," he said. "But you were worried about it. Matrona told me."

"Oh . . . ," Regeane replied. "She simply said we rarely have offspring from love undertaken between ourselves. Most are the product of mixed marriages like I am, but you are a . . . wolf."

"Yes, and only a wolf."

She nodded. "So what sort of child might you father?"

"I don't know. As far as I can tell, I have never had one, and I have known—carnally—many human women."

She shook her head. Her hair was still wet and showered his face with droplets. "Oh, hell," she said, "so much damned water . . . and it's getting cold."

"Change," he said, "and let's sleep."

"You just don't like the way the conversation is going."

"I won't deny I don't care for it. It explores areas I'd rather not talk about. At least not now." He embraced her more tightly, pulling her against his warm body.

She gave a little purring sound, not wolflike at all.

"Ah, that's my beauty. That's my honeyed love, sweet as fruit plucked ripe from the tree, or berries in autumn. Stop worrying about what cannot be changed and go to sleep."

Regeane drifted off, but opened her eyes one more time. "Does no one come here?" she asked.

"No one," he reassured her. "I would know if they did."

Then she drifted down peacefully into dark water, the pool of silence.

She changed as the last rays of sunlight became a fan of brightness on the western horizon. Then he, too, sought his patient brother, the wolf, and slept.

L UCILLA KNEW AS SOON AS SHE SAW STELLA'S FACE. Her hand was at her throat and there was horror in her eyes. "I hate being right," Lucilla whispered to herself. *He is here,* she thought, *and now Stella is frightened of what she has done.*

Lucilla tried to remember what she'd heard about Desiderius's son. Hard, inconsistent, aggressive, and cowardly at the same time. But above all a fool, an egotistical fool, one stricken with the worst disease of power, the belief that his birth alone entitled him to greater privileges than any other man. There he stood.

She bowed gracefully. "My lord."

He smirked at her. "Ah, at last we meet. You are, I believe, the famous—or is it infamous?—Lucilla."

Lucilla would have liked to slap the smirk off his face, but she summoned an exquisite smile and replied, "Whichever you like, my lord. I believe both words indicate a career of some distinction."

The smirk grew broader. "We will have to explore your, I understand, quite amazing talents."

Lucilla felt a thrill of fear. *I'm going to be this man's hostage, and he isn't evil. He's worse than evil, he's stupid.*

"I see you're dressed for riding," he observed. "Good. We will need to leave quickly. I have," he explained to Stella, "only a few men in my entourage, and I think I will not stay until your lord returns."

Yes, Lucilla thought, *because you know he would object to this outrage, the kidnapping of a helpless woman under his protection.* Lucilla simpered, "I wouldn't want to keep your highness. Shall we go?"

He studied her, his eyes opaque, for a moment. Lucilla could feel the perspiration at her armpits and the palms of her hands. *Damn, damn,* she thought. *I caused this idiocy by my own folly.*

"It's too easy," he said. "You're planning something or hiding something. What is it?"

Stella whispered, "Why, nothing."

Damn Stella to hell. She was a lousy liar, but then she always had been.

By day the huge reception hall was dim, the only light coming from heavy glass ports in the Roman concrete barrel vault above, and Lucilla guessed Adalgisus was telling the truth about only ten men accompanying him. But since Ansgar had stripped the town of its defenders, these few were enough, and if they met with any resistance, a massacre might result. They could cut through the unarmed citizenry the way fire roars through dried brush. If Ludolf and Dulcinia had any idea of what was going on, they might both try to stop Adalgisus and be the first to die. That's why Stella was so frightened.

Lucilla managed a smile of gentle resignation. "My lord, you are too suspicious. What could two women, alone, possibly conceal from a man of your excellent strategic intelligence. You arrived, did you not, at the neighboring monastery of Temi and then waited there for Ansgar to ride out. Whereupon you hurried here. Am I correct?"

Adalgisus smiled complacently. "You are a woman of discernment—great discernment."

Lucilla continued, "Only this morning Stella confided in me that she had written you upon my arrival some weeks ago. Yes, I was planning to flee, alone if necessary, but you forestalled me. So I must yield the field to you and consider myself your prisoner. Simplicity itself, my lord, and no need for suspicion. I am truly at your mercy."

Flatter them, flatter the bastards. They lap it up, Lucilla thought. *If only I can get him out of here before he turns the situation into a bloody mess.*

"Still, I think I would prefer that the lady Stella de Imola shares our journey past the borders of Ansgar's lands. I will take leave of you at the villa Jovis, and your husband can collect you there. I have no wish to find myself either harassed or pursued."

"Let me call my maid," Stella said. "I must dress for the journey."

"No! We will not be on the road that long."

One of Adalgisus's men stepped up next to Stella and took her arm. Stella tried to pull away.

"Come, come, my lady," Adalgisus said. "Eberhardt is an old friend. He tells me you met during your sojourn in Ravenna some time ago."

This just gets worse and worse, Lucilla thought. She felt her legs shaking under her divided riding skirt. "Very well. Let us go now," Lucilla said.

Stella looked as frightened as a mouse in the talons of a hawk. Just at that moment, Stella's maid Avernia hurried down the stair. Adalgisus was hustling Lucilla toward the door, Eberhardt doing the same to Stella.

"My lady, my lady Stella—"

Both men paused, and Avernia caught up with them. Lucilla saw Eberhardt glance up the stair, trying to see if Avernia was alone.

"Avernia, go away," Stella hissed. "Don't make a fuss. Hear me? Don't make a fuss or I'll take a stick to you."

"No," Avernia shouted. "What are you doing?" She was growing progressively louder and louder.

Eberhardt threw Adalgisus a look of angry despair. He pulled Stella toward the door. Avernia snatched Stella's other arm and forced him to halt.

"No! No!" she shouted. "No! To arms! To arms! My lady is—"

Lucilla felt Adalgisus release her. His sword flashed in the half-light, the way a lightning bolt gleams against an angry sky. He drove it through Avernia's chest from left to right. Avernia's next cry ended in a horrible gurgle. She staggered back, the expression of surprise on her face almost comical had it not been for the most ugly and uncomical wound. She sat down on the floor, tried to breathe, and a fine mist of blood droplets sprayed from her mouth, spattering Stella's skirts. Then she clutched at Stella's outstretched hand.

Eberhardt pulled Stella away. Stella was a small woman and helpless in the large, powerful man's grip.

"No," Stella whispered as she was propelled through the doors and out into the square.

Lucilla saw Avernia fall back, her body writhing as the she tried to breathe with her lungs filling with blood. She watched as blood foamed at Avernia's lips and poured at last from her mouth.

Adalgisus wiped his sword on Lucilla's skirts and shoved it back into its scabbard. "Move," he said, pointing to the door. "Now."

Lucilla did.

DULCINIA HURRIED DOWN THE CORRIDOR TOWARD Ludolf's room. On her way, she made a decision, an important one. *Drug him? Is Lucilla mad?* No, she was going to tell her lover the truth. The problem was, she didn't find him in his bedroom. Dismayed, she began to search and found him a few doors down, in the library.

Ansgar, though uneducated himself, was a supporter of culture and had forty books, a very large number for the time. Ludolf was trying to find a copy of Ovid's *Art of Love* for Dulcinia, who had never read it in its entirety. He was sure there was one, but the problem was the books were mixed in with state correspondence and Stella's household accounts. When Dulcinia entered, he looked up from the stack of scrolls he was sorting and saw at once that she was frightened.

"Something is wrong, but I don't know what. Lucilla dressed for travel, and she told me to keep you in your room."

Ludolf's face hardened. "Is she planning to run away?"

"I don't know. I can't think so. Lucilla's not a fool, and the countryside's not safe for a woman traveling alone. It's simply impossible, not even to be thought of. Besides, I know Lucilla. If she wanted to flee, she'd go on foot. She can pass for a peasant woman; I've seen her do it. No, no, she looked frightened, not for herself but for me and . . . yes . . . you."

Ludolf dropped the scroll in his hand. "Quick, help me arm myself."

It took only a moment for Dulcinia to drop his mail shirt over his head. He was putting on his sword belt and hurrying down the corridor—Dulcinia behind, almost running to keep up—when they heard Avernia's cries.

Ludolf began to run.

But by the time he reached the stair, Stella and Lucilla were riding hard down the road out of the city. When he and Dulcinia reached the foot of the stair, Dulcinia got a good look at Avernia and screamed. She was a lot better at it than poor Avernia had been.

"She's dead?" Ludolf sounded stunned. "Why? How? What happened? Dulcinia, if you know anything you're not telling me—"

"No, oh, God, no, I don't," she gasped out, shaking her head.

Just then the blacksmith entered. He ran to Avernia but stopped when he could see clearly that his wife was a corpse. Dulcinia's scream had roused the servants. They were gathering, some making the sign of the cross, all gaping at the body.

"What—?" the blacksmith asked. "No, not you!" He pointed to Ludolf's sword.

"No," Dulcinia said. "We were in the upstairs hallway when we heard her scream. We came quickly, as quickly as we—"

"No," one of Avernia's sons said. "We were working at the cathedral across the street. We saw a party of armed men ride in, not many, only—" He shrugged and looked at his brothers. "—maybe eight, ten? I don't know, not a lot. We spoke of it among ourselves, then decided to call later because they were armed and we didn't know them. At least we didn't know all of them. We did recognize one."

"Who?" Ludolf asked.

"He looked, well . . ." The young man seemed uncertain.

"Tell it," the blacksmith said.

"He looked like Adalgisus, the king's son, but we couldn't believe he would be here . . . and with such a small escort. So we doubted our senses, but we did think we should tell our father, so we did.

"Don't leave her lying there like that." He pointed to Avernia.

"No, no," Dulcinia whispered, and pulled off her own mantle.

Avernia was lying on her back, head turned as if looking at the stair, her cheek in a pool of blood. Dulcinia closed her eyes, wiped the blood away from her mouth, and pillowed Avernia's head on her own folded mantle.

"Where is Lucilla?" she asked fearfully.

There were at least a dozen people crowded around the body, with more and more pushing in from the square every moment.

"Yes," Ludolf echoed. "Where is Lucilla, and where in God's name is my mother?"

It took a while to get things sorted out. Avernia's sons remembered bringing a letter from Stella to Florence but knew nothing else about the matter. Their mother had been closed-mouthed about the contents.

"She must have written him the day Lucilla arrived," Ludolf said. "He waited until Father left, then came. But in heaven's name, why did he take Mother? With all due respect to your friend, she is openly the pope's supporter and serves his interests. But Mother—what could Mother have possibly done that would earn his displeasure?"

"Lucilla knew he was coming, and she knew that if challenged you might not yield her up peaceably," Dulcinia said. "She, and probably your mother, wanted to protect us. What would your father have done if he'd been here?"

Ludolf snorted. "I don't think he would have allowed even the son of his liege lord to make light of his hospitality."

"Yes," Dulcinia said. "That's what I thought, and Lucilla knew. He hasn't many men, most are probably with his father awaiting the Frankish king. He took your mother as a hostage for his own safety."

AVERNIA'S BODY LAY IN THE KITCHEN ON THE table where they'd eaten breakfast only a few hours before. Her daughters were washing her, preparing her for the funeral.

"Dulcinia, will you come with me?" Ludolf asked. "We ride within the hour."

"Yes, with all my heart."

He went to the kitchen to comfort the weeping women and pay his last respects to Avernia. Dulcinia ran upstairs to dress.

True to Ludolf's word, they rode out before noon. Even though most of the able-bodied men were with his father, Ludolf was able to muster twenty rather formidable graybeards who had allowed younger men to campaign with Ansgar.

Dulcinia found them a dangerous-looking group, possibly not as agile or high-spirited as the youngsters, but long in experience and grim fury. Adalgisus had murdered one of their own and kidnapped their lord's wife. If they caught him, he would face an unpleasant reckoning.

They stopped at the monastery Temi. Ludolf minced no words with the father abbot. "I don't care who he is," he told the abbot. "He entered my house without my permission, took my mother and a guest of ours, and when one of my servants tried to stop him, he murdered her. I want my mother back. She has done him no harm, and he must be brought to book for his crimes."

The abbot threw up his hands but was unable to do more than point out the general direction Adalgisus had taken, saying bitterly, "All he did was eat a lot, drink even more, then sit around—when he was not sleeping, that is—and demand to be waited upon. He didn't confide in me about where he'd come from, what he was doing here, or where he was going. And if I'd known he was up to some mischief that involved your family, I'd have warned you, because as far as I'm concerned, an unhappy neighbor is bound to be more trouble than a distant king, and your father is well aware of my sentiments. And you should be also. If you're going after him, I'll lend you fresh mounts."

Ludolf nodded, took the horses, and left. Fortunately, the road Adalgisus had taken soon narrowed. It was little traveled and the fresh tracks of a group of horsemen had to have been theirs. The road led into a mountainous wilderness of scrub oak, willow, golden broom, wild rose, and briar. The countryside had a certain strange beauty, the yellow broom flowers twined with the white, thorny ones of briar, and here and there the wild pink rose and blossoming pear seemed to explode among the thickets of oak and still-bare willow.

Dulcinia was a fine rider, but this trail challenged even her skills. Once one of the horses stepped into a hole and tossed his rider into a mound of briars. The horse was only lightly injured, the rider more uncomfortable than hurt, but the gelding had to be unsaddled and left to find his way back while his rider was given one of the remounts they'd been supplied with at the monastery.

"One thing good about this," the blacksmith said to Ludolf. "They can't have left the road. We won't have to hunt them in the countryside."

The road gained altitude quickly but when they reached the notch where it turned down, Dulcinia saw that a river wound through the narrow valley.

"Odds are," the blacksmith said, "he will have taken to water."

Ludolf nodded. "Want to bet his trail vanishes at the river?"

"No," the blacksmith said. "It's a sure thing."

It did.

S TELLA WAS A GOOD RIDER. FOR THAT LUCILLA WAS thankful. She was able to keep up. Adalgisus was clearly frightened. Lucilla cursed her luck and promised herself she would do everything possible to keep up his courage. He was a fool and therefore dangerous, but a terrified fool didn't bear thinking about. For one thing, they were traveling too fast. The pace Adalgisus set would wear out the horses before nightfall. Unless he knew a convenient spot where they could get remounts, he would have to go someplace where the stock could be watered and fed and rested, or most of them would soon be on foot.

On foot in a wilderness, Lucilla thought, observing the overgrown countryside around her. This area toward the mountains had never been thickly settled even in Roman times; now it was deserted. Even brigands here wouldn't prosper—not unless they had a taste for robbing each other.

Not long after midday, they reached the river and drew rein.

"Stop," Eberhardt told Adalgisus. "Our mounts were not the best cattle when we started out, now they are all but foundered."

Stella's and Lucilla's mounts were in the best condition. The women were lighter than the men, but even their horses were lathered; and Lucilla had noticed spurring had little effect on her horse now. At least five of the party had straggled for some miles behind as the horses stumbled and slowed on the rocky ground.

"I suppose," Adalgisus said, looking at his companions. "I suppose I'd best do that."

"Besides," Eberhardt said, "we can use the water to cover our tracks."

Then the two men moved away, speaking together in low tones. Lucilla dismounted, loosed her saddle girth, and began to walk her mount in a circle to cool him off. Stella called out to Lucilla to help her dismount. Stella was a small woman, but once on the ground she followed suit.

Lucilla noticed some of the men with Adalgisus simply allowed their mounts to drink without the cooldown. "Oh, yes," Lucilla whispered. "They will soon be afoot."

"I'm sore," Stella said. "I used to go hunting with Ansgar and hawking with Gerald almost every week, but I haven't done so in some time. Son of a bitch, I'll probably have saddle sores before the day is out."

Then she called Adalgisus several foul names in Roman street argot. "I'm sorry, Lucilla. I'm really sorry I wrote him about you, but when I saw you, I panicked. You see, when Ansgar plucked me from that brothel in Ravenna, it was the most wonderful thing that ever happened to me. I simply couldn't believe my good fortune, and I was sure you'd share my past—what are they, misdeeds?—with him."

"I don't call them misdeeds," Lucilla said. "Men act as if women don't have to eat. What in the hell else do we have to sell, if not our bodies?"

"Well, I don't know about that," Stella said. "I believe they think we should preserve our chastity at the cost of our lives, but I must say both you and I did a lot better than just find enough to eat. You gained Hadrian's company and protection, and I was rather comfortably kept by several high church officials."

"I told you not to trust that bastard Aldric. What happened in Ravenna?" Lucilla asked.

"He sold me into a brothel. His, uh, affairs didn't prosper as he wanted them to. The archbishop called him a turncoat and told him that a man who betrayed one master would turn on another. This was true, truer than true. Only the one he turned on was me. My sale brought him the passage money to Constantinople. Being sold was the most mortifying and humiliating experience of my entire life."

"Not to mention inconvenient and damned dangerous," Lucilla said. "But I suppose a stroke of ill fortune presages a complete reversal of the same bad luck. The wheel turns," she continued. "*Hecuba regina.* We all ride it."

"Who's Hecuba?" Stella grumbled. "I cannot think it was a good thing when Hadrian taught you to read. Ever since, you have been baffling and annoying your friends with odd bits of arcane knowledge and mysterious quotations."

"Hecuba was a queen who ended her life as a slave," Lucilla snapped. "I merely meant nothing is permanent except change."

"See?" Stella was annoyed. "That's what I'm talking about."

"You were telling me about Ansgar?" Lucilla reminded her.

"Yes, well, no sooner was I down then I was up because Ansgar came to the brothel. We 'visited' a few times," Stella said primly. "And then he told that thick-witted pander Milo, the owner of the brothel, that he didn't want me taking any other customers. He wanted to be the only man in my life. Of course, that stinking pig Milo wanted me to cheat, but I wouldn't."

"That must have been a battle," Lucilla said.

"It was, but I won. I know that sort of arrangement is usually dishonest, but a wealthy lord like Ansgar—I didn't want to lose him. Oh, no, I was thinking, no chances on that."

Lucilla took the reins from Stella's hand and led the horses to water. Stella knelt on the bank, drank from her cupped hands, and splashed water on her cheeks.

"He was wealthy even then?"

"Yes," Stella said, straightening up. "He'd tossed that rapacious louse Trudo out of the town and turned the bandit's ill-gotten gains to his own uses."

"One of which was freeing you from the brothel."

"Yes, and it's a good thing I didn't cheat because only a month after we met, I found out I was pregnant."

"Ludolf?"

"Yes. Oh, thank God we got Adalgisus away from the city; I was so afraid for my son! Look at the terribly easy way he stabbed Avernia. Lucilla, do you think she is dead?"

Stella looked up at Lucilla, and Lucilla turned away to fuss with part of the horse's head stall. The plea in Stella's eyes was almost unbearable. She and Avernia had been together so long.

"I don't know," Lucilla answered. "For all I know, she might have been only slightly injured. Listen to me, Stella. When curd brain and his friend who does his thinking for him come back, do you want me to try to persuade them to leave you here?"

Stella glanced around. They had passed the last human habitation, a ruined farmhouse, some miles back. Both sides of the river were thick, overgrown with brush and small trees.

"Oh, God, no. Not in this horrible wilderness."

"Your son might be following," Lucilla said.

"Oh, in heaven's name, suppose he isn't? If Adalgisus leaves me here, I will die. Die on the spot. Don't, please. Don't make such a ghastly suggestion to him."

Lucilla sighed. "Stella, I won't do or say anything that will make things worse for you, but I'd rather take my chances in this wilderness, as you call it, than with Sir Lackwit and his grab-ass friend. By the way, does tall, dark, and stupid really know you from Ravenna? Or can I call his bluff sometime?"

"Oh, God, Lucilla. I don't know. They . . . they were all the same to me. They say it's not a sin if you don't enjoy it. Well, if that's true, I didn't do any sinning at all in Ravenna except with Ansgar." She smiled a little at the memory, and it transformed her face the way a ray of sunlight brightens a flower.

Lucilla felt her heart ache with sorrow. *Oh, God, I am a terrible woman,* she thought. *A vengeful woman to have begun the whole thing.* And then she decided her own opinion of herself was probably correct and regret was the most futile of all emotions.

Just then Adalgisus and Eberhardt returned and they got under way again. As Lucilla thought, they rode into the streambed. The water was shallow but the footing so rocky that they couldn't make any speed. Lucilla kept hoping they would continue to follow the river for a few more miles and give Ludolf time to catch them, but they didn't. Still, one thing heartened her. Two of the horses gave out, and four of Adalgisus's friends had to be left behind. Not enough, but something. She saw Stella's face brighten. *I hope,* she thought, when she saw the fear in Adalgisus's eyes, *I hope he gets what's coming to him. If I can arrange it, he will.*

CHIARA WAS AWAKENED BY BEING SHAKEN VIO-lently. "Yes, stop that," she told the spirit. "It's not even dawn yet, and besides," she continued indignantly as she tried to burrow down more deeply under the covers, "what did you do to Hugo? You had his body in the church last night."

"Hugo is dead!" the spirit said.

This did bring Chiara's head out from under the covers. "You killed him," she said accusingly to the spirit.

"I did not," was the indignant denial. "The lightning brought about his death. And would have killed you and your father also, if I hadn't warned you to stay on the porch."

"I don't believe you," Chiara shouted.

There was a sound that began like the hissing, spitting noises a fire makes when rain falls into it, then rose in volume, taking on deeper and deeper tones until it ended with the explosive roar of an angry bear.

Then Chiara found the covers pulled off, and she was unceremoniously yanked to her feet by an iron grip fastened on her upper arm.

"Up—up—up! And get dressed. Now! You and your father must flee the city."

Chiara replied with a screech of fury. "My modesty, my reputation."

"Damn your modesty and reputation. Neither will do you any good if you are dead. Up!"

She was on her feet, staggering toward the clothes chest in the corner. "Wp-o-o-o-oth!" Chiara gave another yell.

"Abomination and damnation," the spirit roared. "I didn't touch you. What's the matter now?"

"The floor is cold, my feet are bare. I'll catch my death."

"Shut up and stop screeching. Get dressed."

Chiara was lifted by the scruff of the neck and deposited across the room next to the clothes chest.

"Get dressed now!"

"Will you please leave, and don't try to cheat. I can tell when you're in the room, and I won't pull off my nightgown until you're out of here," Chiara shouted.

Just then the door flew open. Armine stood there, candle in hand. It was a fairly bright light, and Armine could see the entire room in the glow. There was a bed, the clothes chest, and nothing else. No one could be concealed here, but undeniably, his daughter was talking to someone—speaking in a loud voice, in fact.

Chiara paused with a gasp, clothes forgotten. "What are you doing here?"

"Never mind," Armine said. "To whom are you speaking?"

"Oh," Chiara said. "N-now see what you've done?" She spoke into the empty air.

Armine made the sign of the cross.

"Damn you for a superstitious fool," the spirit yelled, and boxed his ears violently.

Armine sat down hard on the floor.

"Get up, you idiot," the spirit shouted. "On your feet, too." He jerked Armine up into a standing position.

Armine gave a gurgling yell.

"Now, you stop, you just stop. You leave my father alone, you hear me? I can't think what you hope to accomplish by such high-handed tactics. All you're doing is frightening him."

The spirit paused. "Even now the king is deciding your fate, Chiara. He is angry. Hugo had told him how you rescued the wolf. He's a wild man."

"Who?" Chiara asked, completely bewildered.

"The king, damn it. The king," the spirit shouted.

"Who? What? How? Chiara, are you speaking to someone? Someone I cannot see?" Armine demanded.

"Now stop, both of you." Chiara stamped her bare foot on the cold floor and hurt it. She scooted back to the bed, sat on the edge, folded her arms and closed her eyes, and thrust one small, determined chin forward. "If you both don't stop badgering me now, I'll never speak to either of you again."

Armine edged cautiously into the room, his eyes darting about a bit wildly. "Chiara," he asked, "is there someone in here I can't see?"

Chiara's eyes flew open. "Yes, he's Hugo's friend."

Armine nodded. He moved cautiously over to the clothes chest, candle in hand, and asked, "Is there anyone sitting here?"

"No," Chiara said. "At least—" She, too was looking around. "—at least I don't think he sits."

"I don't."

"He doesn't."

"Yes, well, I do," Armine said, and sat down. "Now, Chiara, tell me what's going on. First, I know that wasn't Hugo who entered the church last night. I'm not sure who or even—" He glanced around nervously. "—what he was but that wasn't Hugo. The man was a worm. He could never manage the look of arrogant self-assurance on that creature's face. And the tender way he assisted me in getting you up to our rooms last night wasn't in any way characteristic of Hugo. Nor was the fact that he was stone cold sober and, moreover, assisted the bishop and myself with the wounded for most of the evening, and he remained sober, too. He ate a little bread and cheese, refused wine, and went to bed. Hugo? No. That's incredible."

The spirit began laughing.

"He's laughing," Chiara said morosely. "He laughs a lot, especially at me."

"Nice that he has a sense of humor," Armine said. "Now, tell me what's on his mind."

"He says the king is going to arrest us . . . not us—"

"You," the spirit said.

"Me," Chiara told her father. Chiara twisted her fingers in her lap. "It seems . . ."

"There's no time for explanations," the spirit said. "We must leave. The king is even now writing out the arrest orders. His counselors are trying to dissuade him from creating a bloodbath, but he won't listen. The more fool he. The only reason the palace guard isn't in this room right now is because the soldiers he sent for—they are at Susa—haven't arrived yet. When they do, he will make a clean sweep of all those he considers his enemies. The bishop is already in chains, poor old man. If you don't flee now, you both could well find yourselves exploring that bottle in the church basement, the one where the wolf was imprisoned. Now tell him, Chiara; if you love him, warn him now."

"Father," Chiara said rather breathlessly, and then repeated the spirit's statements word for word.

Armine listened. Wax ran down from the candle in his hand and splashed on his fingers. "Ouch," was all he said, then tilted the candle so the wax went on the floor. He continued listening intently.

When she was finished speaking, Armine hurried to the window. The palace was full of lights, one in almost every window.

When he turned away, he said, "Get dressed. Now. Hurry. Where is Gimp?" he said into the air.

A second later Chiara said, "He's gone and—" She waved her hands. "—the bear—that's what I call him, the bear—says he took what's left of Hugo with him." She looked up again and listened. "He says they're probably crossing the river now. He says hurry. He'll saddle the horses."

"He can do that?"

"He can throw roses all over my bed, box your ears, sock Bibo, and kick Hugo. I don't doubt he can saddle horses."

LUDOLF WAS HIS FATHER'S SON. IT ANNOYED HIM that he lost Adalgisus's trail at the river but he understood how to handle the situation. The blacksmith and some of his friends rode downstream, but Ludolf rode upstream with Dulcinia and the rest of the men.

The singer thought her horse stumbled in the shallow streambed until she saw the crossbow bolt protruding from its side. She didn't scream but gave a gasp, and a second later Ludolf's arm swept her out of the saddle as he galloped toward cover on the bank. They dismounted in a copse of trees. The trees were scrub oak, thickly twined with briars.

Dulcinia looked back. Her horse was down, kicking, struggling in the shallow water that now ran red.

"I think we've found them," Ludolf said.

Without his order one of the men with him rode back, keeping to cover on the brushy riverbank.

"He will warn the smith," Ludolf told Dulcinia.

"The horse," she said.

Ludolf shook his head. "Probably already dead."

Yes, Dulcinia thought, peering through a screen of thorny vines. The animal was still now. Suddenly she found she was shaking all over. *That—that could have been me.*

Ludolf pulled off his mantle and wrapped it around her. "I'll send you back with one of the men. You shouldn't have come—"

"No," Dulcinia said. She found she was whispering. "No, both your mother and Lucilla may need the services of a woman when we catch up to them."

Ludolf nodded absently. He was peering through the tangle of vines at the other side of the river. "How many do you think?" he asked one of the older men with him.

"Not many, but we are few and it wouldn't take a lot to block the trail."

Just then the blacksmith arrived, riding in quickly and taking cover with the rest. They held a council of war, heads together, behind the thick, stunted oaks and vines.

"How many?" the smith asked.

"Only a few," Ludolf answered, "but two would be enough."

Looking across the river, Dulcinia could see why. It was wide but shallow here; on the opposite bank a steep track ran up to a ridge. If they tried to rush the archers' position behind the ridge, the archers could slaughter them while they crossed the river, and they could be targeted on the slope to the top of the ridge.

"They mean to slow us down," Ludolf said. "They will probably leave, slip away at nightfall."

"No," the smith whispered, "that was my wife they killed. About a half mile farther on there's another ford. My sons and I can go on foot. We will come up behind them. Seem to make a sortie, my lord, let them drive you back. In an hour I and my sons will bring you their heads."

Ludolf turned to Dulcinia. "Stay here. Stay down."

Ludolf and his men got together and ran down the riverbank into the water. Arrows arched over the ridge on the opposite side. This time they were not crossbow bolts. The sortie party fled back to cover.

Dulcinia could hear some of the men chuckling, those who still had breath. The rest were huffing and puffing. Ludolf was laughing.

"We could force it, my lord," one of the men said.

"Yes," Ludolf answered. "They'd run and we wouldn't know where they were going. This way is better. He will take them alive."

"What do you mean?" Dulcinia whispered.

"We will find out where they're going," Ludolf told her.

"Suppose they won't tell?" she asked.

Ludolf and the men around him really did laugh at that. And after a few moments, Dulcinia could see why.

STELLA AND LUCILLA REACHED THE MONASTERY AT dusk. Adalgisus and Eberhardt virtually pulled them from their mounts and drove the women ahead of them into the cloister. The monks were at dinner at the refectory table in the hall. The monks rose to their feet, amazed to see two women enter the dining room. The prior rose to his feet and protested.

"My lords!"

Adalgisus drew his sword. "Where is my lord abbot? Send him here at once."

"He is dining in private with some friends," the prior replied.

"Take me to him. Eberhardt, you remain here. Watch the women."

"I don't know where we'd go," Stella stammered, and threw back her veil.

Every man in the room stared at her, astonished.

"Oh, lord," Lucilla whispered and drew her own veil more tightly over her face.

Stella was still beautiful. Even weary, windburned, and disheveled, she might have been a peacock prancing amidst a flock of crows. She was a small blonde with fair skin, blue eyes, and shapely features. Lucilla was sure none of the men in this room had ever seen anything like her before. Lucilla put Stella's veil up, brushed back her hair, and wrapped her mantle more tightly around her shoulders.

"Please," Lucilla asked Eberhardt. "Find us somewhere we can . . ." She was about to say *stay out of sight*, but changed it to "rest and refresh ourselves."

He also looked nervous. "As soon as I can," he said.

"I'm sore," Stella said, sounding like a child. "And so weary I can barely stand."

Lucilla took Stella in her arms. "Hush, Stella. Everything will be fine."

"Oh, what a dear liar you are," Stella said. "But no, nothing will be fine. Still, I would like to lie down, if I might."

Adalgisus returned. He was with a man, obviously a soldier, big, hard-eyed, and wearing a tunic and sword. He began laughing when he saw the two women.

"Presents for me?" he asked. "What about it, ladies? Eh?"

Stella shrank away from him.

He shrugged. "Ansgar's wife. Why the hell bring her here?"

"I wanted to be sure he didn't follow," Adalgisus said.

"He probably will, but I'll handle him." He spoke to the prior. "Take the ladies to the guest house. See they get something to eat and some wine. Come," he told Adalgisus and Eberhardt. "The pig is so near done it's falling off the spit."

He turned to the monks sitting at the table still gaping at the women. "A round of extra wine for everyone in honor of the king's son." Then he went off with Eberhardt and Adalgisus, arm in arm.

The prior, an elderly man with a fixed expression of disapproval, led them to the guest house.

"Who was that one?" Lucilla asked.

"Dagobert, one of my husband's friends. I suppose he's harmless," Stella whispered. "But he's so big and loud."

The monastery formed a square, church on one side, the monks' quarters across a garden on the other. The front and back were protected by high walls on the inside; the guest house ran the length of one wall, the stables the other.

The room they were shown into might as well have been in the stables. On second thought Lucilla decided it might have been warmer in the stables. At least there would have been hay to lie in. In the guest house, two icy stone platforms served as beds and a small hearth in one corner was intended to warm the room. Or would have if a fire had been present, but since the hearth was dark and cold, the only thing it was doing was creating a draft as the cold mountain air blew through the smoke hole in the roof.

"You can rest here," the prior told them, then turned to go. It was dark now and the only light the lantern in his hand.

"Wait," Lucilla said. "We need fire, blankets, and food."

The prior pushed his way past her. Lucilla jumped in front of him again.

"At least leave us some light," she said as she snatched the lantern out of his hand.

He shoved her aside with his shoulder. "No woman has any right here. I have shown you to shelter; I see no reason to offer you anything else."

He left, slamming the door behind him.

Stella was weeping quietly. Lucilla still had the lantern in her hand. She set it on the hearth and went in search of wood. She found some near the door, wood and kindling both. And in a few minutes she managed to get a fire going on the hearth. When she saw the fire, Stella dried her tears and came to kneel with Lucilla near the blaze.

"That's comforting," she said.

Lucilla blew out the lantern, saying, "The fire will do for light. Stella, I'm very much afraid we won't get anything to eat tonight. This Dagobert, can he be trusted to take care of you until your husband or son can find you?"

"No," Stella said shortly. "Like so many of them, the soldiers I mean, he's a drunk. That's why the prior is so angry, because he's here—he and his men drinking up all the wine the monks have laid down for the year. Nominally he's the abbot, but he never comes here except to stop and empty the cellars. It will be months before the harvest is in and the wine will be gone. Dagobert and his soldiers will sit in the kitchens and eat and drink, especially drink, for the next month. Then the monks will be impoverished. It's not our fault, but the prior doesn't know that, and if he did, he probably wouldn't care."

"Desiderius lets his soldiers do as they please?" Lucilla asked.

"Oh, yes," Stella answered. "Exactly as they please."

Lucilla concentrated on feeding the fire. The room grew warmer. "There's not even a lock on the door," she said. "I think we should sleep near the hearth. It will be more comfortable there."

She had dressed for the journey and had her heavy mantle. She spread it near the hearth for Stella, who came and lay down close to the fire and made a sort of pillow out of her veil.

"Oh, dear," she whispered. "I have been such a fool."

But then her eyes closed and it seemed she slept, leaving Lucilla awake and worried.

Lucilla spent some time trying to find a way to lock the door. She finally had to settle for wedging it shut with a piece of kindling. From time to time she could hear the sounds of revelry coming from near the monastery kitchen. Once it sounded as if a woman screamed. Women? Here? Yes, but then Dagobert and his men wouldn't be traveling without women. Soldiers almost never did. And they wouldn't be worried about sparing the prior's feelings. She suspected the opinions of those whose lives were devoted to work and prayer meant less than nothing to Dagobert and his followers. So she tried to sleep but the floor was cold, not to mention hard, and Stella was hogging most of the woolen mantle, and in addition she'd picked the spot closest to the fire, leaving Lucilla to the cold and dark. But, finally, Lucilla fell into a light doze, so she was the one who was first awakened by the sound of someone trying to open the door.

IT WAS LATE, THE SUN TOUCHING THE HILLS BE- yond the river, when the smith and his sons came across with their prisoner. There was only one. There had been four archers on the other bank, but the other three were dead.

As Ludolf promised, eventually he talked. But even Dulcinia was surprised that it took him so long. She didn't watch the questioning but she heard enough to know pretty much what was being done. The blacksmith and his sons took an active role in the interrogation, but then Avernia had been their mother and they might be excused for being a bit too enthusiastic in their inquiries.

When the prisoner did break, he talked about everything. But even he didn't know where Adalgisus had hidden Gerberga. They gave the man enough grief to be sure he was telling the truth about not knowing where Gerberga and her two sons were hidden, and then Ludolf drove his sword through the mercenary's heart.

By then it was dark. Dulcinia drew close to Ludolf again while some of his men finished stripping the archer's corpse and carried the body away to dump it in a ravine.

There was also a lot of grumbling among Ludolf's followers because the smith and his sons had despoiled the corpses of the other three mercenaries and kept the loot for themselves. Ludolf simply said they did the work and should take the pay.

"I'm sorry you had to witness that," he said to her.

"I didn't see most of it."

He nodded. "I don't think any woman wants to see her man at war, but Stella is my mother. I won't allow her to be abused. Not without recompense. How could I ask to hold my lands if I didn't defend her honor? Are you still willing to marry me?"

"Yes."

"I can see how this nonsense might make me a great lord."

"Hsssst," Dulcinia whispered. "Don't let yourself be overheard."

"No, we're alone now, but if King Desiderius loses to Charles, there is a great deal of empty land between my father's domain and Rufus's. We could split that land between ourselves. Rufus and my father, I mean. And pledge our allegiance to the pope and the Frankish king. One city and at best a dozen towns once stood there. And they can rise again and make the overlords wealthy."

Dulcinia took his hand. "But then you won't want a singing girl for a wife."

He brought Dulcinia's hand to his lips. "Oh, yes, I will. Stella is a good mother to me and a good wife to my father, whatever men may say of her. Yes, I've heard the stories. But I don't care. Besides, you come dowered with Lucilla's trust and Hadrian's favor."

"Yes, Hadrian does like me, and may even contribute to my marriage portion. I believe he would. Especially if you manage to rescue Lucilla and find the runaway Frankish queen. I think he would look with pleasure on your desire to clear the land of brigands and bring it under cultivation. In fact, I think he would be delighted with such an offer."

"Mount up. I will have to deliver on a number of things. We will attack when we reach the monastery tonight. I know the place well. One Dagobert will be there with his men. If my mother is well, I will be merciful. If not . . ."

Dulcinia watched as the same look moved over his face that she had seen when he watched the blacksmith and his sons bring the prisoner up from the river. He hadn't enjoyed what he'd done, but that hadn't stopped him for one very small second. She'd seen the same expression on Lucilla's face and just as often on Pope Hadrian's. They did what they had to do. And if they lost sleep over it, she'd never seen any indication of the fact. Yes, she did still want him. More, far more, than any other man she'd ever known or seen. And if, one day, those eyes rested on her with that same cold resolve, well, she would have to abide the outcome.

L UCILLA WOKE FULLY, COLD AND FRIGHTENED. SHE knew she must have slept for some time, no matter how stiff she felt, because Stella had turned toward her and her head was resting on Lucilla's outstretched arm. The fire had burned down and was only a few blue and yellow flames dancing over the blackened coals on the hearth. The room was almost pitch-dark.

The scratching sound came again. Lucilla closed her eyes and willed herself to ignore it. Something pushed against the door. Lucilla saw the planks shift. Her arms tightened around Stella. This was what she'd been afraid of. One or more of the drunken ruffians from the church had come tomcatting around in what she was sure must be the early hours of the morning.

She cursed the prior and Dagobert for a pair of filthy turds. Why hadn't they given her and Stella any more secure quarters? Or seen fit to set some kind of watch over the guest house? She looked away from the door toward Stella. She was lying there, eyes wide open, looking absolutely terrified.

"Whatever happens, Stella, don't put up a fight," Lucilla whispered. "You're too small; those men are too strong. Please, please promise me."

Stella nodded.

Someone knocked softly.

"They're probably very drunk. Maybe they'll go away."

"Stop whispering together and open the door. You whores have customers. Open up and accommodate us. Otherwise, we'll have to rouse the whole house."

Lucilla scrambled to her feet.

"Come on," Adalgisus said. "No one need know. Just the three of us. Let us in."

Three. Lucilla was willing to bet the third was Dagobert.

"Come on," Eberhardt said in a wheedling tone. "No one need

know. Let us in. We'll have a little romp and then you'll be rid of us. Come on."

Lucilla went to the door and put her shoulder against the planks. "Go away, Adalgisus. I am a close friend of the pope's. You wouldn't want to anger him, and Stella is the wife of one of your father's liegemen . . . We are not unattached . . . and free to—"

Someone kicked the door open.

Stella screamed.

Lucilla was thrown back. Her calves hit one of the low stone bed platforms and she fell backward, supine on the stone slab. Her head cracked against it. She was stunned for a second. Then she found herself trying to fight off Adalgisus.

He snatched one breast, squeezing it painfully. Lucilla screamed and clawed at his eyes and face. He stank of wine, the reek so intense Lucilla turned away from his face, gagging.

Stella screamed again.

Lucilla could hear her pleading.

"Oh, now, stop. Please. I am a man's wife. Please don't try to force me to dishonor my husband." Then Stella screamed, "No. No, oh, God, no. Stop."

Lucilla could see her in the half-light of the dying fire. Eberhardt had a grip on her hair with one hand and the other was around her neck, half choking her while Dagobert was lifting her dress.

Adalgisus was gripping Lucilla's hair also and trying to raise her skirt. Not a very easy thing to do since it was a divided riding skirt.

Stella screamed again. She was clawing savagely at the arm around her neck.

Lucilla got one knee up, lifting Adalgisus's weight off her body, then she turned. He rolled off, and since the platforms were narrow, he went over the edge and landed on his back on the stone floor. He let out a yell of rage, but Lucilla was on her feet and running toward the woodpile near the hearth. Just at that moment, Stella's head slipped down through the crook of Eberhardt's arm and it looked to Dagobert as if she might get away. Her skirts slipped out of his hand, so he stepped back and drove his fist hard into Stella's abdomen just below the ribs.

"There, I'll quiet her down," he said.

Stella didn't scream. She couldn't. Lucilla watched in horror as she doubled over in agony, the color left her face, and her lips, ears, and nose turned blue, and then she fell, landing on her side, curled into a tight little ball of agony.

Lucilla had reached the woodpile. She picked up the stub of an oak branch and swung it as hard as she could at Dagobert's head. He sat down on the floor, blood pouring from a cut on his forehead. Still on the floor near the bed, Adalgisus was trying to get up. This exercise was complicated by the fact that his overloaded stomach chose this moment to disgorge its contents all over the floor.

Dagobert was blinded by his own blood and fuddled by drunkenness. He was still trying to get to his feet, but—possibly a little smarter or a bit more agile than either Eberhardt or Adalgisus—he was in flight. Lucilla saw he was halfway out the door.

Adalgisus remained on his knees, retching violently, while Lucilla hit Eberhardt over the top of the head with her improvised club. Then she hit him in the face, breaking his nose and putting out one of his eyes. She followed this by knocking out most of his teeth with the next strike, and then she managed to break one of his kneecaps. She had to terminate her attack because Adalgisus was up and after her with his sword.

He drove it at her using a simple thrust as he had with Avernia, but the difference was that Lucilla wasn't Avernia, and Adalgisus was no longer sober. She sidestepped the thrust and smacked his wrist with her club. He screamed in agony.

Lucilla screamed back, cursing him with the vilest obscenities she knew. Then she said, "Look, pig, look what you and your friends have done. You have killed Stella."

He stared at the slender, once-beautiful blond woman lying on the floor near the hearth. Stella's skin was gray. She was cold, clammy to the touch. Lucilla knew this because she was on her knees beside Stella. A thread of blood was running from her mouth out onto the floor. Both arms were still wrapped around her stomach and when Lucilla tried to touch her there, she gave the most dreadful cry Lucilla had ever heard.

"No, don't move me. Don't. I'll die. He broke something inside me. I never felt such terrible pain before. Help me, Lucilla. Help me. I'm dying."

She didn't sound frightened but only astonished at her condition. Lucilla looked up at Adalgisus.

"Well, you have played the fool for good and all now, haven't you?"

He backed away from Lucilla, holding the sword in his left hand while he tried to make the sign of the cross with his right. Just then they both heard the screams and shouts coming from the abbey's church.

MATRONA APPROACHED THE POOL IN WOLF FORM. As always, she heard voices. Some of them she recognized; others were strange to her and sometimes she was certain they were not simply language but other forms used to transmit information by beings that could not be classified as human. The languages also were a mystery. She knew a great many and her mind tracked them in their changes over time.

Her own people's language was still spoken now by many different peoples, but it had altered so much over the centuries, the millennia, that it would have been gibberish to its originators. She herself was sometimes slow spoken because her mind idly followed the road through time taken by a concept molded into speech by creatures who first used words to impose order and thought on the continuum, the raw data of life itself.

A thing of power, language. Far more powerful than the men and women who used it so casually would ever understand. Matrona listened to what the voices said. Sometimes they offered warnings or pointed out a path she should take. But most of the time they simply commented on the problems of their particular world or cried out in grief or in triumph over difficulty or in positive achievement.

Now, at this moment, a woman sang a lullaby to a baby, accompanied by the whispering trill of a wooden pipe. Matrona recognized the voice as her mother's. Once the voices haunted her as she had resisted the omnipresent flow of change all around her, but now she accepted her lot as a designated spectator to the human journey and no longer suffered the sense of loss she had known when she realized she would be sundered from all her loves by the inexorable flow of events. She, as Maeniel, had taken up a position outside of time, and unlike him or Regeane, she accepted her portion. By her standards, they were both . . . well, young.

Then she heard Gu! Chanting. Long ago he had taught her the calendar and how to count the years. She made the sound that was his name with the wolf's tongue.

All the languages since then had lost that sound, but it was notable that a wolf could make it, though men had forgotten how. But then he was a master of wolves and in the bleak savage winter of the world, he had run with the packs to live.

"Gu!" she called again but there was no answer. No, he was gone with the rest.

Matrona the mother. We remember when beast and man were one. I am the talisman. I was their talisman. The mountains roared and smoke blinded the sun's eye and the endless winter descended on the earth.

It was our doom. We were careless then. Gu told me. We lived in the sun. We plucked fruit from the trees, the waters were filled with life. We followed the rivers and streams in the dry years. Then, when the rains came, the whole earth was ours and we took joy in its abundance. We needed no clothing because the fur pattern at our groins, head and neck was enough. We were fair with it as cats are, marked with the fine silkiness, gold, black, roan, or silver. It was all we could desire and we caressed each other's bodies without fear, to ask for food or love or even forgiveness and comfort.

The wide savannas were an endless source of beauty and nourishment not simply for the body but the spirit also. Flights of birds darkened the sun. Running herds of horned and hooved beasts rivaled the very thunder of the storms. Trees bent down under the weight of fruit and flowers, offering them to our willing hands.

Until the mountains spoke.

And the long winters came. The long, cold winters.

Matrona couldn't remember the smiling light, the perpetual warmth. She doubted if Gu could either. Many knew the tales of perpetual light and the unending largess of the mother of all life, but they were just that, only tales. A paradise lost. She herself had been born in the farthest south after her people had followed the herds from the north on their annual migration, to hunt them in the gorges and depths of the heavy forest near the sea. They were allowed this margin of land beyond the frozen earth; the ice that gripped the hills, the mountains, and even the plain was held back by the water, the only water they knew that never froze, the roaring sea.

And in the shallow space constricted by glaciers, they could survive the winter until the next time of testing, the long journey when they followed the herds north at the beginning of spring. So one fine spring when they were preparing for the arduous journey into the north, Matrona had been given to the wolves.

Gu had seen the shapes in the fire and the lot fell on her.

She went to the wolves and they accepted her as they had once accepted Gu and named him. So they accepted her and named her. And she ran with the pack to the north as her people did. To the steppes, and there she met the black wolf. They fought.

By then Matrona, hardened by long runs with the pack, fought with the rest for her portion of the kill; and hardened to cold and fatigue by the constant frozen day and night with the pack in the wake of the herds, wearing only her skin, she was at least as strong as any of the wolves. She took no nonsense even from the leader; she was a dangerous opponent for any wolf ever born.

But this one had been special, different from the rest. A last, lone survivor of the ruling pack, the organization of dire wolves who had ruled before her people were even thought of, much less were. The dire. She came to claim her yearly sacrifice, to call Matrona to final darkness and everlasting cold. And now Matrona wore her skin, and her soul looked out through Matrona's eyes at the pool near morning.

Matrona shook herself as if trying to be rid of the memories that clung around her spirit like cobwebs among the trees, and gazed down into the water. There were no warnings—this time. Sometimes the voices she heard were agitated and disturbed. They told her the road was dangerous or that something might happen. She wondered what path Regeane had taken and then heard her voice.

"Is your love a collar and a chain?"

Matrona smiled and slipped into the water. She also came to the same strange forest where Regeane landed, but by now the sun was up and the air warm.

As human she swam across the lake amidst the trees to the falls and studied the same gorge choked with the roots from the monster trees that seemed to floor the entire world. Matrona had been here before. Some scarlet creatures like birds skimmed the waters below the falls taking—what? Insects? Matrona had never known.

Up and up the giant trees rose, tops lost in the clouds before any side branch was to be seen. As Regeane had, she turned wolf in the shallows and started downstream, letting the silence soak into her.

Unlike most humans, she did not habitually think in words. In her world, among wind-blown forests near the sea's margins where she had been born, the word was used to amplify the unending communication of the flexible dance of life over the body. She had not known or needed words when she lived among the wolves, or even after she fought and killed the dire wolf. After Gu came, she had not needed to speak to them or him. So she respected the silence and it brought her news.

The morning wind was tearing to ragged shreds the high mist that concealed the upper portions of the trees. The forest whispered, then spoke aloud to the changing air. The silver-barked trees moved, clattering a little as their meshed branches on the umbrellalike tops struck each other lightly, the sound a timpani of life and delight.

Another night is over.

It is morning.

The splashing of the black wolf's feet in the water spoke whole volumes of haste, urgency. The questions of mobile living things.

She was here.

But she is gone.

She ate a . . . shimmer.

But no harm done.

Among the misty isles of trees, drops of condensation from the night mist fell like rain, slaking the thirst of the ferns and even more primitive plants that hung from holdfasts on the tree bark or nested in the soil caught between the armorlike roots that covered the soil with no openings between them.

A tree died the day she came.

We . . . mourn.

A vast sigh.

We . . . mourn.

She left us at the lake.

Shimmer. And the scarlet birds danced over the water.

Or were they birds?

Shimmer. The forest spoke. *Four foot. Two foot.*

Matrona recognized her own name.

Two foot. Four foot.

Our beloved daughter of silence.

I will go beyond the lake. I must find her.

Strange thought . . . speed. Hurry . . ., the trees mused.

Matrona picked up her pace.

She is in the water. We hear her. Footsteps. She ate the shimmer . . . fruit, cress . . . took part of us into herself. She will return.

MAENIEL DIDN'T FOLLOW THE RIVER AS REGEANE had. He knew of a Roman road. It led, as most Roman roads did, straight across the marsh and made travel very easy.

Disgusted with himself for allowing his own capture and imprisonment, he set a fast pace, wanting to return to the king as quickly as possible. Regeane was hard put to keep up and she knew he must still be angry with her about their argument the night before. Though they seemed reconciled, she felt the quarrel wasn't really over. He wouldn't yield one inch to her, and she continued to feel wronged by him.

When he spotted some waterfowl, ducks with dark feathers and brilliant green heads, traveling in family groups with fuzzy ducklings paddling behind them, he froze into immobility, preparing to make a snack of mother and baby duck both.

Regeane felt disgusted and even the wolf was annoyed. So she broke cover and startled them into flight. The ducks exploded around his face in a flurry of wings and loud alarm cries. As they fled, he swung around and his jaws snapped shut less than an inch from her face.

She recognized this for what it was, a form of intimidation, and stood her ground as he glared at her. She was no match for him and had discovered over the brief time of their marriage that almost nothing else was either. Certainly none of the pack he had gathered around him could match him for sheer lethal ferocity as man or wolf, but oddly, he wasn't nearly as ready as a human male might be to try to overawe her with sheer physical might.

The females of the pack had their own hierarchy. Regeane wasn't at the top of it. Matrona was. But Regeane was a strong second and learning the ropes quickly from Matrona. And one of the lessons was to demand the respect that was her due. Even from him.

So the staring contest ended with him turning away.

And again she fell in behind him.

For the next few miles the road was submerged by the spring floods. No one remained to tend the ditches that once drained it.

So the two wolves found themselves swimming, at times wading through mud. There were snakes. Regeane was indifferent to them, but to pay him back for attacking the ducklings she pretended to be preparing to eat one—behavior that raised his hackles and drew a savage snarl of disgust from him.

Regeane looked up from the wiggling reptile and gave him a look of innocent astonishment, one so meltingly tender that he divined her purpose at once and stalked away stiff-legged with his nose in the air. The snake, somewhat distressed and conveying its fear in rapid snake, the language of movement, slithered away quickly and gave a last tongue flick and an indignant neck curve—*that was very unkind of you*—and vanished into a thick stand of pickerel weed showing the first of its spring flower spikes.

They were united, however, in their feeling about frogs. Both thought them absolutely delicious, so they strolled along, dining as they went.

At length the road resurfaced and the going became easier, though there were fewer succulent frogs to be found. The ground began to rise. It was here they crossed the trail of Armine, Chiara, Hugo, and Gimp. They had only two men with them and were pursued by a half-dozen soldiers and three dogs.

Regeane thought in horror, *Too many for us.* But Maeniel turned onto the trail seemingly without a second thought.

Yes, Regeane remembered. The girl saved his life. They must try to help. Maeniel broke into a run. Regeane followed.

THE BEAR KNEW HE WAS IN A RUNNING FIGHT. He'd become aware they were being followed when Armine and Chiara crossed the river. Gimp was waiting at the ill-omened ford where the family had been killed.

Regeane had observed, *The water must be high by now at the crossing.* It was.

Hugo's body was flung across a saddle, belly down.

The bear swore.

Chiara heard him but for once said nothing. Both she and Armine were frightened. Gimp was, as usual, dozing. He managed this even on horseback.

The bear brought him awake with a loud roar. Then he repossessed Hugo's body. He slid off the horse, staggered, and had to circle the horse three times to work out the kinks. But then he vaulted into the saddle.

Armine's escort noticed almost nothing. They were hideously hungover, and Chiara, Armine, and the bear were pretty sure they would be worthless in a fight. All they could hope for was that the king would be too busy massacring his other enemies to give much thought to them.

Vain hope.

The bear detected the pursuit before the rest. He left the trail, leading them to the Roman road through the marsh. Armine started to protest. He spurred his horse up to where the bear—as Hugo—was leading the party.

"Where—"

"They're after us," the bear replied.

"Oh, no, I'm not worried about myself, but Chiara . . . When I think what might happen to her—"

"I won't let it happen," the bear said. "I won't let them take her."

"Promise?"

"I give you my word," the bear answered, and then a look of ferocity crossed his face, a look that Hugo could never have originated. "I'll kill anyone who lays one hand on her. I promise. I vow, I swear I will.

"Now you, Armine, make sure this carcass stays on the horse while I visit our pursuers."

Hugo's body slumped. Armine got a firm grip on his arm.

The bear never knew how he moved, but he could do so quickly. In a few moments he saw Desiderius's men. They, too, had turned on the Roman road. A footman had charge of the three dogs. They were straining at their leashes. Killers. War dogs. Big, dangerous, vicious. The dog handler carried a whip. They seemed to respect it and him, but they lunged in fury at everything else, including the mounted warriors accompanying them, when they approached too closely.

The bear disregarded them. He'd recovered from his fight with Regeane and Matrona, but it had taken him some weeks. He had been drained near to death or dormancy when he found Gimp and then Hugo. The guardians of the tomb had saved him from— death?—dormancy?—who knows. Some form of nonexistence. A fierce battle with the dogs right now might deplete his energies beyond the point of being able to protect Chiara and her father. And, oddly, this was what worried him the most. The fear that she might fall prey to Desiderius and his mercenary army.

Eventually the king would have her killed, but before she died, the bright, brave little spirit would be broken in the cruelest possible way. The first guilt the bear had ever known crawled in his soul at the memory of the suffering of the "abbot's" prisoners at that human monster's hands. He was being paid out now for his callous support of the madman's desires, but the creature had loved him, worshiped him. This was his connection to the realm of light: the emotions of the creatures whom he was able to make his own. Like the abbot, Hugo, Gimp, and others he had preyed on over the centuries, the millennia, in fact. He could not live without their love, awe, hatred, fear, pain, and yes, even joy.

No true beasts like those maddened, ruined—yes, they were ruined by systematic human cruelty—dogs could ever offer him the energies that sustained his conscious living, human presence. With- out humans he must fade, sink into mumbling stupidity like Gimp and then— He pushed the thought out of his mind. How to stop them? A much easier target was the horses. The men couldn't see him but the horses were a far simpler matter.

He materialized in front of them. He took the bear form and roared.

The results were more than satisfactory.

A few seconds later, he was back in Hugo's body, chuckling. The sound made Armine's blood run cold.

"Try to make the best speed possible," he told Armine. "I gave them a little something to think about. By the time they catch their horses and get the creatures calmed down, we should be well on our way."

Armine studied the man riding by his side. He was clean. He was wearing Hugo's oldest clothes, shirt, dalmatic, and riding pants rein- forced by leather at the rear, knees, and ankles. But the face was so completely changed he could see nothing of Hugo in it. It was the face of a warrior: dangerous, strong, bold, fearless, and oddly handsome. He was leaning back in the saddle, knees clamped to the horse's sides. He controlled the reins easily with one hand, while the other rested on the knife in his belt.

They were moving fast in a straight line down the center of the Roman road. When they reached patches of mud or washouts where the road was gone, he prodded his horse easily into a gallop and passed through without difficulty.

"What did you do with Hugo?" Armine asked.

The thing in Hugo's body grinned in a completely wicked manner. "I ate him."

Armine gave him a weary look. "My lord, don't toy with me. Did you destroy Hugo's soul when you took his body?"

"No, but you are very . . . There are many things about the world you don't understand. I tried to tell your daughter. The lightning killed Hugo. When I returned after seeing the wolf off, I found what remained on the porch. He was still breathing, just barely, but his brain, the part of you that is in the skull, was . . . mush."

Armine nodded. He had more life experience than Chiara. He knew severe head injuries were often fatal.

"I took the body. I can use it." The creature shrugged. "But Hugo is gone. The man you knew resided in his brain; when that brain was destroyed he went wherever it is . . . your God sends them. Heaven, hell, I can't say. He is not my God and doesn't explain these things to me. But trust me, Hugo won't be back."

"I can't say I entirely regret that," Armine commented.

The bear laughed. The hollow echoes of the sound set Armine's teeth on edge.

"Don't do that," Armine said.

"Chiara doesn't like it either," the bear replied. "But—" He broke off, looking preoccupied. "Damn. They are coming again and gaining ground."

IMAGINE, IMAGINE A WORLD WITHOUT BOUNDA- ries, a world without nations, cities, farms, or even laws or rules. The ice shield covered the poles. In the summer it retracted. In the winter it extended itself to the edge of the many seas. In the summer the giant beasts that dominated the limited wilderness between sea and ice spread over the vast plains, the green valleys caught in the folds of the wrinkled, nameless mountain ranges, and the shorelines of the vast wild seas.

This world boasted of incredible riches and brutal hardship. Deer and elk gifted with twelve-foot sets of antlers, wolves that ran in packs and were the size of small horses, mammoth elephants with giant, curved tusks and hairy skin dominated this world.

Matrona and her people hunted, loved, lived, and conquered among animal beings the like of which the world had not seen since the dinosaurs were destroyed and have never been seen since. They wept at the end of each summer, cut off their fingers in token of grief, and slashed their faces. They did this in terror, hoping that whatever gods ruled their universe would see their sorrow and in time give them again the gift of springtime. Then they followed the massive herds of prey animals down in a wild and dangerous journey from the high plains, the mountains, the hills, and the forests to winter along coasts, on islands bared by the shrunken ice-locked sea amid the wind-swept promontories battered by terrifying storms.

In this world a woman must bear four children to raise one; a man must father seven to replace himself. But love they did and snatched joy from the jaws of death and knew transcendent happiness in the shadow of the sword.

Matrona rose from the waters of the swamp like a cicada bursting its shell and confronted the two wolves. Regeane and Maeniel gave each other guilty looks.

"You gave Charles your word," she said to Maeniel.

He cocked his head to one side. In wolf this was *So?*

"It was all your idea," she reminded him.

He hung his head, looking like a scolded dog.

"I don't want your apologies," Matrona said. "Speak to your consort."

Maeniel looked mutinous, but only for a moment, then he turned to Regeane. They touched noses. *Can you handle this?*

She gave a low grunting sound in her throat.

Matrona understood it as well as Maeniel. It was *I will try.*

The head of a cattail landed near Regeane's feet. Someone had swiped a sword through the stem. She looked up. The wolf's eyes saw the outline of Remingus between herself and the sun. He was as solid as he had been on the day when he went to the square with her in Pavia.

"The bear is near," he told Regeane.

The wolf flicked an ear forward, then back. She felt annoyance.

Remingus continued. "Chiara and her father—he is trying to defend them. He will fail. The girl, Chiara, saved your husband. You owe them a blood debt."

Regeane set out at a dead run.

Maeniel tried to follow. He leaped into the air, halted, and was pulled back the way a dog is when he reaches the end of a chain, forepaws in the air, standing on his hind legs. Matrona had hold of his ruff. She held him back. Maeniel's mind dissolved into berserk fury. With the movement of a giant dragon, his body writhed and then broke free. He turned and faced Matrona.

She stood, woman, about eight feet away. Magnificent in her absolute nakedness. Her hair a wild tangle of ebony silk that hung to her waist. Big breasted with dark, strongly marked nipples, a wide rib cage that sloped down to a narrow waist, then spread again into wide, graceful hips. The hair at her groin grew thick, black and curly, a dark silky sable pelt covering her sexual structures. Not protecting them, enhancing them, the hair rising like a wedge whose point terminated just below her navel. For the first time in their long friendship, her femaleness struck him like a club. She smiled, dark eyes glittering with knowledge that made Eve seem a simple, innocent girl. White teeth, canines slightly longer and more pointed than other women's, flashed in a savage, triumphant grin.

"Let her go," she commanded. "It is time. Come. By your own will, you serve a human being. A human king. The more fool you, but it is what you have chosen. So be it. She must now go on alone."

Human, Maeniel thought. No, Matrona was not completely human. She was the . . . other. He studied her, the red rage roaring in his brain. The others. They had not always had fire. They got it from the men. But her people hadn't needed it either. The hair pattern on Matrona's body was that of a creature that had ancestors, close ancestors, comfortable in their own pelts—as were the wolves.

Matrona's ancestors had emerged from the beast state just in time to battle the hideous and beautiful, but mortal and terrifying, agonizing cold. A cold and dark that threatened to sweep all before it and end the life of all land creatures and most of the vegetation they fed upon.

And in this final and seemingly everlasting darkness and bitter cold, only the hunters could live, and the other quasi-humans fell away, dying of hunger when the cold stripped the trees bare of fruit, flowers, then leaves. When drought scoured jungles into deserts and the wide plains were scorched tinder, dried by the unending heat in the tropical latitudes and then burned when heat lightning lanced down from skies darkened by thick dust. And rain never fell.

The rain, the fecund water of the skies, never fell, and the things, being not yet savage enough to kill, died. They had taken another path than the hunters, a more gentle, seemingly wiser road than Matrona's people, but it led only into an eternal night.

Only the hunters, masters of fire and wooden spears, survived. They could triumph, feed on the corpses left by the carnage and chaos, and so survive. The weak, the loving, the kind, the compassionate, the beautiful, and the intelligent served the hunters who mimicked the ways of wolves and dire wolves, or they died.

And the world held its breath and waited for the sun to return.

And Matrona's people strode through the vast desolation and brought humanity to birth and, for a time, humanity cowered in the shadow of their strength. Matrona's people took fire from their hands and it shone as cold, put an end almost even to them.

This Maeniel the wolf understood in a twinkling. As he lunged toward Matrona for the kill.

Matrona threw back her head, white teeth gleaming, and laughed. Laughed as, too late, Maeniel realized he'd flown free of the world of humanity and was flung, following Matrona, into another.

THE SOUNDS OF COMBAT WERE GROWING LOUDER and louder. Lucilla, still facing Adalgisus, bared her teeth at him. "Sounds as if Ansgar or his son might have arrived."

"His son?" Adalgisus asked.

"Yes," Lucilla whispered. "He was present when you took Stella away. She was afraid for him."

"My son?" Stella whispered. "Oh, Lucilla, do you think it could be my son?"

Adalgisus made a lunge toward Stella.

Lucilla lifted the club in her hand above her head. "Touch her, go ahead, touch her," she screamed. "I'll kill you."

Adalgisus backed away toward the door.

Just then Dagobert appeared at the door. He took one look at what was left of Eberhardt and spoke to Adalgisus. "Come. It wasn't a fight, it was a slaughter. How could they get in so easily?" He seemed both distraught and bewildered. And, indeed, he was outlined against the scarlet glow of a fire.

Lucilla heard a long, agonized, animal scream.

Dagobert glanced back in terror. "They are killing them, killing them and burning the church."

Lucilla heard the explosive sound of glass breaking.

"If we don't leave now, we will be next. I can't understand it. The Lombard king is Ludolf's overlord. How could he dare slaughter the king's soldiers?"

"Possibly kidnapping his mother had something to do with it," Lucilla suggested with an ugly laugh.

Adalgisus made another move toward Stella. Lucilla let out a yell of fury.

"Are you insane?" Dagobert shouted. "Look at what's left of Eberhardt and what she's already done to you. We must go and go now. Ansgar's son is in a killing mood. How do you think he'll behave when he finds his mother in the condition she's in?"

"Whose fault is that?" Adalgisus screeched. "You hit her. I didn't tell you to hit her."

The firelight was very bright now, the garden was filling with smoke. Lucilla lowered her weapon.

"That's it, go on arguing. Keep it up until Ludolf finds you. Both of you listen. I'll come with you without a fight if you leave Stella here and do her no further harm, but we must leave at once, hear me? At once. Adalgisus, your father will be furious if you don't salvage something from this disaster, and I will be the something, but you go and leave poor Stella alone."

Lucilla dropped the oak butt she'd used as a weapon and moved toward the door. Adalgisus seized her by the arm and they fled. More glass broke as they ran through the garden. Lucilla looked at the church. Fire had seized the beams supporting the apse above the altar and the whole belltower was involved. Sounds from the rest of the cathedral indicated that some of Dagobert's men had been sober enough to make a stand, but they were losing. More and more Lucilla heard cries for mercy and the screaming of those being slaughtered.

Flames were spreading quickly across the stable's thatched roof when Lucilla and the two men reached it. Lucilla knew they had no time to spare. Still, she had to do their thinking for them. They remained addled by drink, but she managed to get three horses saddled, then snatched up their bridles and led them to a door at the back. The stable was filling with smoke.

Lucilla grabbed Adalgisus's arm. "Up. Up. Mount up!" she commanded.

He was shaking all over. "How . . . How do you know they're not waiting for us out there?"

"They probably are," Lucilla snapped. "But you go first anyway. You, Dagobert, bring up the rear."

Obediently he mounted behind her.

God, she thought as she slipped into her own saddle. The smoke was so thick she could barely breathe. She dropped her head down near the horse's neck, trying for clearer air. It was very dark inside the shed but behind her she saw Dagobert reeling in his saddle. He was still half drunk, too drunk to protect himself from the thick, choking smoke.

"Good," she whispered to herself. "Good."

She sidled her horse toward the door. Then one solid, hard kick from her riding boot opened it. And what Lucilla thought might happen, did. The stable became a tunnel of flame as icy air from the outside roared through the open door. The horse Adalgisus was riding shot through like a loosed crossbow bolt. Her own mount bucked, but Lucilla knew that to be thrown was death. She let go of the reins and clung to the pommel like a burr, and when the beast's hind legs hit the ground he took off at the same pace Adalgisus's had.

Then the air flow reversed itself and the backdraft caught Dagobert. Both horse and man screamed in terror as the fire played on their backs. Her own horse was dug in, his back hooves lunging forward on a wild runaway. Her head was near and to one side of the horse's neck.

Dagobert's head slammed into the lintel of the stable door. His skull didn't so much fracture as disintegrate. Lucilla saw him die. She saw his head split; even the jawbone was torn away by the impact. Then what was left fell, landing in a blazing heap near the doorway. His horse, saddle empty, dashed past her, and Lucilla, a fine horsewoman, caught the bridle and gathered the reins into her hands and led him behind her. Then they were beyond the trees surrounding the monastery and riding through pastureland. Adalgisus looked back, saw Lucilla at a gallop behind him leading the other horse. Lucilla shook her head and then Adalgisus spurred his mount to the best speed possible out across the open countryside and away.

ONCE ALONE, STELLA LAY QUIETLY ON LUCILLA'S discarded mantle, listening to the dying sounds of carnage in the church. She was numb, the pain oozing away slowly in the silence. She was so frightened that she didn't feel fear any longer. Suddenly Ludolf was bending over her.

"Mother," Ludolf said, touching her face.

"Oh, my dear." She caught his hand. Dulcinia glanced around the room. "It's a pigsty," Stella whispered. "Cold, empty, without even a lock on the door. We were offered no comfort at all."

Ludolf nodded and tried to gather Stella into his arms. She made the most dreadful sound that either of them had ever heard.

"Oh, God," he whispered.

"I'm sorry, my dear," Stella whispered. "Don't, don't touch me. Please, please, just give me a few moments. I'm sure I'll be better, but please don't touch me now."

Dulcinia went down on one knee beside Stella. She pulled off her own veil and made a pillow and slid it under Stella's head. Stella was still curled on the stone floor. Then Ludolf covered her with his mantle.

Dulcinia explored Stella's abdomen very gently with her fingers. It was swollen tight and hard.

"Lucilla?" she asked softly.

"Lucilla made them go with her, thank God," Stella whispered. "I was afraid—afraid they would touch me again. They wanted to take me with them. I'm sorry, my son. When I move, I'm in so much pain. Please, give me some time to get myself together."

Stella smiled the shadow of a smile. "I'm sure in a little while I'll be able to ride."

Ludolf stroked her hair. "Yes, Mother. Take all the time you need. I'm in command here. You're perfectly safe. Now, what happened?"

Stella looked distressed. "Adalgisus came. My fault, I wrote him. He wanted Lucilla but took me hostage, too. What he planned I don't know. Don't know even if he had a plan—so many of these warriors are so drunken and foolish . . ."

Stella closed her eyes. She seemed weary.

Dulcinia had never seen a more terrible look than the one Ludolf had on his face. He was cradling his mother's head and shoulders in his arms, trying to keep her from the cold floor. A moment later Stella opened her eyes again.

"In the night, they came in the night—"

"Who, Mother?" Ludolf whispered.

"Adalgisus, Eberhardt, and Dagobert . . ." Stella seemed in very deep distress.

"Don't bother to say it, Mother," Ludolf whispered. "I know what they wanted. Don't distress yourself by saying it."

"They called us whores—"

To Dulcinia the pain in Stella's voice was simply inconceivable. She whispered, "No," and turned away. Her hand was on Ludolf's arm. She felt him flinch slightly as her fingers bit into his flesh. They were both kneeling by Stella.

"Lucilla said not to fight. I was too small, they'd hurt me. But I fought. You will tell your father I fought, won't you? Please? Tell him I fought. Love you . . . my son."

The last words were spoken so softly they were almost not even a whisper, only a breath. And they were the last words Stella ever said.

Dulcinia still had the opium and valerian Lucilla had given her. She mixed them in some good wine, then warmed it. Stella was able to take a small amount of the medicine, and after that she seemed to find some physical comfort. Ludolf and Dulcinia were able to move her gently to one of the bed platforms, suitably padded with feather ticks and blankets looted from Dagobert's stores. In fact, Ludolf received so many bed coverings he had, in the end, to turn them away.

Stella had been deeply loved and not only by her husband and son. There wasn't a mean bone in her body and she had done thousands of kind deeds among her husband's people. Had Ludolf not restrained his men, they would have put every living soul in the monastery to the sword, but he behaved with almost superhuman restraint. Of the culprits, Dagobert was already dead. He was identified by his jewelry and weapons near the stable door. The prior who tried to block the entrance to the monastery Ludolf's men hanged without bothering to ask permission. As for Eberhardt, Lucilla had left him badly wounded. Someone, persons unknown, cut his throat before he was identified. Apparently this was done simply as a necessary housekeeping chore after they finished off the wounded in the church.

The church burned brightly, vigorously, with a roaring blaze that rapidly spread to the all the other buildings except the guest house. The monks, seeing the prior's fate, fled. No one came to make even an attempt to save the buildings. Ludolf's men did only enough to ensure they were able to remove any and all objects having the slightest value. Once the place was thoroughly looted, the fire was guided or cheered on by the very vengeful company for whom it had some entertainment value.

Dulcinia stood in the doorway with Ludolf and watched the place burn.

"Yes," he said softly. "I have sent for my father. I hope he comes soon. She hasn't long."

"What now?"

"We will want you to speak to the pope for us, and Rufus. Neither my father nor I is a turncoat, but we can no longer maintain our allegiance to the Lombard king. He has insulted us too egregiously, injured us too deeply; moreover, if I get my hands on Adalgisus, I'll kill him. There is no going back now."

Ansgar rode in near dawn. Stella never spoke again but she seemed to smile when she saw him. She died not long after he arrived—in her husband's arms.

THE BEAR DROPPED BACK, CURSING HUGO'S FECK-less abuse of his body. It was not nearly as strong as the bear wanted it to be. He was faced with complicated logistical problems. If he fought as a human, he faced getting Hugo's body killed. If he fought as a bear, he was in a much superior position, but even he couldn't destroy six men and three dogs. And one way or another, Hugo's body would die anyway.

They were coming and getting closer. He took Armine aside. "They are too many, even for me."

"If worse comes to worst, abandon the rest of us and take Chiara.

I trust you more than those fools." Armine indicated the two men escorting him.

Considering what Armine knew about him, the bear decided this was a high compliment. Just then they topped a rise and the bear saw that they would descend into another of the small river valleys that threaded through the countryside. The mist still clung to the swampy ground and covered the water. The sun was up around them and shining brightly on the hilltops, but it had to yet to penetrate the sometimes deep water-cut passages between them.

"I'm going to try an ambush down there." He gestured toward the mist. "If necessary, I'll spend this carcass I'm wearing. I can fight on even if it is ostensibly killed. And after that there are other things I can do."

The bear gave another one of those hollow laughs he was so fond of, one of the blood-chilling kind.

"Stop that," Armine said. "Save it for our pursuers. I am sufficiently frightened of you."

The bear laughed again, this time sounding more human. Chiara dropped back to join them.

"We're being followed, aren't we?" She sounded frightened.

"Yes," her father said.

"You were discussing what to do about it, weren't you?"

"Yes," he said again.

"Well, tell me something," she shouted. "I can see by the expression on your faces it's bad, isn't it? Are we going to die?"

Armine looked away and wouldn't meet her eyes. He was pinch faced and haggard.

"Listen to me, Chiara," the bear said. "We're in a tight spot, but no matter what happens, I'm going to be with you. Remember, I can't die, and when you need me, I'll be there. So, no matter what happens, keep on going. Don't stop struggling. I will always come and I will help you."

He reached over and patted her small hand clutching the horse's reins. "Now, you must promise me something."

"What?" she asked.

"No matter what happens, you keep on riding. Don't look back. Just keep on going."

Chiara nodded.

"No matter what happens. No matter what you see or hear."

"Yes," she said.

They had almost reached the wetlands surrounding the river. The bear drew Hugo's sword.

"I'll stand with you," Armine said. "I can use a sword. I've fought brigands a time or two."

"Don't be put off then by anything you see," the bear said.

Ahead a small ruined fortification on the riverbank loomed up in a jumble of stone through the white mist hanging over the water. The bear and Armine turned their horses into the ruins, picking their way among the stone blocks.

Chiara and the two men who were her escorts continued along the road toward the bridge.

REGEANE CAUGHT UP TO THE SIX MEN AND THE dogs following Chiara and her father. The wolf laid her ears back and tried to get the woman to flee. She wanted no part of six armed men, but the three dogs were what really frightened her. To the wolf they were simply insane. Their socialization process had been so distorted by human cruelty that in hatred of all things, human and animal, they would kill at once anything within reach of their tethers.

The wolf was forced on by her human companion, but she was sick with fear. The mercenaries in the king's employ were no better than the dogs. They poisoned the air around them with an aura of horror. The stink of cold iron, dirty hot skin, and maleness permeated their clothing.

The male musk was not something she disliked. She had known within a few weeks of their marriage what her husband's mood was whenever he approached her. Warm desire caressed her senses before he touched her, but this was the male heat raised to warning reek. These men meant murder, and the fact that one of the victims was a young girl only added spice to their savagery. They were in essence being paid for doing what they loved.

Iron, wood, smoke, desire, rage, and a distant hint of old despair all combined to make the wolf want to flee. But the woman shook off her midnight companion's misgivings. She left the road and entered the brush. It was muddy but as long as she stayed on grass, the footing was not too bad. During the chase in the town, she had discovered just how fast a young virgin wolf was. She extended herself and paced the hunters. It was easy. But now what? Six men, all well armed, the dog handler, and three wolfhounds. No—these were not wolfhounds but the more ancient breed—the dogs of war.

Born and bred to kill. It was said that Caesar himself once was struck with admiration for a mastiff belonging to the Gauls that, clad in chain mail, guarded his master's wagon for two days after his master fell in battle. Caesar tried to capture it alive, but it ran onto the spears of Caesar's legionnaires, preferring to perish rather than surrender. As the dogs, so the people. Many perished rather than surrender.

These dogs were descendants of this dangerous breed. The female wolf is sacred among wolves, but these dogs would give no quarter, even to a she-wolf.

The land had begun to drop. At the top of the hill, Regeane heard the shouts of the mercenaries as they sighted their quarry: Armine, his daughter, the two soldiers of his escort . . . and Hugo.

Hugo? Regeane thought. *I'm not going to risk my neck to rescue Hugo.* Still, she continued to pace the party of soldiers, watching as their prey vanished into the mist lingering near the river.

"Beware ambush," the dog handler said to the rest. "I think they may take their chance now. If they don't, they may not get another."

"Loose the dogs," the captain of the soldiers cried.

The dog handler paused; he cracked his whip.

The three mastiffs strained against their collars. Two barked and snarled, jaws foam-flecked with rage; the third was more quiet and looked as if the long distance it had come running alongside the horses might be taking its toll.

The whip cracked again. Then the dog handler dropped the leashes.

Regeane lunged forward along with the dogs. She realized to her shock she could outrun them, and possibly run them down. She crossed the road in front of the mercenaries, a swift-moving, gauzy shadow. One of them flung a spear at her but it flew far wide of its mark. Then she was in the thick weeds and brush, running just behind the last dog. He outweighed her, so she was tentative.

The dog ahead of her leaped a log.

Fear held her back from the pursuit. In the wolf she felt the sense of a precipice. The fear that she was somehow running along the edge of a steep cliff and if she fell, the consequences might be . . . what?

The dog was just ahead. She had only to increase her pace slightly. She'd learned from watching Maeniel. He was born knowing how to use his fangs.

The thug dog had the spiked collar that was supposed to defend him from wolves, but mangling a leg might do as well. She closed with the dog, her fangs sinking into the haunch. The femur that propels the hind legs of every creature from dinosaur to man was her target.

The dog screamed. It shook her. She had not known an animal could sound so like a human. The dog was down, thrashing in circles, snapping at its nearly severed hind limb, spraying blood in circles around its frenzied body.

Suddenly Remingus was with her again. He carried the terrible slashing sword of the first legionnaires. Single-edged, its weight propelled it through skin tissue and even bone. In the hand of a strong man it could quite literally chop a human body in half at one blow. The ghastliness of the wounds it made were legend. It beheaded the dog so quickly even the wolf had not time to blink.

"Go," he said to Regeane. "The battle awaits you."

Above his voice she heard the sounds of hooves on the road; the mercenaries were coming up fast behind the dogs. The bear hadn't picked the best place to make his stand. The ruins were overgrown, thickly overgrown, with briars, ivy, and other creepers. The proximity of the river offering a steady water supply guaranteed lush growth.

The ground was honeycombed with pitfalls for horses and men alike. The two leading dogs and four of the mercenaries came out of the mist to face Armine and the bear at the same time. The horse the bear was riding shied violently as the two killer dogs attacked.

The bear swung Hugo's sword, an arc of silver light, and killed the first, but his mount went down and the second dog lunged across the horse's fallen body for his throat and succeeded in sinking a mouthful of sharp teeth into his arm. Anything Hugo's body could feel, so could the bear, and he let out an inhuman howl of pain.

But Regeane was coming across the dog's back. *I am saving Hugo?* was her astonished thought, but the momentum of her charge carried her forward. She tried for the top of the spine at the nape of the neck, but the spiked collar turned her assault and her wolf canines slipped on the dog's skull. She went tumbling over the horse. The dog, distracted by her assault, let go of Hugo and lunged for the fallen wolf.

The woman never remembered getting her feet under her or knew why her nightmare sister undertook the maneuver that saved her life, but she came up under the dog's chin. It died of suffocation before blood loss took its toll.

Armine nailed the first soldier out of the mist with a stop thrust under his diaphragm. But even before he could get his sword clear, two more were upon him. Instead of backing his horse, he turned it broadside to the pair and they crashed into him. All three went down, a screaming mass of flying hooves and struggling men. Armine, despite his age, was up first and took the opportunity to kill another of his assailants with a thrust, this time through the throat. He closed with the third and knew his own doom. The man had a sword, a shield, and was armored.

Armine had only his sword. His further thrusts were easily turned, then the shield slammed into his body. The wind went out of him in a *whoosh*. He staggered back, knowing he was going to die. He couldn't even run. He was struggling knee-deep in the twisting creepers covering the tumbled ruins.

The mercenary lunged forward to spit him on his sword. Armine saw the eyes glow behind the man's legs, and so frightening were they that he almost shouted a warning. Then the wolf's jaws closed over the mercenary's leg. He wore greaves; this blunted her fangs, but the soldier's tibia snapped with a crack like a dry stick. He half turned to swipe at the wolf with his sword, and Armine, his battle rage at flood tide, beheaded him.

But a second later, the captain of the mercenary band loomed over him. He bestrode the most terrible weapon of all, a battle-trained charger. One forehoof caught Armine's sword arm, and both bones snapped. Oddly, he felt no pain, but the sword fell to the ground from his limp fingers. The second hoof slammed into his shoulder, snapping his collarbone and humerus at the shoulder, and Armine went down. The wolf tried for a hamstring. That's what it was—a try. The charger's heels lashed out.

The wolf found herself airborne. She landed hard, slipping down between two large stone blocks among the twisting tangle of vines. She tasted blood and knew one of her ribs had broken and pierced a lung. But the wolf washed away the frightened woman in a flood of red rage, and she scrambled to her feet.

The other mercenary had joined his captain, but the bear had abandoned Hugo's broken body. As bear he reared up in front of the charger and then made a cruel mistake. He took a swipe at the man, but the mercenary had his shield up. The bear's paw ruined it, crumpling the steel sheath, the leather and wood under it. The charger was trained to attack. As the man on his back threw away the ruined shield and seized his sword two-handed, the big horse reared in front of the upright bear. Another swipe of the bear's claw caught him in the chest, but the horse was armored as well as the man; a corset of scale mail covered the animal's sides and chest. The bear's mighty claws slipped harmlessly across it.

Then one of the animal's steel-shod forehooves slammed down hard into the bear's skull. The other shattered his shoulder. A second later the mercenary's spear drove through the bear's body.

The bear sensed that unless he forsook his corporeal form he was doomed, but he disdained to yield. Better, far better, to go out fighting.

The bear felt a violent shock as the mercenary's sword carved away his whole left paw.

Doom. The bear roared an unearthly cry that echoed through realms untouched by humankind and slammed his right paw into the horse's face, blinding the animal and destroying part of its skull.

The horse floundered in the mass of creepers and broken stone beneath him, still game but dying.

It could yet bite and it did, immobilizing the bear's right shoulder as the mercenary, seeing the opening, drove his sword through the creature's heart.

CHIARA AND THE REMAINING TWO MEN HAD reached the bridge. The sounds of battle erupted behind her. She pulled her horse, worried for her father and the bear. She had promised, but didn't feel it incumbent on her to keep any promise made under what she considered duress.

One of the two men, her father's retainers, reached out and slapped her horse's rump to speed her up. The memory of the dead girl on the church porch flashed across her mind, a reminder of the fate of any woman who lost her friends and kin.

"No," Chiara whispered. She reined in her horse and turned him back.

Her father's man reached for her, but his hand slipped on her sleeve, and a second later she was thundering back across the bridge toward the battle taking place in the ruins.

T HE BEAR REARED AGAIN AS THE SWORD PASSED through his heart but the silver wolf was on the horse's back behind the captain. She had only a second to choose her point of attack. The man was armored.

The bear was going down. To take out an arm would do no good. She went for the throat at the top of the shoulder near the neck. Her left canine slipped on his scale mail and broke, sending a jolt of raw pain through the wolf's skull, but the right entered his throat and pierced his carotid artery, tearing it open. Then he swung hard, slamming his fist into her skull below the ear.

The wolf fell away.

But she had distracted the man long enough. The bear could still bite. His jaws closed on the mercenary captain's sword arm. He pulled the man from the dying horse and threw him down among the rubble and vines, finishing him by biting the man's arm off.

Just then Chiara appeared out of the mist. There was still one soldier left.

Chiara dismounted in one bound, picked up a stone, and hurled it at his head. It connected with a *whack*.

Regeane saw Remingus, a ghost and thing of horror, the dead thing from a Carthaginian cross, stride out of the mist behind her.

The soldier saw him, too. It was enough. He was unwounded and alive but the only one who was. He dropped spear, sword, and shield and rode hell-for-leather out of the cursed mist and back toward Pavia.

Armine lay quiet.

The mercenary captain was dead. Massive blood loss. The horse still thrashed and kicked.

The wolf struggled among the ivy draping a ruined window or portico. She summoned the change.

Chiara gasped. A beautiful woman stood silhouetted against the ruined casement. Chiara never forgot her, because she could see the forest behind her, through the woman's body.

Regeane reached up, trying to catch the ivy stems, and found her fingers passed through them.

The bear roared again, the form he had assumed dissolving into a dark stain among the green creepers and weathered stone.

He is gone, Regeane thought, wondering as she did what was happening to her. Then she staggered. A ray of sunlight pierced the thick, pale mist and she was woman. Solid and real as she had ever been, she sank to her knees gratefully. The ivy creepers falling from the overgrown doorway almost smothered her under their weight. The wolf returned and shook off the thick meshwork of vines.

Chiara was staring in horror at the amorphous thing fighting desperately for existence, coiling, twisting like a maddened bundle of serpents threading its way in and out among the living green.

Again the wolf felt the sadness she'd sensed in the tent when they fought before. The grief at what was going to be lost, a sense of anger that it must end and in this way.

Chiara struggled toward the shadow. "You take your life from us. Take mine. I love you. I'll let you in. Come to me. Don't, don't die. I love you."

Not enough, Regeane thought. And the bear won. What force could not compel, trickery could not accomplish, and threats could not achieve, compassion did.

And Regeane and Chiara both let him join them.

THE WOLF AND MATRONA FACED OFF IN THE SHALlow water at the edge of the lake among the trees. The bones of the planet leaped out here, but the rock ridges were softened by moss, or something that looked like moss. It grew in thick mats between the scattered trees and threw up fruiting bodies densely covered with fine lacework enclosing what looked like jewels.

Matrona became woman to make a meal of the moss's berrylike fruits. She sat in the shade on a green velvet cushion of the same plant and began to ease the sweet fruit from its enclosing matrix. They looked rather like grapes, red, purple, green to almost black, but didn't taste like grapes. They were both sweeter and more spicy.

"Want to quarrel?" she asked Maeniel.

"No. How do I get back? She may need help."

"The answer is you can't," Matrona said. "Not until the journey is completed. Besides, she has help. The dead called her during her journey to rescue you, and they will escort her until she either succeeds or fails in her mission. Let her go, eagle wolf. It is her time. She must find out who and what she is."

Maeniel sat down near Matrona and watched the water rippling across the moss-grown rocks and looked out over the lake. It was beautiful in the cloud-scattered sunlight, an expanse of open water reflecting the changing cloud mountains moving over its surface.

"I want to keep her," Maeniel said. "I love her."

"Keep her safe or keep her stupid?" Matrona asked, laughing.

"Both, if necessary," Maeniel shot back.

"Well, you will fail in both cases ultimately, and she will not be grateful for your efforts."

"So you say," he answered, and was wolf again.

"Don't challenge me, my lord," Matrona said.

Maeniel, more massive even than Matrona, stalked toward her stiff-legged.

"Don't challenge me. Not just because you might lose—and you might—but because you are wrong. You chose this course, the path of human advancement under this king. I warned you that you had all a man could desire. Good friends, a beautiful wife to spoil, prosperity, and even a modicum of power and safety. More than most mortals will ever attain. But it was not enough. You must join the struggles of the masters of war. Well, now you have attained that objective also. The king awaits you. You took the oath. Keep it. I would wander into the mountains, abandon the stronghold, see him fail, but you—who are my leader—chose to accept him. Honor your oath, wolf, else you will regret taking it."

Maeniel turned human again. He reached for one of the fruit-laden stalks and twisted it.

"Stop that," Matrona said as she felt the upsurge of distress all around her. "The moss puts a lot of effort into its fruiting bodies. Don't damage them. Take what you like as far as the fruit is concerned, the moss doesn't care. Spreading them even helps it."

He gave Matrona another one of his long, slow looks. "You talk to the moss."

"You talk to Audovald. You carry on long conversations with him during which you discuss all manner of farm business. Who is pregnant, who will give the most milk, and which one or another will generate particularly fine product for cheese making.

"Not to mention meddling in the personal affairs of your stock. What stallions are favored by the mares as a group for leadership and protection in the high pastures, which of the females—goat, cow, sheep, the stable cat even—is feeling peckish and may have a difficult pregnancy this year, and I cannot think what else. So why should I not speak to moss? Do not offend it. The creatures of this place offer us hospitality, protection, and direction. They advise us on the best routes to travel. Go to your king. You have chosen him against my advice. I will serve him, pleasure him, and protect him out of loyalty to you."

"I am humbled," Maeniel said.

"You are not and will bully Regeane as much as you can as soon as she returns. You have spent too much time as a man and are learning hypocrisy, not to mention greed."

THE SAXON, WAITING IN THE PLACE WHERE HE promised Regeane he would, woke in the night. He could not tell why at first, then he saw the three horses. They were grazing near the trees at the edge of the clearing. One, the dark, nondescript, leggy bay, he recognized as Maeniel's Audovald.

He sat up in his blankets. "Horse, what are you doing here?" the Saxon asked.

Audovald raised his head and prodded the neck of the horse nearest him.

A small animal, the Saxon thought. But then in studying the animal more closely, he saw it was not small. It was simply so well proportioned it seemed small but was actually larger than Audovald. It was outlined against the brilliant sky, its head against the stars.

It studied him for what seemed a long time, while the Saxon yawned and rose to his feet. When he was standing, it galloped downhill toward him. For a second the Saxon had the uneasy feeling that it meant to trample him, but it pulled up short just as it reached him, then reared high above him. If the creature meant him harm, the Saxon couldn't imagine why. But then it seemed that it didn't, because the hooves dropped harmlessly to the ground, and it pranced about in front of him rather the way a dog does when it's time to hunt, when it wants to greet an absent master or just would like to play.

"Friendly?" the Saxon asked.

The horse nuzzled his face, the nose soft on his cheek. The Saxon patted the sleek neck and the horse knelt, going down gracefully on one knee.

"What?" the Saxon asked, astounded.

The horse blew through his nostrils. It sounded impatient. Then, when he didn't react, he was nipped gently but firmly on the instep of one foot. The Saxon was an adequate horseman but not a devoted one. He threw a leg over the horse and it rose with him seated on its back. Then it simply walked around his fire and strolled down to the creek for some water. It drank its fill. The Saxon kneaded his fingers in the horse's mane.

How to control it?

When the horse was finished drinking, it stood expectantly. The Saxon pressed lightly with his right knee. The horse moved left. Pressure with the left knee, the horse moved right. *How wonderful,* the Saxon thought. He tapped with his heels at the animal's flank, and the horse began to trot. The Saxon leaned forward. The horse's pace increased. And then they were going like the wind. They crossed an open meadow, then the horse slowed as they passed into the trees, but once on a game trail, the horse's pace increased again until they passed the tree line and burst out into the open. He could hear the meadow grass crackle under the beast's hooves; though winter was over it was cold enough that the dew still turned to ice. The horse galloped powerfully across the high mountain meadow and then, just at the edge, he stopped and looked out across the world.

The mountains rose all around the Saxon. The snow-covered peaks seemed to glow from within with a light of their own. Above, the arch of the Milky Way flowed, a river of light. The deep valleys below were drowned in hazy shadow. No human light intruded into his vision. Except for the wind and the silence, he and the horse were alone.

The Saxon never knew how long he and the horse stood absorbed in the presence of eternity, but at length he began to find the air cold, and the unending wind seemed to suck the warmth from his body. He felt stiff and half-frozen when he exerted the gentle pressure necessary to turn the horse, leave the high meadow, and return to his camp.

When he reached it, he found the fire built up. Maeniel and Matrona were present. They were both dressed.

The Saxon saw that the other horse was Matrona's mare. The Saxon dismounted and began to rub his mount down with his own mantle. When they drew close to the fire, he saw the horse was a strawberry roan with darker legs, nose, and tail. He found that he needed neither halter nor rope to lead him. It was sufficient to place a hand on his neck and indicate direction. He was rubbing the legs when Maeniel approached him.

"Have you something to say to me, my lord?" the Saxon asked.

They both knew what he meant. Regeane, with the Saxon's contrivance, had followed anyway.

Maeniel sighed. Whatever the Saxon's motives, he was faithful and honorable. No, this was between himself and Regeane. "I have a message from Audovald," Maeniel said.

"Audovald?" The Saxon's eyebrows rose. "Audovald is your horse."

"He is."

The horse dropped his nose again and brushed the Saxon's cheek as if to say, "Listen." The Saxon rose. He was a big man but the horse was two handspans taller at the withers than he was.

"Audovald," said Maeniel, "told me the horse comes from a place far away where the warriors are friends and companions to their mounts and do them no evil. But his human was killed and the family sold him far away. He would not wear bridle nor saddle and never any bit. So he was tortured, kept awake, poorly fed, and beaten to try to break his spirit. He fled and could not be captured, but it was hard for him to live alone. Humans had always cared for him.

"Audovald met him in the high pastures. He told him he knew a human who would understand him. You are the man, or," Maeniel said, "should I ask, are you the man?"

"I am," he answered. He turned to the horse. "There will be only trust between us."

"A saddlecloth might be advisable," Matrona said. "Protect his back, your ass."

The horse blew softly.

Audovald turned to Maeniel.

"He accepts," Maeniel said.

The horse gave a cry and reared, dancing around the fire.

"He is happy," the Saxon said. "He is no longer alone."

"Neither are you," Matrona said.

"Ask him his name," the Saxon said to Matrona.

"He gives you leave to name him when you are ready," she answered. "In the meantime, you ride to the other army, the one commanded by Bernard, Charles's uncle. The gray wolf will lead you. Tomorrow he must attack at Susa. The wolf can show you both what path to take."

BERNARD, CHARLES'S UNCLE, WAS STILL AT IVREA. At this moment he was sitting beside a fire in the open beneath a tall mountain peak. Despite the fire, he was still cold, so cold he was wrapped in a heavy cloak, the all-purpose garment of the people from slave to emperor. A man without this combination blanket, overcoat, raincoat, weapon concealer, and general all-around means of survival was unfortunate indeed. In fact the general term among the Franks for poverty was *naked*, the naked back in particular. Bernard's cloak was undistinguished, rather like the mantles of all the soldiers around him. He'd long ago learned the folly of decking himself out splendidly in battle.

You stand out.

The enemy runs you down and kills you.

The added incentive for killing you, besides winning the battle, is the possession of your magnificent outfit. One aristocratic kill could make the average foot soldier—who usually didn't even own a good sword—a wealthy man.

He'd learned this from Charles's father, Pepin the Short, a man with a permanent grievance against the world because of his height. Any overdressed soldier, no matter how highly connected, was automatically run through bogs, swamps, rivers, lakes, and even duck ponds, or set to—in the event of drought—digging latrines for the army. Pepin's permanently jaundiced view of almost everyone and everything made him a difficult enough individual to deal with on a day-to-day basis without anyone going out of their way to annoy him. Bernard had learned to don protective coloration early.

Bernard was worrying about Charles, or rather worrying about what Charles would do to him if he couldn't attack the Lombard forces at dawn as he was supposed to. Charles, it was told, was somewhat better-tempered than his father, but he was, roughly speaking, about twice as ruthless. Neither Bernard nor any of his officers cared to think about what Charles would do if they failed to keep their appointment tomorrow.

The officers, young men all, showed a tendency to drown their sorrows at supper, so they were sleeping. But Bernard, who had neither the head nor the stomach for heavy wine drinking, sat wakeful and worrying. When Charles had attacked at Susa, Desiderius had predictably pulled his forces away from Ivrea.

Bernard had arrived and found the token garrison Desiderius had left behind completely unprepared to meet him. What followed had been more of a slaughter than anything else. Something, someone, had managed to stampede the garrison's horses. He and his men overran their position in what had been a somewhat worse-for-wear Roman fortress. The defenders might have surrendered had they been asked, but Bernard didn't bother to inquire. He killed them all.

Since then things had gone badly. Bernard had started for Susa with an entire army. It was lost. He had six officers; they were drunk. He had thought he could find guides. As payback for the slaughter at the fortress, Bernard found that everyone in the vicinity of the fortress abruptly decamped at the sight of his army. Then the fog, a springtime feature of warm lowlands near cold mountains, closed in. All armies easily panic, and this army began to hover on the verge of uncontrollability. Bernard was afraid to push them too far, and so here he sat, freezing his ass off by this miserable fire, surrounded by drunken and exhausted soldiers, and wondering what the hell he was going to do in the morning.

Since he considered himself well camouflaged, he was surprised when a man strode out of the darkness and hailed him by name. Bernard's hand tightened reflexively on his sword hilt. He was alone despite the veritable carpet of men sleeping around him, and for a second he wondered if he was going to be murdered in the middle of his army without anyone being the wiser, when he recognized the Saxon.

This wasn't entirely consoling. The Saxon was a large and dangerous individual and hadn't seemed to care too much for Franks.

"My lord Maeniel sends greeting," the Saxon said. "And we have come to take you to Charles."

"We?" Bernard asked, trying not to show he was filled with utter and complete relief.

The largest wolf Bernard had ever seen stepped out of the shadows near the Saxon. "We?" Bernard asked again.

"Yes, wake your men. It's almost dawn. We will leave before first light."

"I trust you will not lead us into an ambush?"

The Saxon's eyes narrowed slightly. "I will ride knee to knee with you. If I do, you may kill me first."

"Your trust in your lord's servants is great indeed."

"My trust," the Saxon answered distinctly, "in my lord is great." Then he turned away, leaving Bernard to make what he would of the statement.

Bernard didn't care to think about its implications. There were stories about Maeniel . . . and his wife . . . and his friends . . .

A wooden bucket near his knee held well-watered wine. It was cold. Bernard took a long drink. Then, lifting the bucket by the handle, he went to wake his men. He decided to rouse his officers first.

B ERNARD WAS NO FOOL. CHARLES WAS HIS NEPHEW. The fortunes of the whole family stood or fell with Charles. As they had retired the long-haired Megrovian kings, one of the other magnates might retire them in their turn. His king needed him desperately. If the devil himself had appeared and promised to lead him to the king for the price of his soul, Bernard would not have turned him down. Bernard mounted every man he could and left his footmen to straggle. If the *scarae* couldn't do it, it couldn't be done. If they won, the infantry could mop up. If they lost, the men were on their own and would have to try to survive as well as they could.

When the world began to lighten around him, Bernard saw the fog had returned with a vengeance. The Saxon appeared before him riding a magnificent roan horse, but Bernard was uneasily aware that the horse had no bridle or saddle on his back. The Saxon rode with neither bit nor rein, and the horse was a stallion. But Bernard asked no more questions.

"The trail is narrow," the Saxon said. "Tell each man to follow the one in front of him, keep up, and don't get lost."

"You heard that," Bernard shouted.

Then at some sort of signal from the Saxon or possibly something else he couldn't see, the roan turned and led them off into the fog. Bernard made the sign of the cross and followed.

"They are madmen or sorcerers," one of his officers said.

Before anyone could blink, Bernard's sword cleared the sheath and, in the same motion, beheaded the man.

"Anyone else care to comment?" Bernard bared his teeth at the rest. It was nothing like a smile.

Then he turned. The roan the Saxon was riding had pulled up and turned broadside and was studying him with one horse eye. The Saxon flicked a glance at the headless corpse still seated in the saddle. Bernard slammed the heel of his hand into the cadaver's chest and it fell. The fog was so thick he couldn't see it hit the ground. Even as he watched, the glowing vapor clouds almost obscured the Saxon from view.

"Let's go," Bernard said. "And in case you haven't understood yet, I could teach the devil a thing or two. So don't try me. Now move."

They did.

LUCILLA FOLLOWED ADALGISUS THROUGH THE NIGHT. She hoped he knew where he was going; she didn't. Toward dawn, she became aware that Stella had died. She knew this because Stella's presence paid her a brief visit to thank her for taking away the two men who had accomplished her ruin, and to say that she lay easy in the arms of Ansgar, the man who, after all was said and done, was her only love.

To weep was futile. They were pushing their lathered horses to get the last few miles from the weary beasts. The trees beside the rutted trace were only shadows against the stars. Every time her mount so much as slowed, Adalgisus cursed Lucilla and struck her horse with his riding whip. She noticed he didn't hit her. She'd managed to cripple and possibly kill Eberhardt, and dear Dagobert hadn't survived long at all when she turned a cold and vengeful gaze on him, so she surmised that Adalgisus might be a bit afraid of her. Besides, the sadness she felt about Stella's fate struck at a deeper place in her being, a place that was uninterested in tears, seeing them solely as a sign of weakness. No. She promised Stella's presence that the pig riding ahead of her and his whole family would forever regret what they had done to Stella. Her fragile beauty would not fade into dust un-avenged. Stella's presence made no comment about Lucilla's resolve, but only seemed to say, *Peace be upon you. I have found mine, Lucilla. May God bless you and keep you safe.* And then she was gone.

Lucilla rode on through the night. She had left her mantle at the monastery under Stella's ruined body, but she was warmed by the cold hatred she felt in her heart. She and Adalgisus reached the villa Jovis near daybreak. They found the household up and stirring even at that hour. The superintendent of the villa immediately placed it at Adalgesis's disposal.

Feeling her age, Lucilla was led to the baths. The water was warm. The bath attendants were two peasant girls who looked capable of bull wrestling. Lucilla didn't even think about escape. Her clothing was taken away to be laundered, and she was given an embroidered linen shift and a dark woolen overgown. Both garments were ample and the overgown was embroidered with yellow silk in a pattern that made Lucilla squint in surprise. Acanthus? No, artichoke leaves. The two girls then conducted her to a room that faced the inner courtyard of the villa. It was lit by four clerestory windows high in the walls. The windows were barred on the outside, as was the door. But inside, Lucilla found a tray with bread, fresh cheese, wine, raisins, and a bowl of onion soup.

Lucilla felt no appetite, but as soon as she tasted the wine and a bit of bread she found herself absolutely ravenous. She couldn't bring herself to stop until she'd consumed the last crumb. When she tried to stand, she found herself reeling. She staggered toward the bed and was asleep before her head touched the pillow.

She was awakened by a scream.

Lucilla got to her feet before she was fully awake. She reached the door and opened it without thinking. Why was it not locked?

Adalgisus was standing in the hall, struggling with a girl who had evidently brought his supper tray—it was resting on a table just out-side the door to his room.

Oh, for heaven's sake, Lucilla thought. *Give it a rest.* Just then the girl screamed again, then crouched down, her back against the wall, sobbing. The light in the courtyard was blue, and Lucilla surmised she must have slept all day. Adalgisus was standing, examining his hand.

"Cunt," he screamed. "Your nails are sharp. I'll have you flogged, you little—" He bit off the word when he saw Lucilla standing there. "She scratched me. All I wanted was a little company." He winced. "Whore!" he shouted again. "I'll wager I'm not the first to have my hand up your skirt."

The girl looked at him, frightened and angry, and answered with a flood of rapid speech in a dialect he obviously couldn't understand. Lucilla understood her. The girl sounded as if she'd grown up near the mountain town where Lucilla had been born. She was babbling about being sore and bleeding.

"The little twit is so backward she can't speak proper Latin," Adalgisus snarled.

"Wait," Lucilla said calmly. "I can understand her. I'll ask what's wrong. What is your name?"

The girl wiped her eyes with the back of one hand. "Lavinia."

"What's wrong?"

"He wants me to lie with him, but I can't . . . I can't . . . I'm bleeding . . . Two weeks ago my courses didn't . . . I was late, so I was afraid. I took a potion. My period came down last night with bleeding and cramps. I'm so sore I feel like if he touches me, I'll die. The cook just sent me to bring him his supper. I'm filthy and dirty. A dozen men had me last week. They use the house slaves here to keep the field hands content. I was in the stable all last week with the other women. I don't know how many had me . . . when I took the potion . . . I think I was breeding . . . I don't want to see its skull crushed. That's what they do here: crush the skull and throw it in the old well."

"Yes," Lucilla said. "Now dry your tears and be quiet and go back to the kitchen. I'll explain to the gentleman."

The girl didn't walk away, she crawled, one shoulder against the wall until she was out of reach of both Lucilla and Adalgisus, then got to her feet and ran off.

"What was she yapping about?" Adalgisus asked.

"Her woman's courses have come down on her. She's cramping and bleeding."

It was almost dark. The last sun blush was fading from the sky. Fireflies danced over the garden beds in the courtyard. A wax light was glowing on the table next to Adalgisus's tray. He was studying Lucilla intently in its light. The shift she was wearing under the woolen gown was semitransparent. Over it, the thick woolen gown was made for a man much larger than Lucilla, and the neck slit at the front extended down to her waist. On either side her breasts rose, pale cups covered only by the thin linen gauze. He was staring fixedly at them.

"They're uneven," he said.

"Yes," Lucilla answered. "Part of one is gone." She pushed the woolen gown aside and showed him her scarred breast. The nipple had been destroyed.

"That must have hurt." He licked his lips.

"It did."

A second later he was bending over, his lips suckling her scarred breast as his teeth nibbled the scar tissue. When he pulled away, his face was flushed, the veins in his neck and temples raised, standing out like ropes.

"What did they use?"

"Red-hot pincers at the nipple."

He made a moaning sound.

Lucilla reached down and caught his erection, wrapping her hand around the spike.

"Ohhhh. Don't." But he didn't sound distressed about her action. "You keep that up," he whispered, "I'm going to come."

"That would be a shame," she said. "A tool like yours is to be used, savored, and enjoyed, before it is at last, alas, allowed its rest."

She backed him into his room and barred the door. The shift and woolen gown landed on the floor a second later. Then she eased him to the bed. *Why didn't he do this before Stella was assaulted by that fool Dagobert?* Lucilla thought furiously. *Why did this stupid piece of pig shit have to play the man among men?* But then, why should she expect him to do otherwise? He had nothing in his character that remotely resembled discretion or good judgment. That a fool should play the fool was hardly surprising.

She maneuvered him onto the bed. She got on top. "Let me control things," she told him.

"All right, but you have to tell me everything they did to you. Everything. I want to hear it while we . . ."

"Fuck?" Lucilla whispered.

"Yes, yes, while we fuck—that beautiful word, *fuck*." He laughed.

Lucilla tightened some very strategic muscles. He cried out, his body arched against hers.

"I've finished," he said, sounding almost astonished.

"Oh, no, my dear, you've only just begun."

He cried out again, sounding surprised as she tightened those well-practiced muscles and he felt his body respond.

"Oh, God," he gasped. "When we reach Verona, I'll have to find a place to hide you. If she finds out . . . she'll kill you."

Somewhere in her mind Lucilla heard a yell of sheer triumph so loud she was surprised Adalgisus couldn't hear it, too. She knew. She knew. Now, now to get a message to Hadrian. And she set out to give Adalgisus the time of his life.

WHEN SHE WAS FINISHED WITH HIM, SHE ROSE and went back to her room. She left him sleeping like a corpse. She'd unabashedly plied him with food, drink, and enough sex to leave him limp as a cooked noodle. She didn't think he would awaken before morning, if then, but she barred the door behind her and found three objects she'd managed to conceal on her person in spite of the observant eyes of the bath attendants.

Now, whom to bribe? She was considering this when there was a timid tap on the door. Lucilla swore under her breath but managed a smile, in case it should be Adalgisus. But it was the serving girl, Lavinia. She entered bringing in a tray of cold chicken, soup, bread, and some cheese.

"The hour is late," Lucilla said, surprised. "Is the cook still up?"

"No, but I was grateful for what you did and asked if I could bring you something when you and . . . the lord were finished. The cook—she's nice to me—made this, and when I saw you come from his room . . ."

The girl's face was red and swollen in the lamplight. She looked as if she'd been crying for a long time.

"What's the matter? Are you in so much pain?" The bath attendants hadn't been able to get Lucilla's small supply of medicines away from her. In fact, they had refused to touch them, thinking her a witch. She might be able to dose this poor child with something, a little laudanum perhaps, that would give her at least one night's sleep in comfort.

A kind voice was too much for the child. She burst into tears again. "I hate it. I just hate it here. Last night I tried to hang myself but . . . I can't bring myself to lean on the rope. I couldn't. I couldn't, but Mira says if I drink enough at the barn . . . Some of the girls make them pay so they have a lot of coppers and buy a big jug of wine. But I can't drink enough to give me the courage to put the rope around my neck and then lean forward."

Lucilla put her arms around the child, who broke down completely, crying in a way that seemed to rend her whole being. Lucilla knew what the child was talking about. It brought back her own past more vividly than she cared to imagine. She'd seen girls in the stews at Ravenna kill themselves the way that Lavinia was describing, tie a rope or even a length of cloth to something low, even the back of a chair, loop it around their neck and then lean forward. She'd spoken once to a girl who had done it and been revived. The first minute or so takes courage but after that the pressure cuts off the blood to the head and sleep follows. In a little time, death. And just to prove how easy it was, the girl killed herself a few days later in that particular way. This time she wasn't found until much, much too late.

"They say you are a witch," the child gasped. "What I saw you do to the lord, I believe you must be. Give me something. Something so I can just go to sleep and never wake up. I was a good girl when I was at home. A good girl. Now I feel filthy. They are always at me. I made a baby. I know I did, but I killed it because I didn't want to see them kill it. I can't stand any more of this place. I would rather die."

Lucilla walked the girl over and seated her on the bed. "Why don't you run away?" she asked.

"I did. I did." The girl began to tremble violently. "They caught me. I went home but there was no one there. The house where we lived . . . was empty. Even the villa nearby was gone. Only the wind, the pines, and the silence remained. I didn't know what to do. I stayed there sleeping by the cold hearth till they came. Look at my back."

Lucilla did and flinched. Her back was covered with scar tissue. She looked almost as if she'd been burned.

"It marked me. I won't run away again. I have nowhere to go."

"I could give you somewhere to go," Lucilla said.

Once, when she had moved into her villa in Rome, she'd found a half-starved cat living in her garden. When she'd offered the animal food, it had been afraid to approach the dish but when she moved away, it pounced. The expression on the starving animal's face was very like the one on the girl's face, frightening in its utter desperation.

"You can—I'll do anything." She fell to her knees. "Anything."

"Take a message to Rome." Lucilla had a ring, a ring all her intimates knew. It had a cameo of Hadrian. She handed it to the girl with some silver wrapped in cloth. "Listen to me carefully," she said. "When you come to the city, go in the early morning among the women drawing water at the fountains. Ask for Lucilla's villa. You may hear slighting remarks about me, you may not. Who knows? But if you do, pay no attention to them. Go to the villa; this ring will guarantee you admission. Speak to Susana, my maid. She is the keeper of the villa and you may trust her absolutely."

"Yes," the girl said eagerly.

"Repeat that back to me—"

The child did, word for word.

"The message is only one word. Only one but you must remember it. Perfectly. Understand?"

"Yes. I understand. What is it?"

"Verona."

"Verona. Is that all?"

"It is sufficient. Just say Verona. If you fail to find Susana, go to Dulcinia."

"Dulcinia the singer?"

"You have heard of her?"

"Yes. Everyone knows of Dulcinia, but these are famous people, my lady. Will they receive me?"

"Show them the ring and they will. If all else fails, go to Simona, mother of Posthumus. She is not rich or famous, but she will be a friend to you."

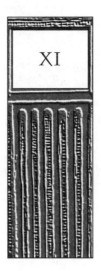

XI

WHEN SHE AND CHIARA BOTH ENTERED THE
bear's world, she heard his roar of fury and terror and
knew, to her amusement, that their entry into his world
brought the same sense of violation that humans felt when he tried to
take control of them. And then she was moving very, very fast across
a level field, and she was part of it, the sense of dimensionality fading.
She was a light twisting in and out of a maze, moving at high speed
toward . . . what?

She had no idea, and then she began to be afraid and tried to
slow her forward progress, but found she couldn't. Faster and faster
she traveled, away from her own life and world, the images speeding
past her in a blur of motion. Her mother's face, Gundabald flogging
her on the floor of her lodgings in Rome, the pope, Lucilla, Maeniel,
and then they were gone—those she'd loved, hated, feared—and still
she was going—being pulled?—traveling faster. She felt the union
woman-wolf-wolf-woman. She tried to scream. Her gorge rose, she
vomited, the pain of nausea reuniting her with her body for a second.
Then the woman-wolf—she was both, she realized to her surprise,
not just one or the other, not either or. Then her muscles locked. She
shed her body the way a cicada sheds the shell that has been buried in
the earth for many long years, the way a butterfly sheds the chrysalis,
the way a bird pecks its way free of an egg.

And she saw the tree. You cannot see the oak in an acorn or the
peach in the thick-shelled poisonous seed, not unless you enter its
life, its being. Even knowing the shape, the form it takes, is not to

318

know it. Nor is it enough to name and remember its parts. The root, the stem-trunk, the rings, the leaves, the fruit, its body naked in winter, clothed in green in the springtime or even the count of leaves it sheds in the bitter autumn winds. By none of these things will you know the tree, for the universe is a tree, and that's why the Irmunsul of the Saxons was planted, that we might remember that we are part of the tree of life and it is part of the earth and the earth is part of the universe and unless you comprehend everything else, the tree remains a mystery.

The universe exploded into life around Regeane. She saw it as part of the singularity that is its heart and beginning. It erupted. Not like a volcano but a flower unfurling around her, world upon worlds, lying beside each other like the growth rings of a tree. And the beings belonging to each world knew nothing and could know nothing of one another. But they were all of the tree, the singularity belonging to its roots. Some things moved between the worlds and . . . she . . . was one . . . of them. The bear was another. He could no more possess her than a man could possess the fixed stars. She was his equal and in some ways his superior.

Unbearable like the flash of orgasm in the flesh, so this was to the mind. Unsustainable, blinding, a light so bright it closes the eye of the mind in its sheer, raw glory.

"I can't—I can't," Regeane screamed.

And she was back in her body—woman—healed whole among the vines, the strange lobe-leafed ivy that covered the tumbled stone of a ruin. She could see, like a double image superimposed on the mass of creepers, what the building had once been to the Romans, and before that the footbridge over a wild river, and yet beyond where no river ran there and the sea lapped a pale sandy shore not far away.

"Stop," Regeane screamed. "Stop!" And it did, and she sat leaning on a stone block looking at Armine lying on his face beside an archway in the tangled green, and the bear in Chiara's arms. He was inhabiting Hugo.

The dead, the ones they had killed, were scattered around them.

"What happened?" Chiara asked. "Where did we go?"

"I think," the bear said, "I just received a lesson in my own inconsequence."

"I don't think so," Regeane said. "No, I don't think so at all. But I'm—give me something to wear."

Chiara handed Regeane her mantle.

"What are you doing here?" the bear roared at Chiara.

"Oh, shut up," she told him, then she glanced at her father, who was sitting up. The blast of energy Regeane had loosed by trying to fuse with the bear had helped him, too. His arms were very sore but no longer broken. Still, he was dizzy and pale with a number of minor injuries.

"And you be quiet, too," Chiara said. She planted her hands on her hips. "When you were both dead and gone, I'd just have been something to use or sell to those men, and the king's money would have spoken loudest. So both of you just . . . just . . . be quiet. Besides, I want to know what happened to me."

"I don't know," the bear said. "I think we were granted some sort of a . . . vision. You saw my world in some way."

Regeane was quiet. She was shaken to her very core by what she'd seen. She had gone farther than either Chiara or the bear.

"I can see," the bear told Regeane, "that any further attempt to capture you or the gray wolf would be futile. I'm not sure such an attempt would be practical with Chiara. She—" He looked at her standing over him. "—she is somehow talented. You said," he spoke to Chiara, "you said you loved me."

"That's because I do." She looked both mutinous and mulish at the same time. "But don't let it give you any ideas. I'm my father's daughter, and I won't just throw myself away on just any wandering evil spirit. I'll expect some assurances, something more in the line of a settlement than just a lot of airy promises."

"Now you be quiet," Armine said. "The bear and I will settle your future between us."

Chiara glared at them both, then began struggling toward the road.

Gimp was found resting against a milepost, sleeping.

"Damnation, they took the horses," Armine said. "He can't even be depended on to look after horses."

"He can't be depended on for anything," the bear snarled.

Then he sat Hugo down. Hugo's eyes went blank, his body slumped.

Regeane peered at Hugo's face. "He looks like Hugo now," she said. "When the bear is in residence, he seems someone else."

"He is," Armine said truculently. "The creature—daemon—

whatever he is, told me Hugo's brain is mush. He was struck by light-ning during the storm. Whatever happened, Hugo is gone. I'm not entirely sure if I believe everything that creature wants me to, but when he isn't present, this—" He pointed at Hugo's body. "—shows no signs of consciousness."

Chiara came back and handed Regeane a dress and shift. Regeane went back into the ruins to change. She hoped to ride along with them for a time, but before she did, she smiled a long, slow smile of satisfaction at Hugo. *It looks as if Hugo is going to live a long, healthy, prosperous life—a thing I wouldn't have bet on a few years ago.*

When she returned, Armine and Chiara and the bear were talking together.

"Can you do what I just saw you do in Florence?"

"What?" the bear asked.

"Leave Hugo's body and be in . . . say . . . a competitor's counting house while he's doing business?"

"Certainly."

"Ah, Hugo, is it? Hugo?"

"It might as well be," the bear answered.

"I hope you didn't kill them, too. I mean the men escorting us."

"No," the bear said shortly. He was holding the reins of four horses. "They are on foot and—" The bear's smile was saturnine, to say the least. "—I think probably running yet."

Chiara sniffed but looked satisfied.

"My dear Hugo," Armine said. "I believe this might be the beginning of a beautiful friendship."

M ATRONA APPROACHED CHARLES'S TENT A FEW hours later. She was wearing a long, flowing robe of white linen. It was deeply embroidered with gold at the neck, hem, and sleeves.

The *scarae* at the entrance heard her. It was Arbeo, who had been Maeniel's jailer when they first met the king. "He won't see anyone, my lady, but he told me if you came, to let you in. It's been a terrible evening. The king's counselors were here, all screaming and yelling for us to retreat, saying the king's plan failed. We're going to lose. We must beat a retreat or attack with our full force tomorrow. The king won't let them do either one. He says he won't waste his best troops yet—" Arbeo broke off because Charles was standing behind him.

"Be quiet!" said Charles. He motioned Matrona into his tent.

She entered and sat down in a camp chair. The model Antonius had built filled fully half of the tent. Next to the model was a table with wine and some cold joints of meat.

Charles gestured toward the table. "Wine? Food?"

"No," Matrona said.

"Well?" he asked.

"The garrison at Ivrea is no more. I stampeded the horses. Bernard finished them. They were slaughtered to a man. None escaped to warn Desiderius."

Charles nodded.

"The lord Maeniel is with Bernard. He will attack at dawn. His army is on the march even now. They will emerge from the morning fog and catch Desiderius in the flank.

"Your plan has worked, my king. In no little time at all, you will be master of the Lombard kingdom."

"I wish I were as sure as you are," Charles answered. He walked over to the wine pitcher on the table and lifted it. The thing was Roman; a procession in high relief was cast around the belly of the pitcher, nymphs and satyrs frolicked together in the rites of Bacchus.

"I am sure," Matrona said. "I looked into my mirror and saw what will be."

The handle of the pitcher was an acanthus flower spike. Charles's hand rested on the handle. "A beautiful thing but pagan, deeply pagan. As you and your lord are, my lady Matrona. If I win, I'll have this beautiful Roman pitcher melted down, that it be made into a reliquary for the bones of some saint or other. Do you know where I got it?"

"You probably took it from the Saxons who, no doubt in the world, stole it from someone else," Matrona said.

"Yes, it was buried among the loot I acquired when I destroyed their sacred tree Irmunsul. So I gave it a reprieve as long as it served me, but I plan to win the world for Christ, and pagan things no longer have any place here."

"Yes."

"So accept Christ and lead your lord and his beautiful wife to the baptismal pool, and I will find a high position for you in my kingdom."

Matrona smiled. "Do you think that a swim in a chilly pool and a bit of bad Latin muttered over us by a bishop will make much difference to our essential natures?"

Charles looked uncomfortable.

"My king, I will be blunt. At this stage in your career, you cannot afford to fail. A king who fails has but one place to fall and that is into a grave. My lord has given you victory and at no little cost to himself. Allow him some peace in return. This is all he asks.

"You attacked the Saxons and destroyed the sacred tree because you needed money to content your nobles, who might have defected to your brother's wife had you been too stingy with your largess when he died. You attacked the Lombards because you needed a victory, and a big one, to impress the most powerful magnates of the Frankish realm. Men who, I might add, hold even your life in their hands, should they choose to act in concert. After tomorrow your position will be secure. Use your strength to be merciful and to grant my lord the peace he asks."

A wave of fury swept over Charles, a rage so intense Matrona, who could feel, smell, and sense his wrath, felt sure he would have killed her if he had a weapon at hand. Then it faded and something like grudging admiration took its place.

"Are you always so brusque with kings?"

Matrona's lips twitched. She knew better than to smile. He was still on the edge of murder. "I never lie," she said. "I may not always tell the whole truth, but I never lie."

He stretched out his hand to her. "Come. There is some little time before dawn, when I must ride out with my troops. What are you wearing under that magnificent gown?"

"Nothing."

W HEN SHE MET MAENIEL IN THE SHADOW OF THE fortress at Susa the next day, she said, "He knows."

Antonius, riding along with Maeniel, answered, "It doesn't matter what he knows. The problem is what he cares to do about what he knows."

"Succinct and, as usual, to the point," Maeniel said.

"Religion and expediency are at war in his mind," Matrona said. "We are very useful to him."

Charles had thrown his bowman and foot at the old Roman fortress. They were taking casualties without visible effect as they tried with little success to force a passage at the river. Desiderius's men on the high ground wielding compound bows were using Charles's troops for target practice.

"This is what I do not like about war," Matrona said. "They are only a diversion, but they will die just the same."

"I'll give credit to Charles: he was in the vanguard leading the attack."

As Matrona and the rest watched, Charles blew retreat, thus tempting Desiderius's mercenaries to abandon the cover of the fortress to press the rout.

It was after daybreak and before sunrise; the fog that had filled the river valleys still meandered in clouds on the wooded slopes and near the water. In some places visibility was very good. In others, both armies clashed in the murk. Bernard and his army attacked at the dramatic moment when the sun's first rays blazed down from the notch in the pass, striking long corridors of light down through the mist and illuminating the whole valley. The river was a pale, lacy maelstrom, the grass an emerald carpet. The forest outliers still hugged moisture and the night's darkness that lay like a stain on the earth. The stones comprising the ancient fortress were burned to almost alabaster brilliance in the golden light.

Charlemagne closed his trap.

Bernard's men crashed, howling, into the flanks of Desiderius's army. The king was among them, upholding the Langobard standard. He fled first. Maeniel was mounted on Audovald; the horse half reared and pranced with excitement. Maeniel gave the loud snort that is *Go* in horse. And they went.

The massed ranks of the *scarae* struck the line first, punching through those few of Desiderius's troops that tried to make a stand.

Maeniel felt the splendid rush that is long-held tension dissolved. He, like the rest of the great magnates of France, led his men into battle.

Battle, such as it was. The erstwhile captain of the king's guard, blindly loyal to his sovereign, tried to put his troops together and make a stand. Indeed, they might have prevailed, had Desiderius shown courage or resolution. Charles had brought the best part of his army over the mountains, but they were less than the experienced troops the lord of the Lombards commanded.

It was a fine mercenary army, and Desiderius had schemed, murdered, betrayed, and extorted wealth from every nook and cranny of his kingdom in order to put together this massive mailed fist, to impose his will on all of Italy. But when the moment, or rather moments, came to strike and destroy his enemies, Desiderius always backed away.

The year before Pope Hadrian had out-bluffed him near Rome, and had Desiderius supported his minions in the Holy City with troops, Regeane and Maeniel might well have died. And Hadrian, under his thumb, might have been forced to abdicate or been murdered. But again Desiderius had backed out of the quarrel and fled.

Both forces came to a stop well out of the pass at Susa on the open plain. The glittering massed ranks of Desiderius's army were drawn up six deep in battle array. The sun was to Charles's back. The Frankish commanders sat on their horses, waiting for the king's signal.

Maeniel watched the Lombard host. By then all of his household were present, mounted, and ready to fight and win. Silvia was there. She was dressed as a man, or possibly the wearing of armor simply made her appearance androgynous.

"Do we fight?" she asked Maeniel. She sounded eager.

"Hold back," he told the rest of his pack. "I don't know."

"On balance," Antonius said, "I think he will run. And then the king will have to decide if he wants to organize a siege at Pavia."

"He has a magnificent army," Maeniel said. "He might very well win, even though in a difficult position. His commander is, moreover, an able man."

"His position isn't that bad," Antonius said. "A tributary of the Ticino is in front of him. His archers can catch the Frankish foot on the boggy low ground and destroy them. His commander has placed his heaviest cavalry on both wings. He's no fool. That's what Hannibal did at Cannae. His center will break, but not far—see those little hills behind them? They will not halt a retreat. But he could envelop the *scarae* and maybe—just maybe—destroy them. The foot will perish easily enough, but Charles's elite troops are better armed than anything he has. And better motivated. No general likes fifty-fifty odds in a pitched battle. That's why both he and Charles are holding back.

"I'm betting he will take the safe way out and run. He can base part of his force at Turin and keep the rest at Pavia. Then he can let Charles beat his brains out against its walls. But his commander is aching to fight. He knows they will never have a better opportunity, and his advice might carry the day, but his king is a shifty, devious little rat. My advice, my lord, is hold your position and don't budge."

Antonius smiled. He shifted his position on his horse's back. "I don't spend enough time in the saddle."

Matrona's mare, Cloris, pranced and tossed her mane.

Audovald spoke sharply to her. She became quiet.

The sun began to burn Maeniel's back through his mail shirt.

Antonius was vindicated.

Desiderius ran.

A beautiful, orderly retreat orchestrated by the captain of his guard. The archers held their position as the cavalry withdrew in double file. The captain of the guard, as he had on the day when he pulled the king away from the mob, left last, in command of the rear guard.

"Nivardd is an able man," Antonius said.

"Nivardd," Maeniel repeated. "I never knew his name."

REGEANE AND THE REST SPENT THE NIGHT IN A tumbledown ruin of a village in the wetlands of the river valley. They sat up late, strangely convivial around the open fire.

"It is peculiar no one lives here," Chiara said. "There is not even any trace of brigands."

"No one has been here for a long time," the bear said. He grinned at Regeane. "I take it you concur, my lady."

"Yes," she said. "I can always tell." The houses, though roofless, were still standing, and they camped in one with its back to the wind.

"Taxation ruined this place," the bear said. "I know. I traveled this way a long time ago with a sorcerer of my acquaintance. The people here fled to escape the taxes, not long before the old empire died. They were vanishing even then and those who remained were at their wits' end what to do to evade the assessment since, flight or not, the amount they must ante up to the collectors remained the same."

"There were fewer and fewer of them to pay it," Armine said.

The bear nodded. He really didn't look like Hugo any longer. He kept his hair close-cropped; Hugo had worn his long. He never drank; Hugo had been a sot.

The bear had been frank about the matter when Regeane had asked him about it. "It has no effect on me, not the essential me, that is. I don't have brain to fuddle. At least not the way Hugo did." He had been cleaning a duck bone with his teeth. "I do enjoy food, though. The taste, I mean. This body would starve without me to care for it. So if I have to eat, I might as well enjoy it.

"What are you going to do now, wolf?" he asked Regeane.

"I don't know." She was cracking open a fish cooked in clay. There were a number in the fire. She hadn't been able to snag any big ones, but she'd taken eight medium-size ones during a quick wade-fishing expedition.

"Give me some of that," Chiara said, extending a piece of flat bread.

Regeane expertly deboned the fish and dropped half into Chiara's flat bread, along with some of the greens she'd used to stuff them.

Chiara ate voraciously. "I'm starving," she said between mouthfuls. "Fighting gives you an appetite."

"That was hardly a fight," the bear said in lofty condescension. "A bit of a skirmish, that's all."

"Somehow I had the feeling, a strong feeling, it was more than that," Armine said. "But my dear friend Hugo, if you want to call it that, I'll humor you. Though at one point I believe both of my arms were broken."

"They probably were," Regeane said.

"I know," Armine said, meeting her eyes across the fire. "What happened?"

"I don't know," Regeane answered.

Armine was doing his best with a bowl of stewed rabbit.

"I think," she continued, "it had something to do with what Chiara and I tried to do for the bear."

Chiara began to tremble and cry. Gimp got what remained of her fish. He was sitting with them, finishing everyone's leftovers, and since none of them were happy with the rather vinegary wine, he was washing them down with copious drafts of the same.

The bear Hugo put his arm around Chiara and began to comfort her. "I'm here," he said, "and I always will be."

"You don't even smell like Hugo," she said.

The bear Hugo laughed. "Ask the wolf, she's the expert."

"He doesn't," Regeane said. "He smells clean. No aroma of dirt, perspiration, or constant drink. He has a dry, sharp smell, rather like some kind of soap."

"Do you smell everything?" Chiara asked, distracted from her grief.

"Everything," Regeane said. "Scents are a constant background to all everyday things. For instance, these ruins, they haven't been lived in for a long time, not by humans at any rate. A fox denned here in the next house, the vixen raised a litter, but they're gone. The latest odor is some months old: a traveler came by last winter. He remained a few days. He dug. He probably had treasure on his mind. I smell an old—again, some months old—scent of turned earth, and . . . and there is an owl in a ruined temple nearby. You can't see the building because it's mostly a mound of brush, but I smell brick and limestone and marble. That says temple to me."

Chiara and Armine both goggled at her.

"No wonder you weren't worried about brigands," Armine said. "You should probably know if there were any within miles of us."

Regeane nodded and cracked open another fish bundle and began to prepare a second meal for Chiara.

The bear Hugo yawned. "This damned body is tired. I would know if anyone came this way, too. That owl has fledglings in her nest. That's where she is, out hunting for them. I don't know where the male is. I was wondering if something happened to him. I don't smell anything, but I perceive temperature gradients, movement, body processes, heartbeat. It does beat. Your intellectual classes are woefully ignorant of how living things work. When I extend my perceptions, your bodies are transparent to me, and, among other things, I sense what you would call topography. The shape of the land and the things living on it."

"There he is," Regeane said. "I think he has a rat."

"The male owl," Hugo bear answered. "She heard him. I felt air displacement by his wings. The human who was looking for treasure was right, there is some here. A small hoard." He yawned again. "In the morning I'll show you where it is. You can dig it up. Am I right?" he asked Armine. "You didn't leave Pavia with much cash in hand."

"No," Armine said. "The king hadn't paid me, and I didn't think it at all healthy to hang around waiting for him to clear his debts. I didn't know you could do things like find buried treasure."

"How the hell do you think I kept that fool Hugo in funds? When we met he didn't have enough money to pay a louse to bite him."

"Show me this right now."

"No, you'll disturb the owls. The rat is a banquet to them. Leave them in peace. This ruin is overrun with noxious rodents. When momma owl is finished raising her young, they will improve the atmosphere of this place no end."

"Is it deep?" Regeane asked.

"No," the bear replied.

"Then I'll get it," she said. "They won't notice me the way they would humans with noise, torches, and trampling the vegetation. Give me a minute." She rose and went through an opening in the ruined house into the darkness.

Armine looked appalled, astonished, frightened, and outraged at the same time. The outrage was because the living arrangements of a family of owls were placed before his wishes.

"Your attitude is original, to say the least. I would think our welfare would take precedence over an owl's."

"Why?" the bear asked. "They have as much right to be here as you have; more, in fact. We're trespassers. This is their home."

"If you look at it that way, he's right," Chiara said.

Regeane forestalled further discussion by returning with a leather sack in her hand. She dropped it at Armine's feet. It ripped open easily, and a collection of silver and gold vessels tumbled out, small ritual objects.

"There's more," she said. "But this was all I could carry—as a wolf, I mean."

"Good God," Armine whispered. "There's a fortune right here. But part of this is yours," he said to Regeane and the bear.

Regeane shrugged. "I have plenty. You should see my husband's strongroom. He could have paid that ransom he offered the king twice over and still have money to spare."

"I don't give a damn," the bear said. "I sense things like this all the time and other, more unpleasant things, too. There are fifteen or sixteen babies in a well not far from here. Times were very hard for the last inhabitants of this place. They couldn't raise any children at the last. That's one reason why they ran away. That's probably why the gold was buried also. They felt sure the tax collectors would confiscate these sacred objects and melt them down. Too bad. Now you will do the same."

"No, I don't think so. Not all of them, at any rate," Armine said. "A great many unpleasant things can be said of the Florentine merchants, but no one ever accused us of being blind to beauty." He was studying an exquisite silver bowl with a pattern of white grapes, the fruit picked out in moonstones.

"I believe," he said, "that we should go into banking, bear. I didn't in my youth. I simply didn't have enough capital. But you will enjoy banking, bear. It's much more interesting than the cloth trade."

"You understand me too well," the bear said. "It doesn't do to bore me."

Chiara moaned. "Oh, lord, but interest calculations are a nightmare."

"Yes, well, I'll give you both charge over the counting house. Your tremendous influence will be envied by every woman in Florence."

"Oh," Chiara whispered, sounding absolutely delighted. "I can see myself going to mass clad in velvet and brocade with an illuminated missal in my hand."

"Yes," Armine sighed. "And violating all the sumptuary laws."

"Oh, nonsense. Mother told me they only crack down when the city goes to war. Besides, banking is against church law, too."

"Oh, yes," Armine said, "but it's easy to get around the church. It's a rare bishop who won't look the other way when he receives a large donation."

Regeane yawned.

Armine glanced around uneasily. "Before we bed down for the night," he asked Regeane and the bear, "are you sure we're still alone?"

"Oh, yes," she said. "We would know."

She and Chiara took the house warmed by the fire. Regeane was a wife, Chiara was an unmarried girl. Propriety demanded they sleep apart from the men.

Regeane and Chiara bedded down together against the wall. "That's a lot of gold," she told Regeane. "Are you sure you won't take some?"

Regeane laughed. "You've seen the way I travel. Where would I put it?"

Chiara blushed.

"What will you do about the bear when you reach the city?"

"I don't know," Chiara answered. "For now I suppose he can go on being Hugo. And, unless I miss my guess, he and my father will soon go into business together." She frowned. "What do you think? Will he ask my hand in marriage?"

Regeane was pushing some grass together to make a softer bed. She could always sleep as a wolf but didn't want to alarm Chiara.

"Because if he doesn't plan on marriage, I won't consider anything else. It's like my mother said, it's all right for a man to go hopping from one bed to another, but women must consider family life and children. Not to mention finances and reputation and all the other things sex brings with it. And besides, that's Hugo's body, and I'm not sure I would like to—"

"How you do chatter," the bear's voice said.

Chiara paused and stamped her foot. "You're getting sneaky. I didn't feel you. Besides, this was a private conversation and you had no business sticking your nose—"

"Enough," the bear said, "little madam shrew. Will you ever be done correcting me?"

"Not so long as you behave like a lout."

"A lout? I, a lout?" the bear roared.

Chiara stuck her fingers in her ears. "I won't listen."

"A fat lot of good that will do you," the bear shouted. "My voice is in your mind."

Chiara removed her fingers from her ears. "Yes, that's true but—"

"Oh, be quiet," the bear said. Then he pulled her away from the fire into the darkness and kissed her. "Now go to bed. And don't worry. I don't need Hugo's body."

He departed, laughing.

"It seems he doesn't," Regeane said.

Chiara walked back to the fire. She was flushed; her long blond hair, which had been up, was down around her shoulders. She looked pleased.

"Look," she said. On her ring finger was a fine band, three swan's necks twined in heavy chased silver. "It's beautiful," she told Regeane. "I didn't really notice it was on my finger until he was gone, but you do sort of have to wonder where he got it. I mean, will the original owner show up in the early hours and want it back?"

"No, I don't think so. It didn't come from the cemetery," Regeane said. "There's a lot more there than I brought. You and your father must get it in the morning." She was also pleased to note Chiara was under no illusions about the bear, which augured well for their future relationship.

Remingus woke Regeane in the night. She found herself in the place of the dead, the thick darkness without moon or star. The town was here as it appeared before it became a ruin. The temples around the forum that was the heart of every Roman town stood on their platforms as they had before they fell to ruins, painted and inlaid statuary intact and gazing away into the middle distance. The statue of an emperor presided over the town, standing on his pedestal forever.

The house where Chiara slept was a shop selling basketry. Regeane couldn't see her, but she knew the girl slept well because her breath steamed in the cold night air, and she sensed the puffs of vapor.

Regeane walked across the empty forum, her feet knowing the stones but not really feeling them. She wore the shift and worn, brown dress she'd borrowed from Chiara. Remingus stood with the boy Robert had killed, the one who had instigated and carried out the murder of the girl he loved.

"He is here with us."

"Yes," Regeane answered. "So I see."

"Tell Robert his mercy was not a vain act," the boy said. "I am not in hell."

"Isn't this hell?" Regeane asked. The chill in her body was piercing. The chill in her heart was deeper still. She had begun to weep. The tears running down her cheeks were droplets of ice, freezing cold against her skin.

"No," Remingus said. "No, this is not hell nor do I know what hell is. But there is no hope here, so there is no sorrow. And he is with us. This is all we had left to ask."

And Regeane looked out from Remingus's eyes as he hung on the Carthaginian cross, looked into the sun. She tried to close her eyes—or Remingus's eyes—and realized she/he had no eyelids. They had been cut away. And even the hardened Roman officers who retrieved his body for burial had been astounded at the things that had been done to him before he was put on the cross. The Carthaginians had exercised all their ingenuity in making him suffer, but still he won. And a door that had been open when Hannibal crossed the Alps swung shut, closing with a finality that rang down through the ages. And so did his pain.

The benediction of her tears blurred away the scene she saw, and when her vision cleared, Hildegard stood in front of her—as she had at the convent when Sister Hildegard came to be seated with her sisters in love, and Regeane hadn't noticed she was dead. The younger woman had guided the elder to her place and put plate and cup before what, to the other nuns, was only empty air.

Now Hildegard reached out and touched Regeane's face with fingers soft and dry as new silk. "Regeane, go to Rome. Lucilla wants you."

Regeane awoke. The night air was cold and clear. The stars hung in splendor across the sky. Her mind as usual mapped them, and the wolf told her it was close to dawn.

Chiara had thrown aside her covers and was now curled up against the cold. As Regeane watched, the blanket was lifted, placed over her, and tucked in, rather in the same way a mother covers a child who has become restless in the night.

"Bear?" Regeane asked.

"Yes. Once Armine asked if I sat; well, I don't sit and I don't sleep, either. That Hugo carcass has to do both, but while it does, I'm at loose ends. I know something came to greet you, because you weren't in your blankets a few moments ago."

"I'm going to Rome," Regeane said.

"Alone? Is that wise?"

"Probably not," Regeane said, "but I'm going anyway. Make my excuses for me."

"Ah yes, as if you left the table early after dinner. A minor matter. Nothing to it."

"I hope not," Regeane said. "Take care of her."

"I will. Will we ever meet again?"

"I don't know, bear. But whatever happens, fare thee well. And when you and Armine become bankers, try not to cheat too many people."

Regeane heard an angry snort and knew the bear had more to say but she was wolf—the change was very easy at that hour—and was gone.

FROM WHERE SHE SAT, ALL LUCILLA COULD SEE WAS a patch of blue sky, but she knew she was in a world of trouble.

Adalgisus had, once they'd reached Verona, tried to hide her from Gerberga, the Frankish queen. To this end, he had placed Lucilla on the top floor of a house overlooking the square. It was a house of ill repute. He felt she would be safe there, since the Frankish queen was a snobbish woman who paid little attention to any but the notables of the city, though there were a number of wealthy women there who would have given their souls to have entertained her in their houses. Gerberga stuck her nose in the air and pretended that only the Lombard lord, one Syagrius, was worthy of her notice. He was an individual of ancient Roman lineage whose great-grandfather had the sagacity to marry a lady who styled herself a Lombard princess—her father had had a lot of loot, and she wound up being his only heir. Syagrius called himself a duke. *Dux,* in the current terminology, a war lord. His family had seen to it that his brother was the archbishop of Verona, thus keeping things in the family, so to speak.

So Adalgisus, Syagrius, and Karl the bishop were the only people the haughty Gerberga would lower herself to associate with. Everybody else was on the outside looking in.

"With any luck," Adalgisus had said gleefully to Lucilla, "she will never know you're here."

Since the lofty Gerberga was in daily attendance at mass, Lucilla got a good look at her every day when she was carried to the church in a sedan chair. She was escorted by four maids and two ladies-in-waiting and her two sons, each accompanied by a nurse and tutor.

"You're her lover?" Lucilla asked Adalgisus on the first morning they went by.

"Why?" he asked. He was looking very vain. "I didn't think you cared."

Lucilla, who wanted to say she hoped so, because Gerberga was welcome to him, simpered and purred. "My darling, I love preening myself that I am the rival of a queen. How amazing."

Adalgisus pulled her away from the window. "Come, sweet, my love, tell me some more stories about . . . torture."

Lucilla gritted her teeth but Adalgisus was busy putting a hickey on her neck. She'd quickly found what buttons to push on the Lombard king's son. She could always stoke his fires to a white heat by recounting the horrors the public executioner practiced on those who annoyed the powerful in Rome. Even Hadrian, who was no fan of torture, used it on occasion, for the same reasons everyone else did: to make an example of someone who indulged in spectacularly vicious criminal behavior, or to persuade the occasional recalcitrant to impart information that they preferred to keep to themselves. Lucilla reckoned herself safe if she could keep Adalgisus's sex life interesting in the immediate future.

She wasn't, and she found out why a few days later.

They kicked open the door near dawn.

Two men.

Lucilla was able to get a robe on—a heavy woolen overgown— and she managed to hide a knife and her medicines. She was hauled before the bishop.

He looked at Lucilla for a very long time, beating a steady tattoo on the arm of his chair with his fingers. "Are you sure this is the one?" he finally asked.

"Grifo and Myra, the proprietors, say the prince visits her rooms every day," one of the soldiers answered.

"She's a bit older than I would expect," the bishop said.

"They say the prince is wild about her. He remains with her for a long time," the man holding Lucilla's arm twisted up between her shoulder blades told the bishop.

"I suppose there's something to be said for experience," the bishop said. Then he studied Lucilla's face. His eyes frightened her. There was nothing in them.

"Let me go," Lucilla said. "I have money."

"Not here," the bishop said.

"In Rome. I could make it worth your while. I have influence also."

"Oh? I know who you are. And you don't have enough of either money or influence to make me betray the king's secret."

I'm a dead woman, Lucilla thought.

"Come here." The bishop beckoned one of the soldiers holding her arms.

The soldier went to his chair. They spoke in low voices.

Lucilla stood quiet. They hadn't tied or chained her, perhaps because she hadn't given them a fight. They were alone in the bishop's hall. In the distance Lucilla could hear the bustle of servants. But besides her, the bishop, and the two soldiers, there was no one else in the room. *Do it,* something in her mind told her. *Think too much and you're lost.*

With lightning quickness she twisted away, out of the soldier's grip, but she hadn't been able to see he held a clubbed mace in his other hand. He was fast; a second later it crashed into the side of her head. She felt the blow. It was so hard she felt a terrible stab of fear that her skull was crushed, then paralysis, and at last darkness.

She awakened in another place, staring up through a steel grating at the sky. She'd been hit so hard that even lifting her head brought fierce, overwhelming pain. So she simply lay quiet, drifting in and out of consciousness for almost a day and a half. When the nausea and dizziness did abate enough for her to sit up, she began almost to wish the blow had killed her.

The cell was somewhere in the ruins of the old Roman city. Most of it was underground. The grating above was its only connection to the outside world. It was floored with overgrown mossy stone, with walls of the same ubiquitous terra-cotta brick the Romans had used to build everything from aqueducts to palaces. It ran some little way underground back into the ruins. There the walls and floor ran out and a fill of rubble and stony soil blocked any possible way of escape.

When Lucilla crawled back to the light, she found they had left her a jug of wine and a basket with a few hard, small loaves of bread. She went to take a sip of the wine and the smell made her jerk her head back. It was laced with opium, heavily laced with opium.

Enough, by the odor, rather pleasant than otherwise, to kill two or three people.

There was one large flat stone, part of a very big column of some temple or other. It was round and fluted at the edges. It made a comfortable seat. She sat down and despaired, closing her eyes and letting her mind drift. She knew what the bishop intended and how she'd been caught. Bishop Karl probably owned the whorehouse. There was a definite affinity between the ecclesiastical establishment and houses of prostitution. The bishop of Ravenna had owned the first brothel into which she had been sold as a sixteen year old, and the bishop was careful to collect his percentage and his ground rents. Such business establishments were lucrative, to say the least. And since Christianity became part of the limited urban scene in the west long before it proliferated into the countryside, much church property was in the cities. So were most brothels. The church, the first corporate body in the west, owned a lot of them.

She should have remembered, but she'd accepted Adalgisus's word that she was safe. She should have known better than that, also. Now she was being invited by the bishop Karl to commit suicide. The wine jug was a sort of mercy left with her so that she could take that road in preference to death by starvation and thirst.

Above, the patch of blue sky was beginning to darken. Night was coming on. Lucilla sat on the figment of ruined Roman imperium, the column drum, sunk deep in physical and emotional misery and despair. She believed in her heart that she was going to die.

Memories drifted across her mind like cloud shadows across summer meadows: vague, fragmentary, and disconnected.

Like a great many others, Lucilla regretted her inability to completely turn off her mind and rest in mental silence and peace. Her father had been a prosperous farmer in the mountainous region of Italy known as the Abruzzi. He was a hard man. She realized now that, given the world he lived in, only a hard man could have survived. The life of a farmer in the mountains was not one forgiving of the weak or even the lazy. Her mother had been a kind and good woman, but she went in mortal terror of her husband.

But Lucilla had been a happy, hard-working child until her father caught her alone in the barn when she was sixteen years old. At first she'd wondered why he was touching her. He was not an affectionate man. But when he threw her down in a pile of hay, she understood, and she fought back. But he threatened her with a horsewhip—no idle threat, as he had one he used to discipline difficult animals, children, and occasionally his wife.

Lucilla lay still. It had been painful, but he had exclaimed at her tightness and been pleased. Like many another girl, Lucilla had tried to turn to the people in her life for help, but her older brother wouldn't even listen. All her older sister said was that it was time she did her share to keep him occupied. Her mother said she didn't believe her. Lucilla decided later it must have been pretense because then and at later times she would never meet Lucilla's eyes, never look her directly in the face. So Lucilla tried to harden herself to the situation. She tried not to care.

But then he began to sneak up to the high pastures to pleasure himself with her tight, young body. To her this was an unbearable pollution. She had charge of their sheep and few cattle because she was fearless. Nothing, not wolves who moved in the cold night or the big mountain eagle who hunted young lambs, nothing was ever allowed to disturb the stock she guarded. And should any stray from the flock, she would climb sheer slopes that wouldn't offer good handholds to a fly, or cross treacherous scree, moving through the dangerous rocks more surely than a mountain goat to bring them safely back.

This was her domain, where she was alone with the wind and the silence, the beauties of wildflowers in spring or the vast ocean of stars on cold autumn nights. The second time he came, she saw him on the footpath from her perch on the mountain. She had collected a large pile of rocks solely for this purpose. She pelted him with them until he turned tail and ran. That evening when she returned the flocks to the barn near the farmhouse, she expected that she would get a beating, probably a dreadful one. She thought he might even kill her, but she felt it was worth it simply to keep her own world hers. But she wasn't beaten. She wasn't killed. Instead she was sold to a slave dealer and in turn, since she was strong and still pretty when she reached the city—a lot of the children they dragged down from the mountains weren't, by the time they reached the coast—she was sold into the sex trade.

Antonius, her son, wasn't only her son, he was also her half brother. If she could have gotten her hands on her father, she would have seen to it that he died in torment. She would still, if she looked into his face tomorrow. But she understood why he had done what he had to her. A tyrant loves nothing so much as ruling, and her father was a tyrant, dreadful as any who ever scarred the pages of human history. They cannot bear to be opposed because it loosens their grip on those they rule. And he saw, mirrored in her, his own strength and determination. So he had needed, as he saw it, to destroy her. He tried and very nearly succeeded—because he knew she would never fully yield.

It was dark now and the sky was bathed in the star blaze. No, she would never drink that flask of wine. Whatever a being does, it cannot deny its essential nature, and she could not deny hers. Yes, she would probably die. But she would die trying to live.

She inventoried her possessions. She still had the knife, more opium and valerian, her cotton shift and woolen gown. Among the debris on the stone floor was some dried grass and a few pieces of wood. She selected one of the pieces of wood and made a notch in it. She would try to keep a tally of the days. Then she piled the dried grass into a bed. A mouthful of the wine wouldn't kill her, and it would probably stop the headache she had and let her sleep.

So she drank that much, then stoppered the flask and put it aside with the bread. She was too nauseated to try to eat anyway. Then she lay down and went to sleep.

REGEANE TRAVELED BY NIGHT AND SLEPT BY DAY. She tried to put the woman out of her mind and become only the wolf. Matrona had told her this was possible, and it worked most of the time. But the things she'd learned from the bear haunted her mind.

Near any human dwelling, she saw shadows. A festively twined temple appeared in her mind even as her eyes gazed on ruins; she could see the brightly painted ornaments and statuary with eyes of crystal, jewelry of gold leaf and semiprecious stones, flesh covered in ivory. Jewels of brass or glass inlaid on the togas and gowns; the painted green leaves of ivy, artichoke, and acanthus decorating the capitals and dados in red or blue glowed before her as if newly created and first exposed shining in the sun.

Sometimes people long dead appeared before her, but these—

unlike other ghosts she had seen—were utterly unaware of her presence. So she found her way, as Hugo had, to the coast, and unlike Hugo, she found the solitude a source of renewal. She had, she knew, come into her own. The criticisms Maeniel had made of her no longer applied. She was a competent hunter and could always find something to eat. She fished well and easily even in the surf.

Other wolf packs were no longer a problem, thanks to her experience with the bear. She would use her augmented sense of temporal positioning to investigate quickly the activity of any pack in the immediate vicinity, finding herself thereafter usually able to predict their movements. The same was true of prey animals. To become aware of a deer was to know where it had been in the last few hours and, therefore, she often knew where it was going.

Her senses, preternaturally acute because she was human and wolf, now stretched even further. Leaping and dancing in the surf near where Hugo had camped, she found that she could sense the presence of each and every living thing: a school of small fish flashing through the shadows, trying to outrun a feeding barracuda; a dozen mussels clinging to rocks in a shallow tide pool; the dark cold intelligence of something cruising the edge of the deeps. Even the ephemeral, feathery jellyfish, wave-borne flotsam and jetsam of the water column, registered on her consciousness.

She turned human and swam along a big sandbar that stretched out far into the sea, drifting among waves burnished by moonlight, then swam ashore near a rocky promontory and had a meal of raw shellfish and whitebait before she resumed her wolf form and slept in a sand cave near the deserted and ruined city where Hugo had his fateful meeting with the bear.

The next day she had to be more careful, because she was approaching the thickly settled countryside near Rome. She found a hilltop and scanned the low, rolling landscape, watching and letting her perceptions range until she felt she'd found a safe route. Then she curled up in an abandoned badger den until dark.

Not long after dawn she was leaping the wall to Lucilla's villa and gliding through the beautiful herb and flower gardens near Lucilla's triclinium. She was pleased when she saw Dulcinia sitting on a bench with a cup of her preferred tea.

Dulcinia looked up when she saw the wolf trotting toward her in a friendly way along the path. "A dog," she murmured. "I didn't know Lucilla had a dog . . . That's not a dog, it's a—"

Just at that moment, Regeane chose to assume human form. "Dulcinia, would you—"

That was as far as she got, because Dulcinia let out a terrible scream and leaped to her feet. Regeane, her mind still involved with the wolf, heard feet running toward them from every direction. She snatched Dulcinia's mantle and wrapped it around herself just as what seemed the entire staff of the villa descended on the garden, at least half bearing weapons or the nearest heavy or sharp object within reach. Dulcinia staggered against a yew tree, hand on her breast, gasping for her breath.

"I'm sorry," Regeane said. "I thought Lucilla would have told you I could do . . . that."

"Do that?" Dulcinia shrieked. "Do that? I didn't know *anyone* could do that!"

"You mean she didn't tell—"

Just then a wave of servants, soldiers, and farm laborers working on the grounds arrived, accompanied by a few strangers or passersby who had heard the commotion and came to see what was happening.

Explanations were in order. Regeane, who was stifling laughter, said, "I startled the lady Dulcinia."

Dulcinia gave her a withering look. "Startled? Yes, I suppose nearly frightening me into a heart seizure might be described as startling . . . but I can't think the lady Regeane means me any harm."

She looked down at the broken glass beaker on the flagstones. "Except for the lady Lucilla's cup, I don't think any harm was done. Will someone please bring me some wine? I feel the need for a bit of a restorative."

Then she left her position against the yew tree and, being careful to avoid the broken glass, she staggered back to the bench and sat down. The crowd dispersed. A tray was carried out, bearing wine and glasses. One of the maids came and swept up the broken glass, carefully collecting the pieces and carrying them away to see if they could be mended. Glass was valuable, a luxury for the rich. Breaking something was a serious matter.

"Where is Lucilla?" Regeane asked. "I came to see Lucilla. I received a message telling me to go to Rome."

Dulcinia gulped half a cup of wine. "She's not here. A message? Who gave you the message? Have you been in contact with her? Do you know where she is? If you do, in heaven's name, tell me. Everyone is very disturbed; we've been—"

"Dulcinia, slow down. No, I don't know where Lucilla is, and the person who gave me the message to go to Rome was . . . was . . . Well, let me put it this way. If the wolf bothered you, this one would really—"

"I'm afraid to ask," Dulcinia said. "And you're right, I'm not sure I want to know where you find things out. You're right; I'm sure it would bother me."

Regeane took another glass from the tray, poured some wine, and spiked it with water. She drank deeply, then said, "Dulcinia, I need food, clothes, and rest. I've been on the road all night. You understand? It's safer if I travel at night."

Dulcinia's answering laugh was slightly hysterical. "Oh, yes, to be sure, much safer. If you meet any people, killing and eating them will be—"

"Dulcinia. I have never—well, only rarely and then almost always in self-defense, almost always, actually once or twice I had no choice, but— Oh, for heaven's sake, Dulcinia. I'll explain later. But I never, I positively never, eat them."

"My, how comforting."

"Stop. You're just getting back at me for startling you."

"Startling me? Oh, yes, remind me to look in a mirror when we get into the house. I'll want to know if my hair has turned white."

Regeane gulped some more water and wine. "Your hair can't turn white. It's an old wives' tale."

"Yes, well, I'm beginning to rethink every old wives' tale I ever heard. Those old wives must know something. Look at you. I thought you were an old wives' tale." Dulcinia sounded outraged.

"Dulcinia, conduct me to the baths. I need clothing, food, and I need to clean up." Her hair was wet with dew, as her coat had been. She shook her head and showered Dulcinia with droplets.

Dulcinia closed her eyes and clenched her fists. "You stop. I will become deranged. You are making me deranged."

"How much wine have you had on an empty stomach?" Regeane asked.

"Too much. I'm not a drinker. I think I am a little tiddly, but why doesn't it bother you?"

"I added water. Besides, if I get too swacked, I can just change, then change back. It seems whatever makes wine wine just burns away."

"Oh, my God," Dulcinia said. Then she rose, not too steadily, and led Regeane away.

Regeane bathed. Dulcinia sobered and found her temper, as opposed to it being lost. She was not a naturally rancorous person and when both women emerged, clean and refreshed, to breakfast in the garden, they were friends again. Dulcinia filled Regeane in on what had happened since she had left Rome, and in return, Regeane gave her a highly edited account of her own activities.

Dulcinia told Regeane what had happened after Stella died. "We tried to follow Adalgisus but lost his trail in the wilderness. We felt he probably rode to the villa Jovis, but it's well fortified. Ansgar and Ludolf didn't want to try an attack there. It's practically a city and bristling with armed men. From there it would be impossible to tell where he went, so we returned and Ansgar sent me on ahead to Rome. Rufus and he are friends. You remember Cecelia's Rufus?"

"Oh my, yes," Regeane said. "I certainly do."

"He arranged for safe conduct for Ansgar to come visit the pope. I think Ansgar is going to switch loyalties."

"Does he blame Lucilla for what happened?"

"Yes and no," Dulcinia said slowly. "He says nothing would have happened if she hadn't come visiting and gotten Stella all stirred up, but he's a fair man and says Stella shouldn't have been so foolish as to send a message to Adalgisus. She knew as well as Ansgar the man was a fool. And this is what happens when women meddle in men's affairs. But, in any case, Adalgisus should have had better sense than to take Stella when he came to capture Lucilla.

"Then Eberhardt and Dagobert behaved as stupidly as they possibly could. They both died, and Ansgar says good riddance. And if he had gotten his hands on them, they would have died a lot harder than they did.

"He blames the men more because he says they should have better sense, but he also says he has to secure his son's future. If he has to swear allegiance to Charlemagne, to do that, he will. And he doesn't object to Ludolf marrying me, if we want, but I'm beginning to have second thoughts."

Dulcinia began twisting an elaborate ruby ring on one finger. "You see, I'm pregnant and Ludolf says he isn't a man to make bastards. He wants his child to be brought up in his city."

"Maybe he won't object if the child is a girl. I mean, to her staying here in Rome," Regeane said.

Dulcinia brightened. "I hadn't thought of that possibility—that it would be a girl. Then Ludolf might not care . . ."

"But I would," Ludolf said as he stepped out from behind a pillar on the walkway around the villa garden. He sat down and looked at Dulcinia.

"Ludolf, this is my friend and Lucilla's: Regeane. She is related to the Frankish royal family, and her husband is the master of a duchy in the Alps."

"Maeniel. Yes, I know. I am honored to meet you."

"Thank you," Regeane said. "And I, you."

Ludolf turned to Dulcinia. "Father is with Hadrian now. I believe they will reach an agreement. Rufus made no secret of his pleasure in my father's offer to join him in swearing fealty to the Frankish king. Between the two of them, they should be able to rehabilitate the wasteland between Rufus's domains and our own.

"And yes, even if the child is a girl, I will still want her and you. I can understand some of your fears and doubts. You have carved out an independent position for yourself, as few women are able to, and I would not take that away from you. But the world is changing, and our town, though newly reborn, looks to be a prosperous one. Our little court might well become a center of art and culture, and I would hope that you would remain beside me to help in the building of such a place."

"My dear," Dulcinia said. "Are you sure? I do love you, but what will the world say to such a match?"

"Nothing. Or nothing that we—either of us—need concern ourselves about. They will talk the usual folly and nonsense as they always do, and we will live together—I hope—in bliss." He lifted her hand to his lips and kissed it. "Nothing ventured, nothing gained. Don't be afraid to try life."

Regeane had an odd feeling. She tried to thrust it out of her mind, but it grew in intensity. The garden around her was filled with people. They walked in shadow but light shifted from one face to another: a magnificent dark-haired woman in pink silk wearing a crown; a dark man with thick, curly hair, black brows, frowning and angry; a pope in the most elaborate dress she'd ever seen, thin-faced, aesthetic, and angry; a warrior, looking more chaste than the pope. And then abruptly, before she could sort it all out, they were gone and she sat beside Dulcinia, as Ludolf held her hand to his lips still.

And Regeane knew time had annihilated itself again. She'd seen—what?

Her journey into the other world had given her godlike powers but they were worthless without a god's concomitant knowledge. All she knew after her vision was that both of these people would leave descendants, but she couldn't be sure if from each other or not. She had been given power to look beneath the smooth, time-driven universe that cradles life from birth to death, but she was far from understanding the meaning of her visions.

Susana, Lucilla's personal maid, came bustling along the porch just then. She was a slender, dark-haired woman. She dressed in the black clothing common among older Italian women. Regeane at first had wondered why she was so retiring, seldom showing her face outside of Lucilla's extensive apartments, until she saw Susana had a harelip. There was a surgery for this defect, but it left its possessor only passably attractive. Susana had been rejected on her wedding day by a suitor whose family thought it would be sufficient to offer their son a wealthy marriage and didn't take into account his reaction when he saw the girl. " 'I wouldn't breed from the bitch,' is what he said," Lucilla had told Regeane. "Her father drew his sword and struck him dead on the spot. Then all parties fell to . . . and during the confrontation Susana's father was killed.

"Hadrian was present. He had to call out the guard to settle the brawl, and all parties blamed the poor girl, as if any of it were her fault. The smart-mouth young whelp should have been taught better manners, and he shouldn't have been deceived in the first place. Susana's family were not much better. They should have realized her little problem would need to be openly discussed before the wedding day. But at any rate, she came here, and I'm the better for it. She manages all my money and estates and has doubled my capital over the years."

Regeane knew the two women were friends and Lucilla reposed

great trust in her, but Susana still covered the lower part of her face with her veil even when she spoke to Lucilla's intimates. "Ladies, you had best come now. Simona is here with someone you need to meet, and you, my lord Ludolf, please accompany me also."

They rose and followed her to Lucilla's tablinium just off the atrium fountain. Simona was standing there with the girl Lavinia. When Lavinia saw a handsome young warrior and three beautifully dressed women approaching, she began backing away. Regeane saw the same mad terror in her face that she'd seen in some animals confronted, not necessarily with a deadly threat, but by the truly unknown. Fortunately there was a thick marble column behind Lavinia. She backed into it and froze.

"Go slowly," Regeane told the rest. They were hurrying along. "She is frightened and ready to bolt."

Simply looking at the girl, the wolf sensed pain and fear: fear for a long time, pain for a long time, so much that they had destroyed her ability to eat and even sleep quietly. This girl was so frightened and so weary she was almost ready to give up on life, to lie down somewhere and die. The rest, sensing the otherness of the child, slowed down, confused and not wanting to frighten her further.

Regeane hailed Simona. "How are you?"

"Very well, my lady." She came forward and kissed Regeane's cheek. "You look to be blooming. Tell me, has he gotten you with child yet?"

Regeane grinned. "No, but we're trying as hard as we can."

"Humph. You mean he's trying as hard as he can."

Both laughed. "And Posthumus?" asked Regeane.

"He and that hoyden Elfgita are at the English king's court. Can you believe it? My son at a king's court. I'm happy for him, yet I do miss him so. But that wench Silvie is breeding, so I imagine I'll have another one to rear soon. *She* won't be what I would call a devoted mother. Too busy counting the hands up her skirt, so she can charge them later."

"Something besides a hand must have gotten up Silvie's skirt. I never heard of a hand making a baby," Regeane shot back.

Simona laughed again, then reached back and took Lavinia's hand. "Come here. Talk to the lady Regeane. She won't bite. Not right now at any rate." Simona chuckled. "Under all those fancy clothes, she's just a woman like all the rest of us."

Regeane stretched out her hand and Lavinia hesitantly took it. Simona's broad talk somehow seemed to have reassured the girl. Regeane inclined her head to Lavinia.

"My lady," Lavinia said.

Regeane could feel tension in Lavinia. The hand alone told her she was trembling like a captured bird. Regeane led her carefully over to a marble bench by the atrium pool. She asked Susana for some bread and wine.

"Now, girl," Simona said, "tell her what you told me."

Lavinia nodded. Her speech sounded rehearsed, and Regeane thought she must have spoken it over and over again in her mind as she lay in ditches, deserted forest clearings among ruins, or hurrying furtively down a hundred paths and byways as she tried to hide from her pursuers.

"I met a lady at the villa Jovis. She was named Lucilla. I told her I was unhappy there but had nowhere to go. She told me that if I delivered a message to Rome for her, her friends in Rome—Simona and Dulcinia and Susana—would help me find work and a place to live."

"We will," Regeane said. "She is Susana, that is Dulcinia—and her intended, Ludolf—and this is, as you know, Simona."

"I was to give you this." Lavinia handed Regeane the ring.

She showed it to Susana.

"It's hers. Hadrian gave it to her."

Lavinia shook her head. "The message she gave me, I don't understand it. But . . ." She looked at Simona. "Maybe they won't believe me—"

"We will believe you," Regeane said. "We know you couldn't carry a long or complicated message. Tell us what it is and see if we can't make sense of it."

Lavinia looked reassured. "All she said was just one word: Verona."

"So," Dulcinia said, and hissed. She and Ludolf's eyes locked.

"Yes," he said, and dropped his hand to his sword hilt.

"Hadrian must be told as quickly as possible," Susana said.

"The pope!" Lavinia exclaimed. She looked ready to die of fear on the spot.

"Shush," Simona said. "That won't be your responsibility."

"It will be mine, and right now." Ludolf kissed Dulcinia's hand again and strode away.

"Lucilla succeeded in her endeavor," Dulcinia said.

"What about the place to stay and work? Work that doesn't involve spreading my legs," Lavinia said harshly.

Regeane said, "We are all grateful to you, little one. You cannot imagine how grateful."

"Yes," Susana said. She drew a necklace of gold links from around her neck and dropped it over Lavinia's head. "This is for you right now. And there will be much more later when you have bathed and eaten. As for a place to stay, remain here. Lucilla would not want me to do less."

"But it might take me some time to find work."

"You are my guest and Lucilla's for as long as you like," Susana said. "Now come. Did they have baths at the villa Jovis?"

"Not for us."

"Well, we do here—for everyone."

Simona shook her head as Susana led the girl away. "Verona. I suppose you know what that means?"

"We do," Dulcinia said.

Regeane was moving out of the atrium, down the pillared walkway at top speed.

"Stop," Dulcinia said.

Regeane paid no attention.

Both Simona and Dulcinia pursued her.

Then she was in the garden. It was siesta time. No one was about. The dress she had been wearing floated away. Simona and Dulcinia found it tangled in a bush covered with white roses. No one saw the wolf leap the villa wall and vanish into the tranquil afternoon countryside.

LUCILLA WAS STRUGGLING TO SURVIVE IN THE HOLE where she'd been abandoned. After studying the grate over the cell, she found it could be pushed up enough for her to get a hand out, but it would open no wider, being secured at both ends by chains and padlocks. The hinges on the other side were new and tight.

She could pick locks, but whoever had placed her here had foreseen that possibility. The keyholes of both locks had been jammed shut with wood. Probably a stick or twig pushed into the hole, pounded down, and broken off.

She then crawled around the walls, examining them. The only weakness she could find was that on one end, the cell was dug into the hillside. On the far end she could see enough to know the ground sloped down and there might not be more than three or four feet of dirt between that end of the cell and the hillside. She considered all the possibilities and then methodically began to dig.

A discouraging task. The ground here was baked dry and almost stone hard. Moreover it was filled with debris of all kinds: wood, pot shards, pieces of brick. Her knife began to wear out quickly. She was dismayed when the tip broke off as she struck a piece of marble.

She was already tired and her head still ached. She sat down on the broken column and wept. She dried her eyes when the thought occurred to her that tears were draining a small supply of water from her body. She knew by bitter experience that one could survive a rather long time without food, but only a very short time without water. If she had no luck with her excavation, she would have only about three days to live. She was tormented by thirst already. She took a sip of the opium-laced wine, forcing herself to make it a small one. Then she sat quietly on the column drum with her back to the wall and closed her eyes.

The opium dissolved her headache and calmed her. She found herself studying the trash she'd already freed from the wall. The piece of marble looked like part of a mortar and pestle. The pestle.

She crawled over and examined it. It was lying next to a piece of wood and assorted pottery fragments. She knocked the dirt off the wood against the column drum; the dirt fell away and she saw the object was cup shaped. Probably it once held a table leg but it made a passable container. She put it aside carefully. It was spring and heavy rains were common in the region. It might be that none would come in time, but they might, and a cup would be a help. Now, as to that lump of marble . . . Lucilla frowned and her eyes narrowed. A half hour later she had several shards of marble from the column drum. One made an excellent digging piece; several had edges sharp as any she could desire in a knife. With them she was able to cut the hard bread into scraps small enough for her to chew.

That evening at dusk she made a meal of small pieces of the hard bread and a few sips of wine. She managed to compose herself to sleep on the bed of dried grass.

The next day was like the first except that she was weaker and more thirsty. All but the dregs of the opium-laced wine were gone. In the late afternoon she found she could dig no more. She lay down on the grass bed and wondered if all that her efforts had accomplished was to condemn her to die an agonizing death by thirst.

Early on the second day she'd begun a tally stick. She looked at the notches and counted: five. Five days she'd been here. She tried to remember if she'd counted the first day or began the count on the second, but then couldn't remember and was annoyed with herself for her lack of mental acuity. Then she laughed silently at herself for being so foolish as to think it mattered. She couldn't laugh out loud because her lips were cracking and her tongue was beginning to swell.

That evening, using a pebble, she was able to coax sufficient saliva from her dried-out body to spit in the jug and loosen the last dregs. They put her to sleep because there was enough concentrated opium in the bottom to knock out a horse, and so she slept, but when she woke in the morning, thirst was a raging agony and her tongue was so swollen it was beginning to protrude from her mouth.

She was able to open a vein in the back of her hand with one of her improvised knives and drink her blood. Not much use, she thought, but it did relieve some of the pain in her mouth and throat.

She went on digging for a while out of sheer stubbornness and to keep herself from thinking about the inevitable end of her struggles. But, again, by afternoon she was too weak to continue. There was one last way to get out a little of the opium caked in the bottom of the jar, and despising herself for needing the drug to erase her sufferings, she went ahead and used her own urine.

The horrible mixture burned her mouth, but she was able to get to sleep. When she woke it was dark. She felt around in the dark for the knife but couldn't find it. She no longer had the strength to search. It was absolutely black in her hole and she wondered if she'd gone blind, but then she was able to see a few stars.

She closed her eyes again and thought about death. She didn't pray. She would not beg and plead with the bishop for her life, and she would do no such thing with God either. She'd come here for a fell purpose. She'd known that when she started out. And if God had judged her unworthy of assistance, he could tell her about it soon enough. If there were no God . . . She remembered what Socrates said about death before he took the hemlock. Perhaps it was only an eternal sleep? If so, he judged it no bad thing, since he had never heard anyone, not even the great king of Persia, criticize the experience of a long, restful sleep. So why should he fear an eternal afternoon nap?

No reason. The man had been right. She had thought so when she first read the *Dialogues* and still agreed. In the morning, come daylight, she would find her knife. She knew where the pulse runs closest to the skin at the elbow and near the thumb. A resolute cut would open a blood vessel there, and she was nothing if not resolute. And it would all be ended. Then she stretched out and relaxed and drifted off to sleep again.

That night it rained.

EVEN THE SKIES SEEMED TO WEEP FOR THE LOMBARD king. Charles pursued Desiderius across a rainy country as the spring downpours broke over the lands below the Alps. Charles kept his army in good order. He rode ahead with a tight guard of his finest mounted men. The bulk of the famous *scarae* followed, protecting the foot columns, and another contingent labored along with the supply wagons at the rear.

Maeniel and a select few of his warriors had a place of honor with Charles's uncle Bernard in the vanguard. The fact that two of the warriors were women was disturbing to a few of Charles's courtiers, but no one really wanted to challenge Silvia or Matrona.

Gavin had spent his time in camp wallowing among the comfort wagons, and his exploits—sexual, gustatory, and alcoholic—were already legendary among certain sections of the court. But he had to do a lot of washing, fumigating, switching from wolf to human and back again to get rid of assorted fleas, lice—seven different varieties—and uncomfortable social diseases he'd contracted during his peregrinations among the ladies and gentlemen of the demimonde.

Matrona currently wasn't speaking to him. Neither was Silvia.

Travel wasn't comfortable and it had been raining off and on all morning. The wind was in their faces. Almost everyone was wearing mail. It had to be padded, and the padding was getting really soggy.

Maeniel twitched his skin in a decidedly nonhuman way to shake off the water on his arms.

Gavin took a long pull on a jug and offered it to Maeniel. "You really should try this, my lord. It's wonderful. I've been sipping it since last night, and I can't feel a thing."

Maeniel sniffed and decided Gavin might be dead. Drinking that might soon kill anyone.

"We bought it from some old man on a farm in the mountains. First he makes turnip wine. Then he freezes it, pours off what doesn't freeze, adds a few herbs and—"

"Pisses in it," Maeniel said.

"Oh, that's just to get the mushrooms in," Gavin told him. "If you steep them, it gets too strong."

Maeniel could believe this, as simply sniffing Gavin's breath made his eyes water. The alcohol content was simply unbelievable and the odor of valerian, mistletoe, henbane, and a dash or two of opium was rank.

"I have to remember that man's name, so I can go back and get some more," Gavin commented. "It's nice for a rainy day."

Just then Arbeo came riding up hell-for-leather. He reined in next to Audovald and shouted, "The baggage train is being attacked."

Charles didn't seem terribly disturbed. "They will want to slow us down. Can you deal with this, my lord Maeniel?"

Maeniel jerked his head. "Yes."

Silvia and Matrona followed him to the baggage train. They arrived to find it in disarray. One man had been wounded, and two bullocks pulling an oxcart of supplies had been killed.

Silvia jumped off her horse and joined in, helping the servants cut the dead oxen from their traces and dragging the cart aside to keep it from blocking the narrow road. One muscular fellow looked as if he might resent taking orders from Silvia, but when she picked up the heels of one of the dead oxen and dragged the massive carcass over to a tree—her intent being to skin and gut the beast so that the meat might be salvaged, but she was going to hang it up first and going to accomplish this single-handed—everyone decided discretion was better than valor in dealing with Silvia. Maeniel didn't think they would give her any trouble. So he and Matrona rode off in pursuit of the attackers.

Even though they were out of the mountains, the countryside was still very rugged, with lots of rocky outcrops, high hills, deep ravines, and small river valleys. They crossed a narrow valley with a brook running through it and paused on the slope of a still-higher hill.

"Robert," Maeniel said. "And I think Desiderius's captain: Antonius gave me his name . . . Nivardd. They know what I can do."

"Ummmm," Matrona said. "Ride to the top of the hill."

Maeniel did so.

The brook they'd just crossed fed into a tributary of the mighty Po. It ran through a thickly wooded valley below the hill. Deep in the forest near the water, Robert and Nivardd watched him.

"My lord," Robert said.

"You know what he can do?" Nivardd asked.

"Oh, yes, he and his wife. But he is too far for a bow shot and, in any case, I wouldn't—"

"No, no, no," Nivardd said. "I wasn't thinking about that. I just don't want him on our back trail."

"Oh, lord, no!" Robert said. "We will take to the river. Even scent hounds can't . . . He's leaving."

At a signal from Matrona, inaudible to humans, Maeniel turned his horse and rode back the way he came. He might as well help Silvia with those bullocks.

Nivardd and Robert rode on and never saw the black wolf watching them from the shadows.

MAENIEL SAT UP LATE OVER HIS WINE, TALKING about matters of state with Antonius. The rest of the pack had adopted his bedroom as a sleep ground. They were draped with abandon over the Persian carpets, the silk sheets, and the folding couch. When he was tired, those in the bed would make room for him. All except Gavin, who was asleep on the floor under the table.

Antonius saw something flicker at the corner of his eye, glanced over, and saw Gavin was wolf again. "He is becoming careless."

"I know," Maeniel said. "The other day when I was dining with the king, someone remarked I had a lot of dogs about the camp."

"Yes," Antonius replied. "The other day Joseph told me it was too much trouble to change just to go out in the dark to take a leak. Besides, it was cold. Fur was much better." He rolled his eyes. "What did you tell the person who made the remark?"

"Not to trouble my dogs. They were dangerous," Maeniel said. "War dogs. Trained to kill. Like our horses, battle trained."

Antonius chuckled.

Matrona entered the tent. Antonius gave a start, though he and Maeniel had been awaiting her arrival. She was wearing a long gown of heavy raw silk. It was red and embroidered with violets and acanthus picked out in gold and thistles in silver.

"You are," Antonius said, "simply, awesomely, staggeringly beautiful."

"Thank you, and I'm delighted you think so. I've been looking for a diversion. That fool—" She flicked a glance at Gavin. "—isn't worth bothering with at present. The king is busy, and the Saxon is still wandering in the high forest. What do you say to some company tonight?"

"My lady, I would be honored and deeply gratified by your presence in my bed."

Matrona extended her hand.

Antonius kissed it.

"Let's hope so," she said.

"I think I can guarantee it," he answered. "I've been celibate for some time."

Matrona gave a purring noise like a large cat.

"Oh, yes," Antonius said.

Then she turned to Maeniel. "It is as you thought. Nivardd and Robert. When I left they were sleeping the sleep of the just. They think they are being clever and, as humans go, they are.

"The pair of them have at least some backbone and are trying to raise the countryside against Charles.

"They move around, collect some men, stage a raid. Then the gang breaks up, and Nivardd and Robert go off on their own, so they will not easily be captured. Between one thing and another, they could cause Charles a lot of trouble."

Maeniel looked at Antonius.

"He hasn't sent out any foraging parties, and he hangs deserters and flogs those that stray. I believe he may be thinking along the same lines we are."

Maeniel nodded.

"Let's go fetch them."

Antonius rose, his mantle fell away, and under it he was seen to be armed.

"Need me?" Matrona asked.

"Not necessarily," Maeniel said. He gave a low growl and Gavin awoke. He gave a huge yawn and then lifted his muzzle toward the sky.

"Don't," Maeniel said.

Gavin paused, then shook himself so hard his ears flapped.

"I need you as a man," Maeniel said.

There was again that strange flicker and, naked, Gavin began crawling out from under the table.

"He's handsome," Antonius said.

"He stinks of women, drink, drugs, the perspiration that goes along with drink, sex, and some really disgusting things only a human would eat. Plus the last four or five women he tumbled, not to mention two or three convenience stations he visited. What about Gavin is handsome?" asked Matrona. "Do you like men?"

"Let's say I believe I may be like Mother in that respect. I have been known not to turn it down," Antonius said.

Gavin was handsome, Maeniel thought. He had red hair and the pale, fair skin most redheads had. He was sinewy rather than massive but gracefully built, with a slender, very muscular body, a clean-cut face, and magnificent eyes.

Gavin was sitting on a bench, tying his loincloth and pulling on his britches. He paused and looked up at Antonius. "What's it like?" he asked. "I've never tried it."

Antonius smiled slowly. He knew most human taboos had no meaning whatsoever among these people. "It can be enjoyable. Come to me sometime and I'll show you. But right now you must accept my regrets. I have a somewhat better offer."

Gavin glared at Matrona. "No doubt," he said, and began lacing up his riding pants.

Matrona laughed. "I'll go as wolf."

A FEW HOURS LATER, MAENIEL SHEPHERDED NI-vardd and Robert into his tent and sat them down at the table. This was awkward because both men were bound, hands behind their backs, ropes looped around their necks. Antonius sat down at one end of the table, and Matrona entered wearing the same scarlet gown.

Their guests didn't come quietly.

Nivardd had fought, doing his best to make Maeniel kill him, but Antonius had caught him with a pacifier, lead wrapped in flexible leather. He had a bloody bandage around his head, over a big bruise and a cut on one side of his forehead.

Robert had run then, but Matrona caught him. She landed all one hundred and sixty pounds of her in the middle of his back. He took a tumble down a steep hillside, slammed into a tree trunk, and broke two ribs. He still tried to fight, but Maeniel was there by then and subdued him.

"I brought you here because I wanted to talk to you," Maeniel told the pair.

Robert gave a snort of pure derision, then found he had a mouthful of blood. His nose was broken also. He turned to spit and saw the canvas floor of the tent was covered by a carpet, a silk carpet. He was too well brought up to spit on a silk carpet.

Matrona rose and offered him a clean linen cloth. He spat and then she tilted his head back and applied a cool, wet cloth to his nose. Her fingers stroked his cheek.

"Be still," she said. "No one means you any harm. We are not men and therefore not cruel. Had my lord Maeniel wanted you dead, we would have run you down this afternoon."

Matrona's fingers and voice worked the same magic they had with Otho. Robert quieted. His nose felt better and had stopped bleeding. She stepped away and returned to her seat. Robert was able to breathe and his head returned to a normal angle.

"Why, then?" he asked.

"Because you are giving the deepest loyalty of your very courageous hearts to a man who doesn't deserve it: Desiderius," Maeniel said.

"He is my king," Nivardd said.

"He is my liege lord," Robert said.

"Do you know the bishop?" Maeniel asked.

"Ebroin, that was his name when he served in the army," Nivardd said. "Yes, certainly I know him. We were boys together."

"Robert?" Maeniel asked.

"I did. He taught me my letters. He had a school for all the boys in the town. My mother sent me. It is most needful in business to know how to read and write. He was a good friend of our family. He was of higher rank than we were, but visited with my mother often in happier times."

"Desiderius hanged him," Maeniel said.

"No," Nivardd shouted. "He wouldn't, couldn't do such a thing."

"No," Robert said, but looked as if he'd taken a blow.

Maeniel drew his dagger, rose, and cut the ropes that bound both men. Then he removed the nooses from around their necks.

"Go." He pointed at the tent entrance. "Return to Pavia and see if I am lying. All I ask is that you refrain from taking any action against the Frankish king until you do so. Robert, where is your mother?"

Robert paled. "She fled the city, at least that's what she told me. That she would flee to Turin and stay with friends. Why?"

"There were five on the gallows. One was the bishop, the second was the law speaker Beningus, the other two I didn't know, but the fifth was a woman."

"Beningus is sacred," Robert said. "To harm a law speaker is an abomination. They take no money, so as to be always free to advise the people truthfully."

"Apparently the speaker was not sacred to Desiderius," Maeniel said. Then he looked at Nivardd and saw the man was weeping open-eyed, tears darkening his gray beard.

"He was one of my closest friends," Nivardd said brokenly. "I cannot remember when I didn't know him. If what you say is true, my king is a monster."

"It's true," Maeniel said. "I wish it were not."

"How can you be there so quickly and back?" Nivardd asked.

"You saw what I did in the church. To one of us, the distance is not so far, once we are over the mountains. I went to Pavia again. This time I was not captured. I can pass through the dwelling places of men like smoke or wind. I was worried about your mother. As far as I could tell, your house was empty. The mice were hungry but could not tell me anything more."

"Mice aren't very smart," Matrona said. "Their powers of observation are limited."

"Or they're not telling all they know," Antonius said.

"We are wracked with grief and you are cracking jokes," Robert said.

"Those aren't jokes. I truly was looking for your mother and I took the trouble to bribe the mice with a small sack of feed. I was able to obtain clothing in the town, and took the opportunity to move about in human form," Maeniel said. "Nivardd was in the church; but you saw us run down the criminals. You both know what we can do. We heard you talking about us yesterday. The sun was not clearer to our eyes than you were to Matrona and myself among the trees."

"Matrona was there?" asked Robert.

"I was wolf," she said.

"Come with me to the king," Maeniel said. "We pay our debts. You were kind and hospitable to my wife, and when it came down to it, tried to help me. I will recommend you to him. I have done him a great service and he will listen.

"If you won't see Charles, we will return your horses and you may go, but the next time you raid the baggage train . . . The king asked me to put a stop the raids." Maeniel brought the flat of his hand down hard on the table with a loud crack. "And I will."

A few hours later they went to see Charles. He was with Bernard and several entrusted with the procurement of supplies when they entered. He dismissed them all except Bernard when Maeniel and the rest entered.

"These," Maeniel said, "are the men who have been attacking our supply wagons." He indicated Robert and Nivardd.

Charles nodded. "So, the obvious question is, Why are they not in chains, not hung, and not dead?"

"With your permission, my lord," Maeniel said. "I would like Antonius to address that question."

"Indeed," Charles said. "His majesty is honored. Antonius is always fulsome in his eulogies of my words and deeds. So must the orators, who once addressed the ancient Roman senate, have sounded when they heaped praise on the world conquerors. You make me feel like I am already dead, Antonius."

"Heaven forfend, your majesty," Antonius said. "Say rather that I err in extending my weak art in honor of one whose deeds are of such magnificence that they render all ordinary praise superfluous."

Bernard burst into a roar of laughter. "Nephew, you can't win. He always bests you."

Charles smiled. "What is it this time, Antonius?"

"My lord, I believe you have in all but name conquered the Lombard kingdom. We will arrive at Pavia tomorrow and, while Desiderius will hope to stand a siege, he will offer no other resistance."

Charles nodded.

"Desiderius is clever. He hopes that starvation will hound your troops as well as his city," Antonius continued.

"Yes, that's why we were having the present meeting. We are troubled about the matter of supplies."

"Once," Antonius said, "there was another great man who led an army against Italia. His name was Hannibal of Carthage, a commander of note."

"The career of the great Carthaginian has not escaped my notice," Charles broke in. "Get to the point."

"The point is he won every battle he fought but the last," Antonius said.

"The only one that is absolutely necessary that any commander win," Bernard said.

"Just so," Antonius said. "And do you know why he lost?"

"I'll bite," Charles said. "Why?"

"Because the brilliant Carthaginian was as noted for his cruelty as his military prowess," Antonius said. "In the end the cities of Italia feared him like death and they turned to the devil they knew, Rome, rather than face the devil they did not know."

Charles nodded.

"My lord Maeniel brings these two brave men to you. Not because they fear you, but because the king in Pavia betrayed them both in an important way."

"I know," Charles said. "He hanged his bishop Ebroin. I thought this action might lessen his popularity. Ebroin was related to half the Lombard nobility."   .

"Was my mother killed?" Robert broke in.

"No," Charles said. "And don't look so surprised, Maeniel. I have independent sources of information in Pavia." He turned to Robert. "Your mother escaped the attentions of Desiderius's executioner. I don't know where she went, but she's not there.

"Nivardd, do you truly wish to enter my service?"

"Yes, but not alone. I would like to bring Robert with me."

Charles turned to his uncle Bernard.

"I can use both of them," Bernard said. "Most of the aristocratic whelps you send me are as ignorant as the average clod of dirt kicked up by a plow. I can use two experienced men who can read and write and are not ignorant of military matters. The great landowners will listen to Nivardd and . . ." Bernard hesitated. He wasn't a man to put things delicately. Robert was not noble.

"Yes," Nivardd said. "But there are those who will listen to Robert, to whom you and I would be only a pair of lazy nobles trying to feather our own nests."

Bernard gave a grunt of approval.

"Then it's settled," Charles said. "They will both join the *scarae*."

"Come on," Bernard said as he rose. "We will find you a place to stay and I'll introduce you to the rest of the boys."

"Maeniel, I wish to see you," Charles said.

He waited until the others left and only Antonius and Maeniel were present. Charles opened his writing case and handed a small piece of paper to Maeniel. Maeniel walked to the door of the king's tent and looked at in the light. The paper had been both ruled and creased.

Gerberga, your late brother's wife, is in Verona. Regeane has gone there.

"Is that Hadrian's hand?" Charles asked.

"It is," Antonius answered. "The pigeons."

"Yes," Charles said. "They were bred in Geneva. I took the precaution of having two dozen shipped to the pope. A special courier brought me this only this morning."

"Will you need me for anything else?" Maeniel asked.

"No."

"I'll be leaving for Verona then, before dark," Maeniel said. "Speak to Matrona or, if she isn't present, Antonius."

Maeniel hurried away.

"He didn't ask leave to quit my presence," Charles noted.

"Would it help if I begged your pardon?" Antonius asked.

"No," Charles said. "It wouldn't help at all."

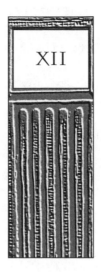

XII

LUCILLA DREAMED AND IN THE DREAM A FACE-
less woman was offering her a cool cup of fresh water. The
taste was the sweetest she'd ever enjoyed. When she woke the
rain was pouring from the border of the recessed grating into her
mouth. Lucilla stood under the grating, mouth open, arms wide in
welcome until she had drunk her fill, then she was able to capture
more in the jug that once held the drugged wine and in every other
container she could improvise from the shards that she'd uncovered
in her days of digging.

At dawn the rain ceased, blown away as the weather front that
brought the rain passed. Then, stacking her precious containers of
water away from the grating, back where during the day it would be
dark, she lay down on her bed of grass and drifted into a natural sleep.

When she woke it was afternoon. She lay quietly, eyes closed for
a time, thinking. She had hope now and hope can be as cruel a thing
as torture if it goes unfulfilled. She struggled with herself not to be
too optimistic, knowing that if the bishop and his minions found out
she had survived this long, they would certainly send someone to kill
her. At length she sat up and checked her water containers. There
were four of them. The wooden cup, a broken bowl, a concave shard
that had been part of something much larger, and the clay flask that
had held the drugged wine.

In the far edge of the cell, a dip held a fairly large puddle. She
crawled over and drank from that first. Then she tied her hair up with

a strip torn from the hem of the woolen gown, picked up her tools, crawled back in the corner, and began to dig.

When it grew too dark to make any further progress, she crawled back, drank from the puddle again, cut another notch in the tally stick, lay down, and drifted off to sleep.

In the morning the puddle was dry, so she drank from the broken bowl and then from the big shard. Otherwise this day passed the same way, except that it was a little colder. She was able to work longer. By now the blisters on her hands had broken and were oozing blood. She drank it, unwilling to let any source of liquid or nourishment be wasted.

On the eighth day all the water except that contained in the wine jug was gone. She drank sparingly from that because she was beginning to feel real hope. She was digging through clean soil now, and it was damp, soft, and friable. She encountered roots for the first time. And she was sure she was close to the surface of the hillside.

That night Adalgisus came.

The moon was out and full when she heard him whispering just outside the grating.

"Lucilla! Lucilla, are you alive? The man I bribed said you'd be dead and stinking but I don't smell anything."

At first Lucilla thought her mind was playing tricks on her, since she had just awakened from sleep. But then the fourth or fifth time he called her name, she knew he was there.

"Lucilla, please, if you're alive, answer me."

He sounded his usual whiny self, and such a wave of sheer fury surged through her that her whole body trembled with an absolute need to kill him where he stood. And then the more cautious part of her mind whispered, *Girl, don't be a fool, as this may be your only chance.* The rage vanished below consciousness as she searched her mind for directions on how to play this one.

"Yes," she whispered.

"God, yes, you are alive. I knew you wouldn't give up so easily as they said."

Again the rage shattered her calm and fury turned the darkness behind her lids red. "I am, but just barely," she answered. "Get me some food, some water. If it hadn't rained two nights ago, I would be dead."

He pressed something down through the grating. Wine in an

earthenware jug, a napkin with a few loaves of bread, some cheese and—blessing of blessings—a hard sausage. She knelt, drinking the wine and tearing the hard loaves with her teeth.

"Lucilla, you have to help me."

For a second Lucilla almost laughed. God, he was a child. Her—help him?

Better find out, her cooler self said. "Why?" she asked between mouthfuls of bread.

"Charles has passed the mountains and has besieged my father in Pavia. It is said that the big landowning families are taking Charles's side and helping supply his army."

Lucilla sighed. Too late for her, perhaps, but what she and Hadrian had hoped for was happening. She'd won. Small consolation. Now, maybe she could use it as a bargaining tool with Adalgisus.

"Get me out of here," she said. "I'll help you make your accommodation with the pope. You might still salvage something."

He was silent.

"If you let them kill me," she whispered savagely, "you're doomed. If you help me, I'll speak for you. Hadrian will listen to me, and Charles will listen to Hadrian. I promise you. But for the love of God, Adalgisus, please—" She was shocked at the desperation in her own voice. "—please get me out of here."

For a moment she thought he might be gone, but then when he answered she was equally horrified by the relief she felt: it seemed to shake her whole body.

"I can't," he whined. "The man I bribed to tell me where you were wouldn't give me the keys."

O Jesus, God, have mercy, Lucilla thought, and it was not a curse but the only prayer she'd uttered since she'd been shut in this hole. He had the man with the keys to this place of hideous torment under his hand and he'd let him go.

The rage overwhelmed her.

"You pig, you pig with the prick and balls of a mouse! Run, you bastard, run. You—you—king? You aren't fit to be the ruler of a dung heap. Run, go to Genoa, Venice, you cock-sucking heap of offal. Take ship and live in exile, rotting in exile till the day you die."

Her voice rose to a shriek. "Till the day you die, you hear me? Till the day you die."

The sound of her own voice shocked her into silence. And just as well, because she heard the sound of running feet, shouting, and she saw the glow of lights through the grating. She snatched up the food from the floor and scuttled to the back of the cell far from the lights, cowering against the wall next to the pile of dirt she'd dug from the hillside. She remained there until silence returned and all she could see through the grating was the light of distant stars and the only sound was the soft churr of insects in the grass and the wind rustling the leaves of a few trees somewhere far away.

And then she wept. For how long she never knew, but eventually she ceased, feeling nothing but a bottomless, endless, hopeless despair. She'd ceased weeping and was resting, limp against the pile of dirt, when she heard the wolf howl.

SYAGRIUS, GERBERGA, AND KARL WERE SITTING TO-gether. They were listening to Audoin, the public executioner. He was speaking of Adalgisus.

"He is gone. And no doubt halfway to Genoa by now, if not all the way. He will probably be in Constantinople by the end of the month.

"You should have heard her curse him—and most appropriate curses they were. So she still has some strength left."

Syagrius looked horrified. "She is still alive? I can hardly credit it. It's been eight days. Brother, I would be happier if you had cut her throat while you had her in your custody. Why this charade?"

Gerberga sniffed. "She hasn't suffered enough. I can imagine her with him, watching me cross the square on my way to mass while they wallowed in their filthy lust. I—I, who offered him a throne. Thus does he use me. Well, Karl has paid him out for it."

Karl chuckled. "I wonder how much longer she will last. It would be interesting to know."

"No," Syagrius said. "Enough. Audoin, take two men and go to the cell. Settle matters now. She should have been garroted when she was brought before you."

"Don't take on so," his brother Karl said. "Everything has worked out perfectly. Gerberga wanted revenge for Adalgisus's perfidy; you wanted him frightened away so we could have a clear field to make our own bargain with the Frankish king. You both have what you want."

Gerberga's mouth twisted. "Do we have to treat with Charles?"

"No, not yet," Karl said. "We must wait, see how this siege goes. I can't think of any lord or king powerful enough to keep an army in the field for more than a few months. Even the Great Charles, the Hammer, wasn't able to keep men under arms for more than half a year. And while his attentions are focused on Pavia, we will be able to strengthen our hand."

Syagrius felt uncomfortable. The woman should be dead, should have been dead. The same for Adalgisus. But Karl was a little too fond of inflicting pain, and someday his dear brother might outsmart himself. Still, he couldn't find any flaw in Karl's reasoning. He bowed to his brother. Karl left with Gerberga on his arm. Well, she was not wasting any time choosing another champion.

He turned to Audoin. "Go and finish her."

"In the morning—"

"Now! I'll sleep better when she's dead."

"But I blocked the locks."

"What locks?"

"The padlocks on the chains holding the grating closed. The bishop told me to. He said she might be able to pick locks. The chain will have to be sawn in half."

Syagrius sighed. "Very well." He was too tired to argue. "But first thing in the morning. No slipups."

"No, my lord," Audoin said. "No slipups."

T HE WOLF HOWLED THREE TIMES BEFORE LUCILLA realized what she was hearing. She crawled toward the grating, stood up, arms extended, hands gripping the bars, and shouted.

"Regeane, Regeane, Regeane." *God, please, please, let it be her.*

There was an answer, a low moaning cry, and a few seconds later something wet touched her hand and a wolf's head blotted out the stars.

A second later Regeane was crouched over the grating. "I knew you had to be near here. I knew it," Regeane said.

"Lavinia got to Rome," Lucilla said. "I didn't let myself dare hope. I thought she had so little chance to get through. Oh, my God, my God, it's so good to know I'm not alone. You will never know."

"Oh, won't I? Lucilla, these locks have been tampered with. How do I get you out? Tell me quickly. I'm freezing."

"Here." Lucilla had been wearing the linen shift. She shoved the woolen gown through the grating up to Regeane.

Regeane wiggled into the gown. "That's better."

"I'll bet it stinks."

"It does, but it's warm. Now, how do I get you out?"

"Is this cage on a hill?" Lucilla asked.

"Yes," Regeane said.

"Good, the cell runs underground a few paces to my right. I began digging there. I think I have almost broken through."

"Show me. Make noise. I can hear things others can't."

Lucilla crawled to the back of the cell and began stabbing at the dirt with her improvised pick.

A second later it gave way without Regeane's intervention and Lucilla looked up into her friend's face.

At first the opening was not wide enough for her to pass through, but it was the work of only a few minutes on the part of both women to create an opening large enough to crawl through.

Lucilla took Regeane's hand and together they stumbled down the hillside to a stream in the valley.

The water was icy, but it seemed to Lucilla that she couldn't get done scrubbing herself. She crouched in the water naked, using handfuls of stony sand from the stream to scrub her face, arms, armpits, breasts, under the breasts, stomach, buttocks, and groin, and in between, what Regeane saw as trying to sandpaper herself raw. She drank mouthful after mouthful of the sweet, invigorating, cold, clear water.

Last of all, she threw the ragged linen shift into the stream and pounded it with a rock, then kneaded it with her feet until it was more or less clean. She threw the tough garment back on, to dry on her body. Then she threw herself down on the stream bank and drank some more.

"Lucilla." Regeane shook her. "Ansgar is not far from here. We must get to his camp. I'm sure you can find clean things there."

Lucilla rose to her feet. "Hell, Regeane—do you know what hell is? It's a hole in the ground with no food, no water. I've been in hell these last eight days. They expected me to die. They wanted me to die. I still can't believe I'm alive. Every day of the rest of my life I will get up and thank God that I am alive. No matter what else is wrong in the world, I will do that."

Then, abruptly, sense seemed to return to her mind. "What is the hour? Good God, what are we doing hanging about here? We might be found and captured. Where is Ansgar's camp? Show me. Stella died, didn't she? Does he blame me? I did what I could. Are you sure it's safe to go there?"

"I don't know what hour it is, but the wolf knows it's very late. Nothing is stirring. I don't think we will be found. Yes." She was helping Lucilla, now suddenly weak, to rise. "Yes, Stella died. No, I don't think Ansgar blames you. Or rather I should say he blames others more. And yes, it's safe to go to his camp. Maeniel is there and in the morning the Frankish king will arrive."

A half hour later they both stumbled into Ansgar's camp. They created quite a stir because they weren't expected. Ansgar had been told Regeane had left Rome, but he had no idea of what she could do, or her probable destination. When Maeniel had joined him, the gray wolf knew she was in the immediate vicinity, but since she did not reveal herself to him, he could only guess at her activities.

After she got into camp and got something to wear from Matrona, she found the Saxon. Did Maeniel . . .

"Obviously not," the Saxon said. "I am here and in one piece."

"No, my lady, he was not bluffing. I cannot think he ever bluffs. He simply decided not to act on his threats. He knows he cannot make me answerable for your actions. He accepts this now. He made me a magnificent present. Or perhaps I should say he introduced me to a wonderful friend."

Regeane met the horse, but she didn't have long to get acquainted with him. Matrona came and told Regeane that Lucilla was calling for her and had become agitated when she did not return quickly enough.

Regeane hurried away to care for her friend.

Matrona stared at Regeane's back through narrowed eyes.

"What's wrong?" the Saxon asked.

"I don't know," Matrona answered. "But Lucilla is a very self-possessed and, let's say, hard individual."

"Hard?" The Saxon's eyebrows came up.

"Yes, she could outface most men. Such behavior is uncharacteristic of her. Keep an eye on both of them, please."

The Saxon nodded and followed Regeane.

Lucilla had taken another bath and while Regeane's clothes wouldn't have fit her, Matrona's did, and so Lucilla was respectable-looking when Charles arrived in the camp.

The Frankish king wasn't a man who was long on ceremony. Ansgar offered him a cup of wine, and he sat down, and they talked for a few moments in the doorway of Ansgar's tent before the fire about the unseasonably warm spring weather. Ansgar noticed the group of well-armed young men who accompanied Charles were very watchful, but nothing happened except that Ludolf arrived—he had been reconnoitering near the city—and was introduced to Charles. He went gracefully to one knee and bowed. They seemed to relax.

Maeniel and Regeane arrived then, along with more food and wine provided by Matrona. Lucilla and the Saxon followed them. Matrona had lent Lucilla a pale blue gown of silk linen weave, very simple but with long, flowing lines and full sleeves. She wore it over a divided leather riding skirt, and Matrona had insisted she wear a light mail shirt between the gown and her shift.

Lucilla had wrapped her head in a heavy linen veil, but when Charles looked into her eyes, something dreadful seemed to leap out of them at him. Whatever it was, for a moment it took his breath away. They glittered like icicles in the firelight, gray-green, blue, all at the same time. Then she bowed and also bent the knee to him.

He invited her to be seated. She sat.

"Ansgar has told me that you have been to the city and can tell us what to expect there."

Lucilla nodded and then, in a clear, calm, well-modulated voice, she told him about the layout of the city, its defenses, how many men Syagrius had, where they were quartered, where the horses were stabled and extra weapons stored. Then she went on to draw a picture on a scrap of paper giving the probable location of Syagrius's and Karl's houses, the cathedral, Gerberga's residence, and the layout of the rooms where she and her women slept, as well as the other wing where the two princes were.

Impressed, he assimilated the information. "The Romans fortified the city well. How do we get in?"

Lucilla laughed. Regeane saw her eyes glitter. She turned to Ansgar. "Have they the slightest idea we're here?"

Ansgar smiled, his smile as cold as the gleam of ice in Lucilla's eyes. "No."

"I thought not. In the morning, every morning, they open the gates to let the farmers bring fresh meat, eggs, vegetables into the city. The watch opens them when the carts appear between first light and sunrise. The road is not far away from here. We are hidden by a vineyard and a large grove of olive trees.

"When you hear the creaking of the carts and the shouts of the drivers, the gates will open. Simply, quickly, before the watch can gather their wits, ride past the farm carts and the city is yours."

"I had been watching them," Ludolf said. "Her plan is workable, but we must move quickly. By day they will see our encampment and raise an alarm."

Lucilla took Regeane's hand and the two women left the tent and the quiet bustle of the encampment behind. They moved silently together through the vineyard. Regeane saw the light was blue now. The vines were just leafing out; the air was as it usually is at first light—very still.

"Are you better now?" she asked.

"Yes, but I need you, Regeane. Promise, don't leave me. No matter what, don't leave me."

"Yes." Regeane was somewhat mystified by Lucilla's fear. What was there to be afraid of now? The wolf's eyes were better than the woman's, but even to a human the blue of first light was growing pale. It was possible to see the ground mist turning to dew on the thick, ropy vines and settling in droplets on the soft young green leaves, and Regeane's eyes could pick out the Saxon and Maeniel mounted and standing among the trees in the olive grove when she heard the first of the carts, the wheels rattling along the big cobbles of the ancient Roman road.

AUDOIN HAD BEEN UNEASY AND HAD SLEPT BADLY. Syagrius had been unhappy about that Roman woman being alive, so he pulled two of his assistants out of bed early and they were nearing the city gates at first light.

He heard but didn't see the gates open. He began to hurry. At the gate, he stepped aside to let a cart laden with firewood pass and found himself looking down the road into the misty predawn light when she appeared. The woman from the cell. She rode out of the foggy morning light with some others, another woman and four men, and he had the sense that others were behind them.

Audoin felt every muscle in his body stiffen and the hair on his neck lift in terror. Of all creatures between hell, earth, and heaven, she was the last, the very last, being who should be here. And he found himself praying she would not see him.

She didn't and rode on, eyes fixed straight ahead. As her horse cantered past him, he realized these people were at the head of a column of armed men that rode two by two into the city. They flashed past him in a thunder of hooves, harness and armor jingling, seeming to fly along. The men of the watch stood and stared, mouths agape, at the procession passing by, until one of them realized he was watching a military disaster happening. But then all he and his fellow guardians did was run, vanishing into the narrow maze of streets near the gate as Charles and Ansgar's men poured into the city. When he saw the watch disappear, Audoin decided he'd best follow their strategy, and he and his two assistants took to their heels also.

Ansgar, Regeane, and Lucilla drew rein in the square before Syagrius's residence. A half dozen of the *scarae* were already forcing the doors. They flew open and Ansgar strode up the steps and followed them into the house, Regeane and Lucilla behind him, accompanied by the Saxon.

Lucilla wouldn't let go of Regeane's hand. "I need you," she whispered. "All hell is about to break loose here. Stay close, you will be safer that way."

The servants and bodyguards of the family didn't get a chance to make even a token resistance. Most fled, a few threw down their weapons and surrendered. A few moments later Syagrius and Karl were herded from their beds by the king's men-at-arms and shoved into the center of the hall to face Lucilla and Ansgar.

Regeane could hear terrible screams outside and smell blood, burning wood, and roasting meat. The wolf grabbed at Regeane in panic. She wanted out. Regeane, though frightened, slapped her down. Burned meat was burned meat. Then Regeane guessed what the charring flesh was and she felt hot nausea as her gorge seemed to rise and start to gag her. The stench was drifting in through the tall windows on either side of the palace hall.

Syagrius looked baffled. "Who are you? What do you want? What's happened? My men? My servants?"

"Your servants are gone." Ansgar sounded almost sad. "Your men . . . I think that's what's left of them, smoke and stink. The king's troops caught them in their beds. The barracks are already burning. I have a question to put to you."

"What king?" Syagrius shouted, "What king is doing this?"

"Charles, the king of the Franks," Ansgar answered quietly. "Now answer my question, please. Where is Adalgisus?"

"Adalgisus? Where is Adalgisus?" Syagrius repeated stupidly. "He's . . . he's . . . he's gone. We frightened him away last night. We sent him to visit a lady friend—"

"Brother, be quiet," Karl said. "The woman." He pointed to Lucilla. "That's the woman."

Syagrius recoiled. "I told you that you should have killed her."

Karl was standing, staring in fascinated horror at Lucilla.

"Adalgisus?" repeated Ansgar.

Syagrius wiped his mouth. "He is gone. She cursed him. We played a trick, pretended to catch him at her cell. She cursed him and he fled. He took what wealth he had stored in his house here. That's how we know he's gone for good. His coffers are empty. He fled toward the coast."

Outside the din was dying down. Regeane could hear some women weeping, others screaming. Above the sounds of human despair, Regeane could hear the crashing, thudding shouts of alarm as houses were broken open and shop shutters were torn down. The looting of Verona was proceeding apace. She suspected all resistance had been snuffed out within a few minutes after the attack, but the agony of the townspeople would go on for some time.

"I see," Ansgar said quietly. "Lucilla?"

"Karl, have you anything to say to me?" she asked.

"My dear lady," Karl said. "You must understand I have rich relatives. They could pay a very good ransom for me. We had no bad intentions toward you. It was purely a matter of business, nothing personal, I assure you."

Lucilla snatched a crossbow from the hand of the nearest of the *scarae*. At this range she could hardly miss. A second later the bolt thudded into Karl's chest.

He seemed to fly backward, then landed in a heap, his body limp before it hit the floor. Regeane thought he looked like nothing so much as a bundle of dirty clothes.

Ansgar turned to Syagrius, who was ghost white and trembling visibly. He'd shit himself. Regeane could smell it.

"Syagrius," he said. "Adalgisus called my wife Stella a whore. So did his friend Eberhardt, and later on Dagobert called on her to do the office of a whore with him.

"Now, they were all young men, none old enough to know my Stella when she was wrongly imprisoned in that house of ill repute in Ravenna. But I remember you being there. And I know someone must have told them stories about my Stella, and I think the someone was you. I can remember the fear in her eyes before I rescued her from that dreadful place. My poor, fragile little Stella. And I remember even more fear when she looked at you, and I see the same fear in your eyes right now. I smell the stench of it on your body, and do you know what? That fear is well justified because I'm going to kill you."

Ansgar turned to the men of the *scarae*. "Take him out and hang him. Use a slip knot and let him kick awhile."

The soldiers had to drag Syagrius away screaming. He broke down at the end.

Regeane ran from the hall. Lucilla pursued her.

They paused because Syagrius was hanging from a second-floor balcony and he was as Ansgar said—kicking. Regeane staggered down into the street. She almost fell because she was staring up at the dangling man, his face turning black, clawing at his neck. Lucilla caught up to her, snatched her arm. Near the palace she saw another house, smoke streaming from every door and window. She ran toward it. The doors were down, lying in the street.

The Saxon caught Regeane's shoulders and turned her around. "Don't go in there," he said.

Regeane glanced from him to Lucilla. Lucilla met her eyes with the coldest look Regeane had ever seen.

"The queen," Regeane gasped. "Her sons! You knew. You knew what Charles would do."

"Yes, and I knew you'd try to stop him and he would kill you along with them. He didn't dare let them live, those little boys. They have as much right to the throne as he has. If they aren't dead already, they must die. Hold her! Don't let her get away."

Regeane gave a frenzied cry. She twisted in the Saxon's grip. He was a powerful man. He spun Regeane around and twisted her arm up behind her back.

"If she tries to stop him, he will kill her and maybe the rest of us, too."

The Saxon threw one arm around Regeane's neck to pin her more tightly. She was incredibly strong. He had never met a woman as powerful as she was.

"Break her arm if you have to," Lucilla commanded. "It's better than her being killed by Charles and his men. Hold—"

The Saxon didn't hear the rest because he slipped and went down on one knee. Regeane had vanished.

"Wait—" he heard Lucilla shout.

He was back on his feet in a second.

"She has some strange powers," Lucilla said. "Find Maeniel."

The world wavered oddly and time became still. Regeane looked at Lucilla and saw her doppelgänger next to Lucilla, being held by the Saxon. The smoke was gone and the morning silence enfolded them. She saw the king, his men, ahead of her knocking down the doors. She glided like a wraith behind him and saw him come face-to-face with Gerberga, his brother's wife, the sometime Frankish queen.

No, Regeane thought. *No.*

But then it didn't matter. She had stepped out of time. What had happened was already over. All she could do was watch the play come to its appointed end. Regeane saw Gerberga run from her own rooms into the central hall. The light was bright now, the dining hall was open to a courtyard garden that looked at the horizon filled with the warm golden light of a hazy spring sunrise.

"Charles," she said, and hurried to place herself between him and the wing where her sons were sleeping. "Charles. Please! Please! Don't harm my children."

"Whatever makes you think I would?" he asked quietly.

Regeane saw he was moving to his left and that Gerberga was turning slowly, her back to her sons' bedroom now. She saw Charles was holding Gerberga's attention.

"Charles, please, please. In the name of Christ, don't harm them.

I'll do anything you wish." She sank to her knees. "I'll go to Byzan-
tium. I'll be your prisoner. I'll go to a convent, let myself be shut
away, but please—"

And Regeane knew with dreadful certainty what was going to
happen.

Charles smiled and stretched out his hand to his sister-in-law, as if
to raise her to her feet.

Bernard stepped out of the boys' bedroom. He carried the small
war ax, the Franka, that gave the Franks their name. This was a
beauty, chased and filigreed in silver to cut down on weight, but the
blade was edged in steel.

It was bloody.

At the very last second, the queen saw Charles's gaze as he met
Bernard's eyes over her head. And Regeane saw, for an instant, a terrible comprehension in her face. Then Bernard swung the ax and
Regeane remembered that the Franka was still the chosen instrument
of execution.

The blade severed Gerberga's spinal cord and she fell forward,
dead at the king's feet. Regeane saw him back away from the
spreading pool of blood. She glided past Bernard and looked through
the door. The two boys were in the bed together. One was so tranquil he seemed almost asleep. But for the yellowish, waxy pallor of
his skin, he might indeed have been sleeping. But the other's, the
older one's, head was half severed from his neck. Blood was still running down the sheets and forming a small, scarlet pool on the floor.
His eyes were open and a rictus of wholly appropriate fear was frozen
on his childish features.

Again Regeane watched the scene play itself out, and then again.
And she knew she could remain here forever seeing this horror over
and over again, if she chose, for all eternity. But no matter how long
she watched, caught like an insect in amber in an eternal instant of
unspeakable horror, she would never be able to change even one
scintilla of the events unfolding before her.

But someone was screaming her name. She wanted it to stop. It
was so irritating. And then she was down, struggling in someone's
arms, and he was dragging her across a room fogged black with
smoke. The only light came from the bloody glow of the rafters burning above them. She fought him even while he dragged her through
the broken doors into the street, clawing, kicking, and screaming,

until she looked up and saw the face, one eye swollen from her fist, skin gashed by her nails, and knew him. Her love, Maeniel.

"I was part of that. I helped," she screamed. "If it hadn't been for me, she—those children—might still be—"

The square around them was chaos. Houses were burning, people running back and forth trying to find loved ones or dumping possessions from the windows, soldiers guzzling drink or gorging on food. But there was no longer any fighting.

"If you love me," she whispered to Maeniel, "take me somewhere clean."

He embraced her and brushed her hair with his lips. The air was full of smoke and no one seemed to notice or even see the two wolves cross the square or run flying down toward the gate. None except Charles, the king. He followed, his horse at a canter. They were only shadows against the wheat sprouting green in the furrows, the olive trees like smoke against the vineyards, and the pastures glowing with long, wind-tossed green grass. Then they were gone.

He shivered, thinking, *The guilt is Bernard's. The blood guilt. They were not his kin. He is my mother's brother. I am free of it. I am free of it.*

But still he sat for a long time, hands folded on the pommel of his saddle, watching the high cloud shadows move over the fair, rich, green countryside he could now claim as his own.

ABOUT THE AUTHOR

ALICE BORCHARDT shared a childhood of storytelling with her sister, Anne Rice, in New Orleans. A professional nurse, she has also nurtured a profound interest in little-known periods of history. She is the author of *Devoted*, *Beguiled*, *The Silver Wolf*, and *Night of the Wolf*. She lives in Houston.